OUT THERE

THE HOMELESS YEARS

DENISE BLUE

PublishAmerica

First printing

All characters in this book are fictitious, and any resemblance to real persons, living or dead, is coincidental.

America Star Books has allowed this work to remain exactly as the author intended, verbatim, without editorial input.

Scripture quotations taken from the New American Standard Bible, copyright 1960, 1962, 1963, 1968, 1971, 1972, 1973, 1975, 1977, 1995 by The Lockman Foundation. Used by permission.

"What a Friend We Have in Jesus." Writer Credits: Charles Converse/Joseph Scriven. Copyright: Stamps-Baxter Music. All rights reserved. Used by permission.

Softcover 1608133133

Paperback 9781681768243

Zoftcover 9781462601813

eBook 9781456063245

PUBLISHED BY PUBLISHAMERICA, LLLP

www.publishamerica.com

To Jessica

Several people made this book possible. Special thanks go to Dr. Marsha Kinder, who read a very rough sketch and insisted I turn it into a book. I am also grateful to John Rechy, who in his Writers' Workshop saw the book's potential and advised me on how best to develop it. For the technical side, I'd like to thank Mike McIntire, with whose help I was able to format the book for the publisher. All were a tremendous help.

"…Wine…goes down smoothly;
At the last it bites like a serpent
And stings like a viper."
(Proverbs 23:31-32)

CHAPTER 1

SUMMER, 1979

I gazed out the window to a vast expanse of sky and sea. Houseboats dotted the water; the Golden Gate Bridge soared off into the distance. I was living in Sausalito, a town nestled on green hills that slope down to the bay. My place was lovely, peaceful. Would I now lose it? Panic and desperation gripped me at the thought.

To quench these feelings, I took a long swallow of my beer and wondered, did I have enough to last the night? Maybe a trip to the 7-11 before they stopped selling alcohol. Wouldn't do to run out. I'd need it tonight. Tonight of all nights. I had to plan a strategy and for that, drinking helped.

I unfolded the note that had been taped to my front door. It was from the landlord. "Dr. Williams: This is an advance notice that I've started eviction proceedings. You have a month to move out."

Terse. Curt. He was actually kicking me out. He'd meant those objections to my frequent overnight guests and their parking on the turnaround. Guests…well. Pick-ups from the local bar. But so what? What made it his business? For a moment, I cringed at the thought of the many men who'd accompanied me here. So many men. Took another drink to blot out the thought of them. Too late now, anyway. And my resentment at his meddling kicked back in. It was my life, not his.

Without a place, what would I do about seeing my daughter? She was only eight, and very dear to me. Last fall, in a rare lucid moment, I'd had to admit that my lifestyle (many men, much alcohol) was not conducive to raising a child. There had been that horrible day when a man I'd been dating had said, "You know, when I meet your daughter, I'll have feelings for her." From the glint in his eye, I'd understood him to mean sexual feelings. Enraged, I'd broken it off with him. But there were other men…could I trust any of them?

I'd called her father. We'd been long divorced. But together, we'd rallied the family to help, and she was now enrolled in a boarding school. I'd been seeing her weekends. Tonight, I missed her sparkly eyes and quick smile, her chuckles as she read *Alice in Wonderland.* Thinking of her now, I felt great longing. If she were here, I could hold her close and feel better. But how could I lay this problem on her? And how could I bring her down with me? Because I knew I was going down.

I reread the landlord's note. "Dr. Williams…" Dr. Williams. He'd been so impressed with my title. "Once a university professor, now working for a magazine in the city," he'd explained to prospective tenants when describing their neighbor. He'd thought I was just the class of person to live here. I'd been so proud. Now was I going to slink away? Rejected, evicted. How shameful.

The beer can was empty. I crushed it in my hand and went for another.

I'd left the university years ago. How exhilarating it had been, the reading and writing and discussing. The focused work on my dissertation. The thrill of the degree. The dream of myself as a scholar and teacher, reputation solid. I felt a clench of pain at the loss of that dream. What had happened? A long, slow descent into drugs and alcohol. I'd told myself that since I'd worked so hard, I deserved it, the vacation. A series of jobs, each less challenging than the last. Finally, I'd been fired from that magazine job. I'd been in charge of the classified ads. But, they said, sloppy work after lunch…after drinks. So unfair—everyone in advertising drank.

Since then, I'd been running a home business, taking editing, tutoring and typing jobs to make the rent. All spring, rent had been an obstacle. I'd finish a job, rush to the bank, then deliver the monthly rent payment by hand, adrenalin racing. It had been exciting, in a way, that month-by-month race. I'd always won it. But the landlord began hinting that I was living beyond my means and "would be happier somewhere else." Now I understood that he meant it.

Somewhere else. The words landed in me with a thud. The big question was, where else. I sure didn't have the money for another down payment. I'd just been squeaking by. Grimly, I walked on into the bedroom, past the heap of clothing on the bed. I'd dressed carefully that morning, tried and discarded different skirts until I found one that would swirl. I'd wanted to be elegant when meeting a potential client. As it turned out, the client had never shown up. I'd begun to feel foolish waiting and had ordered a glass of wine. Several glasses later, I'd given up and left. Face it: business was bad.

The telephone sat placid and still on its table. I willed it to ring, feeling that rising panic again. It had to ring. It would be the client, embarrassed about having mixed up the dates. He'd ask if I could take on a big job; it would be enough to make a deposit on a new place. Please. Oh please. I was trembling.

I considered making a call myself and ran through a mental list of people I could ask for help. That list had gotten shorter in the past year. Whom hadn't I already asked? I'd called everyone in my family already this year. Grandma in Alameda, Dad and Mom in Los Angeles, sister in San Jose, brother in Michigan. I'd even called a former college teacher for a loan to make rent. That had hurt—it was very hard to ask, harder to accept his gracious, "This month I can do it." He'd always believed in me, believed I'd do great things. It had been so awful to admit I was in need—sinking, in fact. Humiliating to feel I was letting him down. I'd had to consume a six pack of beer first.

Of course, I could call family and ask to move in for a while. But could I really? Not with Grandma. I'd lived with her when I first got the magazine job; then the family had told me firmly to stop taking advantage of her. My parents, though, would have to take me in…but did I want to? To live under house rules, at 34? No, too constricting. I couldn't do it. I'd have to accept their advice, look for work, admit defeat—no.

I remembered my last conversation with my mother. I'd explained previously that I was working from home so that I could be a writer in my spare time and promised that if I failed, I'd get a job selling shoes. "Selling shoes yet?" she'd teased me. Failure. The last time my mother and stepfather had visited, it had been to bail me out. They'd paid off my car, paid off my furniture, said, "There. Now you're all set." How could I call now and beg again?

The last time I'd spoken with my father, it had been to ask him to put my new typewriter on his credit card. How blissfully I'd described my future then—I was headed for a life of self-sufficiency with this new home business. Call to confess that once again, I needed bailing out? Total loss of face.

No, I would not admit I needed help again. There had to be another solution. Family was out.

Friends? Friends from the past had indicated their weariness with rescuing me. "Call when you're not in trouble," one had advised when I'd called her for help with yet another rent payment. "Call when you're not drunk," another had said. And then, "I get the feeling these are 'loans' you're not going to pay back."

Why call them with yet another emergency? Why embarrass myself further? I was tired of being in perpetual crisis. Anyway. Another loan would just be a temporary solution, shoaling up what I now believed was a failing enterprise. To hell with calling. I'd come up with something.

I walked on into the bathroom, leaned on the sink and looked into the mirror. The face looking back at me was anxious and afraid.

"Stop frowning," I told her firmly. "It'll make wrinkles." She tried for a more composed expression.

"Better," I told her. "Look—let's face it. What we've got here is a definite downward momentum." She nodded as if relieved to be dealing with the truth.

Downward. How low could I go? I remembered the trip I'd made to London years ago. The truly down and out had gathered around the underground tube stations. They dressed in bits and pieces of old clothing; they found crawl spaces to sleep in; they ran up to passersby to ask for change. I'd been fascinated by them.

Were there homeless people here, too? Probably. But it wouldn't come to that, not for me. My landlord could choke on his own self-righteousness. A new solution would present itself. Having reached that fragile optimistic state, I left for more beer.

***

I put the word out, over the next weeks, that I was getting evicted from my apartment. I kept expecting that someone would offer me a living room couch, a place to stay a while. To my growing dismay, no one did. What was wrong with these people? Finally, I put the question bluntly to a man I'd been seeing. "Look: where am I going to live?" "In your car," he answered matter-of-factly. I was shocked by his callousness. Me, live in my car? Aside from the shame of it, there was the sheer impracticality, the logistics. I owned a tiny vehicle. In such a small car, I couldn't even stretch out to sleep. Ludicrous.

One day, on a hunch, I drove my car down by the waterfront, to a large warehouse that housed an auto repair shop. I knew the owner. I'd been to many after-hours parties at his shop. Once, he'd startled me by pointing to himself and saying "I am your knight in shining armor." We'd both been drunk. But now I was willing to find out how far he'd go with that idea. Putting scruples aside, I'd milk it for all it was worth.

Hearing my vehicle stop out front, he came out smiling as he did for customers.

"Omar, I need your help here," I began. My voice was determined. I'd take as much help as he'd give.

He spread his arms to indicate his competence.

"Could I store some things with you? Stay here myself a few days?"

He frowned. "This is not good, you know. Here is a business. Your things would be in my way."

We negotiated. What I had to offer him was a small car that ran well. I had the papers on it. He had several larger vehicles that might be possible to live in. We made a trade: he'd take the car and give me, in exchange, a van to live in "for now."

He showed me the van. "This one is right for you. See inside. You put a mattress here. You keep what you want for living. So, it is your new house."

He'd been repairing the van's motor. "True, it does not yet run. Better that way. For now, you leave it parked outside my shop. If police ask why it is here, I say I am fixing it."

"Why would the police come?"

He laughed at my ignorance. "Police don't like it, the people who live in old cars. Cars get towed. Here, close to shop, is safe. You have no worries."

"What about my things?"

"Move what you need into van. Take everything else to Flea Market—is the best way." He agreed to help cart my possessions out of the apartment with his own van and a client's truck. I felt tremendous relief and excitement. At last! My problems were solved. But also, in the back of my mind, was a niggling question: Does it make sense to trade a car you own for a broken down van? Isn't it like Jack and the beanstalk—a foolish trade? But I didn't want to pursue that line of thought. The van stood for shelter—and a solution.

After I made the deal with Omar, I returned to the apartment. Now to decide: what to sell, what to keep. All the furniture could go. Most of it was secondhand anyway, and it sure wouldn't fit in the van. Books, records? I went to the bookcase, a brick and board structure holding mostly literature and literary criticism from my university years. Carefully, I picked out my favorites: the complete Shakespeare. The first editions Mom had gotten me. Some German poetry. The rest I'd have to give up—hopefully, some poor grad student would buy them at the Flea Market and give them a good home. All the records would have to go. There'd be no electricity for the stereo. Regretfully, I packed up my jazz and classical and rock and roll—hours of comfort. Resolutely, blinking back tears, I packed up my daughter's clothes and toys to mail to her grandparents, where she'd be spending the summer. Once we got the van running, I promised myself, I'd pick her up and we'd go have an adventure on the road.

The closet was a challenge. So many clothes, and I couldn't take them all. I stood indecisively for a moment, then rummaged through picking out my favorites and carrying them in armloads to the car. As for the rest—most of my fancy work clothes—someone else would get a chance to be glamorous in them. Packing and sorting was very difficult. I willed myself to be heartless, as if I were clearing out a place where someone had died.

My last day in the apartment, I woke early and fixed myself coffee with brandy. I turned the radio as loud as it would go and danced as I drank, singing along to the music. My mood was brave defiance.

When Omar and his friend came, I was well into the brandy. They lifted, loaded, moved resolutely through the apartment while I pointed out what I was keeping, what selling. It all happened in a blur.

I looked around the place for the last time. The picture window— how I'd loved it. The hardwood floors. The cozy kitchen. The bedroom whose window looked out to the stars. A painful, cracked sob welled up—I was losing my dream cottage, and with it, my dreams.

"Dee! We go now!"

I walked out to the porch, closing the door behind me.

"He who is gracious to a poor man lends to the Lord,
And He will repay him for his good deed."
(Proverbs 19:17)

CHAPTER 2

I lived in the van that hot blue summer. It was bright orange on the outside, industrial gray within. It hulked in front of the garage, hard to miss.

When Omar had a lull in regular business, he'd work on its engine. From time to time, it would mutter, promising movement. Encouraged, he'd make an adjustment and pound on it some more. I was hopeful. Once it ran, I'd lead a happy, gypsy life. I'd be able to pick up my daughter and take her for rides. We'd be carefree, joyous—a team again. I'd stay away from stray men and we'd laugh together and explore new towns. It was a lovely fantasy that comforted me and assuaged my guilt.

When things got too noisy with Omar's banging, I'd walk out by the marshland along the bay. Seabirds skimmed the surface of the water; an occasional heron paced deliberately by. These were peaceful interludes. I felt calm and at one with nature. I could forget the aching worries that my money was running out, that I had no work and no real stability. During my walks I just pushed all cares aside. This was a good life, I'd tell myself. Who needed the scramble for rent, the need to impress others? I was free of my burdens, with no responsibilities. Yes—this was real living.

People from the nearby houseboats noticed my occupancy and began dropping by. Some were suspicious of me. Who was I? Why had I just appeared on the street? Was I an undercover cop? Others accepted my presence and came to make suggestions.

Paula was the first. She'd met me when I lived on the hill. I'd taken a last-minute job editing an impassioned speech to the city council on the needs of houseboat dwellers. She'd come to pick it up.

"Nice place," she'd commented. "I do odd jobs myself. Some odder than others. Listen, while I'm here, would you mind if I used your shower? The Gate 5 showers are acting up."

She had visited me several times after that to use the shower and dress for nights on the town.

Now she came to get me straightened out. With a casual grace, she climbed in the back of the van. Her glossy brown hair was pulled back with a bandana; she'd tied a paisley scarf around her waist. Her ability to create a Look with whatever was at hand was impressive.

"Here I am," she announced, sure of my gratitude. "You helped me out before; see, I haven't forgotten. Now I'll help you."

She looked around the van's interior: a mattress balanced on boxes and boards. A stack of clothes along the wall. A box of candles, some books and a photograph album. It was a life pared down.

Seeing my new home through her eyes, knowing she was comparing it to what I'd lost, I felt a pang of sadness mixed with shame. I'd been the gracious lady on the hill, once. Now here I sat, with a bare minimum, in a van. Gone were the furnishings, the decorations, the music, the refrigerator filled with food and wine. But she made no comment on the van. It was my life she wanted to rearrange.

"Look, you have to get yourself organized," she advised. "Go up to the courthouse and sign on for foodstamps. While you're at it, listen: apply for that crazy money. SSI."

"No way," I said firmly. I was getting by with the last of a dwindling bank account. What I'd do next, I didn't know, but it wouldn't be appealing to the government for crazy money. Forget it. SSI was a government check, given to those who could demonstrate that they were without resources and unable to function in society. It was for those who could be deemed mentally incompetent. People who received the monthly income dropped out the bottom of one world to land at the top of another. To those who had nothing, they seemed wealthy. They became the aristocrats of the down and out. That would be all right, but not the first part, not saying I was incompetent. Never. Not me. How dare she even suggest it? Feeling huge resistance, I glared at her.

Paula patted my hand. "Don't get huffy. It's a good check coming in every month, which is more than you've got now. Go on, apply. Tell them you hear voices and 'can't cope.'"

Crazy money. I rejected Paula's advice with a visible shudder. As long as I'd known her, she'd had one Plan or another going on, involving herself and anyone else around. She loved to organize people. Quite simply, she was wrong in my case. I wasn't crazy. I wasn't desperate. Things would get better. This van was a stopgap measure, a temporary…

"*You* seem to manage all right out here," I told her reproachfully. "So will I."

She smiled at me with kindness and pity. "I know how to work it, and you don't, Dee. I know how to find a guy with a boat who's a little lonely, needs someone to be sweet to him a while. Then I know when to leave for the next situation. The timing is important."

"I'll get by fine, Paula. Please don't worry."

I poked my foot into the wheelwell of the van and began to fiddle with the sleeve of my t-shirt. I had to get her off this subject. It hurt to think about what I had lost and where I was now. I didn't want to face it, not at all. Why didn't she leave?

Paula seemed to sense that she'd pushed me far enough. "Think it over, Dee. Okay?"

I did have something to ask her. It weighed heavily on my heart. "Listen, Paula. I miss my daughter. I haven't seen her for months now. I keep waiting for things to get better. What do you think? Shall I try to get her here with me?"

She frowned. "Dee honey, you can barely take care of yourself right now. Where is she? Is she safe where she is?"

"It's summer. She'll be with her grandparents. Then they'll take her back to boarding school."

"I'd leave things the way they are, then. You'd be doing her no favor to bring her to this van. It's not really safe out here for a child."

I felt sadness at her assessment but also relief. No, I didn't want to put my daughter in any danger. That made me protective, rather than a woman who'd abandoned her child. I could live with "protective."

"Now. You're not even feeding yourself right. Come along with me for some dinner."

"You're cooking?"

"I'm going to the Open Door, babe."

"You go ahead without me," I said quickly, repulsed. The Open Door was a soup kitchen supplied by the churches in town. Housed in an old, boarded-up storefront, it was open for a few hours several nights a week. I'd seen people hanging out in front of the place, waiting for it to open. They had nowhere to go, and it showed. Me, join them? Unthinkable. They just weren't in my class. I felt myself go rigid with the thought of eating with them.

No, the Open Door was not for me, not at all. I'd be too ashamed... and someone from my old life might see me. That would be dreadful.

"It's just not my kind of place, Paula."

She reached for my hand and pulled. "I don't like to go alone, Dee. I need a friend with me. Come on, help me out here. We don't have to stay long."

If she really *needed* me to go with her, that was different. I supposed I could escort her so she wouldn't get jumped by somebody.

Outside, it was twilight. Purple shadows lengthened on the road we walked, softening the landscape. On the left were the houseboats close to shore. On the right, the Sausalito hills rose up, deep green shapes. Here and there, lights twinkled from the houses on the hill. It was a beautiful evening. In my former life, I might be walking along with a friend to a seafront restaurant. We'd have the catch of the day—well, cocktails first.

I was dawdling. Paula nudged me. In the soft, dissolving twilight, she was a reassuringly sturdy presence. "Come on, Dee. Think of those good Christian ladies who made us dinner. We have to do our part, here. We can't disappoint them by not showing up." Reluctantly, I quickened my pace.

We approached the place, which looked small and shabby. Graffiti covered its outer walls. A lanky man leaned against the door frame watching two well-dressed women get out of a car. One woman handed the other a covered plate and then carefully lifted out a large pot.

Paula narrowed her eyes at the guy who was playing doorman. "Who brought you up?" She hollered in her carrying voice. "Where are your manners? Help the ladies." He straightened quickly and reached out for the heavier pot. The woman relinquished it, making sure that the towel she had tucked around its handles stayed put. All three went into the open door.

Paula tucked her arm in mine, pulling me along with her. "Be nice to those church ladies, now," she whispered, "so they'll come back." I walked slowly beside her, feeling myself tense up. Repulsed. Oh, what was I doing here? How had she talked me into it? Again the thought gripped me: what if someone saw me? Someone I knew from my days on the hill? I searched for an excuse, some acceptable reason to be here. I could say…I was researching the place. Doing a job for a paper. Yes, research. That would do.

We reached the door as the women were leaving. To my great relief, I had never seen them before.

"How good of you ladies to bring the food tonight," Paula said, sparkling with social grace.

"Very thoughtful," I murmured.

The women beamed. "Oh, all the churches take turns," said the taller of the two. "Hope you will enjoy it." They climbed back in the car and drove off.

I hesitated at the entrance to the Open Door. I'd done my part: I'd walked her here. It wasn't too late to go back to the van. Inside the door were the noise of many voices and the tinkle of piano keys.

Paula took my arm and guided me over the threshold. Inside the place, I blinked. It was very dim, lit with candles on low tables. On the floor, bodies were strewn about—people were lounging, some lifting up on one elbow. Against the far wall was an old piano with someone curled up under its bench and a woman seated on the bench, trying to play. The back of the room had a counter which held a large coffee urn. Behind the counter, a woman was ladling out food from the donated pot. My breathing grew rapid. Was this an anxiety attack? What if I fainted and flopped down on the floor next to those grubby bodies? Oh good God, what was I doing here?

"Come on. Let's get in line before they all do," Paula suggested.

My eyes were readjusting to the dim, flickering candlelight. My breathing was slowing down. No one had accosted me or bothered me at all. Maybe I could go through with it. I had to admit that the food smelled good.

"Don't they have lights in this place?"

"They do, but they only turn 'em on when it's time to leave. People come here to crash, Dee. Eat and crash. This place is only open a few hours. Most people try to get warm here to prepare for the night ahead."

Cautiously, I joined her in the line that had formed in front of the long kitchen counter. The man in front of us was causing a delay. He'd stopped by the coffee urn and was busily scooping sugar into his cup.

Paula took a bowl from the counter and handed one to me. "Here's hoping they didn't scorch the bottom, reheating it. That happens a lot. Oh good, somebody brought doughnuts."

"Nobody scorched dinner; get on with you now," said a soft voice from behind the counter. "It's good spaghetti from First Methodist, still hot." I looked to see who had spoken. It was the woman who was scooping food from the pot into bowls. Her dark hair was slicked back tightly from her plump face and hung in a ponytail down her back. Her eyes were hidden behind thick glasses, the frames black and pointed. She wiped her hand on a flowered apron and held it out to me.

"I'm Virginia," she trilled. "I staff this place, along with my husband. This your first time?"

I shook her hand.

"First time, yes. I'm Dee. I'm—just here with a friend."

Virginia nodded as if it were perfectly natural I be here. I felt oddly comforted. She wasn't looking down on me or judging me at all. She filled our bowls and motioned to the plate at the end of the counter.

"Get yourselves a doughnut now, 'cuz they'll go fast." She turned to a man who was hunched over the doughnut tray, stuffing his pockets with crullers. "Richard! That's *enough* sugar, good heaven's sakes. Get some nourishment in you."

Paula led me to a spot in the corner. The few low tables were filled. The whole place was crowded, I could see as my eyes began to adjust to the dim light. People sat on cushions around the room; some still sprawled unconscious on the rug.

Paula briskly filled me in. "House rules are no drinking or using inside the place, but it's ok to come loaded and sleep it off. No fights."

As if I would start one! Still, it was reassuring that fighting was forbidden here. Sleep it off…so that's what the seemingly dead bodies were doing. I clutched my bowl, wishing I could transport myself to a cafe uptown. What would I do if someone grabbed my ankle? I sat, tucking my legs firmly underneath me.

Paula relaxed against a cushion and began to spoon in the spaghetti. "Hank and Virginia are pretty cool," she observed between bites. "They keep this place open. That's Hank inside." I looked where she was pointing. Past the kitchen was a small office. Inside, a bearded man was talking on the phone and making notes.

There was a glow in our corner; it came from an illuminated fish tank that stood against the wall. I began to eat the noodles and sauce while I watched the tank for fish. Small sleek dark ones darted to and fro, appearing and disappearing into the waving water plants. A large, flat green one edged along the bottom, keeping close to the moss.

"Soothing, isn't it?" said Hank, who'd emerged from the office. He crouched near us. "We brought this tank from our son's room. He's back in Minnesota now, got married last year."

"I like it."

"Yes, they sure live in their own little world." A striped fish curved up to the top, catching a flake of food. They're safe and happy, I thought. I'd like to climb in there with them. Then I could observe the place from my sheltering water, just turn pirouettes and be unconcerned. Just wait until someone fed me. I'd be snug with a thick pane of glass between me and the people here. I could drift…

Hank was using the light from the tank to sort through the notes he'd made. He rose and waved them at the crowd, which quieted. "Messages for Rudy and Coach. Anybody seen them?"

"Who wants to know?"

Hank grinned. "Didn't leave a name, just a number to call back. Maybe it's the Mounties."

"Maybe it's a parole officer."

"Maybe it's Aunt Jane."

He waved them to silence. "All right, pass the word if you see them. Phone's open for an hour, local calls only, and I do the dialing." He headed back into the office.

"What's that about?" I asked Paula.

"People use the Open Door as a message center. There's a machine for messages. See?" Paula gestured to a group now milling outside the office. Men and women vied for Hank's attention. One man in a red baseball cap was leaping up and waving his arms as if to say that his was the most important call to be made.

Most men wore caps; the women bundled with layers of clothing: jeans, overskirt, shirt, vest, jacket. All together, they were a scruffy hodgepodge. How could Hank tell them apart? Yet he seemed to; he was passing out message slips and calling people by name.

"They conduct their business from here," Paula explained.

"All kinds of business," murmured a sepulchral voice from the floor. A man who was either stocky or very well-bundled was lying prone under the fish tank, half hidden by the pillows piled around him. He had a knit cap pulled low over his forehead. His large dark eyes flashed in the candlelight. Those eyes were intelligent, knowing. I felt a surge of excitement pass through me. Attractive? Oh, surely not. How could I be attracted to a bum?

"So that's where all the pillows went!" Paula laughed. "Don't be a pig, Miguel. Pass us a couple."

He handed out two cushions from his nest. "Saul was looking for you, Paula."

"Yeah? Where is he?"

"Just outside."

She handed him a doughnut. "Here, it's barely used. You can finish it for me. I need to talk to him." She turned to me. "Gotta go, Dee. See a man about a boat. You know the way back." She tossed me both pillows and was gone.

My lifeline had vanished. I felt betrayed, outraged. I'd only come here because of her. How dare she leave me stranded here? In fact, *did* I know the way back? In a momentary panic, I studied my spaghetti bowl it as if it held the answers. Should I leave at once? Would anyone try to stop me? Surely not; I was unknown here. I could just slip out unobtrusively, go back to the van and lock it up. Huddle into my sleeping bag and never come back.

"How do you like the Open Door?" Miguel asked, biting into the doughnut Paula had given him. Try not to offend him.

"It's—different."

"Think of it as a private club," he advised. "Very exclusive. Only a select few qualify." He grinned at me and sank back down into his cushions. A private club…that did make it more…acceptable.

I finished the last of the Methodist spaghetti and leaned back against the wall, using both cushions. I pulled my knees up so as to occupy as little space as possible. I'd pretend to be invisible. If I bothered no one, no one would bother me. In a minute, I'd make a dash for the door. In a minute…a certain lassitude had taken over my limbs. In spite of my resistance, the fish and the warmth and the murmur of voices were soothing.

On one low table, a couple of men were playing chess. A discordant tinkle from the far corner came from the old piano. The player sat very straight on the bench; I could only see her back.

Free-form jazz filtered through the room. The striped fish came out of hiding and began pirouettes inside the tank. If I were in a night club, I'd be relaxing over brandy. I'd know the piano player; I'd be popular with the band. I'd dance, talk wittily…

A woman was making her way around the room, collecting empty bowls. She was large and fair, dressed in a denim overall. She lifted bowls from sleeping bodies, from the edges of the tables, from the floor. I gathered the ones closest to me and handed them to her. That's it: I'd help the staff. Maybe she'd think I was a zealous volunteer from First Methodist. A missionary, perhaps. Under that cover, I could then make my excuses and go.

"Would you like some help?" I offered.

"Next time, dear. Tonight we have a crew on dishes. Let's just set these on the counter."

"Are you from First Methodist?" I asked.

"No, I work here with Virginia and Hank once a week. I like street people."

I willed myself to show no reaction. Or should I say I liked them too? Luckily, she was in a talking mood. I'd let her carry the conversation.

"I used to be one," she confided, getting herself a cup of coffee. "A street person." She stirred in powdered cream. "I'm from Chicago. Dropped out of school there and got deeply into drugs. Wouldn't think it to look at me now, would you?"

I wouldn't have. Her light blue eyes were clear and focused. Her denim suit was clean. Her body exuded health. I'd have pegged her for a farm wife.

She leaned toward me confidentially. "It's been ten years now. I was scrawny and paranoid and sick. Saw demons everywhere."

I looked furtively around me. "Uh—they went away?"

"I got help. Thanks to the good Lord, I went into rehab and left Chicago. Sometimes, you just gotta leave the surroundings. Just get out of temptation's way. I came out here, went back to school, got a degree in social work. That's what I do, days."

She beamed at me, pleased with herself. "This way, working here, I get both worlds. I'm clean; I have a life back. But you know, sometimes I miss street life. I don't miss the drugs, those ups and downs. But the people—they have a certain quality. A tough humor, an acceptance, a pluckiness. So I come here as a volunteer."

"Sharon—" Hank poked his head around the office door. "I need your help in here. Now." His pleasant voice became firm and urgent. There was a flurry of movement behind him, a flailing of arms. "I think this guy's in seizure," he called, going back into the office. She moved quickly to help him, closing the door behind her.

Deserted again. I scanned the room for Paula, who had vanished. Without her, I was lost and afraid of people. The Open Door was a whole new world. I didn't fit in, nor did I want to. Did I?

"She won't be back tonight," said Miguel, who appeared at the counter. "If you want any more coffee, drink up. They'll be closing soon."

I was amazed. I'd stayed through to closing time? I must have been hypnotized by the fish.

"Goes by fast, doesn't it?" As he spoke, the room blazed with light, darkened, lit up again. Hank was flicking a switch on the wall, on off on.

"Ah, the light show. It's closing time."

Bodies on the floor rolled, groaned, rose. They reminded me of sleepwalkers who resisted waking from a warm cozy dream. The player closed the piano lid. The place began to empty.

In full electric light, I could see how shabby it was here. The walls were badly scuffed, the cushions were worn, the carpet was stained.

"That's it for tonight, people." Virgina folded her apron over one arm and headed out the door, carrying the empty pot. "Good night, Miguel. Hope to see you again, Dee."

I stepped outside. The night air was cool on my face. Sharon was already driving away. Hank held the door. A man was grabbing onto the knob.

"You'll be all right now," Hank told him. "Come on, let go. You know we don't have overnight shelter here."

The man shook his head from side to side.

"No more fake seizures, Max." Hank pried the man's fingers from the knob, closed and locked the door. Defeated, Max slumped against it.

"That's right. We'll be open again in two days." Hank held up two fingers. "This is Monday. Tuesday, Wednesday. Come back Wednesday night." The straggler ducked his head, then ran in a loping half-crouch out into the street and away.

"Hank!" called Virginia. "Come help me load up. We've got to return these things to the church yet."

Miguel pushed his knit cap an inch up his forehead. "Allow me to walk you home, Dee." He rolled his eyes. "Who knows what evil lurks in the heart of man?"

"The Shadow knows," intoned Virginia, slamming the trunk. "Let him escort you, Dee. Miguel's a gentleman."

It was a short walk to the van. I wasn't lost after all. Miguel hummed as he strode along, arms swinging. Then he stopped abruptly.

"Here's your van."

I climbed in, carefully closed the inner latch. I could hear Miguel singing as he continued on down the road.

***

Late the next afternoon, I was sitting in the van reading an old *New Yorker* I'd gleaned from my moving boxes. The article was about welfare scams. One woman, apparently, had successfully applied in four different counties, describing a variety of starving children to different social workers. On the first of each month, she'd take the subway to make the rounds and collect her various checks. Her downfall, I decided, was in getting overly elaborate with her tales of woe. She'd described one of the mythical children who had developed serious health problems, warranting a raise in the welfare payment. The social worker, alarmed, had tried to trace the child and found that neither she nor any of the others existed.

I read with interest. Who knew, I might need this information, especially if Paula kept after me about applying for benefits. "Keep it simple," I murmured. "No fancy stories." Amazed, I realized that I was identifying with the con artist, not the welfare people. Whose side was I on? Yet, I wondered about the woman who'd been caught. What had her real situation been?

"Your door is open; I take it that means you're receiving visitors?"

I looked up to see a slight figure framed by the van's large sliding side door.

"May I come in?" she asked.

"Yes." I indicated the curve of the wheel well, padded with cushions. "Have a seat." Good—I could still be gracious and entertain.

She was a small blonde woman, taut with energy. I'd seen her coming and going from Omar's, where she was a frequent guest, but I had not yet met her. As well as running his auto body shop, Omar informally ran a social center from his office. People dropped by at all hours.

She gestured toward the garage. "He's carrying on about some people who won't pay him. I'm bored with it." Holding out her hand, "I'm the Poet. 'Bout time we met. What are you reading?"

"Just some research."

"Ah, leave it for now. Want to hear some of my stuff?"

"Sure."

She threw her arms out to the side, as if to clear a space for herself, then declaimed:

There the heron
Blue and straight
Stands one-legged at the gate
to the ocean wild.
Does it see this child

watching it?

I go stumbling by

fingers to the sky

feet in mud.

Rolling, reeling on two legs

I journey on, to make my way

This thirsty day

She paused and looked expectantly at me.

"That's beautiful about the heron checking you out. I like to go out and watch them, too. What's that line about a thirsty day for?"

"You'll see—listen to the end:

The coast is clear

I need a beer.

Got any money? I've got nearly enough for a quart here."

I laughed at her sneaky appeal for change and felt in my pockets. "I've got 75 cents."

"We're rich; let's go."

She took me to her favorite place, Bait and Tackle, a small supply store near the dock. We purchased beer with combined change; then, we sat on the large oilcans outside the store and watched the sun set on the water. I felt increasingly light-hearted. Here we were, two ladies of leisure, celebrating our freedom from society's rules.

"Otis Redding composed a song here, right on that dock. She dropped her voice several octaves and began to sing.

We sat there till dusk, alternating "Dock of the Bay" with heron imitations. She told me that she stayed here and there, sometimes with Omar "when he's feeling prosperous. Lately he hasn't been, so it's time to look around again."

So Omar sometimes supported her. With his business, he was a comparatively rich man on the waterfront. I suspected he picked up people who amused him, then dropped them and found others. I also suspected he dealt in more than used cars.

***

The next morning, I was wakened by a polite tapping on metal. Morning light filtered in, bringing a reflected orange glow to the objects inside. I felt a pleasant anticipation. Who was my visitor this beautiful day?

I lifted the lock and slid the van door open. Omar stood outside; with him were a man and woman who peered in at the nest I'd made.

"Introductions," he said grandly. "Here we have the Estermanns. They brought me this van, long time ago now." Turning to them, "Here you see Dee. She's been taking good care of it, yes? You see how is possible, to make it a house."

"We're interested in doing something similar," the woman explained.

"Now we talk, me and you two. Dee might like breakfast."

The man responded quickly to Omar's hint by reaching into his wallet. "Please have a meal on us," he said courteously. "Unfortunately, we can't join you; we have some business to discuss."

A restaurant meal was an attractive proposition. I took the *New Yorker* with me and settled in at the nearest cafe: propping the magazine against the salt and pepper shakers; savoring hash browns, eggs, coffee and fruit; enjoying it all. I was a paying customer and could afford to take my time. I felt entitled, privileged.

Returning, I lingered along the bay, hoping to spot a heron. I wanted to check its posture against our bird imitations of the night before.

When I got back to Omar's, all the doors were closed. Out front, where the van had been, was a large empty space. Stacked neatly on the curb were a few boxes and an electronic typewriter that I'd used in my business on the hill. Shock and disbelief coursed through me. My home was gone. Stolen?

From inside the mechanic's shop came loud diligent banging of hammer on metal. With my fist, I hit the door, timing the thuds to be heard in between the clangs within.

"Open up, Omar! I know you're in there." I shoved, using my shoulder, shaking the door. I felt extra-powerful. I would get answers. This was an outrage. It couldn't be happening.

Finally, his door opened partway. Inside, the garage was dim and cool.

"Very busy now," said Omar. "Many dents on this one."

"The van is gone."

He shrugged. "Here is business. Those people, they brought me the van in the first place. Traded. Didn't think their van would ever go again."

"So you got it going."

He beamed. "Magic, I make. It goes this morning. They want it back; we talk; I sell."

"That's bad magic, Omar, to disappear the van. We had a trade of our own. My car for the van." I was starting to panic and willed my voice to keep steady.

He shook his head. "Your old car for the van a *while*. All fair: you had a place to live all summer, right by the water, no rent. What that would cost you is more than two old cars. Plus, you see," he pointed me outside to the typewriter on the curb, "you still have your way to make a living."

Omar closed the door, and I heard the inside lock snap into place. I went to the curb and sat with my things, stunned. Afternoon deepened into early evening. Then, with a sudden rush of energy, I lifted the typewriter to a group of outlets around the corner. I set it carefully on the ground and crouched to plug it in, pleased to hear it catch and hum with a surge of power.

A jeepful of musicians spun round the corner from the opposite direction. They were headed for a nearby storage shed to set up for a practice session. The drummer leaned his head out.

"Hey, Dee! Get outta there! We'll need that outlet for the guitars."

I touched the machine, then rose and turned to face them. "Back off, Marco. It will take you half an hour to set up. Leave me here with my instrument."

"Let her be, man," advised the driver, who backed and completed the turn to place the jeep right by the shed. "We'll be a while." I sat on the ground, crosslegged at the power source, and made a rhythm with my fingers on the keys. It was the sound I was after. I let the machine's steady hum fill the background, and alternated percussive keystrokes with a three-four cadence that flowed from me onto the keys and into the twilight. When I was played out, I unplugged the machine and carried it back to the curb. "Here's my contribution to the street," I said grandly, and walked away.

The next morning it was gone, and I was out there.

"Do not lay up for yourselves treasures on earth…but lay up for yourselves treasures in heaven…for where your treasure is, there will be your heart also."
(Matthew 6:20-21)

CHAPTER 3

I stayed up all that first night, huddled in a bus shelter. A nearby streetlight gave the illusion of warmth. The horror of my situation kept me awake. First the apartment, now the van. I was out of resources and had no idea what I'd do next. "Homeless," I kept repeating to myself. How did homeless people behave, how survive? I didn't know. I'd have to learn, and learn quickly.

For months now, I'd distanced myself from the truly down and out, feeling superior from the confines of the van. That last barrier had vanished, and with it went my pride. I shivered in the night wind and hunched myself tighter into the bus shelter.

From the boxes left on the curb, I'd pulled out a photograph album, and I pored over it all night. There I was as a bride, with flowers in my hair, beaming at the camera. I'd been so confident that love could conquer all. There was my ex-husband, so young, holding an impossibly tiny new baby. We'd been so excited at her birth. There she was, wide-eyed, eager, reaching out for a bright toy. How funny she'd been, and how easy to entertain. There she was again, grinning happily, perched on a rocking horse.

With a wrenching grief, I studied each face, each pose. I caressed the photographs. I held the album up to my heart as if I could transport myself to another time, happy and secure.

Come morning, I tucked the album under my arm and went searching for a peaceful place to sleep. I was stiff and cold from the bench. I felt now, not panic or despair, just curiously numb inside. I welcomed the numbness. It was protecting me from feelings of grief and fear that I could not afford if I was to survive.

I was next to a park, green and cool, with a row of weeping willows bordering the shore. The park was grassy, with a playground and a pergola painted white and blue. It opened onto a small rocky beach.

I'd visited the park when I lived and worked on the hill. I'd brought my daughter here to play. She'd loved the swings, had shouted to go higher and higher. And sometimes, after delivering a rush job to a lawyer's office, I'd gotten a sandwich from a nearby deli and lunched here. It was a pretty park, I remembered. Maybe it would be a good place to begin the day. Didn't people sleep in parks? I was one of those people now. The fact hit me with a fierce jolt, shattering my numbness. I was unprepared for it. Was anyone ever prepared?

I made my way there and headed for the pergola. Around it, seated here and there on the grass, were people I recognized from the Open Door. Grimy people. How was it possible to get that look of lived-in dirt? Would I?

One man was wearing a red baseball cap and gesturing to the ocean. There was something bright in his hand; it glinted in the sun. As I neared, I saw it was a harmonica.

"Beautiful day," I ventured nervously.

"Ain't it, though? Made to order." People shifted on the ground to make a place for me. Before, I'd never have gone up to a group of strangers in the park. I'd have ignored them and they me; I'd have sat on a bench near the water and read a book. What was different? Social barriers seemed to have vanished. In me, a new boldness was emerging. Now, I wanted to fit in. I wanted to learn from these people. They knew how to survive; I didn't—not yet.

A woman whose jeaned legs stretched out below a flounced skirt reached into a bag on her lap and handed me an orange.

"Have some vitamin C, hon. You look bushed. This one's fresh picked from a tree near camp." She winked at me.

"Thanks." I began to peel the fruit, using my teeth. Juice squirted into my mouth. Aah, heavenly.

"You were looking at my skirt." She smoothed it out around her. "Found this in the Free Box over by Gate 3. Been there?"

"Not yet."

"Great place. It's just behind the drydock, a wood shelter that looks like a playhouse. Full of clothes—the Junior Leaguers drop off whole boxes full. The way it goes is, you just take what you can wear. So," she gestured to her outfit, "I put on everything I like. Check it out."

"Colorful."

I made myself at home on the grass. The group resumed its activity, passing around what food and drink there was, playing harmonica and singing. When a wine bottle came my way, I reached for it gratefully, then hesitated an instant. Germs—but it would be rude to ask for a separate cup. Unrealistic, too. I took the bottle and drank deeply. Blessed comfort. Maybe things weren't so bad…

One of the group was weak and quite far gone. He lay on the ground in their midst, almost unconscious. When the Orange Lady introduced me to him, he barely lifted his head to nod.

"This here's Squeaky. We call him that 'cause of his voice."

"What's wrong with him?"

"Who knows? We're keeping close watch on him today. Twice now he's rolled into the water."

All that day, people took turns making runs out of the park to panhandle and then bring back more wine. Someone was always assigned to stay near Squeaky.

The group was a smoothly functioning unit. I thought of how overwhelming it had become for me to manage the chores of life when I still lived on the hill. In contrast, the people around me here were untroubled by grocery lists, planning, saving. As a need appeared, they met it.

People were discussing whose turn it was to go by the doughnut shop. The Open Door had an agreement there; any unsold day-olds would be donated if someone picked them up.

"It must be time. Look how low the sun is on the water."

"Bert has to go; they know him."

"Why don't we all go?"

"Who'll stay with Squeak?"

The Orange Lady turned to me. "It's your turn to stay," she said firmly.

I hesitated. "What do I have to do?"

"Just make sure he doesn't roll over and get his head in the water. It's easy." She was impatient to be gone.

My first job. Could I do it? Would I let them down? I was no nurse. But she was right—it was my turn. I stayed with him, feeling very fastidious at first. I didn't want to catch anything. He did tend to roll, so I finally propped his head on a jacket and sat up against him. I bent down to hear him breathe, curiosity winning out over disgust. It was like listening to the ocean. There was a lot of fluid in him—each breath had to rise up against a lungful of it.

When they returned, someone else took over watching him. I had learned the first Rule of the Street: Never leave another street person in trouble.

"Never leave one of your own," the Orange Lady had counseled, and her words went deep inside me. "One of your own…" so it was true. I was not visiting this world as a tourist. I was becoming part of it, and I trembled with the knowledge.

My eyes were sore, and the wine combined with my tiredness to make me very sleepy. I pulled away from the circle, positioned myself under a willow, and slept.

I awoke suddenly, disoriented. There were shouts and grunts off to my left. That must be what had wakened me. What was going on?

Two men were wrestling on the grass. "Keep out of it!" yelled one. "No way!" panted another. He reached out for an empty wine bottle that had rolled nearby. He raised it and swung it down onto the other man's head. I gasped in horror. Would it kill him? What was I doing at a street fight? Should I hide? I found I couldn't move, was too petrified to move.

The one who'd been hit rocked back on his heels, stunned. The bottle had opened a gash in his forehead, and blood flowed over his face. The other man gave him a shove.

"You're bloody…go clean up," he said in disgust. The wounded man rose unsteadily and staggered off to the drinking fountain.

"That's the end of that fight," commented Orange Lady matter-of-factly.

"What was it about?" I asked shakily.

"You, babe. The one guy started to mess with you while you were sleeping—was taking your pants off. My old man stopped him." I was unnerved. So I'd almost been raped and had been the cause of violence. Irrationally, I felt guilty. So it wasn't safe to sleep then? Maybe just not in the open.But where?

Later that night, as I searched the drydock for a place to crawl in and sleep, the harmonica player came up to me. "We lost Squeaky."

"You lost Squeaky? He can't have gone too far."

"He's dead, is what it is. We watched him but, you know, it was getting late. We set him in some bushes propped up, but he slipped down and rolled over on his face. Then he drowned in his own fluid."

I'd only known Squeaky as a sick lump of a man, but hearing of his death saddened and shocked me. It seemed so unnecessary. We'd been so careful to watch over him. I felt a spurt of anger. Why did he have to die? He'd been harmless.

The drydock was shrouded by the various shapes of boats needing repairs. The newsbringer leaned against a weathered dinghy. He nodded.

"Just thought you'd like to know since you were there with us near the end. He's gone. I'm going out by the water now to play a few songs, send him off."

"What will you play?"

"Taps, I guess. Could say a prayer. You know any?"

I searched my memory. I had been out of churches so long. But once, in the 7th grade, I'd gone to a church program and we'd been told to memorize a psalm. "I know part of one. 'Yea, though I walk through the valley of the shadow of death, I shall fear no evil, for Thou art with me...' That's all I remember."

"Cool. Come on along. We'll send him off in style."

I realized that I was deeply shaken by this death. If it could happen to him, it could happen to me. There was no protective shield between me and the elements now. I recited what I could remember of the psalm, broken in spirit.

***

It was another twilight, my favorite time. I'd been walking all day, without destination. I'd rested whenever I found a nook. Out past the marshes, near the bridge to Mill Valley, was a large tree whose branches curved out and down, forming a natural shelter. I'd hidden inside it for much of the afternoon, noticing the bark and the leaves and the pattern of sunlight through the green. I dozed, drifting in and out of a dreamy state of mind.

Occasionally people had passed by, sometimes so near that I could have touched them. I observed them from my hiding place. They were so near and yet they were, I thought, existing in a different world. They were dressed in running suits or work clothes. They were purposefully walking. They'd call out to each other, wave, speak of children and jobs and projects. I stayed very still so as to be invisible to them. It pleased me to be an unseen observer. We were physically close, yet they were in one world and I was in another. With a certain wonder, I thought: I can see them. They don't even know I'm here. And if they knew, they wouldn't care. Quick! Move on. Don't linger with that thought. Don't give yourself time to get sad.

I made my way back to the Open Door. Was this a night it would be open? Hope flared. I had come to rely on the Open Door. I held up two fingers and moved them like a pair of scissors, snipping off the days. One, two. Had it been two days?

"Snip," said a voice. "Are you giving haircuts?" I looked up, startled out of my reverie. A man was leaning against the pillar across the street from the Open Door. He was tall and sturdily built, with sandy hair and beard. I thought he was the one who called himself Coach. I was suddenly shy.

"No, I was…just figuring something out."

"If you're waiting for the Open Door, you've got a long wait. It won't open 'til tomorrow."

My hope crashed. No hot food, no refuge, no company. I nodded sadly and turned to leave. He pushed himself away from the pillar and extended his hand.

"Coach," he said.

"Dee."

"Yes, I've seen you around. You're the one with the van. What do you have in there, surveillance equipment?"

I laughed. "I had odds and ends from an apartment in it, but it's gone now."

"We had some bets going that you were a cop, spying on the street."

I was offended. "Not me."

He considered for a moment, then seemed to make up his mind. "You know, hanging out in the same area all day, people get into a rut. Their minds close up. Ever noticed that?"

Insulted, I wondered if he were talking about me. Closed-minded? "Do you mean the people who wait for the Open Door to open?" I asked belligerantly.

"Exactly. It isn't the only spot in town, you know. Let me show you something. Come for a walk?"

I considered. I had nothing else to do. "Why not."

We went through the industrial section, past Omar's, around the modern office buildings, past the supermarket. Sidewalks were smoother now; buildings were landscaped. A hiss signaled the starting of automatic sprinklers, which began to spray clear water on the lawn of the Sausalito Center.

"Ever been woke up by one of those?" he asked.

"No."

"It happens. Here and in the parks. Once I passed out with my head right over the sprinkler. That's a sudden wake up! If you use the park for sleeping, listen for that start-up sound and get ready to run."

He turned the corner and pointed. "That's where we're headed—the Pelican."

It was a waterfront restaurant-bar, popular in town. The sounds of Happy Hour spilled out into the street as the door opened and closed with people coming and going.

I gave him a questioning look. He nodded. "Excellent place. For a dollar, you can buy an hour of good living. I can front you the dollar."

I accepted at once, amazed. A dollar was a lot of money. Where had he gotten two dollars? Best not to ask, not to pry. I'd just accept my good fortune.

Sure enough, at the Pelican, between five and eight, the purchase of one drink gave access to a tableful of food: little tacos, meatballs in sauce, chips with salsa. We bought two dollar draft beers, one each, filled several plates and munched calmly, surveying the crowd.

In my former life, I reflected, I could well have come into this bar. I'd be on a bar stool, my companion intent on impressing me and vice versa. We'd brag of our achievements, our backgrounds. We'd move on to dinner, and then negotiate the matter of bed. It had been hard work, maintaining a good front. Now, I didn't have to. Being here was just a matter of survival.

After an hour, Coach took my arm.

"Time to split…we don't want to eat too much and wear out our welcome. The bartender's starting to give us the eye."

As we headed out the front door, our way was blocked by a crowd that had gathered. Directly out front was a police car, red and blue lights flashing. Through the crowd, I glimpsed a man with his hands on the hood of the car. As I watched, a policeman cuffed him and pushed him into the car.

"C'mon, muttered Coach. "Let's take the side door. We don't want to get involved in this scene."

I allowed myself to be hustled away although I didn't understand Coach's urgency. What did we have to be afraid of?

"What was that about?"

"Could be drugs, could be drunk & disorderly. Now cops'll be all over the place. Let's take the back road."

I looked over my shoulder to see if anyone else was being arrested.

He gave me a tug. "Time to move it. We don't want to get picked up for loitering. If you hang out to watch, you could get pulled in yourself. They don't need much excuse."

It was foreign to my nature to fear the cops. After all, we weren't doing anything wrong. I thought he was being paranoid. But, to humor him, I went along with Coach, who'd taken it into his head to tutor me.

***

One day, I visited the Free Box on my own. A jumble of shoes lay on the floor. On a ledge, clothing was piled high. A few jackets hung from nails in the wall. I was delighted by the sheer quantity. All this, free for the taking.

Paula was there, studying herself in a floor-length mirror. I supposed it was a mirror. It was made of metal rather than glass, tarnished and fly-specked in some place, clouded in others. At certain angles, it created a distortion, rippling her form.

"That's like a fun house mirror."

She grimaced, then made a half turn, pivoting like a model on the balls of her feet.

"How about if you be my mirror. What do you think?"

She was wearing a quilted bed jacket in a lush peach shade over a gauzy skirt.

"It makes quite an impression."

"It does, doesn't it. I thought maybe with these boots…" She held up a boot of soft brown leather. It was knee-length and laced up the front in a series of hooks.

"Just the thing."

"I thought so, too. Would you mind helping me find the other one? It must be in here somewhere."

We began to go through the shoes on the floor. As we searched, we sorted: men's shoes in one corner, children's in another, women's in a separate pile.

"About time somebody organized this place. Here's a hip boot, Dee, if you want to go wading. Where's my other one? Let's see if it got folded into the clothes."

We proceeded on into the piles of clothing. I marvelled at the variety. Checked wool shirts, a few rather limp semi-formals, two mu-mus, a tangle of jeans.

"Here, it was under the thingy." She lifted a bowl of artificial fruit. "And here's why the owner got rid of the boots—this one has something spilled something down the side."

Indeed, the leather was puckered and stained along the insole. She tossed it to one side.

"Too bad; I guess I'll go with these black pumps." She slipped bare feet into them, took a few steps. "They'll do." Now that her outfit was complete, she surveyed me, arms akimbo. "I'm glad to see you here, Dee. Gotta take care of yourself." She held up a shirtwaist dress. "How's this for you? It'd be good for when you go up for foodstamps. It helps when you look like you're making an effort."

"Mmm," I said, trying to stay noncommittal. In her mind, she was doing me a favor. I felt a deep resistance. I still didn't want to go up to a welfare office and declare myself indigent. I'd be ashamed. Despite my situation, that pocket of pride remained.

"Here." She packaged the dress by rolling it up and placing it in a straw tote bag. The bag had sea shells fastened to the side.

I remembered clothes-shopping trips in the past. The whole point had been to transform myself, to create a good impression. When I'd just finished graduate school, I was preparing to fly to Chicago to a big convention, to interview for teaching jobs. I'd looked through all the clothes on the racks and had finally selected two skirt and sweater outfits—long skirts, one in brown and one in blue, with sweaters to match. I'd felt so elegant.

Now I was getting clothed for another interview, for welfare benefits. Lower end of the scale, but still—another interview. Same principle applied: Look your best. Same tension applied too. Facing strangers, being convincing and persuasive. Maybe I'd just put it off.

"I'm going to spread this glamor around." She strode away, skirt fluttering.

I set the tote bag in the corner. After some deliberation, I selected a red and white gingham shirt and a pair of jeans that almost fit. Wait. Was that a red felt hat in the corner? To be sure it was. A black flower drooped from the brim. "Fluff up," I said, flicking my fingers through its petals. I set it on my head and turned to the mirror. If I positioned myself carefully, I got a partial reflection.

I looked like someone who'd found a dress-up box. The colors were bright. My face was very brown from being outdoors; it had a curiously blank and hardened expression. Was that a distortion? Or had I really become so empty, so tough? My hair was growing long and wild. I pulled the hat tighter and leered at the mirror. "Hold a mirror up to nature," I murmured. On the way out, I picked up a long green jacket that hung by the door.

I thought I could find the Pelican again. I didn't have a dollar that night, but the ladies' room would probably yield one. I remembered being approached myself, once—it seemed long ago—by a woman who said she'd lost her purse. I'd given her a few dollars, and so, I reasoned, would someone to me. The ladies' room was a place for small confidences. I could say—hm. I could say I'd come to meet a friend who was late, and "Could you possibly loan me a dollar until he shows…?"

As I walked, I tried out different stories. I could say I'd locked my purse in my car, perhaps? I was getting desperate. Could I hide that desperation while lying to cadge a drink and food? Would I be able to fool anyone?

I wondered if Coach would be there. I was nearing the market, which I remembered as a landmark. I saw some familiar people out front. They conferred briefly by the newspaper stands, then stationed themselves by different entrances. Coach was with them. Perhaps he'd like to join me again for hors d'oeuvres.

As I got closer, I realized they were stopping passersby to ask for money. Egad! How lowdown. Oh no, too embarrassing. Of course I knew it was done; it was how people survived. But I'd never done it. I hated asking for money, had even had trouble selling Campfire Girl peanuts as a child. I decided to pretend I hadn't seen them, and I quickened my pace. The ladies' room seemed a safer bet to me. There, I could shield myself with a genteel fiction that, for instance, my date had walked out on me and he had the cash. ("Help me out with the price of a drink? My boyfriend went off in a huff...") There. I'd perfected my story.

What this group was doing in front of the market—collecting change—was so dreadfully public. Everyone could see them. I was close enough now to hear.

"Say, could you spare some change?"

"God bless you, ma'am."

"Excuse me, we're short 58 cents, could you help?"

Each person had a preferred approach and would repeat it over and over again. I pulled my hat to one side to cover my face and walked faster.

Then, to my chagrin, Coach saw me and vigorously waved me over.

"Good, Dee, you can help. Nice jacket. Here, stand here. If we get a couple, you ask the man and I'll ask the woman."

"I can't do it."

"Sure you can."

"I don't want to, Coach. Let's just go to the Pelican instead."

He indicated the others, who were darting out to the shoppers.

"We're working, Dee. Can't just stroll in for free food *every* night, for sure not with this whole group. We'd wear out our welcome quick. Look, tonight we have another plan."

I was stiff with revulsion. He patted my shoulder.

"Stop worrying. These people don't really see you, girl. We all look alike to them."

True enough: Just as the shoppers were not quite real to us, as they strolled out laden with goods, so we were not quite real to them. Most people looked right through us, or intently past us, or quickly down to the shopping list in their hands. That evening, words froze in my throat. People went by in a blur. I felt a nudge.

"Dee, you're slowing me down now. Look at that one you just let by. Listen, don't stand so close this time. Stand over there, and just ask the ones you can."

Reprieved, I went over to the newspaper stands and pretended an interest in the headlines. Nearby, a woman was loading her trunk with groceries. I watched with longing. There was a box of cookies in there, several loaves of French bread, a deli chicken. I remembered what it was like to walk in with a list, to select rye or French bread, beans or broccoli, to consider chicken and decide on pork chops, to add a few last-minute items just because they looked good. Oh! She had some barbecue-flavor potato chips. What would she say if I asked for a handful? Did I dare?

She looked up, saw me watching her. "Fine night," she said.

"Isn't it? Lovely." I couldn't do it. It was so much easier to just pretend to be another shopper.

As she drove off, Coach shook his head at me.

"Dee, we aren't out here to chitchat."

Under pressure to bring in something, I rushed up to a man who stood poised near his car, reaching for keys, his shopping bags balanced on the hood.

"Excuse me…"

He frowned. At the same moment, I lurched backward and heard a hiss in my ear. "Don't ask! I got this guy going in." Coach, who had grabbed hold of my jacket to pull me away from the car, now positioned himself in front of me and bowed from the waist.

"We beg your pardon, sir, and thank you again. Drive carefully, now."

Thus I learned the second Rule of the Street: When panhandling, never ask the same person twice.

***

My awkwardness was forgiven. "After all, she tried," claimed Coach.

With a small group working one area, the majority of people passing get asked for change, and cash accumulates faster. As we worked the storefront that night, though, I noticed that our own group had thinned. Coach noticed too.

"We've got a hole now by the second exit. Let's spread out—Brian, can you cover?"

At last we had enough—we could stop. I felt immense relief; tension left my body. It had been hard work.

"Okay, we've got it. Let's knock off." That night's goal was a bottle of brandy. The group had agreed, prior to my arrival, that the night was cold enough to warrant it. We moved around the corner, behind the store, where rusted-out shopping carts loomed at odd angles. We formed a circle, and Coach opened the bottle, drank deeply, and handed it to me.

"Yes, she gets in on this. She stayed with us, which is more than—" a new body moved in near me, reached out for the next swig. Before I could pass it along, the bottle was plucked from my hand.

"Oh, no you don't." The hand dropped, and the one who'd sidled up to me was edged out as the circle tightened.

"Get out of here, Max." The newcomer stepped a few paces back.

"Yes, get OUT. We saw you man, you know better."

"I was with you."

"Yes, you were with us, before you sneaked away to spend our change on your precious Night Train. Get out, Max. Go cry in your empty bottle. Guzzled the thing without passing it, just like last time. That money should have come to us, man. We were out there an extra half-hour because of you."

Max took a half-step forward, and a growl rose up from the circle. Defeated, he slunk away out into the field behind the store. It was the ultimate rejection: to be kicked out of a homeless group.

That was how I learned Rule Three: When panhandling with a group, bring back all proceeds to that group.

***

Coach had told me that the pavement outside the supermarket where we'd been that night was "For everyone. Use it anytime, Dee, and don't let anybody tell you different. Keep off the mini-mart, though."

"Come on, Coach. That's where I get morning coffee."

"Yeah, fine, go there to buy if you've got the change. But don't work the front, Dee, never work the front for change in the daytime. That's Matt's spot, and you got to be careful of him."

He leaned closer, eyes sparkling with urgency.

"He's a killer," he whispered. "Vietnam vet."

Chilling. Would he kill me in my sleep? Mix me up with the enemy? I knew who Matt was from the Open Door. He was very scruffy and weatherbeaten, but he stood straight in his khaki jacket. His skin was deep brown and creased from years of living outdoors. He had piercing blue eyes and would hold people in his gaze. He panhandled all day, at a steady pace. He'd retreat around a corner if asked to leave but never went far from his territory.

Other tramps varied location, working a storefront one day, a bus station the next. Not Matt. The mini-mart near the boats was his; when he was there, no one else had better be. He persevered, with a fierce claim on the place. It was the only store that carried his white port.

The next day, as I strolled along the dusty Gate 5 road, Matt approached me.

"Good afternoon, ma'am. Could you spare any change this fine day?"

It flattered and pleased me to be asked. I forgot my fear of him. His question elevated me; I became in that moment a lady out for an afternoon stroll, a woman of wealth and leisure whose charitable nature was understood. At the same time, since I was becoming a street person too—a fact I alternately resisted and embraced—I was completely free from obligation.

"Sir, had I any change it would be yours."

"I appreciate the thought. Are you very busy right now?"

"Not really."

"You could do me a favor, if you would. In here," he patted his military coat, "is what it takes to purchase one bottle of white port. Took me all morning to get the change. Problem is, I'm barred from the one store in town that carries my brand."

"How dreadful."

"Yes. You, however, are free to enter the store. Unless...?"

"I'm allowed in, yes."

"Excellent. If you were to take my capital here" (again he patted his pocket) "and invest it for me in a bottle of white port—not the red, now—I would be in your debt."

"I could do that."

Once inside the store, I headed for the wine section. Night Train, Ripple, Boone's Farm and red port were all in evidence. Where, now, was the white? A clerk who'd been eyeing me came up. "Did you want something?"

"White port, if you have it."

"Running errands for Matt, are you? It's here, on the low shelf."

I deposited Matt's change on the counter and carried the bottle back to him, knowing that the brown paper bag did not conceal the nature of the errand. I'd gotten cheap wine with his morning's change, I realized belatedly.

My earlier fantasy of being a charitable lady vanished. My green coat, I noticed, was crumpled, and bits of the field where I'd slept stuck to it. By appealing to my vanity, Matt had gotten me to work for him. That was my introduction to Rule Four: if you give yourself airs, prepare to be used.

***

The basic sleeping area was a strip of marshland, bordered by the freeway on one side and a backwash from the bay on the other. It was an unlovely spot in a lovely town; I used to think of it as the scene that had been deliberately omitted from all the picture postcards.

Gray and flat, it looked to be a graveyard for abandoned vehicles. Old rusting cranes were there, and trucks and cars which were empty shells, having been stripped for parts.

One afternoon, the Poet and I had a run of luck. We'd stopped by Bait & Tackle just as a boat party arrived. They were stocking up for a fishing trip. "Leave some beer for us!" she called out to them. Laughing, they deposited a six pack on her lap. We were astounded and laughed aloud with pleasure.

"You aren't drinking that here, I hope you know," called the man working the counter. "Go someplace else and leave my customers alone." That day, we were unphased by his rejection. We wanted to enjoy our giddy good mood and good fortune.

"Let's find us a luxury car," she said, "and celebrate in style." We set out for the auto graveyard and crawled into a Lincoln that had pulled off the road at a slant. A rumpled front fender showed why it had ended up there.

"I spotted this one earlier. Look, it comes with blankets." Under the backseat was a bedroll. "We'll share them later."

We drank, and after dark she distributed the blankets. "Now all we need is Mom to tuck us in. You may have the front seat," she added graciously. "If I snore, honk."

We were awakened that night by a great thudding sound. Someone who'd previously claimed the car was hitting the roof and windows with a baseball bat. I was terrified. What if he hit me with it?

"Dirty car thief! Wake up. Yeah, you too, get out of there. Get out before I smash your heads in."

"Okay," the Poet's muffled voice came from the back. "We're going, so lighten up, man. No need to air condition this thing."

He jerked the door open and stood to the side, leaning on his bat.

"Use the other exit, Dee," she cautioned. We crept out from the opposite side of the car and ran for the highway. "Keep your damn blankets!" she called back to him. "They've got bugs."

So it was through both instruction and experience that I learned Rule Five: Never invade another's territory.

***

Miguel knew cars. He knew them inside and out. When Omar had more business than he could take care of himself, he'd send out word that he was hiring by the day. Miguel was one of his regulars.

Miguel lived in a Pontiac along the dirt road on the edge of the auto graveyard. He'd claimed it by the tactic of staying in it most of the time. He'd nestle up inside with blankets and books—the *Life of Abraham Lincoln*, the *Aenid*, the *Lives of the Saints*. Most days he'd be there, sleeping and reading. His forays out took place at night.

Because of his stability, he was the unofficial landlord of the area. He knew which cars and truckbeds were occupied, which were available, which were likely to be towed. I decided to consult him and tapped on his car window.

Looking up from the book he'd propped on the dashboard, he nodded at me and unrolled the window halfway.

"Last night, the Poet and I were chased away with a baseball bat."

"So I heard. Word is now, you've both got bugs."

"A lie," I said indignantly. Word on the street spread quickly, and now I felt the urgent need to disprove it. "Poet only mentioned bugs to scare our attacker."

"Be careful what you say, then."

"Can you recommend any place for me to sleep?"

"Maybe."

"I've noticed a large truck now, near the corner. What if I slept there tonight?"

"It was once used for transporting chemical waste. You'll notice that it lacks a back door. Winds come through at night."

"I'd thought of going way deep inside."

"Around 2 am, a loud group of drunks often seeks shelter there. If they find you, they'll assume you came to entertain them."

I shuddered at the thought. I didn't know whether or not to believe him. It could be that he was trying to scare me away. But I wasn't willing to run the risk.

"As it happens, you did right to consult me. The line of cars parked along the edge here are all likely to be towed soon. The Lincoln, as you know, has been claimed. I do know of an opening, though. Just a moment."

He pulled a knit cap over his head, and got out from the driver's side of the car. Unfolding a length of cardboard, he placed it over the books and blankets in the front seat.

"This way." I followed him off the road, into the overgrown lot where machine bodies rested among clumps of wild anise that grew as high as a person, releasing a licorice scent. "Just past this crane. Yes, here we are." He gestured to a sea-green station wagon, flecked with rust. It tilted on flat tires. "This one, now, was the home of a guy who left this very morning for a stay in jail. How he got the car is another story. What matters is that he expects to be away six months and asked me to keep an eye on it."

He moved around to the back of the wagon. "The back seat folds down, leaving room for someone your size to stretch out." I thanked him, filled with gratitude. He nodded and was gone. The anise rustled with his retreat. It was then that I understood Rule Six of the street: Everything is temporary.

***

The next morning, I woke to a pale light that filled the car. "It's very early," I realized, "and I'm free. The day is open before me." It settled in me, clicked into place. "I can do as I please; there's no one to impress." I felt giddy with possibility.

I was hungry, but panhandling by the market would be too arduous today. Trying to bum a coffee at the mini-mart would mean I'd run into Matt, who'd used me already. What did that leave?

I headed straight for the dumpsters. These were considered extremely territorial. The idea was to get there first. That morning, I would.

There were several dumpsters placed near Gate Five. All were large, and either metallic gray or bright orange. Thanks to the nearby mini-mart as well as a pizzaria and deli, they were reliably stuffed with leftovers.

The one I'd had my eye on was housed in its own little shelter. I unlatched the gate and, seizing the top edge of the dumpster, used its outer ridges as steps to climb up. Then I carefully lowered myself in.

"Supplies," I decided, "will make my new place home. I'll stock up." Moving quickly and precisely, I began to sort the garbage. Salad stuff went in one bag. "This batch I'll rinse off," I murmured, noticing some leaves coated with French dressing. "That's a peculiar shade of pink."

Bags were plentiful, so I used another for substantial food: ends of salami and pizza crusts. Into a jumbo sack I put the separate bags I'd filled.

I worked my way down through levels of garbage, pausing over a carton of dogfood that rattled. "Still something in here, but I don't have a dog." Considering, I put it in my sack anyway. "I'll set it on the ground by the dumpster, where any hungry dog can get at it." It was comforting to think aloud. It didn't alarm me that I was talking to myself.

A head poked over the top of the dumpster. It was Brian, he of the baseball bat. "Finding anything good in there?" he asked wistfully.

"Lots," I answered. "Need any dogfood?"

"No thanks."

I relented. "Care for some pepperoni?"

"No, keep it. I'll check the next dumpster down."

As I watched him leave, I felt for the first time that I'd truly been accepted. Brian had honored my territorial claim to the dumpster.

As I worked, I cleared a space until I'd made my way to the bottom where the bottles were. With deliberation, I decanted the wine. Choosing a large wine bottle with dregs ("Almaden, not bad") I poured into it the remains from other bottles. Then I tilted my head back and drank. It made enough for a decent start on the day.

"How blessed is he who considers the helpless;
The Lord will deliver him in a day of trouble."
(Psalms 41:1)

CHAPTER 4

AUTUMN, 1980

I woke up in the abandoned car which had been my shelter for a year. Amazingly, it had not been towed away. Each night, I was reassured to see it waiting for me. The original owner had never returned to claim it. It was mine. My photograph album and a few books filled the front seat; I slept in the back.

The air was cool this morning, and I knew we were well into autumn. There was something about today, something I had to do. What was it? Something unpleasant. My stomach clenched with dread and resistance. What was it?

I peered glumly over the dashboard to see if anyone else was up. Yes, there went Matt, headed for his territory around the mini-mart. I wished I were he, going about the normal routine of a day.

Foodstamps, that was it. Paula had organized a caravan to go up to the Civic Center. I'd stalled for a year, but today was the day. From the houseboat area, a rooster crowed, shattering thoughts of sleeping through the morning. How did Miguel manage to do it, sleep all day? And he, as far as I knew, never took any kind of government assistance. If he could make it, why couldn't I? Surly resentment filled me. But I'd given my word.

I slithered outside, shivering. Maybe the Open Door would know where to get more blankets. I slid my bedroll under the seat and stretched my cramped muscles.

I made my way to the faucet by the dock. I braced myself for the cold water and splashed my face and hands. At least I was dressed, having slept in my clothes. I had to laugh at that, despite my grouchiness. Sleeping in the same clothes sure simplified life.

Getting ready had once been a major procedure. I remembered how elaborate it could get: buffing nails, showering, conditioning hair, slathering body with lotion, examining face with a magnifying mirror and tweezers. Toner, creamer, make-up base. Eyeliner, mascara, maybe some dramatic shadow. Then deliberation by the closet and the careful assemblage of an outfit. After setting it out on the bed, I'd apply polish and lipstick, coordinating the colors. Then came the choice of scent, the careful dressing, the purse, and what to go in it: always money, and some extra tucked in a hidden pocket just in case. Lipstick, eye drops, container for contacts, keys, tissue. Last came puttting in my contact lenses and a final viewing of the finished product.

What had happened to my contacts? I wondered idly. They'd become too much bother. I thought they must be tucked away in the van I'd lost. I'd long since stopped wearing them. Too much bother to keep them clean. I'd lost my glasses too, so the world was blurry.

Today, I shook the water off my face and I was ready. The sun was higher now. I felt warmer. Maybe I could just take a walk into town, forget the whole trip. Would I be missed? What if I didn't show up? I contemplated the idea. No go. Paula would be impossible and get after me, after me until I went through with it. All right. I'd go by the parking lot and hope the others had forgotten. They well might have—who had a watch, after all, or a calendar? Out here, promises were often made and not kept. I'd hope for that, an abandoned trip.

On the way, I passed Miguel's car and looked in. There was a round hump in the backseat, a pile of clothes at one end covering his head. So that's how he did it; he just blocked out the sun and the noise. As I watched, a foot twitched. Yes, he was in there.

I went up to the mini-mart and turned right into the Gate 5 parking lot. Rats. I was disappointed to see a small crowd gathering around a rusty pick-up truck. Some people were climbing in the open back of the vehicle. Paula was seated up front. When she saw me, she beckoned.

"John's going to take anyone who needs a ride, and he'll bring us all back this afternoon. He's asking $5 a head."

I was instantly and intensely relieved. "Then I can't go. I don't have $5. Thanks anyway." I turned to go, lighthearted.

"He'll take the $5 on credit, Dee. None of us has it. When your stamps do come in, he'll collect. Ok?"

"Yeah, that's fair." I saw no way out now. I'd have to go.

Paula was pleased to see me, but distracted, even as she organized the cluster of people into the back of the pick-up.

"Let's get going," she said. "I have to get my own grant straightened out."

I liked the idea of calling charity money a grant. It made the trip much more acceptable, put a nice gloss on things.

"What's the problem?" asked Coach, who, an organizer himself, was ceding to Paula since she'd arranged for the ride.

"My daughter turned me in to the Welfare people. She's thirteen, and she decided that since she's the reason I get paid AFDC, I should give her $100 of it in cash. When I wouldn't, she called the AFDC people and told them to cut me off, that the money wasn't getting to her."

"Major problem."

"Yeah."

"You've taught her well," said Coach, laughing. "She knows how to go after what she wants. Will they put you back on?"

"Oh yes; I convinced her to sign a statement that it was just a disagreement we've resolved. But I have to re-apply and convince them of my good intentions."

"You can do it."

She nodded, confident that she could.

With a pang of longing, I thought of my own daughter. She'd be in school today. What was she doing, how was she doing? Did she miss me, call out for me? It grieved me to think of her. I remembered first taking her to the boarding school. Driving away, I'd felt such loss that it had been tempting to turn the car around and ask to sleep there myself in one of the bunk beds. Lately I'd been having nightmares about her; she was in a concentration camp and I couldn't get her out. Desperately, I wanted to see her. But did I want her to see me? Like this? Could I bring her into this world I now inhabited?

I had tried. I had called her school, asking them to put her on a train to San Francisco for a weekend. The administrator had told me that my father and ex-husband had gotten custody of her and had stipulated that I not be allowed to see her alone. I had been enraged at the news. How dare they declare me unfit? How dare they separate us? Then, slowly, I'd come to accept it. I tucked the pain of missing her back inside of me, deep inside.

A figure loped toward us, walking with the rolling gait of those who are more used to the motion of a boat than the surface of land. He held a container of coffee from the mini-mart.

"All loaded up? I checked on my boat. It'll be in drydock until late this afternoon, so I'm yours till then."

"We're ready, John, " said Paula firmly. "Whoever's here goes; we aren't waiting for stragglers."

He nodded and climbed into the driver's seat. The engine turned twice, then caught. He revved it.

"We'll get there," he called over his shoulder. "Thing's just cold. Hold on, people."

The truck bumped out of the dirt lot, steadying and gaining speed as it reached the paved road. He pulled onto the freeway, and I watched the town and shore recede as we headed uphill. We were off. I felt a steady fluttering of apprehension.

Coach stretched out in the back and closed his eyes. I positioned myself against the cab to avoid the brunt of the wind. Despite my anxiety, I found it exhilarating to be moving so fast. I saw the exits for Mill Valley, Tiburon and Corte Madera; over to the right I glimpsed another harbor. Then we curved back inland, joining the morning traffic. The cars going in the other direction, toward Sausalito and the Golden Gate Bridge, were moving slowly, but we kept on at a fast pace.

I'd grown accustomed to the stationary vehicles which stayed where they'd been abandoned on the strip of dirt road. This trip in a moving car was opening the world back up to me.

Once, I'd travelled the freeways without giving it a thought. I'd just climb into my car and go. The towns were close together in Marin County, and I'd loved to travel. Over there... Wasn't that the restaurant where I'd negotiated with a client? He'd gotten the best of the deal, as I recalled.

There, for sure that was the shopping mall where I'd gone to buy a dress when I first came to Marin. I'd been going to a reception. I'd been afraid the check would bounce.

As we moved through the wind, past various landmarks, I felt as if I were moving through my past. It was as if someone else had travelled these roads, had returned home to pore over the accounts and pay the bills. It was another woman who'd waited by the phone, rushed to meet deadlines, tried to maintain a polished appearance for clients. I felt a curious detachment from that past self. We were so different, she and I.

We rounded a curve and I jostled into Coach, whose eyelids flickered. He lifted his head to see where we were. We'd passed the turn-offs for San Rafael and were riding through low brown hills. "Almost there," he commented. "The Civic Center's just ahead of us. You been there before?"

"No."

"Oh, it's the pride and joy of Marin. Frank Lloyd Wright designed it. See what you think." The wind caught his words and whirled them past me.

"A ma-as-ter-piece," he shouted.

The pickup slowed, turned for the exit, and chugged up a low hill. The others in the truck bed, who'd been hunkered down against the wind, stirred and raised themselves again. One woman pulled out a comb and began pulling it through her hair, which she'd tucked up into a knit fisherman's hat for the ride.

"There's the palace," she drawled.

I blinked and stared, unwilling at first to believe that the building we were approaching was real. It was a delicacy of pale pink and blue, with a golden spire—fanciful, ornate. It rose from the hill like a doge's palace, and it was impossible to associate the place with the business it housed: the grimy details of existence, foodstamps and general relief, accumulated tickets, jail and bail, court sentences, probation. (Since this writing, San Rafael has built a new jail in a different building.)

"Jail's over to the right," Coach remarked. "Prettiest jail in California, from the outside, anyway. Inside, it's just another place with bars."

"It looks like a big birthday cake, with all that trim."

"That's why we're here—to get us some of that cake. Got your story all ready?"

"Story?" I was puzzled.

"Yeah. The tale of woe. They like to hear the pathetic details before handing out the checks." He climbed out of the truck bed gingerly and limped a few paces, grimacing.

"What's wrong with your leg?" I asked, alarmed.

"Nothing that general relief won't cure. I'll tell them I take jobs on fishing boats but can't work when my gimp leg acts up."

"How'd you get the gimp leg? Last time I saw you, you were walking fine."

"I was sleeping near a guy with heavy boots on. We told him to take the things off, but he was too drunk to listen. Kept saying we'd steal them if he took 'em off. Sure enough, he got convulsions in the night and started kicking out. Iron tips."

I shuddered to imagine a vicious steel-tipped leg kicking out. Keep yourself in that car you've got as long as possible, I warned myself. Stay away from groups. Had it been accidental, that kick, or had it been payback for a grudge? I thought the latter. Coach was bossy, liked to be leader. Not everyone appreciated it. It would be easy to kick and then claim, later, to have been asleep. Sleep...the most vulnerable time.

"I may just call it a war wound. Depends on who's doing the interview. I can usually tell if the person's the type who checks up. It'll be easier for you, though, Dee."

"Why?"

"They're tougher on guys. Expect us to all be working; always ask about when's our next job interview. I only came today because I thought maybe I could play the leg. But chicks, they love chicks. Tell 'em they can save you from prostitution. Tell 'em you've got five crying kids at home."

"No way," said Paula, striding toward us. "Don't listen to him. If you mention kids, they'll want to see school records."

"They never did with my old lady," Coach protested.

"Your old lady! I've heard you talk about her, man, but I've never seen her. I think you made her up."

"I never," he said. "She's taking care of her sick mother in Barstow."

Paula snorted. "Sick mother. Ha!"

The driver waved his arms at us.

"Listen up, people. I've got some business in town. I'll be back here at 3:30 and wait fifteen minutes. I'll park in this same spot, or as close as I can get. Anyone who isn't here walks home."

His truck emptied quickly, and he drove off. Paula took my arm. I was glad of that. My nervousness had returned now that we'd arrived. What would I say? Could I convince them?

"I'll show you where to go, Dee. I've got an appointment, but I'll get you started first."

"An appointment? You mean they're expecting you?"

"Oh yeah. They know me well up here. I've been doing this routine for years."

I envied her savvy. I felt very naive by comparison.

"Will they let me in without an appointment?"

"Oh sure. You'll just have to wait, is all. Where you're going, they take people one by one, in order of arrival. That's why we came up here early."

She led me inside the building, up a set of wide stairs, up an elevator, past a maze of corridors, and into a small waiting room.

"Here's a kiss for luck," she said, brushing my cheek with her lips. "It's a day for business—try to get as much done as you can while we're here."

My heart plummeted as she walked away. I was alone. What could I say in an interview? Could I do it without someone coaching me? I felt squeamish, as if I were here to panhandle. But wait a minute. I was good at interviews. Wasn't I? In the olden days, at university, I'd convinced people to give me fellowships and scholarships—convinced people to give me a teaching job. So. I could do this too.

I signed in on a clipboard and joined the people who were already waiting. Bright orange chairs in hard plastic lined the walls. About half were already filled with women and children. Several women were, as I watched them, composing their faces into expressions of distress. It was like watching them put on their psychic make-up.

I wondered if, when it was my turn, I should try to cry. Once, in a high school play, I'd had to cry. Backstage, I'd applied drops from a bottle of glycerin to make my cheeks shine. It had worked then. Perhaps, though, the workers here would be hardened to such tricks.

"Go on, now," said one mother to her small son, "blow." She patted his nose with a tissue, then pushed him toward some battered toys in the corner. At her feet, a baby slept in a detachable car seat.

"You musta left your kids at home," she commented to me. "It's sure easier that way, but, you know, I figure if I bring 'em, the worker will believe I really need that check."

"Good point."

A woman appeared at the counter and called to me.

"Do we have you on file?"

"No."

"Then you'll have to fill these out." She handed me several forms, which I took back to my seat. I pondered them a while, as if they were test questions.

"Name"—I considered an alias. Brenda Wynn? Mabel Lowry? Hm. Too risky. Carefully, I printed my own name: "Dee Williams."

"Social security number:" Heck. I remembered some of it. Perhaps the whole thing, give or take a digit, would float back to the surface of memory by the time I'd filled out the questions I could.

"Driver's license:" that one was easy. I put "lost." "Others in Household." Now, here it was. Did I mention my daughter, pretend she was still living with me, go for a bigger check? I felt a stab of guilt. How could I use her that way, for my own survival? Then practicality took over: better not. They'd be sure to check. I put down "self."

"Family income:" Another easy one. I put "zero."

Most items I left blank. I was uncomfortable with the survey of my life. It looked so stark. Once, I'd been proud to talk about myself. Academic honors, good references—but now, I felt, my life wouldn't bear much scrutiny.

Around me, women came and went, most with children in tow. There were no men in the room. The wall was covered with regulatory posters, each a sea of small print, and, incongruously, travel posters. I gazed at one advertising Holland: a field of tulips, a windmill on the horizon. Yes. If I could, I would escape into it.

I waited. Once I thought I saw Paula, hurrying down the outside corridor. Finally I heard my name and followed the worker into a small cubicle.

She glanced through my forms, frowning.

"Income zero? What happened?"

Shame. "Oh, uh. I had a business, but I couldn't keep it going. There just weren't enough clients who showed up. I got depressed, got to drinking a lot..." Was that a mistake, to mention drinking? Surreptitiously, I watched her expression. She was a master at keeping her face impassive.

I went on. "Then, the landlord got sick of rent being late, and I got evicted. I had nowhere to go...so...I ended up in an abandoned car on Gate Five Road."

She frowned at that. "Had you no friends you could stay with?"

"I hate to impose."

"Impose! You had a personal emergency."

How could I explain my dread of ending up in someone else's place, hemmed in, having to abide by his or her house rules? Or, worse, accepting charity with the understanding that I needed some kind of rehabilitation. I couldn't bear the humiliation of it. Nor did I want to enter a program, to be rehabilitated. I was fine the way I was. Why couldn't people accept that?

"I thought—I thought it would be better to take care of myself, if I could. For a while, I had a van."

She looked pleased at that.

"So you have property."

"No—it got sold out from under me."

She was frowning at the form. "I see here that you're educated. Now, Dr. Williams, it's hard for me to believe that you couldn't get a job."

I furrowed my brow, studied my hands. "Yes. Well, I lost my glasses." That sounded weak. Hm. "And my contact lenses too." Weaker. "And I just lost my...ability to work, I guess."

She tapped her pencil on the forms.

"Residence, Gate 5 Road. You live on a road?"

"I told you—I live in a car."

"Is it yours?"

"No. It's just an abandoned car. I'll stay there until it gets towed."

"Well, you're not high priority. We mostly take care of families with dependent children here. What I'll do—" she began crossing things off the form, scrawling in what I supposed were the answers the system required—"What I'll do is give you a provisional three months of food stamps."

Now she studied me gravely. "Try a little harder, Dr. Williams. Get cleaned up and see if you can't find some work. Even part-time somewhere."

With that, our interview was over. I was reprieved. All right. It had been relatively painless. I could tell she felt she'd done her part by giving me a pep talk. I was relieved to have signed up for food stamps but uneasy too. Was I now beholden? Having entered the welfare system, had I given that system the right to check up on me? Firmly, I set the thought aside. Let's not get paranoid. I'd gotten what I'd come for, and that would get Paula off my back.

I wondered how the others were faring. For that matter, where were they? In various cubicles and waiting rooms, I guessed.

Outside the office, I saw a sign for a cafeteria on the top floor and rode the elevator up to it. My stomach was rumbling. I was hungry and longed for the days when, seeing a sign for food, I could have simply stopped and purchased some. Oh, if only I could today. Maybe I could try to rely on my wits. I'd go check it out.

At midmorning, the place it was mostly empty. I looked around for tables that had not yet been cleared. There were a few, but they held only empty plates and saucers. There! Along the wall, two women were rising to leave, their heads bent together as they continued an intense conversation. I hovered while they gathered up their things, and then I pounced on the table.

The women had left their coffee cups with some liquid in the bottom. Quickly, I poured the remains of one cup into the other. Aha. One had left the outer ring of her cinnamon roll. I transferred it to the saucer of my cup and carried my score to a corner table.

The cup had a smudge of maroon lipstick on the rim, but my new table provided napkins, and I wiped it off. Shaking, but impressed with my own daring, I took a sip. The coffee was cool and somewhat bitter. I poured sugar into it, stirred vigorously.

Someone had left the Sports Section of the *Marin Journal* on a chair. I folded it and, eating and sipping slowly, pretended to be a lady of leisure. I'd enjoyed such mornings when I'd first moved to Marin. I'd buy a trendy paper, order a cappuchino, relax and be seen. Now, I hunched over and read of the local high school's recent victory.

I turned the page and read the banner: Girls' Team Wins. I studied the grainy photograph of a young woman making a basket. The ball had just left her fingertips, which stretched up to project the desired arc. Her feet splayed out, midleap, off the ground. Poised in midair, her body curved up toward the basket; a spasm of desire distorted her face.

In fact, she would have landed then, and teammates would rush to congratulate her. In my mind, however, she kept on going, rising in the air. Miraculously propelled…and maybe I could, too…

I read the accompanying story with care. Indeed, the ball had dropped into the basket and resulted in decisive points. In the background of the photograph, people in the bleachers had tilted their heads to follow the course of the ball. Their eyes rolled upward as if in prayer.

I bit into the cinnamon roll and stretched my legs out, pointing my toes. What if I were to elevate from my seat and keep going? What if God lifted me up? I'd fly out the skylight and up, over the green hills. The pink and blue building would become a miniature; its gold spire would glint in the sun as I circled it, rising higher and higher, out and away.

Voices broke into my reverie. The cafeteria was filling; it must be break time or early lunch. I placed my feet back on the ground and bent my head to the paper. Horseracing.

There didn't seem to be a time limit in the cafeteria. No one had come to move me along, to hustle me out. The food counter stretched along the wall opposite my table; servers were intent only on lifting lids from containers and, through the steam, scooping entrees onto plates. The cashier at the end of the line had her back to me. Good. I felt safe and warm at my table. A respite.

I was comforted to see Coach's head in line. I watched his progress. He grinned at the cashier and seemed to be negotiating with her. The line piled up behind him; finally she waved him on. He scanned the room, plate in hand. Spotting me, he lifted a hotdog from the plate and waved it in triumph.

"Dee. Any luck?"

"Looks like you had some."

71

"It was so smooth. I got a new worker and just insisted on emergency stamps."

"What are those?"

"Same day issue. They can do it, they just don't advertise it. The cashier didn't want to take the voucher at first, but I talked her into it. How about you?"

"I got a three-month okay for stamps."

"Mm," he nodded, chewing thoughtfully. "Have some chips." I ate some, liking the way their saltiness contrasted with the last sugary drink of coffee.

Coach's hot dog squirted out a stream of mustard onto his cheek. Fastidiously, he wiped it away.

"Seen the others yet?" he asked.

"No. I couldn't find anyone else."

"Gotta know where to look," he said knowingly. "I've talked with most of them. Paula got reinstated."

"Good."

"It is, yeah. I knew she'd do it. Lady's like a rolling tank once she gets started on something. Bert got in on emergency stamps along with me; he's crowing outside about it. Jan's in deep trouble, though."

"How come?"

"Aw, she got them going with some story about losing her houseboat, big drama, her and her kids with nowhere to go. She really had that social worker believing it. Worker got all excited, ready to help, got on that phone, got them to draw up the check and everything. Was all ready to pay the landlord, you know?"

"And?"

He shook his head. "Worker asked for the landlord's name, and Jan gives her old man's name. Of course the worker looks it up, finds out the old man's in jail for dealing."

I clicked my tongue against my teeth, unconsciously imitating the woman who'd interviewed me.

"Yeah. Real nasty. Jan said that check disappeared so fast, and then the worker got tough."

"What'll happen now?"

He laughed. "Oh, nothing. They'd have to catch her, and she took out of there like she was on roller skates. You know they aren't going to send someone out to Gate Five to track her down. That maze of boats and piers? No way. Best place in the world to get lost in."

"Otherwise—Frank's waiting on his probation officer, but everyone else is through. Last I saw Paula, she was going to try to reach our ride, get him to stop by earlier. She knows the people he went to visit."

He shoved his chair back. "Let's go see."

We rode the elevator to ground level and walked into a square, green, indoor garden. Ferns, thick-leaved trees, and flowering shrubs proliferated, some of the taller trees reaching up nearly to the skylight.

"It's like a jungle," I murmured.

"Cool, huh? Bert tried to sleep here once—almost made it, too. But they ousted him."

We made our way back to the parking lot, where Paula and the others were gathered.

"I got hold of him," she said briskly. "He'll be coming along."

"You mean you pried him away from Mirella? Woman, you are gifted. I'm surprised she let him go. She only gets him off that boat once a month."

"Said I'd give him a bonus. Have you seen Jan?"

"Yeah, she's on the run. She said she'd hitch back, not to wait."

"I heard about it. Too bad, she just got greedy. Wanted that check *now*. I told her she could've used John's name for landlord. He'd have gone along with it."

Bert swaggered up. "Same-day service, can't beat it."

"Beginner's luck."

Paula focused her attention on me. "Get everything accomplished?"

I filled her in; she nodded crisply.

"Good work. They'll send you foodstamps each month. That's the best. These same-day guys are happy now, but you watch. They'll sell the stamps at half price, get loaded tonight, be broke tomorrow."

Our ride honked and we piled back in, settling down for the return journey. When we neared the Sausalito/Marin City offramp, a motorcycle roared right up to the truck, aimed straight for us. I cried out and ducked down, bracing for the collision, panic and adrenalin racing through me. At the last moment, the biker veered left, missing the bumper by inches.

"Happy trails!" he taunted as he passed us.

Coach shook a fist at the biker. "That man's going to bite it one fine day," he muttered. "He just don't care."

"Who is he?"

"Andy? He has a boat anchored out. Does pretty well, living off his inheritance and drug sales. Man's crazy, Dee. Avoid him."

Our driver pulled into the Gate 5 lot. "That's the end of the road, kids."

Coach climbed out quickly. "I'm off to unload these stamps. Best place is in Marin City; woman there gives close to a straight trade. Most people want 2 for 1, stamps to cash."

I was weary of his advice and fed up with people, with their presence and their stories and the fragments they tossed out from their lives. I wanted to curl up tight like the bugs did, the roly polys. I wanted to be somewhere dark and hidden, where no one would upend my covers to poke and prod at me.

I got out of the pickup gingerly; I'd banged my knee when I dove for cover. Paula was deep in conversation with the driver, gesturing, probably working another deal. I made for my car, checking Miguel's as I passed. He was out, but a book lay open on the dash. I checked the title. He'd moved on from Vergil to *Life of Abraham Lincoln.*

I crouched behind his car, peering out around the back wheel to make sure the road was empty. Then I crept into the anise, breathing deeply, inhaling the spicy scent. I moved through it to my car. I got in and covered myself with the blanket. Lying still so that no one would guess at my presence, I went to sleep.

***

Several days and dumpster forays later, I was huddled up in my bedroll with a sharp pang in my belly. Hunger—would the Open Door be open tonight? I didn't want to leave the body warmth I'd generated, but I had to get out of the car. The thought of hot soup pulled me upright.

I reached into the backseat for a jacket and, pulling it on, left the car to run down the dirt road that led to the Open Door. With deep relief, I saw the yellow porch light shining at the front door.

Still disoriented from sleep, I went through the door and into the familiar candle-lit gloom. There was Miguel, playing chess at one of the low tables. There was Matt, curled up in his usual place under the piano, an empty bowl by his side.

Virginia was behind the counter; she called out to me. "Dee! Come get yourself some hot stew before it's all gone."

I helped myself to food and coffee and ate quickly while I watched the chess game. Miguel was losing. A frown of concentration wrinkled his brow. I got up to refill my coffee.

As I stood at the urn, I felt a hand on my shoulder. I turned my head and jumped back, repulsed. Stark terror rushed through me. There behind me was a leering, evil face. It was folded into itself with monstrous wrinkles; a trickle of blood glowed from the temple to the chin.

The apparition laughed. "Trick or treat," it intoned. I grasped the counter for support, feeling foolish now instead of terrorized.

Virginia laughed. "Rudy, you prankster. I wondered if anyone would remember Halloween. Here, I saved you a doughnut." I'd spilled my coffee. Virgina handed me a towel to clean it up. Halloween...once, that had been my favorite holiday. I refilled my cup and went to sit on the piano bench, placing my feet so as to avoid Matt's prone body. Across the room, the candlelight flickered over the monster mask as Rudy sneaked up behind others in the room.

I plinked down on a piano key. Halloween. In childhood, we'd always deliberated on costumes throughout October. What to be? Once I'd dressed up as a farm girl, painting freckles on my face and pulling my hair into pigtails, carrying a large milk pail to be filled with candy and popcorn balls. In the school parade, there'd always been at least one child dressed as a hobo—black greasepaint to indicate stubble on the chin and a red bandana tied to a stick to make a bundle of the bum's possessions. It had seemed romantic, to be a bum.

Stepping over Matt, I went to refill my cup again. It would be cold tonight, and I wanted to get as much warmth in me as possible.

"The righteous is concerned for the rights of the poor;
The wicked does not understand such concern."
(Proverbs 29:7)

CHAPTER 5

NOVEMBER 1, 1980

In the 80's, a traveller driving through Sausalito would exit the freeway at one end of town and drive along the main drag until reaching the headlands and the Golden Gate Bridge at the other end. Such a traveller, on exiting the freeway, would see a strip of road with abandoned trailers, winches, and cars. Beyond the road, the eye would see a seeming vista of uninterrupted nature—marshland dotted with occasional fields which grew up to the shore and the ocean.

That area, which would look deserted to the casual observer, in fact teemed with life. Along with the shore and marsh birds were the humans who lived in the cars, slept in the fields, and who were expert at ducking out of sight. In fact, the whole area was inhabited. (Today, this area has been "cleaned up" and built up; the homeless are even less visible.)

To those who lived in the abandoned cars along Gate 5 Road, or who camped in the fields and parks beyond, it seldom mattered what date it was, or what day of the week. If such knowledge became necessary—if, for example, there was a court date or an appointment with a social worker—we could peer in through the glass of a coin-dispensed newspaper stand and read the top of the paper. "Monday, November 1," it would have read that morning.

On this first of the month, however, there was no need to seek out a newspaper to verify the date. There was no mistaking it. The dirt road, normally quiet in the early morning, was bustling with people heading out to pick up their welfare benefits and begin the process of trading and selling food stamps. Joy, good will, and a high, tense excitement prevailed. Festivity crackled in the air. I was hopeful that I, too, would be part of the celebration. My social worker had said to expect foodstamps on the first of the month. Had she kept her word? Would I find them in the mail? Or would I go to collect them only to discover that there had been a mistake? Hope welled up; caution tamped it down.

With a tense, springy pace, I made my way to the Post Office in town. I left the abandoned cars to walk along the main street. On my right, vehicles sped by, commuters eager to get through town and across the bridge. On my left was a seeming wilderness of trees and bushes which, I knew, concealed others who were taking a more circuitous route.

When I reached the small, sedate midtown building which flew a flag for the U.S. mail, I saw a line for General Delivery snaking out the door and into the street. I joined it, furtively checking the others for cues on how to behave. Superstitiously, I believed that the approach was important. If I looked too eager, I might be disappointed. Most people were waiting with an air of quiet confidence, casually talking with those next to them.

I imitated them. "Fine morning," I remarked to a woman near me. She gave a preoccupied nod. She'd braided her hair and looped the braids around her head neatly. She was carrying a string bag; I knew she was planning to fill it with groceries before the morning passed. I wished I had her certainty and tried to look as if this stop were just a minor detour on my way to market. If I could hold that hope steadily, it might come true. I focused on her braids and tried to quiet my heart's anxious pounding.

We began to inch forward. Brian, whom I'd thought of as Baseball Bat since our first territorial clash over a car to sleep in, was standing apart from the line, scanning it. He spotted me and approached.

I looked straight ahead, pretending I hadn't seen him, but he tapped my shoulder.

"Seen Ralph?" he asked intently.

"Not today."

I ignored him and surveyed the others. The man in front of me was bundled against the wind from the bay, his hands shoved into the pockets of a plaid wool jacket. As if he felt my eyes, he turned his head and spoke to Brian.

"You're the third person chasing Ralph this morning, man. I think he got smart and had his check sent straight to the bank—direct deposit."

Brian hit his forehead with the palm of his hand and whispered a curse. Then he took off at a run, pushing people out of his way, and sprinted uptown. I was grateful to the man in line who'd sent him away.

"What's that about?" I asked.

"It's all about Ralph this morning. Come the first of the month, he's the most popular kid on the block. He gets the big check, SSI."

"Crazy money?"

"Yeah, the lucky dog. At the end of the month, when he's broke, he tries to buy on credit. Speed, mostly. People know he'll have money on the first, so they front him what he wants. Then, come the first, they have to track him down."

He grinned again, appreciatively. I could tell he hoped that Ralph would evade his creditors.

"Go, Ralph!" chimed in a woman further up the line. She wore the costume favored by female houseboaters, shabby jeans under a long, full skirt, topped with a jean jacket. To mark this as a day of celebration, she'd draped her shoulders and neck with a wisp of lime green chiffon.

"This line's nothing compared to the one at the bank," she added. "That's where the real vultures are. If I got the big check," she went on dreamily, "I'd have it sent to another town. Mill Valley, maybe. I wouldn't tell anybody where it was being mailed. Then I'd get me a motel. Nobody'd see me for days."

I nodded agreement, trying to look knowledgeable. The big check— once, I had scorned it. Now, I thought what a triumph it would be. What if I got it? What if I met with a Social Security doctor and really wowed him with a story about hearing the voices of dead poets, say? I could go further; say I saw them, say they came to visit me in my car. In my mind a bearded psychiatrist looked grave, jotted a note, said "You are badly out of touch with real life." Aha. I could just see him signing the magic papers with a flourish and okaying me for crazy money.

People would notice me then. I'd be courted, pursued. I'd be one of the elite out here. I felt a stirring of excitement to contemplate it. When had I changed my mind? When had crazy money become desirable? I didn't know, but I had changed.

The line moved again. I was almost up to the door now. There was John, who'd driven us to the Civic Center the week before. His alert face noted each person in line as he lounged against the wall, rolling a toothpick in his mouth. He was taking no chances on collecting the fares due him from his passengers.

"I remember," I said in passing. "Five dollars."

He winked.

Then I was inside, with a view of the counter. A harried clerk stood behind it, handing over fat envelopes. Oh, please let there be one with my name on it. Please. The walls inside were covered with posters and lists of regulations.

In here, it was even more tightly packed with people. One man sat on the floor, carefully peeling a banana. When the line moved, he slid forward on the floor.

My anxiety increased. What if I were standing in line for nothing? What if I got up to the counter and there was no envelope for me? Everyone would see that I was leaving empty-handed; I'd feel a fool. I tensed in apprehension.

Way ahead of me, up at the counter, was Omar the car mechanic. He was smiling benignly, standing to one side. He appeared to be guarding another man who was getting mail. The man was thin with a thick walrus mustache. It seemed to tremble while the clerk searched General Delivery.

Then the clerk handed over an envelope. Omar immediately took the man's arm and steered him to the door.

"Now we go to bank," he instructed.

"Hey, Carl," called the woman near me. "Got yourself a bodyguard this morning?"

The man shook his head, embarrassed. Omar beamed.

"Yes, I guard him. You see?" He pointed to the wall, where a poster advertising one-day airmail showed a hawk poised for flight. The bird's eyes were fierce. Its beak pointed aggressively toward a destination that, the poster assured us, would be reached in a day.

"That's me," Omar said. "Like that bird. I make sure that my friend's mail goes right to bank."

So Omar, who had a romantic side, liked picturing himself as the fierce guardian bird. Mr. Mustache probably owed Omar money. No one was going to mess with them, not with barrel-chested Omar guarding every step to the bank.

"From the bank right into your pocket," murmured the woman in chiffon, not loud enough for Omar to hear. She'd interpreted his actions the same way I had.

There was shouting now at the head of the line. Matt, his head burred from nights in the field, was gesturing wildly at the postal clerk, who shook his head and disappeared behind a partition.

"Government fraud!" Matt shrieked. Coach, looking disappointed, was trying to calm him down.

"Come on, bro. It just didn't get here yet. It'll come in tomorrow; you know how it is sometimes. We'll come back."

"What's this *we*?" snarled Matt, narrowing his eyes. "It's *my* check they lost. I tell you, they're tracking me. They're holding my check to read the code on it."

"Move it!" called the next man in line. He'd waited long enough. A redhead all in denim, he clenched his fists and wiggled his red eyebrows as if willing Matt to accept his bad luck and move aside.

Matt wheeled around, eyes blazing at the crowd.

"Watch out, all of you. Don't get a private post box!" he warned the line. "They raid it. They check it for secrets. It's unsafe."

"Of course it is," drawled a woman who'd just come through the line. "It's very dangerous. There are always spies around."

It was the Shadow Lady. She was tall and thin, with a curtain of long dark hair that fell to her shoulders, often obscuring her face.

Once she'd agreed with him, Matt stopped shouting. She leaned against the post office wall, counting her food stamps.

"Come on," she said. "I'll get you some wine. You can pay me back tomorrow."

She pushed off from the wall and walked languidly out the door. Matt followed her eagerly. Coach hesitated, as if weighing his chances of joining the new partnership. He decided against it and went to talk with our driver instead.

This was a new view of Coach. I was disappointed in him. Why had he been with Matt, except to mooch off his expected check? I'd seen Coach as a leader up till now, as a gentle and generous guide. Now I saw he, too, could be a predator.

This whole line, I now realized, was made up of two groups of people—those who were expecting benefits and those who were preying off the former. It saddened me that Coach fit into the latter category. I avoided his eyes as he passed.

The clerk reappeared; our line moved forward again.

"There's a scene like that every time," said the clerk peevishly. "I hate the first of the month." He looked warily at the remaining crowd.

"All I do is hand over the mail that comes," he said, aggrieved. "If there's nothing in the box, if the check's a day late, what can I do about it?"

"Nothing, man," said the redhead appeasingly, stepping up to the counter. "You're doing a great job. Got anything for Callahan?"

The clerk turned and began to shuffle through the "C"'s. All the general delivery mail had been set out alphabetically, I noticed. I tipped my head back and squinted, trying to see if there was anything there under "W."

"Someday they'll cut us all off," intoned the woman up from me, fingering her chiffon scarf. Her voice was funebral and it struck a chord of despair within my heart. "My worker said so. Next budget cut, we'll be the first to go."

I wasn't even properly on benefits yet, and now I'd be cut off? What if the cuts had come even while my worker was preparing my paperwork? I was increasingly agitated the closer I came to the counter. It could well be that my worker had changed her mind, or had been playing a mean joke on me. Then again, perhaps my paperwork had been lost. I grew rigid, and I forced myself to pray. "Dear God, please. Let there be good mail for me." Was that a valid prayer, if it was only for myself? I considered. "Ah, God…please let there be mail for *us*."

My turn had come. The clerk fingered through the stack of mail and oh! yes, yes, passed across an envelope for me. Immensely relieved, I stepped past the line and tore my mail open.

There, to my delight, were packets of brightly colored foodstamps—brown, yellow, green, blue. They reminded me of a monopoly game. With the booklet was a letter telling me that my temporary allotment would come on the first of each month for three months. It urged me to complete and mail the enclosed form to guarantee the next delivery of stamps.

I did so, using the pen at the postal counter. My hand shook; I put my left hand over the right, to guide it. Squinting at the form, I signed my name in spiky loops.

I felt a mix of joy and sorrow-tinged fear. Joy in that my booklet had come and I was now flush with stamps. Hallelujah! I was like the others; payday had come for me. No dumpsters for a while. I was flush. Yet I felt sorrow too in that I was now part of a shaky system and feared that I'd be dropped. Also—was it true, what Matt had said? Once I'd signed, would I be tracked by social workers who'd follow me secretly? Was I already being spied on? Above my head, the eagle glared balefully.

As I counted the stamps, my mother's voice echoed in my mind—"When we were growing up, in the Depression, all six of us kids would share one orange. Things were really hard, but my folks never lost hope, and they never signed up for charity. They said that was for people who'd given up."

I shivered and felt a spasm of guilt. I was breaking with family tradition. Perhaps if I used a different name? An alias? Too late now; I was already registered. I sealed the envelope, tasting bitter glue, and dropped it quickly in the outgoing mail slot.

Once outside, I paid our driver, who was offering another trip into Marin City for those who wanted to sell their food stamps for cash. I decided to hold onto mine. The going exchange rate was three stamps to one dollar. I'd spend the cash or get robbed and be without anything by the end of the day.

Feeling very prudent and pleased with my decision, I headed back down the road. Way ahead of me were two figures walking. They looked to be a man and a woman. They were stumbling along, supporting each other as best they could, and singing a Janis Joplin tune together. They were laughing as they sang.

The woman lurched forward and fell to the ground, pulling the man down with her. She recovered by kneeling and waving her arms as if in prayer.

There was a rustling from the bushes to their left. Three men emerged. One jumped the man on the ground; the other pinned the woman's hands behind her back. The third began to search the couple roughly. Appalled, I leaned back into the shrubbery.

The woman screamed. The man holding her down bashed her sharply in the head and she ceased. I gasped at the violence. Her companion began to cry. Within seconds, the three attackers leaped up and ran away. It had been a quick hit.

I was trembling with shock, horrified to have witnessed the attack. Should I have intervened? But if I'd been any closer, the thieves would have gotten me too.

So I'd stayed far back, unwilling to become a third victim. Now I approached the couple. The man was openly weeping and feeling the woman's head. She seemed to have passed out on the ground.

As I got nearer, I saw his tears running down his cheeks and clogging in a tangle of brown-grey beard. I touched his shoulder.

"Is she all right? I saw you were attacked."

He leaned his head back and howled. "Our checks! They got both our checks, just cashed this morning! Baby…" he leaned down to arouse the woman. Her eyes flickered. "Baby, they got our checks!"

She rose to her elbows, blinking. "God hates me!"

She was red-faced. Her long brown hair fell forward as she put her face her in hands. They both reeked of whiskey.

I felt ashamed that I had not been able to help them. My first impulse had been to stay as far away as I could; I'd pressed myself back into the bushes while the robbery was occurring. Now I reached in my pocket and withdrew a twenty-dollar food stamp.

"Would this help?"

The man lifted his tear-stained face. "We don't want to put you out."

"No, Randy, take it. She's being a good Samaritan. Let her help." The woman turned bleary eyes to me. "Thanks, sweetheart. This'll help some."

She took the stamp and tucked it into her blouse. "Man alive, we never even saw those guys coming. We'd just been to cash our checks and get a few drinks and boom. And swear to God: same thing happened last month."

He was now cradling her head in his lap, and they began weeping together. I straightened up and left them to their sorrow. Two big checks gone. That was a lot of money to lose. Now they'd be reduced to panhandling all month.

Hard luck, but it was their luck, not mine. I hardened my heart. I still had a nearly-full issue of stamps. I'd have to act as if I didn't have any, be very cagey and clever. No one would get my stamps.

Should I find an unobtrusive market and shop right away? The closest one was right up the street, but I couldn't go there. It was the one I'd used when I lived in the apartment on the hill. The shopkeepers, a married couple, had always genially inquired about my health, about my daughter, smiled and commented on the weather. I couldn't show up now, after all this time, with foodstamps. I imagined their faces: Mr. Chan would cough and look away. Mrs. Chan would gaze sadly at the colored paper. She'd pick it up with one finger, as if it might contaminate her. And as for their queries about my daughter, what would I say? That I no longer see her, that I can't take care of her, that it breaks my heart but it's true?

No. I'd go back to Gate 5 and use the big market there, where no one knew me. On the return trip, I detoured through the oceanfront park where Squeaky had died. Today it was full of picnickers on the grass, all people who'd just been issued foodstamps. Several celebrations were well under way. People sat on the ground, laughing and drinking in clusters. A man in a knit cap was climbing a tree and stashing a wine bottle in its upper branches. He was wearing a loose overcoat which flapped in the breeze as he climbed. I guessed he wanted to save something for later.

In one group, a woman with a floral mu-mu over her jeans was holding forth, waving a bottle in one hand and a booklet of food stamps in the other. Wasn't she cold? No, she was flushed with wine. She was the rich one today, the queen of the group. Around her, in a circle, were her hangers-on. She was instructing a runner who crouched expectantly at her side.

"Go to the big market this time. Take a ten and get a piece of licorice. When they're busy, they'll give you all the change in real money."

So that's how it was done: use a big foodstamp for a little purchase; get the change in cash; spend the cash on alcohol. The ground was strewn with small packages of chips, candy bars, popsicle sticks. It looked like a slow process, building a pile of change one item at a time.

I passed through the park rapidly, not lingering in any group. I hoped to disassociate myself from the food stamp crowd. I'd planned it out, dreamed of it, how I'd wheel a grocery cart through the market and shop like a regular customer, sedate and purposeful. Above all, I wanted to avoid the disapproving looks and raised eyebrows of other shoppers.

People buying candy and junk food for change, people using the change to get bottles of wine, got whispers and tsks from the regular shoppers. I'd heard them.

I remembered once being in a supermarket line and hearing the other customers comment acidly on a food-stampee's purchases. "They shouldn't allow these people to get expensive cookies with foodstamps."

No one, I vowed, would murmur disapprovingly about me. No one would jab me with a disdainful look. I continued resolutely on to the market, which was very active. People outside were clustered in their usual begging stations by the entrances. Today, however, they were not panhandling but discussing strategy. What to purchase to get the maximum amount of real money back in change?

"They ran out of gum."

"An ice cream bar comes to $1.18. Try using a $5."

The Poet was among them. Seeing me, she ran up, a gleeful expression on her face. She leaned closer and spoke in an exaggerated, confidential tone. Her fair complexion was flushed. Drunk. Did I look like that when I drank? Sound like that? Why, it was…pathetic. I steeled myself against her request.

"I've been working all morning as a runner for change. Good, huh? I'll let you in on it. Whatcha got?"

I clutched the stamps, wishing I'd kept them out of sight.

"Well I—just thought I'd get a few groceries."

She nodded vigorously.

"Do, sure. You do that. Get what you need. Gimme me a few stamps and I'll make change for you."

I hesitated, drew back. So Poet was one of the hangers-on. She'd made a job for herself today, offering her services as a foodstamp shopper. I was sure she was expert at getting real-money change from stamps.

"Spicy gum!" she whispered urgently. "I'll get you some, huh? It's the best. Real change for it is almost seventy-five cents."

I began to edge away from the Poet. For the first time in our friendship, I was embarrassed by her.

"Market Day," she hummed. "Whaddya say?"

"I'd rather not, thanks. I don't want to shop to make change, Poet. I just want to shop for real."

She blinked, looked hurt. "I'm good at it, Dee. I'm the best there is."

"Here." Impatiently, I tore out a food stamp. "Get whatever you want, okay?"

"Sure," she said slowly. "This bothers you, huh? So jus' pretend you don' even know me."

She pushed off from the dispenser, tilted unsteadily to one side, then gathered her energy and dashed into the store. I detached a cart from the rack and pushed it deliberately through the automatic doors. The wheels squeaked as I went from aisle to aisle. They seemed to announce my presence.

I passed the Poet once. She was examining the frozen food section and kept her head down as I went by.

My conscience jabbed me as I squeaked away. I held myself straight, trying to salvage what I could of my shopping fantasy. I remembered accompanying my mother to the grocery store as a child. She'd hold her list in one hand and steer the cart with the other, making well-planned stops. I'd thought then that someday, when I was a big person, I'd come to the grocery and fill that cart with whatever I wanted.

I tried to milk the memory, to step into that childhood dream, but the joy was gone from my shopping. I placed a few things in the cart, being very careful not to add them up. I wouldn't total them, wouldn't be like the others, buying whatever would bring the most change.

The checker at the market looked as harried as the postal clerk had. Her bleached blonde hair fell in limp waves across her forehead. With a droop of her shoulders, she accepted my foodstamps without comment and, lifting her cash drawer, made change in kind.

Outside the store, the Poet was slumped by the newspaper dispensers. Without looking up, she held out her fist.

"Your change," she said formally.

"No, keep it."

She measured her words carefully.

"I wasn't asking you for charity, Dee. Here is your merchandise—" she deposited a chocolate drumstick in my grocery bag. "And here is your change. Eighty-four cents."

She dropped the money in the bag as well. I remembered how we'd shared our change the first day we met, how we'd passed a quart of beer back and forth and sung together. My annoyance with her ebbed away; remorse rolled in to replace it.

I tried to repair the situation. The Poet had hoped that she and I could have fun with my foodstamps, buying junk food and making lots of change to buy wine. I felt I'd seriously let her down and, worse, set myself above her by refusing to play.

How could I preserve our friendship now? How salve her wounded feelings?

"Would you like to come eat with me?" I asked.

"No, thanks all the same," she replied stiffly. "It's a busy day for me."

She walked away, head held high, her blonde cap of hair glinting in a ray of sun.

"At least take the ice cream!" I called after her.

She didn't turn around.

I lifted my bag of groceries from the cart. Getting the food, which I'd fantasized for so long, looking forward to the half-hour of respectability it would give, had lost me a friend. The stamps in my pocket felt heavy.

Then there was the drumstick, melting in my bag. I took it out. It was quite soft, chocolate and nuts running together, cone soggy to the touch.

I shifted the groceries to my hip, hearing the change jingle down to the bottom of the bag. The drumstick dripped from my right hand as I walked through the parking lot. When I'd cleared the cars, a Gate 5 dog ran up to me. I set the drumstick on the ground; he sniffed it warily.

"Eat," I said. "It's a gift."

He sniffed it, circled it, sniffed again, then walked away from it. I wiped my sticky hands on my pants and walked away too, leaving it, a dark puddle on the pavement.

"For the Lord…does not despise His who are prisoners."
(Psalm 69:33)

Chapter 6

Autumn, 1981

One night, I could not shake the uneasy sensation that I was being followed, being watched. I had a little cash on me; I'd sold a packet of food stamps in Marin City the week before and hadn't yet spent it all. (My issue had been renewed, and I'd long since lost my scruples about selling stamps.) Why should I become a victim? I'd fool my hidden pursuers with stealth, taking back roads to the corner market for wine. Paranoia? Or proper caution? Either way, I felt very crafty plotting my route.

I could follow the fence by the boat yard. I thought it went all the way through to the back of Omar's garage. From there, the market was just across a parking lot. Excellent plan, I congratulated myself. You've developed good street smarts.

Clutching my jacket around me, I started off.

"If you're moving at night," Miguel had told me, "Stay in the shadows. Avoid bright light, and if you hear a movement, hold very still. That's how animals do it."

There was a big patch of anise growing along the fence. It threw a deep shadow, and I ran for it, then paused. No movement, no footsteps. I scurried quickly into the next shadow, then the next, until I'd reached the familiar shape of the garage.

There was no banging from inside, no music or voices either. Omar must be out. The closer I got to my destination, the safer I felt. I left the fence and walked down the middle of the road, whistling "Oh Susannah" to embolden myself and prove to the bogeymen that I was unafraid.

I'd gone a few feet when a car screeched around the corner of the garage. Panicked, I jumped to the side and quickened my pace. To my dismay, the car cruised right alongside me, its red and blue top lights flashing. A policeman leaned out.

"Where you headed?"

"Ah—the Open Door."

"That's funny," he commented. "It's in the other direction. Hold up. We want to talk to you a minute."

I sped up; so did the car. The driver turned it to block me off; his partner jumped out.

"Come on," he called. "Don't be afraid. See the side of the car? 'Protect and Serve,' it says. That's us. We just want to talk with you a minute."

"Let's not do a chase scene," the car's driver called out laughingly. "This is a lousy road."

Warily, I decided that running wouldn't get me very far. Anyway, why panic? I hadn't done anything wrong, I reminded myself. The men were even enjoying themselves. Were they laughing at my expense? What was so funny? I resented them.

"So, what are you doing out on this road?"

"Just walking."

"Uh huh. Your name?

"Dee Williams."

"Got any ID?"

"No."

I'd been so careful once to carry a purse with identification. Where had it gone? Lost, of course, in the process of moving from apartment to car to van to abandoned car. Well, it shouldn't matter much. Should it?

He shone a flashlight on my face. I squinted against it, feeling like a rabbit impaled by the light. His partner was repeating my name into the car radio. I heard the hiss of static. They consulted briefly.

"Remember me, Ms. Williams? Officer Gainer. I gave you a warning on your car registration twice, couple years ago."

Forever ago! I did remember being stopped on my way to deliver an editing job. I'd forgotten to mail in a check for registration and had been issued a fix-it ticket. Was this the same cop? How could he possibly remember me?

The car radio hissed again. Of course. He didn't remember me; the information had come over the radio.

"Where's the car now, Ms. Williams?"

"The car's long gone."

"Mm hm. Well, you've got a warrant out. Looks like you never took care of it."

This couldn't be happening! It was too absurd. A ticket for a car I no longer had? "Yes, but—but there's no car anymore." I was stammering, and I longed for an eloquent flow of speech that would convince them and send them on their way.

Swiftly, his manner changed.

"Hands on the hood."

I shook my head and looked for any escape. With his hand on my back, he pushed me up to his car, grabbed my hands and fixed them on the hood. Briskly, he whacked my jacket pockets.

I whirled around and dodged under his arm. His partner leapt from the car and pinned my arms behind my back. I heard a click and felt cold sharp metal. I was handcuffed.

"No! You can't arrest me! You can't take me to jail. I'm no criminal."

My voice was loud and panicky. It squealed out into the night and ricocheted off the police car back to me. I was horrified to have made such a sound, equally horrified by my situation. Good people didn't go to jail! Outrage and disbelief surged up within me. I twisted my wrists, and the cuffs bit back. I was trapped.

The driver returned to his seat. Gainer opened the back door.

"Please," I pleaded frantically. "Let me go. I tell you, there's no car anymore! D-don't take me in."

He nudged me toward the open door. Limply, I acquiesced and slid into the back seat. My resistance flared briefly as he closed the door.

"You're making a terrible mistake," I called. "Just terrible. You really can't do this."

The driver laughed.

"We do it every night," he assured me. "We checked you out first for loitering. Then it turned out you had a warrant."

The car started up. I closed my eyes and leaned back into the seat, feeling raw panic surge within me. Jail. My God. It was bitterly unfair. Maybe when I got there I could talk my way out of it. Find someone who'd listen. Explain that it was all a mistake. Better yet, I thought fiercely, I'd tell the papers. Expose these guys for false arrest, or for... something.

It was dark outside, and I was suddenly confused. Where were we headed? The jail, of course. But what direction were we going? From the freeway, dark shapes seemed to whiz by.

Then I began to recognize the route. It was the same one we'd taken up to get food stamps. I longed to be back in that day, involved in an innocent errand. If only Paula were here. She'd know what to do. Well, I wouldn't wish that. But if only I were riding along with her in the truck.

I leaned back. The handcuffs chafed my wrists. I wriggled my hands, trying to find relief.

I remembered hearing that the jail was right next door to all the offices for social services. Yes. Up ahead loomed the graceful shape of a building which seemed to grow out of the hill that was its base.

The car curved off the freeway, through a huge back parking lot, and into a space under a covered archway. We were here. Oh God. What would I do now? I'd had no experience with jail. How did one behave? Should I act tough? Demand a lawyer? Or should I be gentle and plead for understanding and release. The cops had laughed and joked as if we were playing a game. This situation, though, was no game for me. Did they really enjoy bringing in innocent people? I was aggrieved. My fear had turned to self-righteous indignation.

"We're home," said Gainer. "Out you go." He led me over to the side of the building, where others were waiting for an elevator. There were two guards standing watch. The rest were men in street clothes who, like me, were handcuffed. They all looked resigned; several were laughing together as if this were a familiar joke. I slumped against the wall.

Gainer handed some paperwork to one of the guards and spoke with him, then waved at me.

"Be good," he said, and loped back to the car.

I closed my eyes, not wanting to be there, willing it to end.

"Hey, sister," said a soft voice. "You're out late."

I opened my eyes. A tall, thin man in a baseball cap and denim jacket was leaning up against the wall. He winked, then wiggled his fingers at me. His hands were cuffed in front.

"It's all a mistake," I said earnestly.

He chuckled. "Oh yeah. Wrong place, wrong time."

A guard marched up to us. Gainer had been relaxed and jovial. This one was serious. His iron-grey hair was clipped close to his head; his pale eyes snapped.

"No talking among prisoners! No fraternizing. Just wait for the elevator." He glared at us to make sure his orders were followed.

There was a snort of laughter behind him. He turned and marched in its direction. The man next to me winked again and lifted his cuffed hands to his shirt pocket. He tipped out a cigarette and raised his eyebrows in a question. I nodded. He placed one in my mouth and lit it. I was impressed with his dexterity.

"Lots of practice," he whispered.

Instantly, the guard was back.

"No smoking!" he barked. "No fraternizing and no smoking. No passing of contraband."

The cuffed man dropped his hands and spat out the cigarette he'd placed in his own mouth, still unlit. The guard hit him in the chest with the heel of his hand so that the pack popped out. He squeezed it in his fist and threw it to the ground.

"What—what are you doing?" I gasped, shocked at the vicious response.

The one in cuffs rolled his eyes heavenward, shaking his head at me. The guard spun round and pulled the cigarette from my mouth, threw it down, ground it out.

"Are you deaf?" he barked, face inches from mine.

"Are you human?" I hissed back, emboldened.

There was silence, a collective holding of breath, as the others watched me and the guard. He looked at me impassively for a moment. Then his face twisted. He gave a short burst of derisive laughter and slammed my shoulders up against the wall.

"You're in jail now," he growled. "Follow procedure. I said no smoking."

Tears sprang to my eyes. People weren't supposed to act this way. I felt a wetness on my cheeks. Oh no, I was crying. I stiffened, fighting for control of myself. I didn't want the bully guard to think he could make me cry. Nor did I want the others to see me as a weakling.

The elevator clanged open and he herded us in. The one who'd offered me a smoke continued to shake his head at me. He held his finger up to his mouth, as to caution silence. I ignored him. Better angry than crying, I thought. From my corner of the elevator, I glared at the guard.

What could I say to him? How could I reach through his toughness? Threaten to report him? No—he'd have others inside just like himself. He'd just laugh at me again. I struggled for the words. Then it came to me.

"Your mother would be ashamed of you," I said.

He drew himself up straight.

"My mother's very proud of me," he retorted stiffly.

Our elevator bumped to a stop, and he got out. The car proceeded on, jerkily. It had left the metal shaft. It was a crosshatched cage now, a container of people moving slowly upward.

We could see outside of the elevator cage. Officers were moving along a corridor, not paying much attention to our ascending crate.

"Where are we going?"

"Jail's on the top floor."

As we ascended, I called out again.

"This is a bad mistake! You'll—you'll regret it." A guard turned his head up toward me, bored.

"Look around," he said. "*You're* the one in handcuffs. Doesn't that tell you something?"

"Save your energy," advised my friend inside the cage. "You'll just make it worse on yourself."

We stopped again. A guard slid our cage open and led the men down the length of the hall. Another brought me into a brightly lit cubicle. She unlocked my cuffs and left, clanging bars behind her. There was a bench on the wall; I sat down to wait. At least my wrists were free. I rubbed them.

I reviewed my situation. I'd been stopped just for walking down a road. This business about car registration seemed like just an excuse to pull me in. A bad excuse. What should I do?

A guard entered the holding cell. At the same time, another guard appeared behind a crosshatched grate in the office beyond.

"Hands on the counter." She proceeded to search my pockets, pulling out a comb and a pencil and foodstamp cash from my jeans and putting them in a small pile on the ledge.

"Sign here for your property, Williams."

The guard behind the counter pushed a paper toward me. Shakily, I signed for the tumble of articles on the counter.

The guard who'd searched me opened the barred door.

"Follow me, Williams."

She led me into a little room which was brightly lit and filled with paraphernalia.

"We need to get you printed. Step up to the counter now and let your hand relax. Let me do the work."

Set on the counter was an ink pad and a stack of white cards. She took my hand and rolled the fingers in greasy ink.

"Relax your hand, Williams, or we'll have to do this over."

She grasped my hand and rolled it again, then pressed my fingers one by one onto one of the white cards. Bleakly, I watched as the imprint of my fingers filled the card. I had a record now. I thought of my past academic life, the honors I'd won. Now here I was: Dr. Williams, felon.

"Other hand."

As if in a very bad dream, I let myself be printed.

"Okay, you can wash up at the sink here." She handed me a paper towel that she'd squirted with cleanser, and I wiped the deep black ink from my fingers, then soaped off the rest.

"Now step up to the red line. I'm going to take your picture."

"Do you have to? I'm here on a very minor offense."

She escorted me to the red line, impatiently. "Standard procedure. This'll just take a second."

She stepped behind a large black camera. An intense light shone in my eyes, and I blinked into the flash.

"Now. Wasn't that easy? I'm taking you back to booking."

She led me back to the waiting room. I sat tensely on the bench and began to watch the corridor for another passing guard.

"I need a phone call," I insisted, whenever one went by. Finally, the window inside the room opened again.

"Here, then," said a woman, pushing a telephone onto the counter. Trembling with hope, I called the operator and got the Open Door number.

"Open Door. Hank speaking."

"Hank! Dee. I'm in jail."

"What are you doing there?"

"I was just walking along and they took me in. Can you come get me?"

"No. Don't worry, though. If it's just for loitering, they won't keep you long."

"Yes, but I shouldn't be here, Hank. It's just about some unpaid registration for a car."

He laughed at that. "These things have a way of catching up to you, Dee. Don't worry, now. At least you'll get a warm place to sleep. It's noisy here; we're about to close. We'll see you when you get out—we'll pray for you."

A deep, desolate loneliness rushed through me as I hung up. I'd thought my one phone call would make a difference, would fix things, but I was still here alone. No one was rushing to my rescue. With a hard, cold certainty, I felt the reality of where I was.

The guard pulled the phone back into her office and left, to reappear outside the bars. She unlocked the door.

"Okay, Williams. You'll have to go to court on this warrant. You're lucky; it's Thursday night. Court's tomorrow. Follow me."

She took me into another room. It had concrete floor and walls. There was an open shower in the corner. She left again, re-emerging behind another glass window. These people love exits and entrances, I thought. The frequent appearance and disappearance of the guards was disorienting. It was designed, I supposed, to mark my difference from them. I was enclosed; they were not.

She pushed a bundle of clothing onto a counter. "Leave your street clothes in the corner," she instructed. "Shower over there, then change into these. We'll have to hold you overnight."

"But—but why are you keeping me here at all?"

She glanced at a sheaf of paperwork in her hand.

"Looks like a traffic offense." She looked up at me, briefly puzzled, as if the evidence in front of her did not match the paperwork. She shook her head.

"Get moving; I'll be back in five." Then she was gone again.

I went into the shower stall, hoping its walls would hide me from view. The overhead light, I thought, might contain a camera. Shivering, I went over to the shower and turned the tap.

A torrent of hot water surged out. I stood under it, delighting in the spray. It pelted my skin and my tense muscles. I luxuriated in it and felt my resistance melt. It had been a long time since I'd taken a shower. When I reached for the bar of rough soap, the water stopped.

"Hit the button," said the guard. So she was in the room with me. I looked out; she was gathering up my clothes and dropping them into a plastic bag. Baffled, I looked for a button.

"Here," she said, slamming her fist into a metal circle on the wall. Instantly, the water gushed out again.

Showered, I toweled off and stepped into the clothes she'd left me. There was a sweatshirt and some drawstring pants, very clean and raspy with starch.

Again the door clanged open. "Come on, I'll take you to your cell." Outrage and fear had gone; I felt limp and passive now. I just followed her.

In the dim light I could see the outline of two bunk beds against the wall and a table in the middle. Behind a low partition were a toilet and sink.

Two of the bunks were occupied, upper and lower. The body on the lower bunk groaned and covered her eyes with her arm.

"In here," said the guard. She handed me a flimsy nightgown and bedding. "Court call comes early. Be ready."

Her footsteps echoed down the hall. Still trembling, I made up an empty bunk and climbed into it. Across from me, the woman on the upper bunk reared up on her elbows.

"Don't even think about getting acquainted now," she ordered me. "We don't care why you're here; we just want to get some sleep. Save it for the morning."

She lowered herself back down with a definitive thunk. "Fine by me," I replied with bravado. "Good night."

I huddled into a lower bunk, willing myself not to snore and offend them. It hurt my feelings that they didn't want to hear my story. Well all right, if they wanted to be that way. I'd feign indifference too. Court tomorrow—I'd be eloquent. I'd get right out of here. The judge might even apologize to me. With that comforting thought, I rolled over and went to sleep.

***

There wasn't much time to get acquainted with my cellmates in the morning, either. Breakfast came, rattling in on a cart. An inmate handed our plates in to us, through the bars, and we ate on the table in our cell. I was very pleased to have a hot meal. I tried not to be—after all, I shouldn't even be here—but I was pleased nonetheless. Hot meals were rare. Gratefully, I sipped coffee and spooned hot cereal into my mouth. I was dubious about a side dish of stewed prunes, but the orange balanced on the plate seemed safe enough. I'd save it for later.

"Room service, yet," sneered one of my roommates. She was an attractive woman, very slender with long dark hair and an aquiline nose. "I'm afraid to get used to it. I get transferred to C.I.W. next week."

I didn't want to betray my ignorance so didn't ask her what C.I.W. was. She eyed me tolerantly.

"California Institute for Women," she said. "The real place, the prison. This dinky jail is a country club."

"No golf," pointed out the other woman, munching toast. She was a redhead, shorter and stockier than the glamorous one. "You don't want your coffee?"

"I'll trade you for the orange."

They swapped and chattered on, ignoring me. I felt slighted. They belonged; they knew what they were doing. I didn't. I was awkward, tongue-tied, in contrast with their glibness. Out of place.

Right after breakfast, I was called for court. The courthouse was next door to the jail. I was taken to a small chamber downstairs to wait. Another woman was standing in the stairwell.

She pointed at the door in front of her.

"Courtroom's right through that door," she said. "When do you think they'll let us in? My lawyer's supposed to meet me. Where do you think he is?"

Upstairs, to my roommates, I'd been a novice. In this woman's eyes, I was an expert. Pleased, I tried to adjust to my new role.

"Oh—he'll be along."

She thrust out her hand.

"I'm Amanda. They told me to wait here. I hate waiting, don't you? Do I look all right? I'm so glad they let me put my street clothes on. I wish I had my makeup, though. I feel so pale. How do I look?"

She had blonde hair, frizzed all around her head in a halo. Her eyes were enormous and bulged slightly outward, very pale blue. They reminded me of robin's eggs. Her face was sharp and thin.

She was in a constant motion, her hands pulling at her sweater, pushing at her hair. I wondered if she were coming down from the effects of a drug. She looked and sounded hyper.

"You look fine. Look at me, I'm in jail clothes. Next to me, you look—innocent."

"Oh, I hope so. I don't know what to tell the lawyer." She plucked at her hair and poured out another rush of words.

"Listen! I'm in a really bad dorm. Upstairs. The women scare me. Should I tell the lawyer about it? Can he do anything? I couldn't sleep all night. They're so tough in there—I think they belong to a gang. They keep saying they're going to beat me up or rape me. Oh, I couldn't sleep. Should I tell him?"

She stopped plucking at herself and started plucking at me, tugging at my sweatshirt. I wanted to get rid of her, but there was no place to go. Was she exaggerating about the gangs? It made me profoundly uneasy to contemplate. What could I do?

"Sure, tell him everything."

"If I tell him, will he get me out? Will he believe me? Listen, what if he doesn't believe me?"

I began to wish fervently that her lawyer would come and get her away from me. If she acted this way inside the jail, I could see how her roommates would be very tempted to scare her silent. Yet, my attitude amazed me. How quickly I'd become cynical. What if she was in real danger?

"I'm no expert, Amanda. The ones in your cell were probably just trying to get a reaction—trying to scare you."

"Well, they did!"

"Yeah."

A gray-suited man appeared. He was as frenetic as she, also thin and angular, also in constant motion. He gestured with one ringed hand, twitched his briefcase with the other.

They began talking at each other. Her voice rose in pitch. His hands waved faster in the air.

"It's important that you let me do the talking," he insisted.

She darted a glance at me.

"I'm going to tell him," she said.

"Good. Do. And after you tell him," I made a motion with my finger across my mouth, "Hush up."

I was acting as if I knew what I were doing. The lawyer grinned appreciatively at me and drew her into the courtroom. I felt good and tough. Here I was, already advising a defendant. I'd do just fine with my own case, I thought confidently.

A guard came down the stairs, trailed by a group of male prisoners who were linked together on a long chain. The guard escorted us all into the first three rows of the courtroom. Amanda and her lawyer were over to one side. She looked pale and resigned. I wondered what the real trouble was.

The room was overwhelmingly brown. The walls were paneled in a deep shade of wood; the benches and judge's desk were an even darker wood. A flag in the corner gleamed with the only color.

The judge entered, looking tired, and began to call the cases forward. My earlier confidence had faded. Everything was so official. Would I get swallowed up by the system? My hands were clammy; my stomach fluttered. Now my only hope was that he'd call me soon so I could get out of there.

"Milton," he said, rustling through a set of folders in front of him. "Milton, James."

A black man in the front row lifted his head briefly. He was in his sixties, I guessed. His head and face were covered with white stubble. The guard had unfastened the chains, and Mr. Milton folded his hands in his lap and sat politely, looking briefly at the judge and then down at his shoes.

A man from the lawyers' table stood. "It's a case of dine and dash, Your Honor," he said.

The judge winced.

"All right," he said. "Step forward, Mr. Milton."

The prisoner walked up to the judge and stood, keeping his head bowed.

"Mr. Milton, you're charged with entering the…" he checked his notes. "Entering a Red Barn Restaurant and ordering a meal, then attempting to leave without paying for it."

Milton nodded, still looking down.

"How do you plead?"

"Yessir, I did it," said Milton. "I was hungry. I'm sorry I did wrong."

The lawyer stood.

"We plead guilty, Your Honor," he clarified. The judge nodded impatiently. He grimaced as if Milton's situation pained him.

I was intrigued. That was one way to get fed—order a meal and then sneak out the back. Could I do it without getting caught? Be worth a try sometime.

The judge seemed embarrassed by the situation. What would he do?

"Mr. Milton, you've been in jail since Wednesday evening?"

"Yessir."

"Time served," he said, clunking his gavel in front of him.

The old man rose and a guard led him out. The judge passed his hand over his face for a moment. Was he regretting that a man had gone to jail for being hungry?

"Williams, Dee."

I stood up. Tension coiled within me.

"Please approach the bench. The charge is driving with a lapsed registration. I see you had two warnings on this violation. How do you plead?"

"Guilty, but I no longer have the car."

He looked up at me.

"You don't have the car?"

"It was stolen." That seemed simpler than explaining I'd traded it in for a van that was taken away from me.

He snorted "pah" and rolled his eyes at the bailiff as if pleading for some real cases.

"All right, Ms. Williams. Still, when you had the car, you were driving with lapsed registration. Are you pleading guilty?"

"Yes."

"That will be a fine of $350 or 3 nights in jail. I see you've already spent one night."

"Yes. I'll take the jail." As I spoke, I felt deeply the difference between myself and those well-dressed civilians who were here at court voluntarily, to take care of tickets. I knew they'd simply pay fines. With my acceptance of jail, I was marking myself as a woman who had no choice. Overnight, my attitude had changed. Going to jail had seemed outrageous, impossible, insulting. Now, it was just expedient—the only way out.

The judge nodded and motioned to the bailiff.

"May I speak?"

He frowned at me. "Briefly."

I turned quickly and pointed out Amanda. "There's a woman here who's been threatened in her cell. Please take care of her."

The bailiff bustled me out. Amanda waved.

On the way back to the cell, I wondered why on earth I'd spoken. For all I knew, Amanda had been making the whole thing up. I cautioned myself to be more careful with my sympathy, not to be so gullible. I could get into trouble that way.

Back on the women's side of jail, the automated barred door gave a hiss and then clanged shut behind me. Desolation thudded through me at the sound. It was so——final.

***

My cell mates were sitting at the table, laughing over the newspaper. The short redhead was reading aloud.

"Video Theft in Richmond," she giggled. "Here, they mention my name:

Janet Morgan and Wilson Frede, both from Oakland, were apprehended in Richmond after a high-speed chase. Police found stolen video equipment and boxes of videos in the car. The couple was captured after raiding stores in both Oakland and Richmond.

"Well, you're famous," congratulated the glamorous one wryly.

"Yeah. I told him, you know. I begged him. 'Honey,' I said, 'Let's go home now. We have enough. Please, let's stay out of Richmond'."

"Why Richmond?" I asked, butting in. I wouldn't let them ignore me today.

"Ah, that place. They hate mixed-race couples there. But he had to go, wouldn't listen. There we were in a red convertible, racing along. Then the cops started chasing us, and he"—she shook her head fondly—"he tried to outrun them."

She set the newspaper down on the metal table. "I saw him right outside of court yesterday," she confided. "He was all messed up; his arm was in a sling. He told me he was sorry. 'I love you, baby,' he kept saying. 'Do you love me?'"

Glamour, the dark-haired woman, laughed appreciatively. "Don't they get romantic when they're locked up? Mine has been sending me love letters. I keep 'em under my pillow. They're really hot. I hope he keeps sending them…we've got two years to go. I'll be glad to get moved out of here so I can settle down to do my real time."

My cellmates were waiting to be transferred to a real prison, and they were so calm about it. I'd be out in another two days. I tried to let that sense of perspective cheer me and lift the bleakness that had descended when I returned to the cell. My sentence was nothing compared to theirs.

"What's he in for?" I asked Glamour. She'd told me the night before not to mention our own offenses, but maybe I could get away with asking about her partner.

She gave me a level blue-eyed look. "Grand theft. He's a thief, a good one. He'd never get caught. It was some people we were staying with who turned us in. I just got 'Receiving Stolen Property.'"

"How about you?" asked Richmond. "How'd it go in court?"

"Three nights in jail," I replied.

"Three nights? What were you, drunk?"

"No," I said. "It's political." The lie came easily. Being a political prisoner seemed dramatic, interesting. I'd impress them with my special status.

Richmond raised her eyebrows at Glamour, who snorted to suppress a laugh.

"Yeah? How come you didn't just bail out?"

"Oh," I waved my hands airily. "I didn't have the money on me when I was picked up."

"So call a friend."

Anxiety welled up inside me. I didn't want them to know I was destitute and lost in here. Churning with turmoil, I searched my mind for a way to win their respect.

"Yes, yes," I said airily. "I have called. Actually, I manage a theatrical troupe. They were very upset to hear I'm in here. They're out raising the money right now. They may show up at any time, really."

"Uh huh." As one, they rose from the table and turned their backs to me. Nudging each other, they settled on the lower bunk.

"I'll read you these letters," said Glamour to Richmond.

"Don't leave out any good parts."

Excluded. It had been a mistake to lie. But the truth was so banal! Now I was trapped. I looked around for something to read myself. I'd pretend I didn't care that they left me out.

"Two more days!" Richmond moaned quietly. Glamour patted her on the shoulder, commiserating.

They were talking about me—about being stuck with me. I felt ashamed and profoundly lonely. I was unwanted even here. Maybe it had been over the edge to mention a theatrical troupe. Possession of drugs would have carried more weight. Oh well. They didn't want me here, but they'd just have to put up with me.

Having said that my troupe would rescue me, I began to hope someone would. However, no one came. It was a long, slow day and night.

The next day, after lunch, we were taken out to the yard. It was a cement oblong, with a few tables set up in the sun. Above us were loops of barbed wire which cast sinister shadows on the ground. These chilled me. It was impossible to pretend to be anywhere else but jail.

Several of the women bounced a basketball around and made half-hearted attempts at a game. Most sat on the sidelines, smoking and talking. I was still ignored. I traced "out" with my foot on the ground.

What would it be like to get used to this life? Nothing happened here, it seemed. It was tedious, with constant reminders of locks and bars and the dreadful looped wires. I thought it would wear me down to nothing if I were to stay here any length of time.

On our return indoors, I asked a guard about Amanda. I learned she was on a bus to another facility. I wondered about her and about the others in here. There were about thirty women, from what I could tell. Thirty lives suspended.

We ate dinner in our cell. My cell mates were both expecting to be moved soon. They were eager to go.

"They won't leave us in this ritzy place," said Richmond. "It's really just a glorified holding cell. You now, you get out soon."

She asked me pointedly if my friends had arrived, but Glamour silenced her and offered me her own orange. I was grateful for the gesture. I accepted the fruit graciously, peeled it slowly, ate each section. It's an apology, I thought. The orange of peace. I beamed my thanks.

That night I lay huddled in my bunk, trying not to make a sound. Sleep came slowly. Guards periodically paced the corridor outside our room, checking that we were still there. Where would we go?

I was still confused by what had happened. I'd been walking down a road, whistling, playing a hiding game with the shadows. Then I'd been scooped up and put in jail. It amazed me how quickly it had happened. In an eyeblink, it seemed, my freedom could be taken from me. Was this the way it would be from here on out? What could I do about it? Stay on guard. Be vigilant. Keep hidden.

The next morning, I was released. A guard came for me.

"Bye," said Glamour, somewhat wistfully. "Now be good out there, and don't come back."

"Break a leg," added Richmond, a sarcastic grin sliding over her face.

I was taken to the shower room to exchange my jail clothes for street clothes. A new guard stood behind the counter.

"Ms. Williams," she said. "Sometimes people leave clothing here, so we have—a few extra items. I wonder if you might like to wear some of those."

"Why?"

"Well, they're laundered. Of course, if you prefer your own…"

I thought she was being very tactful. She was offering me charity clothing. These guards on the women's side made up for the bully of two nights before.

"I'll just leave a few things here, and you can decide."

She passed me a black garbage bag that held my clothes and left a folded stack on the counter. I opened the bag. A warm, moldy, sweaty odor. Was that how I smelled, out there? Disgusting.

Firmly, I tied the bag back up and dropped it in the trash. The clean clothes she'd set out were a pair of tan slacks, a bulky red sweater, a jersey. Clean socks, and tennis shoes—I put them on. The red sweater was my favorite.

"Those fit fine," she said, returning. "Another woman is being released this morning. You can go on out together."

The door opened. In walked a tall black woman I recognized from the yard. She changed quickly into her own street clothes that the guard passed to her—no charity treatment for her, I noticed. She must have come in clean. She put on a short green knit dress, black heels, a long trench coat that she belted loosely.

"That's better," she said. "Where's my property?"

The guard set two plastic baggies on the counter, tagged with our names. We opened them, surreptitiously looking at what the other had. Her bag held long green earrings that she immediately fastened on, a pocket knife, a make-up kit, loose change, and a tangle of spangled bracelets.

She slipped on the bracelets quickly, one after another, and shook her arm, making a tinkling sound.

"These are better than the bracelets you provide," she told the guard. "I had a purse, too."

The guard passed it across, and the woman dumped the remaining contents of her baggie into it.

My property consisted of a twenty dollar bill that was left from when I'd cashed in my food stamps, a few pencils, and a charm I'd found loose on the ground. It was a miniature Eiffel tower. There was also a one dollar food stamp that must have come loose from the original booklet.

Heartened, I put it all in the pocket of my slacks.

The guard rode with us down in the elevator; it was a much quicker trip this time.

"Goodbye, ladies," she said, and we stood together on the sidewalk, blinking in the bright autumn sunshine that came slanting over the hills. Freedom!

I was out. For how long? It was disorienting to be standing in the cool morning air, without bars or slamming doors. I'd walk differently from now on, with a consciousness of who might be behind me, following me, waiting to take me in.

But for now I was free, and I felt joy and excitement bubbling up within. Colors were brighter. The hills were golden. Life was good.

"Huh," said the woman next to me, indicating the departing guard. "She can be nice when she wants to be. Like anyone else, I guess. What's your name?"

I told her. She shook my hand, gravely.

"I'm Tanya. Where you headed now? You got a ride?"

"No. They never showed up."

"They never do," she agreed. "I'm going to Marin City."

"Sausalito."

"Right next door. We could share a cab."

"I hadn't thought of that."

"Can't you afford it?"

"I can, actually."

"Thought you looked flush. Me too. Lucky—I don't always get pulled in when I've got money on me."

She looked me over.

"Nice pants," she said. "They don't really go with that sweater, though."

I looked down at myself.

"No. I didn't put this outfit together. My own clothes got…torn, and so these came from jail. Someone left them."

"Uh huh. I thought they looked familiar."

We rounded the corner. She walked purposefully to a pay phone, jingling her pockets for change.

"Is this Bay Cab?"

She spoke forcefully into the receiver, describing our location. As she hung up, she grinned at me.

"A cab's the best. Go home in style when you can, girl. We don't want to straggle back on no bus."

A cab pulled up a short time later. The driver leaned over in his seat and peered at us. I saw us through his eyes—two women, just out of jail. One all dolled up, one nervously neat. Both teetering on the sidewalk, preparing to re-enter the world. He paused, then got out and gravely made a point of opening the door for us. "Morning, Tanya. I thought it must be you."

"Yes, sweetheart. Give us a nice ride now, me and my friend here, and we'll give you a big tip."

As we rode along, she opened her plump, soft leather bag and began applying make-up.

"Never go back looking puny," she advised. "Here." She reached over and sprayed me with scent. "If they ask where you were, just tell 'em you needed a little rest."

The cab rolled on; she applied mascara and a deep glossy lipstick. She was transforming herself completely. She'd been somber in the yard, with a grim and off-putting expression. Now she sparkled.

"I'd hardly recognize you."

"That's it, girl. Keep 'em guessing. Oh, you mean from in there. Well, no. I don't socialize inside. Say one word in there, and it gets right out. You'll hear it in the yard the next day. Hah! I don't need people knowing my business."

She leaned forward and tapped the driver's shoulder.

"Slow down," she said. "Here, go slow. There's someone I know."

Obligingly, he slowed. She opened the door and leapt from the cab, bag flying behind her.

I was stunned by her flight. The cabdriver laughed.

"She's good at that," he remarked. "She cuts out before paying. I should have known. She did it so you'd have to take care of the fare yourself."

I felt bitterly foolish. Tanya had scoped me out in jail, when we were getting our property back. She'd marked me as someone who could pay her fare back home. Her seeming friendliness had been calculated to put me off guard.

"Where to?" asked the driver.

I looked at the meter.

"How much more to take me to the mini-mart in Sausalito? The one right by the freeway."

"About five dollars."

Recklessly, I decided to spend what I had. "Go ahead, then."

He dropped me off where I'd requested. Paying him took most of my cash.

"Next time," he advised, "Get her share of the money up front."

Ha! As if I'd be tricked that way again. "There won't be a next time," I said firmly.

"That's right," he agreed cheerfully. "Learn from experience. See you."

"And it came about that as he journeyed, he was
approaching Damascus, and suddenly a light from
heaven flashed around him; and he fell to the ground,
and heard a voice saying to him, 'Saul, Saul, why are
you persecuting Me?'"
(Acts 9:3,4)

CHAPTER 7

The cab pulled off.

I'm all right, I thought, trying to convince myself. I'm a free woman. I'm the sort who takes cabs home. I'm a woman of style. Then came the reality: I need a drink.

I stood in the parking lot for a moment, reorienting myself. It was so good to be outdoors again. Details were bright and bold. In front of me, the hills rose pale green in the early morning light. Behind me were the bay and the shrill cry of gulls. I breathed deeply of salt air. I'd been locked up for only three nights, yet I felt different, shaky, knowing this world I enjoyed was precarious, could be taken away.

Had anyone seen me arriving in style? No, there was no one I knew in the smattering of people milling around the mini mart. I straightened up, counting my change. There was just enough for a small bottle of wine. What a relief. I purchased it.

Things looked different this morning. The shadows, the running, the panic, the sudden bright glare of police lights, the outrage—all had receded. I unscrewed the cap on my wine and took a long drink. Instantly, I was flooded with warmth and comfort. Then I went on the alert: better be careful. Didn't want to share it, didn't want to get picked up again for having it. I hid the bottle in its brown paper bag. I'd nurse it all morning.

From where I stood, I could see the road that curved through a tunnel into Marin City. The town was known for its Flea Market, held every Sunday in a vacant lot. The Market bordered both Marin City and Sausalito and attracted many people. I could see a steady stream of them, some on foot, most driving vans and pick-ups, all on their way to find bargains.

"Dee!" It was Paula, hailing me from the road. "Come on!"

"Where are you heading?"

"The Flea Market. It's a good time."

She drew closer. "I heard you got pulled into jail. Best thing is not to dwell on it. We all go in at one time or another."

Did Paula have an answer for every situation? Yes. But I felt reluctant to go along with her today. I felt still half-in and half-out of jail. I needed time to assimilate what had happened, to make sense of it. I wanted to hole up and finish my bottle.

"I don't know about the Market. I haven't got any money left."

"So what? It's just good to get out and mingle. After 4, lots of people leave things they didn't sell. It's good for scavenging then."

She patted my arm. "So, come on. I know a guy who'll take foodstamps for a falafel. I'll get you one."

Some food? Tempting. I'd begun to get used to regular meals in jail. Funny, that. I nodded and matched my step to hers. It was easier to give in than to resist. I felt the same passivity I'd experienced in jail. What had happened to my spirit? Oh well. I'd tag along and then, when she wasn't looking, I'd finish the bottle and duck out again. The Flea

Market meant crowds of people, and I wasn't quite ready for people. Jostling, pushing...

I walked mechanically, my mind buzzing with the noise and color of my surroundings. Jail had dulled my senses. Now they were jangled with the barrage of sensation. Cool morning air. Brightly colored cars. People laughing, talking.

We crossed the highway and headed up the hill, through the smooth tunnel that led to the Flea Market field. We passed the bottle back and forth; I'd decided against hoarding it since she was going to feed me. The inside of the tunnel was smeared with graffiti. The names of the two towns, Sausalito and Marin City, were distorted in here. "Sleaze-a-lito" someone had scrawled in red. "Moron City," another had painted in retaliation.

Paula sombered in the tunnel. "Did you hear about Andy? This is where he got killed, just a few days ago."

I stopped, feeling sick at the news. Dead.

"What happened?"

"He was loaded and he wanted to ride his motorcycle. People tried to stop him, but he had to drive it. He took off on that damn bike, took the turn too fast, and wham! Creamed out. Right here."

I stood very still, horrified and chilled to be at a death scene. I looked for bloodstains, but there were none. It was just a road. I hadn't known Andy, but I remembered him as the motorcyclist who'd buzzed the truck when we were returning from getting foodstamps. He'd been a daredevil that day, jeering at us and trying to scare us as he pretended to run us down. He'd been invincible, I'd thought. Now he was gone—splattered onto the highway. I shuddered. Coach had warned me that Andy was dangerous. "Keep away from him," he'd said.

It was appalling, the suddenness of death. "Gruesome, Paula. You knew him?"

"Yeah. He let me stay in his boat once for a few weeks. He used to be an artist, you know. Had shows and everything. By the time I met him, though, he'd stopped painting. All he ever wanted to do was get high and ride."

"Sad." I thought of paintings abandoned for the quick rush of a high and the wild feel of wind on a bike.

"I don't think he wanted to live any more, to tell the truth. Not the way he was going, always taking a risk. I'll miss him. He was good to me."

We walked somberly on, my mind filled with images of quick death and loss: the speed, the thrill, the fast turn, the skid, the terrible impact.

Once we cleared the tunnel, the noise level increased. Paula began calling out to people she knew, and soon we were in the midst of the crowd. People jostled one another as they moved from one display to the next.

The Flea Market had taken over a vast flat lot in Marin City. Displays of furniture, of old shoes, of clothing and toys, of tools, of records and lampshades were all crammed in next to each other. Some sellers had their wares spread on out the hoods of cars. Others, more professional, had brought campers. They sat on camp chairs, surveying the goods they had displayed on folding tables. They sipped beer or soda and kept an eye on the crowd, watching out for buyers and for thieves.

I felt a sudden surge of loss and grief. I'd brought my daughter here once for a Sunday outing. We'd found her a stuffed animal; her sweet face had lit up. She was growing, changing. Would she even recognize me now?

I was subdued, saddened. Paula, however, was in good spirits. She stopped by a rack of clothing and held a dress up to herself.

"Any place I can try this on?" she asked. A straw-hatted woman directed her to the back of a camper.

"Stand guard, Dee," Paula called, climbing in. Crouching in the half light of the camper, she began to undress. I stood by the door, taking my responsibility seriously. Here was a job I could do well. No one would spy on my friend while I was around. She emerged wearing a purple sweater dress with a high, soft cowl neck.

The asking price was $5; she talked the owner into accepting a $10 food stamp "until I can get the change."

"Come on, Dee. We'll make that transaction at the falafel place." I followed along in her wake, wondering at her ability to bargain. Next to her organized confidence, I became mute. Would it always be this way? "Come along," and I'd come, like a pet. In my fantasies, I was always brave and quick. In life, I was always just following along. It irked me. When would I develop some gumption? Soon, I promised myself, and quickly finished off the wine.

Try as I might to feel a part of the Flea Market bustle, my mind was still back in jail. The noise, the bustle, the shouts and laughter all were jarring to me. I thought of the yard, where inmates slowly circled, where the shadow of barbed wire fell on the ground. This scene was so vivid and lively by comparison that I felt lost.

At the next booth, Paula charmed the falafel maker into two plates of food and an even trade of food stamps for dollars. We sat at a rickety table to eat. I chewed glumly, removed a piece of gristle. Juice from the meat and vegetable mixture oozed onto the paper plate.

"Lighten up, Dee. It was only three nights in jail, for Pete's sake. I spent a couple weeks there last summer, and it didn't do me any harm."

I wiped juice from my chin, insulted. "You're used to going in, Paula. It was a shock for me. I never thought I'd be arrested."

"You'll get over it." Paula's eyes roamed the crowd. Then she darted up to a man who was smoking and bummed a cigarette. Returning, she puffed on it and then, winking at me, held the cigarette briefly to the hem of her new dress.

"Well, look at that. It's damaged. I'm going to go back and try to talk her down on this dress. It's got a burn mark on the hem, here."

Another scheme. I nodded and waved her off.

Across from me was a display of hats: bowlers, sloping felt cloches, elaborately feathered creations, and a black straw with bright red cherries on the brim. The cherries matched my sweater. I walked over to it, touched the brim.

"That one's only $3," said a woman from her lounge chair. I felt for the foodstamp in my pocket. "Will you take this stamp as a downpayment?"

She shook her head vigorously and retrieved the hat.

"Cash only."

Disgruntled, I moved away. Why didn't it work for me? Paula had a way of bargaining that made people want to accommodate her. I didn't have the knack. To me, shopping was still what it had been before—in a store, one paid the price or didn't buy. I lacked the confidence to make my own rules, to talk people into doing things my way. When I offered the food stamp, I'd expected to be turned down. It embarrassed me to bargain. "Better change," I muttered to myself. "Better learn to survive when you've got nothing." I shook my head to free myself of self-pity. "Snap out of it."

I moved through a press of people over to a table full of books and records. Beatles, Rolling Stones, the Canadian Brass. *Catcher in the Rye, Bell Jar, Fear of Flying.*

"Books a quarter, records fifty cents," said the merchant, straightening record jackets. I moved on quickly. All the merchandise was creating a longing in me. Nice things. What would I do with an album? Yet, I'd wanted one. I watched the people near me loading up sacks of goods, and I envied them. I made my way through the aisles, walking dazedly as if in a dream.

At the end of one aisle was a booth selling soft drinks. I saw a flash of green. It was Tanya, her earrings swinging as she moved her head to the reggae music which boomed from across the way. She saw me and waved.

"That you, girl? You get home all right?"

"I got there."

"Sorry to run out on you. I only had some change. You thirsty?"

She handed me a tall cup of cola.

"Drink up. I've got to make room in the cup, get the level down."

I took another swallow. She drew a pint of vodka from her bag and poured it into the cup.

"Here, have yourself a real drink. You look out of it."

"I am. It's all the people, all the sound."

"Just takes a little getting used to, being in and then out again. All these people, what do they know?"

I drank and shrugged.

"Nothing, that's what." She nodded firmly. "Today, I'm just killing time. Sundays are always slow. You shopping? Seen anything you like?"

"A hat. But she wouldn't take a food stamp for it."

She shook her head impatiently.

"Girl. All you had to do was ask me. Don't you know that? Show me that hat."

We walked back to the hat booth. She picked up the black straw, moved it side to side so the cherries bobbled.

"Mm hm. You can do some dancing in that." As the hat woman approached, Tanya set the hat on my head.

"This here's my friend's. She'll take it, but look, these cherries are loose."

"Two dollars, then."

Tanya handed the money to her.

"Now. Don't you say I never gave you nothing," she admonished me.

"I thought you just had change?"

"I've done a little business since then. Take another sip of this, then I got to be going. It's a slow day, but a woman's gotta try."

Feeling restored, I made my way to the outer edge of booths. A long picnic table displayed art books. I flipped through one that featured Salvador Dali. There was a picture I knew, watches drooping on the landscape.

Here was one I hadn't seen before. I bent to look more closely. It was of Christ on the cross. The cross was gold and immense, and the perspective was such that it and He loomed over the landscape, dwarfing it. It was a painting of stunning victory. I was amazed; I'd always thought of the cross as tragic. How was it a victory? Yet, it must be. Here was the truth of it, the mystery. I looked up, imagining that this huge cross was suspended over the Flea Market, over me and all the people.

The picture showed a man who had defeated death, and I was suddenly exhilarated. I wanted the protection of that cross. I wanted to huddle under it. No, I wanted to climb aboard, to ride it...I was suddenly filled with joy.

"Help you?"

"I'm just…looking. This picture!"

"Yes. Really brings it home." So he understood. My self-pity, my gloominess had vanished. I had nothing, but I was all right now.

A cold wind rushed through the aisles. The light had changed; it was getting later. As the wind intensified, people began packing up and loading their vehicles. The bookseller closed his picture books and began stacking them into a box.

The Flea Market was breaking up. The crowd of couples, families, and lone bargain hunters began moving for the exits. A few rushed back to make last-minute purchases.

There was a rumble of car motors starting. On the grounds, cars and vans wheeled about, laden with unsold goods. In their leaving they created vast swirls of dust which rose and obscured my view.

The crowd waned and the sellers drove off. Through the clouds of dust, I could make out the silent forms of street people. First one, then another appeared, pacing the lot and quickly sorting through all that had been left behind. It was as if they had been waiting in the wings. Now it was time to scavenge.

I saw one man rushing for a set of cartons which stood abandoned on the empty lot. I blinked and looked more closely: more and more shapes appeared, moving quickly in the billows of dust, to pick through the debris that remained.

The Flea Market had vanished; in its place was a field strewn with odds and ends. Street people moved like phantoms through the grounds. They darted, dove, gathered and vanished. Two men staggered off, holding either end of a rolled up carpet that had once held merchandise.

I saw Miguel, bending with the load of a box.

"Need any help?"

"Here, you can take an end."

We walked toward the tunnel, carrying the box between us.

"Stop," he said. "There's something I want to check out. Will you wait with the box?"

"If you hurry. It's getting cold."

He headed for a jumble of odds and ends that had been dumped on the ground. I saw a lampstand upended, a bowl of plastic flowers, a pile of old boots. Miguel was tugging one of the boots onto his foot.

The wind came up strong behind me and whisked off my hat. I chased it. It landed on the edge of the swamp, which bordered the Flea Market field.

It was dead water, oily and scummed. Tires had been tossed into it, round humps sinking deeper into the mud. The sun, setting, gave a deep red glow to the swamp.

"Look," said Miguel, clumping up behind me. "The Red Sea. Think it'll part?"

He took a stick from the shore and waved it over the water. In its breeze floated a record jacket, partially submerged. He used the stick to fish it out. The cover showed a nightclub and a man blowing into a saxophone. Miguel gave it a shake.

"Empty," he snorted, and tossed it back in.

We headed back to the box. I stooped to pick up a small piece of carpet that was covered with tire tracks. Quick! Grab it! I could brush it off and put it in front of the car I slept in—make a little patio with it. I put the carpet and my hat under one arm and lifted an edge of the box with the other.

"Sunday night," said Miguel, as we walked toward the tunnel. "The Open Door will be open for sure. I hope it's not soup."

"Steak and eggs," I suggested.

"Broiled lobster," he countered.

"Shish kabob."

"Leg of lamb."

"Veal cutlets with new potatoes."

"Ham, yams, potato salad."

"Chef's salad."

"Dream on, " said Paula, joining us. "Where are you staying tonight, Dee?"

"The car I've been using. Why?"

She turned to Miguel. "You didn't tell her?"

"You do it," he muttered.

"Dee, the tow truck came through and cleared off the cars on Gate 5 Road. They got yours."

The wind blew at my back. Then it hit me. My photographs were gone. All this time, I'd saved them, savored them. They were my last link with my daughter. How I'd pored over them in the safety of the car home. Now they were gone. I couldn't bear it. Deep grief welled up inside me; a terrible sense of loss engulfed me. The photographs had been such a source of comfort to me. Going through them, I'd been able to remember the love and laughter my daughter and I had shared. Gone now. How could I bear it?

I felt despair, too, at the loss of shelter. At least in jail I'd had a place to sleep. Where would I go now? I looked past them to the now-desolate field. Make a nest there in the far-off shrubbery?

"Why didn't you tell me sooner? Now I have to find a place in the dark."

"Didn't want to wreck your day. Listen. You know that shack behind Omar's place?"

I nodded, numbly. My mind wasn't functioning.

"Well, it's open. The people who were staying there just left. I saw them a while ago; they caught a ride to Salinas. If you hurry, you can claim the place."

Miguel dropped the box, rummaged through it, gathered three books into his arms, and took off running.

"Oh, that pig," said Paula. "*His* car didn't get towed. You'd better go by there right away, Dee, before you hit the Open Door. Otherwise he'll have his stuff all over the shack."

Panting, filled with urgency, I made my way running back through the tunnel, across the highway. Tanya was sitting in a bus shelter near the freeway, her trench coat wrapped tightly against the wind, drinking straight from the pint bottle. Could I get a sip? Just to console me?

"Sunday night," she said. "Not many clients out tonight. But you never know. I've got to make up for that time I lost inside."

A passing car slowed. She tossed the bottle in the trash and stood on the curb. The car pulled to a stop. She leaned up to the window.

"Hi," she said brightly. "Want a date?" The driver opened the door, and she slid in. Then he peered out at me.

"How 'bout you, too?" he asked. "We can go to a motel and you can both work on me."

Tanya gave me a questioning glance. "Want to come?"

"No thanks," I stammered, embarrassed and feeling out of my league. So this was her work. "I've got something to see about."

Tanya shrugged. The driver made a resigned face and slammed the door. They took off without a backward glance.

I crossed the highway and began to run again, holding the piece of rug against my chest. It was a cold night. Jail had been warm: showers, clean clothes, meals. I felt a twinge of nostalgia. Did I actually miss jail? I shook the thought away. Just that little bit of time indoors had softened me up.

The Open Door was lit. I was tempted to stop, to get warm. If I did, though, someone else might take the shack. Better not. I forced myself to keep going, determined to stake my claim.

I knew the place Paula meant. Long abandoned, it had become a popular spot for squatters. As I neared it, I saw a flickering light through the window.

Miguel had lit a candle. It made a pool of light in the dark shack. I saw two old couches with missing legs, sloping at angles to the ground. Miguel was on the floor, rinsing out a needle with water from a plastic bottle. He looked up when I entered.

"Point's almost broken off," he complained.

I gathered my inner resources. I needed this place. "Look, Miguel. Paula told me about this place first."

"So what?"

"I plan to stay here."

"Take the green couch; that's my stuff on the other one."

I was frustrated and upset that he'd gotten here before me and already made the place his own. Now I'd have to fit in with his plans, his schedule. Tension and loss combined produced hot tears which rolled down my cheeks.

"You don't really need a place, though, Miguel. I do."

"Yes, I do too. My car doesn't hold much. I'll meet clients there, and stash things here in my second property."

Impervious to my tears, he flushed more water through the syringe.

"We have a better chance of keeping the place if there are two of us," he added practically. "Go on to the Open Door if you like. I've got things to do here."

"I bet you do." I looked at the needle. He must have some crystal meth stashed here. With longing, I thought of the euphoric escape the drug provided. I could just get high and forget about the loss of my photographs and car…

"Don't ask, Dee. I've only got enough for me tonight."

Maybe if I agreed with him, I could bargain for something else I needed—a blanket, say.

"Have you got an extra blanket here, Miguel?"

"I'll see what I can find when I go out later."

He bent his head down to the light, trying to straighten the point on the needle with the edge of a knife.

It bothered me to watch him. He was going to get really high. There was nothing for me. I was too weary to argue, too beaten down by shock and loss. Resigned, I left.

I went back to the Open Door, which was quiet that night. There were usually raucous voices as people came in to sober up and jostle each other in the soup line. Tonight, most people were resting on the floor. One man was curled up below the coffeepot; I had to step over him to miss his capped head. The only sound came from a woman who was hunched up by the piano, humming and rocking herself. I got a bowl of soup and drank it standing.

I spotted Virginia, who seemed to be staffing the place by herself. "I feel inspired tonight," she said to me, removing her apron. "Watch this."

She climbed on top of a low table that usually held a chess set. The woman who'd been rocking in the corner stopped and pointed at Virginia.

"What're you doing on the table?" called Rudy in alarm. In answer, she clapped her hands over her head.

"Listen to the story of Paul," she began, high above the prone bodies. One or two heads lifted up.

"He was once named Saul, and he was a *terrible* man," she declaimed, wrinkling her nose in disgust. "He went around killing people, torturing them, throwing them in jail."

"I know the type," muttered someone from the floor.

"Ah! Yes, but then, you see," she continued, her voice rising with excitement, "Then, on the way to Damascus..."

"Over by Mill Valley," added a man, rolling over and leaning back on his elbows, enjoying the show.

"That's right," she said. "On his way, a dazzling light shone upon him, blinding him."

"It was the cops, I bet."

"No. He was a cop himself. A mean one. This light was something else, something new. He heard a voice saying, 'Saul.'"

"Bet that freaked him right out."

"Well, it did. He fell to the ground. 'Saul,' said the voice. 'Why are you persecuting me?'"

She looked at us, triumphant and pleased.

"He knew it was the voice of Jesus. So! He fell to the ground—" she dropped, knees on the table top.

"Right then and there, he changed. Yes!" She stood back up on the table with a flourish. I heard her knees crack as she rose.

She stood facing the clock on the wall, then slowly turned around, so that her back was to the clock and her face to the piano.

"180 degrees," she pronounced, demonstrating again. "That's how he turned. He went from an evil villain to a voice for the Lord."

"Turn again," said the man on the floor.

She executed the turn, moving her feet carefully on the table top.

"See? The one way was a bad way. He turned completely around, and began on a good way. So can you! So can you all."

She climbed down from the table, patting the man on the head.

"If he could do it, so can you."

"Good show, Virginia," he said, sitting up to clap.

Others joined him. Virginia was popular—she was known to be fair with the doughnuts, making sure that they went around and no one got too many. Now she flushed with pleasure at the applause.

"Remember that bright light!" she said. "It can be your light too."

Matt, who'd been lying in his favorite spot under the piano, leaned out.

"Did you say light?" he asked. "Is it time to leave?"

"Not yet, Matt. I was talking about a different kind of light."

"Yeah," he said, voice slurred with wine. "Tell me when it's time to go," and rolled back under the piano.

Virginia turned back to me. Her glasses caught and reflected the candles flickering in the room.

"Every now and then the Spirit moves me," she explained. "When it does, I just have to speak out."

Her statement amazed me. I realized with a start that I loved Virginia. It seemed to flow naturally from her love for us. It was so brave of her to be here alone, just one woman in a room full of street people. What if a drunk attacked her? What if a gang threatened her, demanding cash? She's fearless, I thought. Why does she do it? The answer nudged up into my consciousness: it has to do with her faith, with her Christ. I wanted that certainty of hers, longed for it.

She moved toward the office and I made my way to the door, stepping over more bodies as I went. There was one guy, lying flat out. There was another, curled up like a fetus. It was like walking through a mine field. Matt groaned when I bumped into his foot.

The shack was dark when I returned, but there was an old woolen coat spread over the green couch. Bundling it around myself, I settled in.

It was a new place; I slept fitfully. I was used to the close confines of the car. Here was more space. Could I make it into a home? I hoped so. Every so often a cold blast of air would come through as Miguel opened the door, coming and going. I heard him rustling around, dropping off loads of scavenged goods. I kept my eyes closed. He was high and I wasn't; there was no point in starting a conversation.

I burrowed deeper into the coat and dreamed of Virginia, spinning around like a top.

"You can too!" she called. "Round and about! 180 degrees!" She spun faster and faster, becoming a blur of motion.

"God is our refuge and strength,
A very present help in trouble.
Therefore we will not fear…"
(Psalms 46:1,2)

CHAPTER 8

OCTOBER, 1985

For the next few years, Miguel remained my roommate. We developed a close rapport. When we got high, which was as often as we could, he'd play flute and I'd dance, wild dances with much spinning and leaping.

We moved constantly. We were chased from the shack because I'd left a candle burning in it, and the business next door feared fire. We lived in abandoned vehicles as they opened up. We lived in derelict boats, one of which sank while we were in it. Often, there was no place to stay, so we'd reverse our sleeping schedule, remaining awake all night and sleeping in parks in the daytime. Each place became, briefly, home. We'd decorate with scavenged items. Then we'd lose it, to accompanying grief on my part. Despite the reality—being constantly on the move—each time I hoped I'd found home, so each loss was hard on me. In this Chapter, we are in a shed by the boatyard.

***

The morning was gray and damp. To my dismay, I saw that soggy piles and cartons were strewn about the floor. There was barely room to move. Miguel was nowhere in sight. This shed was in real disrepair. There were puddles on the floor where the roof had leaked. Miguel's salvaged debris was strewn about chaotically. One pile seemed to consist of nothing but bicycle parts. This was impossible! I wouldn't touch any of it. Firmly, I decided to leave it all for him to sort out.

I was groggy. Maybe I could find someone to buy me a coffee. I'd start with coffee and move on to wine as the day progressed. How? I'd offer to get Matt's white port in exchange for a large coffee, that was it. He wasn't going to get free labor out of me again.

Cheered to have formed a plan, I set off for the mini-mart. As I walked along the dirt road, I could see it in the distance. It was perched by a parking lot; cars were pulling in and out as their drivers stopped by for coffee and doughnuts. Miguel and the Poet were working the entrance, with some success. I joined them.

"Does Matt know you're here? I thought he had this spot reserved."

Poet shook her head. "Matt's in the hospital, didn't you hear?"

"What happened?"

Miguel took over the story. "Ah, the fool was really drunk and he tried to light an old camp stove he had. He was using gasoline. Thing blew up on him; his camp caught fire; he got burned all over."

I was aghast. Grimly, I pictured the burnt flesh. Monstrous image. "Like one of those monks."

"What monks?"

"Those monks we used to see in the news, during the Vietnam War. They'd pour gasoline on themselves and light it, go up in flames."

"Yeah, well. So maybe that's where he got the idea. I think he was just drunk and careless—spilled gas on himself, tipped the thing over."

Miguel was scornful of drunks. In his mind, they were sloppy and vulgar. He saw no point in getting high on anything but meth. That's what gave him the hyped-up energy for his late night scavenging.

The Poet spoke up again. "He'll go to his brother's when he gets out."

Her statement baffled me. It went against everything I knew about Matt. He was so self-sufficient. Was it really possible he had family nearby? "He has a brother out here?" I asked incredulously.

"Oh sure, his brother's a businessman. Lives in town. Commutes to the city every day, has a nice place on the hill."

Then how…"So why is Matt camping out in the field?"

Miguel shrugged. "That's the way they do it. His brother went one way; Matt went another."

The Poet grinned. "You take the high road, and I'll take the low road."

"That's about it. Every so often his brother will come down, offer Matt a meal and a place to clean up. Once in a while, Matt goes with him, but never for long. He comes right back out to his field and the dirt road and the white port."

The Poet began to hum an old tune, then to sing, changing the words.

"With a white port coat and a red carnation…" she sang in a clear soprano, spinning around as if waltzing with an invisible drunk.

We three panhandled together. The mini-mart was doing a brisk morning business. Poet was the boldest. She'd bounce up to a customer and give him a sweet smile. "Want to help some starving artists get breakfast?" she'd ask. Miguel was more low-key. He lounged against the entrance, his cap pulled low over his forehead. When a customer neared, he tilted the cap slightly. "Morning, ma'am. Could you spare a quarter?" I positioned myself on the steps which led to the parking lot. "Excuse me…any spare change?"

We made enough for a coffee each, and withdrew to the steps to sit and drink. Miguel, who I knew had been up all night, looked surprisingly dapper. He'd found a place to shower, wore clean clothes, and managed to give the impression that he was not really with us but was just lingering until something better came along.

The Poet tried to interest us in a trip to San Rafael. "You know, they've got a place that gives free lunch there. St. Vincent's, it's called. It opens at 11, closes around 3. If we left now, we'd make it. We could get a ride over, eat, come on back."

She smiled triumphantly at Miguel, with the air of playing a trump card. "From there, we could walk to the charity place that has clothes and books. It puts the Free Box to shame. Good hats, good coats, good shoes…a whole tableful of books."

Miguel began to show interest. "I suppose I could ask around about a ride over," he said.

"Yes, see if you can find someone. If you can't, we could work on bus fare."

Late morning sun was breaking through the clouds. When I lifted my head to the horizon, I saw the world in bright, clear outline. The hills were clumped with distinct shades of green.

In front of them, bordering the highway, were tall wooden utility poles. However, I did not see them in their functional form, as poles carrying electricity, but only in their shape. They were a series of tall crosses, planted near the hill. Crosses in a row. I beheld them in wonder. Once there had been three crosses, on a day of dreadful death. Who had been on them? Two thieves and Jesus. Miguel once had told me the story of the Good Thief who felt compassion for Christ and ended up in heaven with Him. Which cross might belong to whom? I lost myself in meditation.

As I gazed at them, awestruck, a bird swooped down to rest on one of the wires connecting the poles. It was joined by three more. There were four wires, I saw now, one above the other. They were dotted with dark birds.

The birds were holding their bodies in place as if they were musical notes. I tried to match the score with my humming. As I did, the birds shifted position. One flew higher, one lower. Two more landed midrange, further down the score.

"Bird music," I murmured. "They're making a composition on the cross." This was wonderful, exciting. I was in on the moment of creation. Their movements were quick, and I hummed as best I could to keep up.

Then came a long pause. Six birds ascended together, straight up and away, leaving a single bird on the lowest rung of wire. It held position for four long counts and then also flew away.

I needed a way to note the formation. This was holy music coming. I had to write it down before it all passed away. I saw a paper bag in the parking lot below me and chased after it. Weren't there pens in my pocket? No, but there was a pencil. I pulled it out. Quickly I drew lines for the wires and filled them in with circles for bird bodies, as best as I could remember their movement.

I sat there, poised to record the birds. When one side of the bag was covered with marks, I ripped it open and began on another side. I worked frantically, as if to lose a movement would be to lose a promise of salvation.

People came and went up and down the steps. I ignored them; they were only passing feet to me. Once, I thought I heard a shout. I ignored it too, totally absorbed in what I was doing. The birds had an endless variation in their repertoire. Obsessed, I continued to track them, getting another bag when I'd completely covered the first.

At last, weary, I put my head down to my knees to rest and absorb what had happened. Had God been speaking to me? Why me? Was it because I'd gone into a deep meditation on the crosses? My legs were stiff and numb; I shivered. I was cold. The music had ceased.

An orange flare in the sky signaled the coming sunset. I blinked as if coming out of a dream. I'd been sitting there an entire afternoon. It had seemed like moments.

I felt keenly my inability to read music. I'd been able to recognize that the birds' changing patterns on the wires could be read musically but only to approximate in my humming how such music might actually sound.

Perhaps at the Open Door I could find a pianist who'd help me sound it out. Then we could fill in the jottings of the different movements. We could take, say, three consecutive afternoons, and piece a score together. What a triumph that would be!

The Open Door was not far. Eagerly, I walked down the dirt road, hoping that this was an open night. Days and nights passed and blended without any real way to mark them.

I remembered Hank's holding two fingers up to show us one, two days before the place opened again. It had seemed so obvious and clear to him, the passage of time. But to us, day became night became day. We met, parted, scavenged, slept when and where we could. There were fights or fires. There were, at any given time, different alliances of people who'd teamed up for some purpose—getting a bottle, primarily—but who, in a few hours, would separate. To say, "Two nights ago it was open, so it will be open now tonight," while very simple in one frame of mind, was not possible in another.

The door was still closed, but to my joy a number of people were waiting outside it, so chances were it would open soon. I saw Miguel leaning against the side wall, eyes closed, face turned to the last of the setting sun.

"Miguel! Want to work out a piano piece with me?"

He stayed very still, but I didn't think he was asleep.

"Miguel?"

He frowned and waved me away with his hand, without opening his eyes.

"I have a good plan for a musical piece," I insisted.

His eyes flew open. "Will you leave me alone, Dee? I'm talking to God."

I walked away. "Excuse me for interrupting a private conversation," I muttered. I was hurt by his curtness. How dare he brush me off like that? So highhanded. I had something great to share. Couldn't he have interrupted his prayer for at least a hello?

"I'd leave him be, Dee, if I were you," the Poet offered, turning the corner of the building. She was holding a small bottle of wine by the bottleneck. She passed it to me and continued her warning. "Be careful with him. He was really angry at you this afternoon."

"What for?" I asked, taking a hit off the bottle.

"Didn't you hear us? We found a ride into San Rafael and called out to you to come with us."

That must have been the shout I'd half-heard and pushed away when I was tracking the birds' movements.

"Did you all go?"

"You were totally ignoring us, so we left without you. It was okay. The food place, St. Vincent's, is open every day, not like here. I'm thinking of moving out to San Rafael for a while."

"It was that good, huh?"

She made a face. "Steamed rice, vegetables, a glop of stew. Thing is, it's steady."

"That's an advantage, all right."

"Why didn't you come with us? We were yelling at you to come on, and Miguel tugged your shoulder, but you just sat there in a daze."

"Sorry; I didn't really notice you. I was focused on something else—a kind of bird music."

She studied me a moment.

"Yes, I get that way sometimes. When I'm making a poem, I just want people to leave me alone. I've been working on one, a scary one. Want to hear it?"

"Sure."

She reached inside her jacket and pulled out a piece of crumpled paper. It looked like a computer printout that she'd found in the trash. She bowed her head briefly, then began to read:

> I tell you we're the refugees
>
> I tell you we're the tramps...

"Hold on, that isn't right." She peered more closely at the paper. "Not tramps but strays."

> I tell you we're the refugees
>
> I tell you we're the strays
>
> I tell you we're the cast-offs
>
> And we never go away.
>
> We haunt your every nightmare
>
> We raid your garbage cans
>
> We roam your streets and alleyways
>
> Do we upset your plans?

Pretend you cannot see us
Pretend we are not here
Pretend we're from another town
We're from another sphere.

I clapped; she bowed. "Refugees, get it? 'Cuz we get kicked out and have to move from place to place, looking for refuge. It's not quite done. When it is, I'll take it around to the different soup kitchens."

She reached for the bottle of wine and took a big swallow, finishing it. "So, Dee, I know how it is when you're composing."

I was deeply grateful to the Poet for understanding. Miguel, however, continued to ignore me—paying me back, I figured. All right. Fair was fair. I'd ignored him. And he couldn't keep a grudge forever. Could he? I followed the Poet's advice and kept out of his way all night.

When the place closed, he'd vanished. I doubted my welcome at the shed but decided to try. After all, I reminded myself, bolstering my confidence, it was my place too.

When I got there, it was dark and deserted. Miguel must be out scavenging again. I felt for a stub of candle and lit it on the fourth try, glad for the packets of matches in my pockets.

The floor was covered with piles of varying sizes. More seemed to have been added. Miguel had been hitting the dumpsters with a vengeance. Maybe some of this stuff came from San Rafael, as well.

I held the candle closer to investigate. There were heaps of sodden clothing beneath an oilcloth. There were engine parts strewn about. There were pieces of lumber leaning against the walls and boxes full of odds and ends: an iron with a frayed cord, some magazines whose pages had stuck together. Maybe this loot was destined for the Flea Market.

It was overwhelming, and I was tired. He'd taken over the place; I conceded defeat. If I could find my old coat in all the disarray, I'd take it and just head out. Most of the abandoned cars had been towed, but there were still a few vehicles left on the road. I'd take my chances, I decided with a sudden daring.

Soggy cardboard boxes were piled high. Was that the coat underneath them? I began to tug at it. One box spilled over, dumping shoes on the floor.

There in a corner was an old tote bag. I'd better retrieve it now and get out of here. Let him simmer alone.

Footsteps, coming closer. I turned to face Miguel.

"So you thought you'd come back?" He asked, glaring at me.

Don't show fear. "I came for my coat. Miguel, I'm sorry about this afternoon. I didn't realize what was happening."

He looked at me coldly. "You disrespected me in front of people. I arranged for a ride, and then you made me look like a fool."

Pacify. "I'm really sorry. I'll explain to the others, if you like. I wasn't trying to be disrespectful."

"The damage is done," he answered in a tight, grim voice. "You just sat there like you were wanting to get picked up by somebody else, like I was nothing."

"You've got the wrong idea. I was composing—well, in a way."

He snorted derisively. "Composing. You don't compose. You don't do anything. Just sit on the steps like a zombie, like a whore. You could have been useful. You could have sorted through all this." He gestured to the soggy bundles strewn about the shed.

"What?" I looked around me in disbelief. He couldn't be referring to these piles.

"Clean it up!" Miguel screamed, his face contorted. "Look at this place! It's a mess. You were supposed to clean it up."

His face had reddened and he grimaced at me.

A jolt of anger shot through me. Did he think I was his maid? Total injustice. "Miguel, what are you talking about? I'm not the one who went out and scavenged all that stuff. I'm not the one who dropped it there. I really don't want it there at all. It's damp, it's starting to mildew, it's gross. Listen, man. You brought it. You take care of it."

I was totally taken aback. It was shocking that Miguel's body contained this ferocious personality. It was as if a stranger had possessed him. Yes, I could understand his hurt pride, but I was disgusted with the unfairness of his demand.

"Get out, then," he roared. "Get out, go away forever."

Fear coursed through me. I grabbed the tote and ran. I moved blindly at first, without direction or purpose other than escape. When I stopped, panting, to catch my breath, I saw I'd come quite a way from Gate 5.

The main road through Sausalito was high above me. I could hear the zoom of traffic along it. I was standing a cliff's drop below it, on the dirt footpath.

It was what I thought of as "the low road." I'd taken it out of instinct, first running then walking until I had put a good distance between myself and Miguel. Was this the end of our partnership? Sadly, I realized how much I'd miss him. Maybe he'd relent, come to his senses.

High above me, a bright white moon lit the path. On my right was the cliff; on my left were eucalyptus trees whose strong scent perfumed the night.

As I went along at a slower pace, I wished for someone to talk to— someone who could help me make sense out of what had occurred back at the shed. He'd been hurt, then angry. I'd responded in kind. Well, my claim on the place had certainly proven to be fragile. It was a cold night. I was lonely and shaken from our fight.

I began to talk aloud. Perhaps if I spoke as to a companion, one would emerge.

"He's like a kaleidoscope, is Miguel," I said. "There's the flute player, and the reader of epics, and the teller of Bible stories. Then there's that creature who appeared tonight, all snarly and unreasonable."

Just ahead, I could see the large building which housed the Army Corps of Engineers. I made my way to the loading dock and sat down. It was good to rest. I had to regain my composure, to figure out what to do next.

I sat facing a whole grove of eucalyptus that hid the cliff from view. The trees rustled in the wind. As their forms shifted, shafts of moonlight came and went, illuminating the area.

I was relieved to discover that, with distance, the fight with Miguel was losing its power to disturb me. A thought nudged: Perhaps, after all, it was true that he'd been seriously offended by my behavior that afternoon. Perhaps I'd been wrong. Well, given time, he'd get over it. I might even apologize again, when he was in a more reasonable frame of mind.

Opening my tote, I found an empty food stamp packet...no! There was a five dollar bill tucked inside, left over from when I'd last cashed in food stamps. Oh, joy! I was rich.

I shivered. It had gotten really cold now. Too bad I'd had to leave the coat back in the shed. Was it safe to return? No, that would be foolish. Better not risk it.

The cement loading dock had soaked in the cold and felt icy beneath me. My fear returned. I was like a sitting duck here, and I was freezing in place. It was time to move on. Above me, on the high road, was a

7-11 store, open all night. I could hang about outside of it. The lights would give the illusion of warmth.

I returned to the path and forced myself to hum a carefree tune. "Don't show fear," a neighbor boy had told me when I was small. "A dog will smell it. Just walk along whistling."

The hill slanted up on my right; from above it came the sound of late night traffic along Bridgeway. Then came a rustling from the shrubs on the hill, and a dark form hurtled toward me, crashing into my side like a cannonball and knocking me down. It was Miguel.

I moaned and gagged with pain and clutched my side. He must have been lurking in the bushes, watching me. He peered at me, wild-eyed. I covered my head with my arms. He took a swing at me and missed; took another and connected. I huddled tighter, to be less of a target, only concerned with self-protection. His punches slammed into me. He kicked my side, then dropped to his haunches to examine me. "Where were you going?" he snarled suspiciously.

"Away from you!" I panted, doubled over on the ground. My side hurt ferociously where he'd rammed into me. I was terrorized, frozen in place.

"You're not hurt," he said scornfully. "I barely tapped you. I thought you were coming to invade my hiding place."

Sudden, blessed anger flooded me. "Who cares about your hiding place, you idiot? You were watching for a chance to ambush me."

I was shaking from shock and pain. How could this be happening? I drew back my arm and took a swing at him. He ducked and I missed. With dismay, I knew I had no skill at fighting. I'd never been trained in it, never thought I'd need it. What use was all my education? I needed to know how to fight.

"Got any money?" he demanded.

Enraged, I took the tote, opened it, shook it in his face.

"Empty," I said.

"I saw you put something in your pocket."

I pulled out the front pockets to my jeans, distributing lint and shreds of tobacco on the ground.

"Empty."

He kicked my legs in frustration and cuffed my head, but there wasn't much force behind his swing. Good, he was already tiring. He spat in disgust and wheeled away from me. He strode off, muttering.

"Fool," I whispered after him, glad for a minor triumph. I felt for the five dollars in my back pocket. Yes, it was still there.

"Ha," I panted. My heart was racing with adrenaline.

It took me some time to stand up. I hurt, I was mad, and I was deeply chagrined. I'd thought of him as a close friend, had not believed he'd be violent. Could still not believe it.

I hunched over on the ground and began to rock to and fro.

"Friend to fiend," I snarled. "Just drop the r."

The rocking helped. I did it faster. "Rrrrrr," I said, rolling the r's, remembering a French class. Mme. Blaise had taught us to roll our r's.

"Rrrr," there we go. It sounded like a motor, ready to take off. "Rrrr." I am a motor, I repeated as I rocked. Then, slowly, I balanced, lifted up, and began the hike up the hill to the 7-11.

"Rrrr," I exhaled. Breathed in, then "rrrr," breathed out. Halfway up the hill, another bush rustled.

"Drop that r," I shouted, surprising myself at the loud sound I made. "Drop it right there." The bush was still. I glared at it fiercely and continued on.

"Friend—fiend, friend—fiend." Alternately singing and growling to fend off attackers, I made it to the top of the hill and ran across the street to the blaze of light that was the 7-11.

I loved that store. It was open all night, providing light and warmth. There were always people there, going in and out. There'd be safety in numbers.

A large coffee cost seventy-five cents. I'd have one. It gushed out the tap into a big white cup that was decorated red and green.

I put in several packets of cream, taking my time, opening them and pouring them in. I lifted the sugar container and dumped a lot in. I took a stirrer and swirled the mixture until it frothed. I scooped up the empty containers into the trash.

What else could I get? I took sips from the hot, sweet coffee, willing it to heal me, and perused the freezer compartment. There. A Super Burrito, $1.75. I took it out, shivering at the cold air from the freezer, and placed it in the microwave. When the machine beeped, I took the hot package and walked around to the cash register.

A teenager was staffing the place, alone at the register. He was tall, and his upper lip was fuzzed in patches as if he were growing a mustache. He rang up my purchases. I carried my meal outside and crouched by the corner of the store. I was on eye level with the license plates of cars which drove up and then away again.

Ignoring passersby, I ate my burrito and drank my coffee. "Grr," I said, biting into meat and melted cheese. "Mmmm. Grr. Mine." I'd be an animal guarding my territory.

A woman approached me cautiously. "Grr," I rumbled at her through the soft burrito goo. Startled, she backed away.

All I had to do was get through the night. I couldn't go to sleep; I certainly couldn't go search for an abandoned car. My enemy knew that territory too well.

I was, I thought, in shock. My life up to this point had not prepared me for violent attack. It had been horrifyingly sudden and unexpected when Miguel had jumped me. The terror of it began to seep into me. Then there was sadness. If I couldn't trust him, whom could I trust? No one? Surely someone? Virginia trusted Jesus. I had to try to do the same. I remembered my earlier elation at bird music, my fascination with the telephone poles shaped like crosses. That had felt so good, had lifted me out of my surroundings. Had been transcendent. But then my partner had turned on me. Did faith get a person in trouble? It was mystifying. Still. Whom did I have now but God? With His help, I would get through the night.

I began to pace in the parking lot to keep warm. To stay awake, I chanted different versions of my new song. It wouldn't scan properly, so I abbreviated it.

There is a fiend

Was once a friend

The End

"…the needy will not always be forgotten,

Nor the hope of the afflicted perish forever."

(Psalm 9:17-18)

CHAPTER 9

Finally, it was morning. I'd thought the long night would never end. I was exhausted. The teenager behind the counter had gone home; his replacement let me get a free refill of coffee. Numb from my night outdoors, mind reeling from the violence, heart hardened from betrayal, I carried it to the bus shelter and waited. My one urgent thought was to get out of town. I felt empty, disoriented. I'd thought Miguel was a trustworthy ally. Why had he attacked me? Was it the drugs? Would he try again? Where should I go from here? My rage and sense of injustice had rumbled down to a low undertone within. My thoughts raced toward my next move.

When the big green and white bus pulled up, I got on, using the last of my change. I'd ride it to San Rafael, try St. Vincent's, the free food place. I was totally focused now on survival. I could not afford to dwell on having been attacked.

But at the last Sausalito stop, Miguel boarded. My heart lurched, slamming into my chest. Imminent danger. How was this possible? Did he have eyes everywhere? I sat frozen in my seat, suddenly terrified and unable to move. Why was I so passive?

He nodded curtly and hurtled forward as the bus started up again. Moving from pole to pole, he stopped at my seat and slid in next to me.

I would not be afraid. I'd scare him away. I turned to him and grimaced, showing a gap-toothed snarl. I lifted my hands to form claws. There was still rage in me; good. "I'll curse you," I hissed, not even knowing where my ferocious gesture came from.

"Don't threaten me, Dee; I'm in no mood for it," Miguel snarled. In one motion, he pulled back his fist and hit me in the head. My head slammed into the bus window, making a loud thunk. Miguel stared fixedly forward. I heard a gasp from the seat behind me.

Feeling sick and dizzy from the blow, I half-stood and turned to face the other passengers.

"Doesn't anybody care?" I shouted. "I've been hit! Help me!" They stared at me in shocked silence and then looked away. A woman rummaged in her purse for a transfer. A man pulled out his paper and hid behind it. With dismay, I realized that no one was willing to interfere. The bus turned left onto the freeway.

"Don't make a scene," said Miguel complacently. "Wake me when we get there." He leaned back in his seat and closed his eyes.

I hated him. A surprising deep calm came over me, and within it were two things: my hatred and a determination to get away. I sat very still and watched his head bob down, jerk back with a snort, nod back down. He must be coming down off his drug. Slowly, carefully, I raised myself up and edged out of the seat. Grabbing the upper railing, I made my way to the front of the bus and asked for the next stop and a transfer.

The driver nodded. We were on the freeway now; the bay curved behind us. Mini-malls flashed by. I clung to the pole, swaying with the turns of the bus. Fighting off dread, I prayed Miguel would stay asleep, that I would escape.

At last the driver pulled to a stop. The doors whispered open, and I ran out. They whispered shut again; the bus pulled away. Miguel was still on it.

I looked around. I was in Corte Madera, in front of a shopping mall. I was tired and hungry and sore. I didn't know where to go next. It was confusing to be outside of the territory I knew every inch of. I'd come to think of the Gate 5 area as my home, my turf. I was now many miles away from it, in an alien land. What next? Try not to panic.

It must be after nine, because the parking lot to the mall was starting to fill. I was dazed and wanted only to sleep. I leaned my head against the wall of the bus shelter and began to slide in and out of consciousness.

I dreamt I was inside the mall, buying things for a new apartment: curtains, teakettle, brightly colored towels. I selected a soft fluffy towel. It was long, full body length, pale green. Or did I prefer the rose color?

The scene dissolved, and I was in a luxurious bathroom. The tub was full of hot scented water. I got in, feeling the warmth, knowing that when I emerged, all soft and clean, I would wrap myself in the towel.

I jerked awake at the sound of a bus pulling up to the stop. Several people got out, one a woman with a stroller and an older child. Her child looked curiously at me and tugged his mother's skirt. "Mama," he said urgently. "Looka dat lady." She hushed him and, lifting him up, hustled away. I must have alarmed her.

Was I still in the towel? Was I wet? No, no. My legs were covered in very dirty jeans. My jacket had a dribble of dried coffee down the front. Hanging over one eye was my black and red scarf. I tugged it off and rose to board the bus, legs wobbly.

The driver motioned me aboard. Her visor was squarely positioned on her head, shading her face. Below it I could see broad cheekbones. Her face was solemn.

"Get on or off, now," she commanded. Flustered, I stepped up and fumbled in my pocket. Where was my transfer? Had I lost it while I slept? I felt a quarter and held it out to her.

She furrowed her brow at me, shifted into gear.

"I'll take you as far as the terminal," she said. We rode on in silence.

The San Rafael terminal was underneath the freeway. Gray stone buttresses arched overhead. Rows of benches lined the sidewalk. Directly across from them was an overgrown area, a storm drain littered with trash and bordered by a wilderness of bushes.

I held onto a bench and surveyed the area behind it. Down in that wilderness would be a good place to hide for a while. Determined, driven only by a need for sleep, I picked up a paper bag to serve as a pillow and crawled in under a bush. Pulling the branches down around me, I made myself into a tight ball, fists clenched against enemies, and passed out.

When I came to, I didn't know where I was at first. A deep, steady rumbling overhead was…what, what? Ah, the freeway. Yes, I was under the freeway. Cautiously, I emerged from the bush. I didn't want to slip into the storm drain. I edged my way back to the waist-high fence which separated this wilderness from the bus terminal, and I climbed over.

I leaned against the fence to get my bearings. From the light, I guessed it was late afternoon. The benches were full; many people were waiting for a connecting bus. I joined them. I felt desolate. They all had someplace to go. I had no place.

A sharp-eyed woman was making her way along the benches. She was very thin; she seemed to be all edges. She was wearing baggy jeans and a long vest; her arms and elbows angled out from its garish plaid. She scooted in next to me and began talking with the woman to my right.

155

"Excuse me ma'am, I wonder if you could help. I'm trying to get to Novato, and I'm short on the fare."

My neighbor shrank back and held tighter to the purse on her lap. Undaunted, the vested woman hopped to the next person.

"Sir, excuse me…" The next bench over yielded results. A woman nodded and handed over a dollar.

"Yes, honey. I been down myself. Here you go."

A bus pulled in, and the bench population shifted. Those who'd been waiting got on; those exiting milled about. The panhandler stopped to let them settle. Her eyes never stopped moving. Then she was next to me again.

"Listen, sleeping beauty. I'm working this place. Whyn't you move on."

I was indignant. She wouldn't chase me off so easily as that. "Listen, work your heart out. I'm just resting. Deciding where to go next. Any shelters in town?"

She considered. "You missed the sign-up. There's a bus that takes people to one of the churches in town. You gotta sign up first, though, and you only get in for three nights a month. You ain't been yet?"

"Not yet."

"You can probably get in then, but you missed the sign-up for tonight, like I said."

"Where do I sign up?"

She pointed me south.

"You go down past the bus station here. Turn right and look left. It's on that street—an old yellow house, with steps. Downstairs they got clothes, like a thrift shop. Upstairs they got offices. That's where you register."

"Is it far?"

"Nah. You'll find it. I can't take the time to show you, kid. Don't want to break my rhythm here. I'm on a roll. Besides, it wouldn't help you to go with me. They all know me there. I've registered under four different names, and they've caught on."

She grinned and, before I could thank her, she was off again, moving down the benches. I set off in the direction she'd indicated. I felt better now. I was rested and I had a purpose.

I found the yellow house without difficulty. On the lawn were racks of clothes and a table of books. I wondered if this was where Miguel got his supply. I spotted the stairs and climbed them, opened the door marked "Office."

It was a light, narrow room with a few small desks. A woman was standing behind one, straightening papers, packing up her things as if to go.

"We're closing, dear—gave out all the groceries. Come back tomorrow."

I would not be brushed off. "Ah—I came about shelter."

She shook her head briskly.

"Tomorrow. Come between 1 and 3 to sign up."

"No, I mean—a woman's shelter. For women who've been beaten up. Don't you have a place?" There must be one.

She narrowed her eyes.

"It's not a walk-in shelter. You have to be screened. Is this an emergency?"

I felt stubborn. I *would* get help here. I sat in the chair across from her and simply decided to stay in place until she helped me. I flashed on the people in the bus who'd looked away. That would not happen here.

"Is this a crisis?" she repeated. "Are you in danger?"

I nodded.

"Are you being followed?"

I hesitated.

"If I go back where I was, I'll be followed. A fiend…" If I said any more, I'd cry. My defenses were suddenly down. My hands, I saw, were trembling. Shock was wearing off. Good. Maybe that would persuade her.

"There's no one outside right now, waiting for you?"

"No."

"All right, I'll see what I can do." She reached for the telephone and dialed.

"Yes, Marla? Joan here. I've got a possible intake; can you see her? Don't know—she's disoriented. Possibly delusional. Mentions a fiend."

I sat up straighter in my chair, sharply resentful. Delusional? How dare she label me that way? I was perfectly sane.

There was a long pause while she listened to the person on the other end. Then she smiled. "Ok, when? Yeah, thanks."

She hung up and turned back to me.

"There's one place that might have room, but you'll have to be interviewed first. She's going to meet you in half an hour. There's a coffee shop two blocks away—the Heavenly Bean. Go there and wait for her; she'll find you. Her name's Marla. Here," she reached into a drawer and pulled out two dollars. "Get yourself some coffee." I was filled with gratitude, forgave her comment about being delusional. A gift. Just holding the cash gave me strength.

She walked out with me, locking the door behind her. She pointed me in the direction of the coffee shop and I set off again, putting one foot in front of the other, feeling like a sleepwalker. My legs were leaden, and my thoughts would not focus. Just get there, I told myself.

"One, two." I counted. "One, two."

I stopped at the sign for Heavenly Bean. Inside was a square room, redwood and lots of ferns. I sat down to wait, holding the two dollars in front of me like an offering.

Heavenly Bean was crowded. People were nestled at redwood tables, talking together, sipping from mugs. They were mainly couples, I noticed, with a few solitary ones mixed in. Those who were alone brandished newspapers to read with deep concentration. No one came up to me. After a while I realized that customers placed their own orders at a counter in the back of the room. I didn't want to move for fear of missing my contact, so I sat where I was, undisturbed.

A woman entered and stood at the doorway, scanning the room. She wore a denim dress and sturdy sandals. Under one arm she'd tucked a clipboard. Her light brown hair was cropped in a business-like manner around her face; her eyes were covered with large, rectangular, red-framed glasses.

She spotted me and headed directly for me, shifting the clipboard so that she could hold out her hand.

"I'm Marla," she said. "Were you waiting for me?"

I nodded, feeling a mixture of relief and apprehension. Would she help? She surveyed me calmly. "Have you eaten anything?"

I shook my head. Abruptly, she got up and went to the counter. She returned with a bottle of juice and a roll from which sprouts and tomato protruded.

"Eat, drink," she said, setting the clipboard on the table and taking out a pen. I did, wolfing it down but without tasting the food.

"So you are…"

"Dee Williams."

"Age?"

"37."

"Address?"

"Not at the moment."

"Hm. We may not be the best place for you. Can you tell me what happened? The violent episode?"

"Someone I thought was a friend starting hitting me, following me and hitting and kicking me. It was very scary."

"Is this person a partner?"

"We were roommates in a shed."

"In a shed?" She was startled.

"Once I was in a car, but it got towed and anyway if I got another, he'd find it."

The situation was clear to me but seemed to puzzle her. She frowned. I grew nervous. Would she turn me down? I shouldn't have implied I was homeless. No wonder people made up stories, backgrounds, events. They had to make themselves fit the shelter's rules.

"So you have no place to live."

"Right."

She tapped her pen on the clipboard.

"We aren't really a homeless shelter. We provide space for women and children who need to get away from domestic violence."

I thought it was a lousy way to qualify for shelter. Should I cry? Tears were close to the surface. Too late to make up a family, husband, home.

She sighed and spoke with reluctance. "We're usually full, but a family left this afternoon. It may be that we could give you a bed for a night or two. You'll have to sign a statement promising that you won't reveal our location to anyone."

"Okay." I'd sign anything to get a bed for a night.

She held out a form, and I signed it, hardly daring to believe my luck. My hand was shaky. But I was in. Would she want to blindfold me before taking me to the secret place?

"I'm going against my better judgment here," she confided to me. "We're not really set up for street people. I'm surprised at the referral. Our purpose is to help women with children, women who have their own homes but are victimized by their spouses. Homeless people are in a different situation, and—don't take this personally—tend to be disruptive in a home setting."

Rejection loomed. "Oh, I'll be very quiet," I said urgently. She tapped her pen again, made a note on the page. She sighed and looked toward the service counter, as if hoping that someone there would provide a solution. How could I convince her to take me in?

"If I stay outdoors tonight," I said firmly, "I'm likely to wake up dead. You'll read about it in the papers."

I had shaken her composure. Good. She hesitated, then made another note.

"Well. I hope I won't regret this. You won't tell your friends where we are?"

I shook my head and twisted a sprout in my fingers.

"I suppose we could try two nights. You understand that it's temporary. If we get another family in, you'll have to go."

I began to push the sprout along the table top toward a heart that had been carved in the surface. "E. M. and L.T.," it read, the initials gouged deeply. There was a word carved beneath the initials—"Forever." I rolled the sprout onto the edge of the heart.

"Come on if you're coming," she said. "We'll have to drive." I urged myself to remain calm, to act poised. I didn't want to show her how much I needed her to decide in my favor. I didn't want to reveal my deep relief at being accepted, lest it be taken from me.

We rode in her car, curving along side streets, delving into the residential section of town. It felt strange and luxurious to be in a car again. We passed neat houses with green lawns. Amazing—I'd forgotten people lived this way.

Marla pulled into the driveway of an ordinary house. There was a child's scooter on the porch.

"Here we are. Let's get you situated."

I followed her up the walkway. She unlocked the front door and we went into a living room whose dominant feature was a big color television. Several small children were seated in front of it, watching cartoons. They looked up curiously at us. Marla waved at them and ushered me on into a middle room.

"Have a seat here, Dee." She placed a clipboard in front of me. "We do have some paperwork. While you fill it out, I'll go get someone who can show you around."

I looked at the form on the clipboard. Always paperwork. Why? Who ever read it? Marla had filled some of it in. For "residence" she had put "Sausalito (no address)." The part she wanted me to fill in was titled, "Describe violent incident:"

My hand was still shaky. Gripping the pen tightly, I printed, "A friend hit me and kicked me all over. Then fiend hit my head on bus." That was the best I could do. To retell it was to relive it and to feel the fear and anger and pain again.

I set the clipboard on the table and looked around. There was a picture on the wall of a woman on a horse. Her hair streamed back; she was going fast. She wore armor and carried a spear. "Joan of Arc," said a placard on the frame. Hm. Would she protect me?

I contemplated her. She'd been a great warrior, winning battle after battle. But then her enemies had her burned. Burned! My problems were minor compared to that. Imagine, through—a woman who was a fierce fighter. If she'd been jumped by Miguel or hit in the jaw, she could run the fiend through with a sword. I wished I had that kind of strength.

She was fighting for God, she said. Following the voices in her head. Today, that would be called crazy. Yet, she won.

The door opened and Marla reappeared. She lifted the clipboard and read what I'd written.

"Does this fiend have a name?"

I was silent.

"The information here is confidential, Dee. It's just for our records. Are you afraid he'll hurt you if you say his name?"

I nodded. It was a rule of the street I was unwilling to break. Reporting people to the authorities was forbidden. Miguel would track me down and beat me up worse. Others would look at me with scorn and distrust, would scorn me as a snitch.

"This is just between you and me."

"I don't know his real name."

She frowned again.

"I was hoping for more cooperation here. Why don't you think it over. Perhaps tomorrow we can find another place for you to go."

"Okay."

She stood; the interview must be over. I was relieved. I'd been uncomfortable during it. How could I explain the intensity of what had happened? A trusted friend turning on me, becoming so dangerous. My inability to fight back. The thunk of my head against the bus window, as if it were an inanimate object. The panic and pain transforming into an urgent need to escape.

She opened the door into the kitchen.

"Your bed's this way, Dee. Rachel, could you show Dee the room downstairs?"

Rachel was loading plates into a dishwasher. She straightened and looked me over.

"Ginny's old room?"

"For tonight, yes."

"Huh. Okay, follow me." I walked behind her, watching her glossy black braid. It swung to and fro as she led the way out of the kitchen and downstairs into a refurbished basement.

We walked through a children's playroom. Shelves along the wall were filled with stuffed animals and games. A miniature table and chair were pushed off to one side; a crate of toys was next to it. My daughter would be too old for these toys by now. She'd be playing other games. My daughter...good thing she'd not been with me. I felt intense gratitude that she had not been exposed to the violence.

Just behind the crate was a door which led to a narrow room. It held a cot and dresser.

"Here you go. Bathroom's down the hall."

She opened the dresser and began to set items from it onto the cot.

"Nightgown. Towel. Toothbrush. We'll have to see about clothes later."

I sat on the cot, overwhelmed by these details.

"We've had dinner. If you're hungry, there's a fruit bowl upstairs."

She looked at me sternly. She knew I didn't really belong here; she let me know she was just tolerating me.

"We eat only healthy snacks. Don't go bringing junk food in here; we got kids to think about. We'll set you up with chores in the morning." Then, grudgingly, "If you want, you can come on up and watch tv."

I nodded but did not move.

"Ok, then. I'm going back up."

I heard her footsteps on the stairs. I sat on the cot, surveying my new surroundings. I appeared to be underground. There were no windows. Above me came the sounds of more footsteps, voices, the throbbing hum of the dishwasher.

Next to me was a pale, flowered nightgown and a plastic bag that held a toothbrush and comb. More than anything, I wanted to sleep, just to escape the events of last night and today. I pulled down the cover and climbed in, clutching the nightgown to me. I made a cave with the blanket and, listening to the swish and whir of the dishwasher, went to sleep.

I dreamed I was drowning. Long watery arms pulled me deeper and deeper, at a dizzying pace. I struggled at first and then gave in; I was headed for the center of the vortex.

I awoke to a bright light in my eyes and far-off voices. "Look, she's still got her clothes on."

"That's fine, take her that way. Put this coat on her." I was being bundled up and herded along. I was propped up against someone who kept her arm around me until she'd fastened me into a seat belt. I didn't know if my mouth would make words.

"Wheh we gwing?"

"We're going to the hospital. When the night staff checked on you, you weren't breathing. Try to sit up now. We'll be there soon."

Someone lifted me onto a stretcher, and I lay there in a trance, drifting in and out of consciousness. Doctors and nurses moved around me in soft-soled shoes. I'd begin to slide back into the deep, watery place, only to be pulled back.

After a long time, an arm came behind me to lift me up. It was the woman who'd driven me here.

"Come on, we're going back now."

"Back where?"

"To the women's shelter."

I was baffled, disoriented. My driver, a middle-aged woman, was very strong. She wrapped a coat around me; it was scratchy tweed. She half-supported me back to the car. I was interested in how wobbly my legs were. Funny! I could get them to move, but it took some doing.

The sky was streaked with red and gray. It must be early morning. My companion started the car.

"Goodness, we were in there all night. I had no idea—I only volunteer at the shelter one night a month. It's been quiet until now. You gave us a scare, I must say."

"Sorry." I didn't feel sorry, really. I felt vaguely curious as to why I'd been treated. Mostly, I felt lucky to be with a woman of compassion and kindness. Her voice was gentle.

"Well, it isn't your fault. It turns out you have pneumonia. Pneumonia, for heaven's sakes! And the hospital wouldn't treat you at first. I really had to insist that they take you. Had to ask for the supervisor. That got things moving. They wouldn't keep you overnight, though."

"Why?"

She turned her head to look at me. "Because you're—because you have no address. If you'd gone in on your own, I don't know what would have happened. No money, no insurance…I had to promise that the shelter would be responsible, and it took forever."

"Thanks for your help." How wonderful, that someone had fought for me.

"Oh, I'm glad I was there. I'm just really angry about it. I had no idea, really. What do people do, if they have no one to speak up for them?"

I thought of Squeaky, alone in the park. "They die."

"And they went away and found a colt tied at the door
outside in the street, and they untied it…And they
brought the colt to Jesus and put their garments on it;
and He sat upon it."
(Mark 11: 2, 7)

CHAPTER 10

I rested at the battered women's shelter another week, staying in bed
and keeping out of the way. I was determined not to give Marla cause
to regret her decision. I felt weak and defeated. My brush with death
had frightened and sobered me. I was badly shaken. I knew that if I'd
been alone, sleeping outdoors, I'd have gone down into death without a
struggle. With no one to identify me, I'd have been tagged "Jane Doe"
and forgotten. I was intensely grateful to the volunteer who'd taken me
into the hospital.

Once the medicine had made me stronger, the staff transferred me
out. So it was that I found myself on a night bus, heading for a Christian
shelter in Novato. I felt quiescent, as if I'd given up my fate to the hands
of others. It was a strange sensation. There was no fight left in me. I'd
just gone along with this new plan to transfer me without protest. I
relaxed in my seat, limply, listening to the roar of the bus engine.

Novato is in northern Marin, way out past the courthouse. It's full
of green rolling hills and pastures. I thought of it as horse and cow
country. I suspected that I was being farmed out. Marla, I knew, had
wanted to get rid of me. Here I was, unwanted baggage, being foisted

off on a place called New Life. Would I fit in? Would it really be a new life for me?

My bus stop was near a 7-11 store, which comforted me. 7-11s were my friends. They had sheltered me. Up the hill from the store was a residential section of Novato. No one was about. It felt eerie to be walking the empty sidewalk at night, inspecting the houses for addresses. Me, in a house? I was suddenly skeptical. I didn't know what I was walking into. Still, I continued on.

I found the right place, a white stucco house with green shutters and door. I rang the bell. After a long silence, during which I could hear the bell reverberating through the house, the door was cautiously opened by a young woman in robe and curlers.

"Dee Williams? I've been expecting you; come in."

She led me into the living room, where the television flickered with the movie of the week. She lowered its volume and motioned me to sit on the couch.

"We're a halfway house, Dee. We've got only three women staying here now; four counting you. Two of our residents have children. The women take turns with meals and household chores, and each of them has found work. One at the market, one at a local deli...This is a place where you can get your life back together."

I braced myself for a recitation of house rules.

"There's no alcohol or drugs allowed. People eat and sleep here, and go to work during the day. Otherwise, you stay on the premises. Wednesday night is mandatory Bible study with the director; you'll meet him tomorrow. Any questions?"

"Who are you? A resident?"

"Oh, sorry." She extended her hand. "I'm Kyla Jones, acting housemother. I'm only here at night—I'm a student at College of Marin. Sociology."

She looked at a sheaf of notes in her lap.

"Marla tells me you have some interviews set up to get you going with Social Services. Our day staff will make sure you get there. Then we'll help you get a job—the director is very big on everyone working. The idea is to become self-supporting."

Work—ugh. Would I have to wear a uniform?

"You said there was Bible study. This is a religious place?"

"Oh yes, it's a Christian center. It's run by one of the local churches. The Bible study is required of everyone who stays here. Will that be a problem?"

"No." I could deal with a discussion group—if I stayed that long. I'd been here five minutes; already I felt cooped up, as if the walls were closing in. Rules, regulations, rehabilitation…I cringed.

She rose from her armchair. "I'll show you your room, Dee. We have an early morning, so everyone's in bed."

In the hallway, she turned. "I know you've been a street person. I hope you'll try your best to cooperate with the house here. The director won't tolerate any trouble."

I kept silent and tried to stare her down. It rankled that she was younger than I and telling me what to do. A college student! I could have been her teacher, once. Could have told *her* what to do. Write that essay! Read that book! Ha. Who was she to talk to me of trouble? I felt my rebellious nature flare back into life.

She stared back; then, to my satisfaction, she looked away first. A small victory.

"Here's your room. I've set out a nightgown for you. Good night, Dee. I may see you in the morning."

"Good night." Good riddance.

There were two bunkbeds squeezed into the corners; the furniture was sparse. A night light of Bugs Bunny beamed from the wall. A small shape in one of the beds sighed as I entered the room, but it stayed asleep. My heart softened to hear the child. How I wished it were my own child, safe in bed and near me.

Wistfully, I changed into the nightgown and sat on the bunk. It would be useless to try to sleep. I was revved, filled with adrenaline and curiosity. I'd explore the house. Quietly, I made my way back down the hall and into the rear of New Life.

I found a dining room and adjoining kitchen. Inside the dining room was a low bookcase, which I inspected. Its upper shelves were filled with bibles. On its lower shelves were heaped stacks of comic books. Pleased, I opened one and sat on the floor to read it.

It was a picture book about Jesus—no surprise there, in a Christian house. On the cover, Jesus had long wavy brown hair, big brown eyes, a sweet expression. Realistic or greeting card? How to find out? Who knew, really? He had on a long flowing robe. He wore sandals and his feet were delicate and strong, like a ballet dancer's. I flipped the pages fast in my lap, to make a cartoon movie. Jesus twirled and leaped.

"You need some jazz," I told him. "Some saxophone." I imagined a faint echo of horns, then the room filling with sound. Delighted and soothed, I held my knees and rocked to and fro with the silent music. It was sublime and comforting. I felt a rare peace encircle me.

Then, I leafed through more slowly. I watched him go under water and come out to receive a dove on his head. Swoop, went the dove. What would that feel like, sudden sharp bird-feet on the scalp?

There he was travelling, walking along with bearded guys in robes. Tramp, tramp, tramping along through the country. Sleeping out. Sleeping rough.

Funny. Jesus had chosen the same way of life that I had. Street person. Both of us would walk miles in a day—would hunt for a place to sleep each night. Well, such a life has its advantages, I agreed. No rent, no house rules, no job pressures. Out of doors and always on the move. A certain freedom. It pleased me that we were alike in this way. We could even maybe be friends? Might meet en route?

There he was making bread and fish. Little sardine sandwiches. Make some mustard, I suggested, to go with the fish. I must be hungry. I set the book down and went into the kitchen, where a fruit bowl stood on the counter. I chose a banana and returned to the comic.

There he was filling up his lap with children. A fellow who likes kids. I was glad he had some happy times. Little sturdy bodies climbing on him, nestling on his lap. My daughter's face flashed in my memory. Mentally, I placed her there. "Christ, I've been unable to care for her. To hold her. To cherish and comfort her. Will you?" I fervently hoped so.

There he was walking along in a crowd. A woman was crawling after him. The book said she was bleeding to death—repulsive. Drip drip gush, all day long. No blood showed, though, in the picture. On the shelf were some crayons. I put a red puddle around her. Let's be realistic.

I turned the page; she was up and smiling. "Good," I said to her, relieved. "You got your strength back. So will I."

"Your faith has made you whole," he told her. Oh! my favorite part. It was thrilling. I wrapped my mind around the story. What I loved about it: Jesus tells her she herself did the healing, because of her faith. That was classy. He gave her the credit for getting strong again. Didn't claim to have done it himself. No, he told her, she'd done it herself, through faith. Good going, I told her. I could feel hope build in me.

I skipped a few pages. There he was now, in a frenzy of anger, tossing down tables and money boxes. He was outraged. Wood splintered; coins were hurled far and wide. Scary. I wouldn't want to get him mad at me. I ducked my head to get out of the way of that wrath.

I knew the really gory, sad part was coming up—whips and nails. When I was a child and visiting friends of my parents, I'd seen a super-realistic crucifix on the wall. That day was my first experience with Jesus. I'd stared in horrified fascination. I'd shuddered; I wanted to lift him off the cross and away from the pain; I couldn't move. This night, reading the comic book gospel, I flew back in my mind to my childhood wonder about Christ.

On the last few pages, there were some women crouching outside an empty cave, poking at body wrappings.

"Where have you taken him?" asked one. I turned the page excitedly. There he was again, talking with her. Then he was gone. Back again, talking to the men—and gone again. What a marvel. Oh how lovely, to be able to appear and disappear. Vanish, and reappear to surprise people. What an advantage. My spirits lifted. I laughed out loud, then looked around guiltily to make sure I hadn't woken anyone. I didn't want to be chased back to bed.

I turned to the very last page. There he was again, going up like a rocket into the clouds. "Bye for now," I said.

A flicker of love stirred in me. I wished we could be friends, day by day friends. Was that even possible? I reflected on it, aware of a deep yearning now as I curled up in a corner.

In the early morning hours, I heard rustlings from the front of the house. I went to bed as the others were rising for work and school.

In the late morning, I re-entered the dining room. There was another application form set out for me on the dining table. These forms were so tedious! Name, it said. Address, telephone. Place of employment. Insurance. Next of kin. Boldly, I laughed at it.

"If I had all that," I told it, "why would I be here? Come off it." I filled in my name, crossed out all the rest, and for "occupation" put in "Dancing with Jesus to jazz." This was a Christian place—all right. I'd dare them to accept my faith. My passivity was gone.

That day I met the director. He had a light brown suit, light brown tie, brown hair and eyes. If I looked at him too long, he seemed to melt together. I thought of him as Mr. Beige. He read my form, pursing his lips. He looked up at me sharply, suspiciously.

"What's this about dancing with Jesus? You're turning the form into a joke."

I smiled benignly. "It's real to me," I said. In the late night hours I'd seen the dancing feet and heard the jazzy sounds even more clearly than I was now experiencing Mr. Beige. Of that I was certain. I was sincere, but how to prove it? It was a puzzle. I gave up.

"We do serious work here, Ms. Williams. We believe that a firm Christian foundation is the most helpful way to get people back on their feet and off the streets."

I waited. I nodded. I knew there was a catch.

"Now. Marla, the supervisor of Hannah House, has arranged an interview for you. It's a session with a doctor to determine whether or not you qualify for SSI benefits."

Hooray! A burst of joy. And it was thanks to Marla. Grudgingly, I had to admit, despite friction with Marla, that she'd worked on my behalf, setting things up to get me what I wanted: the Big Check. This was good news indeed.

"Well and good, but we also expect you to go out and get a job, Ms. Williams. The 7-11 down the road needs a checker. After your doctor's appointment, and once you get on medication, that's your next stop. Understood?"

"Perfectly." He didn't want me lounging around the place, being a bum and reading comics. Despite my bridling resentment at being bossed, I remained impressed by the speed with which I'd be going in for an interview to get benefits. I knew people on the street who'd been waiting a long time for a talk with a Social Security doctor. These shelters had strings to pull. As for getting on medication, I could just throw the pills away.

He set my form flat on the table and crossed out my entry. "We'll complete your form when you've stabilized, Ms. Williams. Our Bible study should help you with that. The purpose, of course, is to find God's will for your life. God has a plan for you, rest assured. Here, we'll help you find it."

I suspected that it was Mr. Beige who had a plan for me: By day, checking merchandise in the 7-11. By night, listening to him explain the Bible. We'd see about that. I felt highly suspicious about a plan that was made without consulting me. Whose life was it, after all? As for Bible study, I was good at interpretation myself. I'd give him a run for his money.

I'd read the Bible, believing that no one was truly educated without it. My favorite character was the baby donkey who carried Jesus to Jerusalem. Just a little humble new one, yet such a big part to play.

***

New Life was true to its word. I was taken to be interviewed with a psychiatrist who approved me for SSI benefits. I was elated, and I threw away the prescription for medication. I wasn't crazy—just pretending to be crazy. I felt a little guilty at the deception, but not much.

I was less than pleased, however, by the push to find a job. Mr. Beige insisted that employment was God's will for me and that I should submit. "Submission" was a word and a concept I abhorred. It meant weakness. It meant giving up and taking orders from another. Was that really what God wanted? Or was it what Mr. Beige wanted? I wasn't sure. All I was sure of was that the house was becoming very confining and that I wanted my freedom back, freedom to rove.

One morning, I saw my chance to escape. I could legitimately leave the house to go to the 7-11, claiming I was going to inquire about the checker job. From there, I could disappear. The plan exhilarated me. Would I get away with it? I was impressed with my daring.

Heart pounding, I left the house early, closing the green door carefully behind me. Morning mist had rolled in, covering the other houses on the block. Shivering, but with a great sense of jubilation at escaping, I walked down the street to where the 7-11 gleamed brightly on the corner.

The place was bustling, with commuters pulling in and out for morning coffee and papers. I edged over to the front of the parking lot, looking for a likely score. In a few moments, I saw one—a pleasant faced man in suit and tie who stooped getting out of his sports car. I darted up to him.

"Excuse me, sir. Could you spare some change for bus fare? I have to get into the city."

He patted his pockets and then, to my delight, pulled out a dollar. How much was busfare? Probably $1.25. If I scored another dollar I'd have enough left over for coffee.

I had a sense of urgency. I didn't want anyone from New Life to come by and see how I was getting along here. I scanned the cars again, ready to pounce.

There, coming out of a cream-colored sedan, was a lady dressed all in red. She wore a cherry-colored suit with a red and gold scarf tied at her neck. Her shoes were red to match and, as I got closer, I saw that her nails and lips also glowed as if with blood. Surely here was the rest of my busfare.

"Ma'am, could you spare some change for the bus?"

She jerked upright and glared at me. "For the bus? I hope it's for the bus and not for a drink."

I stood up straight to match her erect posture. Put on my most honest expression. "It's for the bus—I'm leaving town."

She gave me an assessing look. "I'll give you some change if you tell all your friends to stay in the city," she instructed me. "The city is bad enough, with all the panhandlers. I don't want to see that here."

"I'll do that," I said, amazed that she'd think I had so much influence.

Still annoyed, she fumbled in her purse for change and handed it over to me. She huffed into the store then, and I saw her talking in an agitated way to the clerk behind the register. Turning me in?

I ran around the corner and ducked down behind the 7-11 dumpster. Sheets of cardboard and empty boxes jutted out from the top, and I thought how potentially useful they'd be for someone setting up camp. Cardboard made a good cushion against the cold, hard ground or cement. Good, I was thinking like a street person again—thinking of survival.

I heard the store manager and the lady in red coming out the front door.

"I'm sure sorry you were bothered, ma'am. We don't allow panhandling in front of the store. She was in the parking lot?"

I peeked underneath the large dumpster. I could see red pumps and what I supposed were the manager's black shoes. Good, they were headed away from me.

"She was coming up to the cars, bold as anything. I don't like to be disturbed that way! I don't expect it out here."

Their voices were fading. I thought the clerk was making soothing noises. I waited, heart racing, and then peeked around the edge of the dumpster.

The clerk had gone back inside. Red Lady was talking now with my first score, the man in the suit. In my own way, I'd been the cause of a 7-11 romance. Had brought them together. He patted her hand and walked her to her car.

Reprieved. Now, though, there was no point in trying to get a cup of coffee. I'd be chased off. My best bet was to wait for the bus and board it. I leaned back against the dumpster, panting. I'd been holding my breath. A stench of sour milk filled my nostrils. How disgusting! Yet, I'd climbed into dumpsters when I was hungry. This wave of nausea must be because of my stay in the shelters, my frequent bathing. Given a time outdoors, away from showers, the sense of smell was blunted until everyone smelled the same and stench could be ignored.

When I heard the familiar sound of a city bus, I slipped out to meet it. There was a strong smell of exhaust and a creaking of brakes. Joyously, I boarded.

"What a friend we have in Jesus,
All our sins and griefs to bear,
What a privilege to carry
Everything to God in prayer."

Chapter 11

Early 1986

I rode to central San Rafael, where I tumbled around on the streets and in the parks for a few months. During that time, I made one of my infrequent calls to my mother, who told me that my daughter had entered a private high school in Carpinteria, near Santa Barbara. My hopes rose, and with them my good intentions. What if I went there, and cleaned up, and was able to visit? Could I do it? In that part of each drunk when all things seem possible and the drinker superhuman, before the world grows blurry and woozy and dim, it seemed that I could.

I asked other street people for the word on Santa Barbara and learned that it had both shelters and free food places. "If you starve in Santa Barbara," said one informant, "it's your own fault."

So, determined to become a good parent, I got a bus voucher for out of town. I'd noticed, in my travels, that most cities will give a bus voucher. I reckoned that their gift was motivated by a desire to have one less homeless person around. Still, it was a gift I needed and gratefully took. I rode to San Francisco and then onto a Greyhound bound down the coast to Santa Barbara.

Santa Barbara, here I come.

I had been to Santa Barbara once before, as teenager. A group of us had wanted to join all the other young people who gathered at Balboa Beach over Easter weekend. There would be a beach packed with glistening bodies, and young people from all over, and a good chance that some had their own places to stay—unchaperoned. There would be parties, liquor, the boardwalk, chocolate covered bananas, and hours of each day to lie in the sun, get bronzed, gossip, flirt, speculate.

A friend's mother, as a ploy to keep us away from the scene of wild unchaperoned teenage parties, had rented a place in Santa Barbara instead, a good hour north of the forbidden action beaches. So we'd gone there. I remembered it as being calm and peaceful that spring, with vast stretches of empty beaches, little red trolleys, miles of sidewalk right along the beach. There had been nobody much around—our Easter week did not coincide with the local college's—and we'd been bored.

Now I'd be going there by choice. In Santa Barbara, I dreamed, I'd find that calm and peace again, and it would be a relief. I'd escape street violence and running from danger and just relax a while. Maybe shape a whole new life. Maybe find a little place where my daughter could come and visit. I'd do all that as soon as I got off the bus and got a drink in me.

My destination loomed golden before me. In one week, there at the General Delivery would be a big check waiting for me, and I'd be rich, rich! Oh, not rich by society's standards, but compared to normal street life, awaking each morning with zero, I'd be wealthy. In a beach town. All I had to do now was get through the week. I could certainly do that. I felt resourceful and brave—a pioneer.

I dozed through the morning. When I woke, I saw that the bus had stopped along the way, and I'd picked up a seatmate. She was a plump, bustling woman in her sixties who carried a bag of knitting and another of gifts.

"Late Christmas presents," she explained. "For the grandkids. My son's in school at Santa Barbara. Am I proud of him? You know it. To go back to school with three youngsters in the family! Takes gumption, don't it? Of course, Sara—that's his wife—is such a doll. He couldn't do it without her. They live in student housing, Isla Vista. Not far away—he said he'd pick me up from the station."

It began to rain once we passed Santa Maria, and my seatmate told me we were driving right into Santa Barbara's rainy season.

"I thought we were heading south into sunshine and palm trees," I said sadly.

"We are, dear. It's a beautiful climate, beautiful town—a real resort community. It does need that rain, though, to keep the flowers so nice."

"How long does the rain last?"

"Oh, 'bout two months. January, February. Thereabouts. They get flooding sometimes. You might have seen it on television last year?"

"No."

"Lower State Street was flooded—that's the main street. People were kayaking down it. A homeless camp got completely washed out, too. One man drowned with his dog. Sad, really. I mean, I'm sorry he died and all, but those camps are such an eyesore. It took a flood to do what the city couldn't."

I bridled, feeling quick anger at such callousness. "Get rid of the homeless camps?"

"That's right, dear. Sounds heartless, I know. But those people are just so pesky on State Street, always 'Got any spare change?' It makes a body nervous about going shopping."

She patted her purse. Did she know I was one of the people she dreaded? I inspected myself: I'd showered not too long ago; my long khaki jacket was neat enough. My denim pants were to that comfortable grubbiness where they fit me like a second skin.

The rain intensified the farther south we drove, blurring the landscape and turning everything gray. I contemplated it gloomily. I hadn't counted on the weather. Forget about a night with a nice bottle, under the stars. I began to adjust my plans. I'd try for a shelter in town.

As my seatmate chattered on, I began to concoct my story. "New in town…had some bad luck…getting life back together…gotta check coming in a few days…need a place to stay while I look for work…" I'd use my best manners and stay sober until I had a bed. I'd just have to wait out the rain.

When we pulled into Santa Barbara, it was late afternoon. It was a small station. A blind couple was in the waiting room, placidly sitting side by side. Their dog, a golden retriever, sniffed me as I passed.

"My new life is beginning," I said to myself, determined to replace depression with hope. "My new prosperous life." I opened the station door into a gust of wet, blustery air. Black clouds massed overhead, but there was a lull in the storm.

I saw no one to ask, so I went into the Fire Station to request directions to the Salvation Army. It was just around the corner from the bus station—good town planning.

I walked confidently past a retirement hotel, turned the corner, and, marshalling my wits, made a right into the Salvation Army.

"May I help you?" asked the woman at the counter. Her voice was impossibly high and sweet. How could a woman sound so? Did she have no problems, no worries? Would she break into the strains of Amazing Grace? Was she genuine? I decided that yes, she was. She was living in a world apart—bodily present here, but really living in some other realm.

She was in uniform—black cap with a red rosette, red and black jacket and skirt. Dressed as for a parade. Why? Surely she wasn't marching in this weather. She caught my look and brushed an invisible speck of lint from her jacket.

"I'm dressed for the flag ceremony," she said happily. "Every first Tuesday. It's a special service when we bring out the flags and explain their symbolism. Did you come for the service tonight? Better get in line now."

"I just got into town," I announced, enunciating carefully. My confidence held. The words, rehearsed all the way down the coast, rolled smoothly off my tongue. "I've been going through a rough stretch, but things will improve."

"Oh praise the Lord, sweetheart," she beamed. "You know they will."

I was taken aback. "Uh, yes. In that I'm expecting a check any day now."

"Isn't that wonderful? Now, that will help. God is so good."

"Yes. So what I need is a place to stay—for a week." There, it was out. I looked at her with, finally, pleading in my eyes.

She nodded thoughtfully. "We're full, of course. We're always full, this time of year. It's amazing how many folks get religious during rainy season." She laughed, a tinkling sound that reminded me of wind chimes. She was bewilderingly light-hearted.

"Could you refer me to another shelter?" My confidence was faltering. I'd been told this town was homeless paradise, town of shelters and soup kitchens and multiple camps. Had my informants lied? I shivered. No way could I sleep in a downpour.

"They're all full too, dear. It's a shame, isn't it?" She looked regretful. "The best I can do is offer you a spot on the porch. It's covered," she added helpfully. "That is, it's got a roof."

I nodded, weak with relief. I wouldn't have to go out into the storm. She was going to help me.

"You do have a bedroll?" she asked.

"No."

Her smile rippled over her calm face. "God is good! I knew I'd be able to help you with something. What a blessing! God sent us someone who came by this morning with a whole pile of sleeping bags to donate."

"Great," I agreed, very pleased that I wouldn't be sleeping with only my jacket for a cover.

"Dina." She stuck out her hand to me.

"Dee."

She craned her neck, looking past me. "Oh, my. You'd best get out there in line, Dee. We have service at 5:30, dinner at 6:00, and once you're through eating, you can go on out to the porch and claim a spot. That's how we work it here. It's first come, first served, and the line is really growing."

Outside, the line of people was stretching down the block. I joined it, huddling into my jacket as best I could. Soon, others were behind me.

I had planned a story for agency people, but I had nothing prepared for other streetpeople. It didn't matter. The others were incurious. No one needed or wanted to hear a tale of woe. I was one of them; they simply accepted my presence. It seemed to be another Rule of the Street: keep your own counsel.

The main topic of discussion was where to sleep that night. Some had staked claims on the Salvation Army porch; most were planning to go to the train station's roofed porch. A tall man with an orange beard was insistent that the station was the best place.

"There's no hassle there," he kept repeating. "No one comes by. The gas station is right next door, and they got all-night coffee. I'm tellin' ya, though, if you don't have cardboard yet, get some. That concrete gets hard and cold."

I was disoriented to be in a new town, but figured I'd learn the local customs soon enough. By listening, I'd pick up tips. And the ritual of lining up for food was comforting.

Down the sidewalk came an older man supporting himself with two metal canes which fastened to his wrists. He was slight in build, and a silvered black beard covered his face. He looked at the long line in dismay.

"Here," I beckoned. He looked up hopefully.

"Step in front of me," I said. "No one will mind."

He grinned at me and tipped his baseball cap. "Thanks, lady. That's real kind of ya."

A rowdy group joined the end of the line. They were several men and two pit bulls, whose leashes tangled whenever they spotted other dogs.

"It's the Daltons," said Orange Beard. "Them and their dogs. I hope they ain't coming to the station tonight."

"The Daltons?" I asked.

Orange Beard pulled a 12-ounce beer can from his pocket. He took a long gulp, then surreptitiously propped the can behind him on a low wall.

"That's what they call themselves," he said. "Like the Wild West gang. They think they're tough."

Hm. People to be wary of. He reached back for his beer. One of the Daltons, a rangy blond man who had a solid black pit bull on a leash, spotted the movement and was instantly by Orange Beard's side.

"Give over, bro," he commanded. Silently, the Beard passed the container of beer. The Dalton drained it, crushed it, and tossed it into the bushes behind him.

"Thanks," he said. "Good to know who your friends are." He winked at me. "You're new," he announced. "You with these people?"

I shook my head, intrigued by his bravado. "I just got in today from San Francisco," I said. "I'm travelling solo."

"Quickest way to get around," he agreed, and would have said more but the line began to move quickly now. Dina had opened the doors. I relaxed in the sudden warmth and began to let down my guard.

We filed in past the office into a room that had been filled with folding chairs. On each, an old green hymnal had been placed. I took a seat in the third row, wanting to get as close to the front as I could. If I understood Dina right, the first in were the first served, and the first through with dinner were the ones who'd get a spot on the porch. I felt a firm resolve: that was my goal. Stake a claim on that porch.

I wanted to stay as close to shelter as I could until I grew familiar with the town. The train station and gas station and their delights would wait until I'd gotten my bearings.

Luxuriating to be indoors on a stormy night, I looked around. Up front were a podium and several flags, some that were new to me. These must be the Army flags Dina had mentioned.

On the wall to my left hung a large, pastel print of Jesus in the Garden. His long robes were sparkling white. With the sweetest of expressions, he lifted clasped hands upward to a stream of gold which came from the heavens in a steady shaft to spotlight him. He was surrounded by foliage; I wondered if his mates were hidden in it, snoozing. I peered at the bushes, hoping to see some evidence: a foot, a hand, the top of a head. Wait a minute. Wasn't this picture showing his night of agonizing prayer before death, where beads of sweat stood out on his forehead like drops of blood? I looked more closely. He was benign and calm. Perhaps things were just getting started.

I was surrounded by much rustling, coughing, and low chatter as people found places. Curious, I looked for the Daltons. A few of them had made it in, but the dogs must be still outside. In the row behind me, there began an intense discussion of laundromats.

"You know, there's a clothes washing day here at the Sally."

The Sally? Ah, a nickname for the Salvation Army.

"Laundry? I think it's Tuesday mornings."

"Aw, forget it," exploded an exasperated voice. "Like I'm supposed to keep track. If the sun's up, it's morning, all right? When is Tuesday at 8:30? You know anyone's got a watch?"

"The laundromat on Chapala is open till 10. We could go after dinner."

"And wear what while the clothes dry?"

"Maybe Dina'd let us take something to wrap in."

"You're so full of it. She might have some clothes in the box, though."

"Whatever, man. I gotta get these washed. My socks been on me so long, they're stuck to my feet. If I wear 'em one more day, they'll need to be surgically removed."

I listened closely. My own pants smelled of myself and long journeys. They stuck to me when I walked. As for socks, my feet slid in my shoes as if I were slipping in mud when I walked. I felt chagrined to be so dirty. But at least I was not alone.

The talk of laundry intensified my awareness of the whole room's smell. As unwashed bodies packed in, it grew warm and close and nauseatingly ripe. I held the hymnal to my nose, seeking another smell. The book's odor of sanctity was, in this case, a faint tang as of spaghetti sauce and a deeper smell of mold.

A man in a suit walked to the front of the room and looked expectantly about him. He lifted his arm and the room silenced, which amazed me until I realized that unless we passed through this service obediently, we would not eat. So, of course, everyone obeyed.

"Good evening, folks," he began. "For those of you who are new, here are the rules: no drinking or smoking inside. No foul language, no weapons. Gentlemen must remove their hats indoors; ladies may keep theirs on."

Dina, who stood behind him, patted her cap and beamed at the group. There was a grumble of protest as men pulled off baseball caps.

"That's the rule," overrode the speaker. "It's in the Bible, so don't blame me. Now. Tonight we are truly privileged to have a very honored guest."

I sat up straighter, thrilled and expectant. Could he mean me? This was a welcome indeed! But no, he left the podium to usher in a very small, very old woman. She was dressed in black—long black dress and black hat with a veil. She was hunched over, almost deformed, but she walked with grace and poise as he held out his arm and escorted her to the piano.

"Miss Lucinda McCabe," he pronounced, "has been a career Army woman since birth, right?"

"Just about," she twinkled at him.

"Her folks were Army, so she was born into it, and people, she's given her life to it. She outranks me, so I'd better watch my p's and q's tonight."

There was a smattering of applause. Miss McCabe bowed to the group and then turned to the piano. She played beautifully the opening chords to a hymn.

"We are honored to have her as our pianist tonight, people. I see she's chosen the opening hymn, so please turn to number 44."

I felt a stab of jealousy as we all picked up the books and found the page. It had been exciting to think that I was going to be introduced as the honored guest, and now here was this little old lady hogging the spotlight. Of course, it had been an irrational hope. Who would honor me, after all?

I couldn't really play piano, but I could have fingered out "God Bless America" like my grandmother had taught me when I was small. I hummed it under my breath, defiantly.

She drowned me out with another opening chord. The hymn she had chosen was "Are You Washed in the Blood of the Lamb?"

"No," whispered someone from the row behind. "We're dirty. We need a box of detergent."

"And quarters for the machines," hissed another voice.

The speaker and pianist moved valiantly into the song, and straggling voices from the crowd picked up the lyrics.

I began to shake with suppressed laughter as we sang out a question about spotless garments. Anyone with a nose knew the answer to that one. We were far from spotless.

"I ask for detergent," continued the whisper behind me, "and they offer me blood."

I let out a burst of laughter. Dina, standing at attention by the flags, cast me a mournful, disappointed look and put a finger to her lips. "I expected more of you," said her gaze. I squelched my laughter but continued to shake through the song's stanzas.

My mirth dissipated with the next song, "What a Friend We Have in Jesus." The words, as I scanned them on the page, troubled me deeply.

"What a friend we have in Jesus,

All our sins and griefs to bear…"

What kind of meanness was this? The poor guy already had that cross to carry, that bitter vinegar to drink, those nails going into his hands and feet. I was supposed to add to his troubles by having him carry my grief? And who said I was a sinner? I was just down and out.

It was the second stanza I found particularly galling.

"Oh what joy we often forfeit,

Oh what needless pain we bear

All because we do not carry

Everything to Him in prayer."

No. Every atom in me revolted. That was too much. This song was claiming that what I'd gone through, I and the others in this room, was pointless and unnecessary. "Needless pain!" I burned with rage at the implication. The song was telling me that we were fools to suffer outdoors, fools to walk along the streets with our hurting minds and bodies. We were jerks to do it, because it could all be avoided if we would simply pray. How about getting beaten up by Miguel? Had that been needless?

And yet——and yet. Had I not longed for friendship with Christ? Yes, but I did not understand the blood. Or prayer. Or sin. Well—was friendship always easy? No. With that thought, my rebellion against the songs subsided. Maybe it was just…ignorance. Maybe it was just something I couldn't understand yet. I felt calmer, though still puzzled. There was much I didn't understand.

I looked again at the painting of Christ in the garden. "If it's possible," I whispered, "to let me into your world…"

Dina was next on the program. She had such a high voice and was so sincere as she explained what the colors on the flag stood for. I tried to understand why it mattered so much to her. I guessed I could. People who signed up with the Army were safe for life. I'd asked an Army bell ringer I'd seen in Marin County why she was doing it.

"Doesn't the ringing drive you nuts?"

She'd shaken her head. "It's better than the ringing in my ears from someone bashing me in the head all the time," she'd explained.

"You're still asking for spare change."

"It's for the Lord now," she'd said in a voice that brooked no further discussion.

Dina told us she'd have a special session after dinner for people who wanted to learn more about the flags and how to join the Army. She looked significantly at me. I sighed deeply. Here already came the downside of accepting help: being expected to join and conform. It happened each time I sought shelter and was why I was, normally, loathe to accept help. Of course it would please her, but there was no way I could sign up. Already, the concept of cleansing blood and life-changing prayer were more than I could understand.

Now, just for a place on the porch, I had to hear the indoctrination lecture? This was an expensive place. Just to get onto the porch required time in line, disturbing songs, a sermon, a talk, another talk...I was disgruntled.

What would an indoor bed cost?

By the time the service ended, I was edgy and fatigued. I wanted to eat and to sleep, maybe to sleep forever. Wouldn't it be something if I could sleep for the week? What a beautiful idea.

We closed with a final hymn. The woman next to me had a piercing, off-key soprano, and the man behind her hit her over the head with a hymnal, which sent Dina into a paroxym of grimaces and headshaking.

Finally, the service was over. The side doors opened. With a whoop, people rose from their hard seats and formed another line. I looked for the man with metal canes, and again motioned him to get in ahead of me. He beamed.

"Your mama raised you right, dear. Much obliged."

Dinner was tuna casserole, which I ate hungrily. I shoved it into my mouth, wanting to chew and be done with it so I could claim a spot on the porch. Hastily I cleared my plate, dropped it off at a counter that was filling with dirty plates and dishes, and looked for Dina. I found her by the door.

"Why, hello! Are you ready for the special talk on the flags?"

I steeled myself. "No, actually I'm ready to stake out a place on the porch. You mentioned a sleeping bag?"

She gave me an assessing look.

"I don't want to end up on top of somebody else," I told her. She pursed her lips, then left to return with a green nylon bag which I clutched eagerly. It was slick, it was new, it was lightweight, it was mine. Heavenly.

"Where do I go?"

She escorted me out another door to a small roofed porch. Benches were set into the wall; beneath them were large tin jars. "Ashtrays," she sighed, indicating the tins. "I'd like it if no one smoked, but then. We can't have everything. I suppose a lot of these fellows have hard lives, and I'd hate to deprive them...but smoking is only outdoors." (The Salvation Army now has a non-smoking policy.)

The porch was empty of people, to my enormous relief.

"You see? You had nothing to worry about. We don't even open the porch until people are through with dinner, and the ones who are here tonight get first pick."

"I have the very first pick," I marveled.

"You do. Put your bag down...not there!" I'd placed the bag on a bench; she pulled it off and spread it out directly underneath. "You don't want to be on a bench, dear. What if you rolled off and hit your head. Now, just leave it here for the moment. When it's time for lights out, we'll bring out some mats and I'll make sure you get one." I was filled with gratitude. She was a kind woman. Now if I could stay on her good side for a week, not alienate her like I tended to do...

The porch had three walls, which it shared with the Salvation Army rooms; where the fourth wall would have been was open to the street. A gust of wind blew in, wet with rain. Dina smiled and moved my bag further back.

"Thank you, God," she said sweetly, "for showing us not to place it too close to the edge."

I sat down on the sleeping bag. "I'm very tired," I announced firmly.

She smiled sadly. "It'll be warmer inside, you know. I'll hope to see you back in the service room. We start in 10 minutes."

I nodded to get rid of her, and then I was briefly alone. It had been a long day; I was exhausted. New people, new town—would I be able to get by here? I felt a tumble of emotions: hope for a new future, guilt for brushing off Dina, confusion over the hymns, fear that I wouldn't be able to adjust to this new town.

The porch livened up as people finished dinner and came out to smoke or to stake out their own territories. I decided my best bet was simply to stay where I was. If I left, someone might steal or move my bag. Dina was dreaming if she supposed I'd subject myself to any more sermonizing than necessary to get in here. I ignored, too, the chatter of the others. I rebuffed any attempts to draw me in.

People got the message and left me alone. I lay with my back to them, my face to the wall, hunched up into myself. I wanted a smoke, a drink, but I was afraid to move, so I stayed put.

As it became later, people came in from the street, and soon the porch was as full with bodies as it could be. I could hear dogs' voices mingled with human, so I thought some Daltons must be here, but I kept my eyes closed and my back to the people.

Talk got raucous. Men called out that they were lonely and wanted sweet young bodies near them. I just kept rigidly turned away. It had become a test of endurance now, to see how much I could block out and for how long. It took all my strength to remain aloof and rigid.

I needed a friend! Not a lewd threatener, but a friend…how did that go? "What a friend we have in Jesus…" My last thought before sleep was that the porch comments were just noise, noise, just noise washing over me. A sturdy, warm dog nosed my hand; I allowed myself to pet its head and it burrowed in near me. Dogbody warmth.

"Give strong drink to he who is perishing
And wine to he whose life is bitter.
Let him drink and forget his poverty,
And remember his trouble no more."
(Proverbs 31:6,7)

CHAPTER 12

Now that I had a spot on the porch and meals, all I had to do was wait for my SSI check—crazy money—to come. I felt a strong anticipation. Soon, my life would change. I was sure of it. Optimistically, I asked Dina to use the phone and called my daughter at her new school. Her voice was skeptical and cool.

"Hi, it's your mother. I made it to town."

"Oh, really?"

"Yes. I'll be working on getting a place. So we can visit. How do you like school?"

"It's all right. I have a lot of homework. I'll talk to you later. Call me when you're settled."

When I hung up, my hand was shaking. I felt let down. She hadn't believed me. Well, what had I expected? A warm welcome after years of not seeing her? I'd have to work at slowly winning her over. Could I do it? Sudden doubt gripped me. The task seemed daunting.

And the problem remained, how to fill the days until my check came? I didn't want to cluster, like some, in the main hall and watch television. In the tv room, the smell was bad, I could not see the tv without glasses, and I was afraid to be hit on—especially if word got out that I had money coming. I felt very canny and shrewd. I'd keep that secret.

So, I walked. Dina had found me a huge poncho which covered me from head to foot. Large, gray, hooded, I felt like a specter moving through the streets of Santa Barbara.

I passed a bar, gazed in with longing. I craved a drink. I'd decided to stay sober until I'd gotten the business with my check completed. If I got drunk, I might miss out and lose the money. It was difficult. My body needed the alcohol; I was trembling inside.

I'd arranged to stay at the Army until the check came. I'd met with the director, who explained—

"Like all shelters, we have rules. First—no drinking. If you come in drunk, you forfeit your place. Understood?"

I nodded. I'd just have to stick it out. How long had it been? Three, four days? Proudly, I told him as much.

"Well, that's good. Keep it up and you can stay here."

"I thought the Salvation Army was created for drunks, originally," I challenged.

He grinned at me. "It was. But when we let drunks in, they get very disruptive. No one can hear the service. They start screaming and try to start fights. That brings me to another rule: no weapons of any kind."

Back in school, I had studied revolutions, and understood peasant revolts—mobs brandishing pitchforks. Now, I realized, I was one of the peasants. I was disenfranchised; I was among the poor and hungry. The smell of tomato soup wafted into my reverie.

During my week at the Army, I made the acquaintance of Shelley. She was an enormously fat woman who looked like a baby. She dressed in ruffly pink, yellow and blue dresses, which she covered with shawls ("hand-crocheted by my sister," she told me.) She and her sister had had a falling out; apparently the sister was roaming the town in their remaining item of property, a '76 cruiser ("black, honey—it looks like a limo.")

Shelley had big blue eyes and a circle of blonde ringlets around her face; she looked like an overgrown Shirley Temple, and it was difficult not to call her Shirley. She and her sister, who were twins, had quarreled about the car. Shelley had been driving it one day and had left it overnight in a spot she'd forgotten and had been unable to find for a few days.

"I went into the Mexican bar, you know, for a few dances, and after a while, I just forgot where I'd left it. It got towed and Sharon had to pay to get it out of hock. 'I'm sorry, I'm so sorry,' I told her, but she hasn't spoken to me since."

"She took the car?"

"She took it, and now she's the only one who can drive it. To be fair, babe, it's her car. She used to let me drive it. She can be a real bother sometimes. She wants me to quit drinking, and she's right, babe—I have a weak heart. Still, if she'd lighten up about it. She can be very unforgiving. She's my sister, though, my very own twin, and I love her, babe."

"I know you do."

Shelley and Sharon had been living on savings. They'd been caring for an elderly uncle who died, leaving them debts instead of an inheritance. To escape creditors, they took off in the cruiser, which Sharon had had the foresight to get transferred to her name.

"If that's your last property, I can see why she was miffed you lost it," I said practically. I wasn't going to buy into her sob story.

"I can understand, babe, sure. Only forgive, that's what I say. She dropped me off here, and she ain't been back in a week. That's hard."

The same night she'd lost the car, Shelley had lost her SSI check.

"I cashed it, babe, at the liquor store. Then I started buying drinks, because people had been so good to me. When I went to check my purse, what do you think? Gone. I'd just ordered a round of drinks, too. Life is so unfair, don't you think?"

Conversation with Shelley was easy. She took the burden of it on herself. That was good because, without alcohol, I found talking difficult. Indeed, the very basics of living were difficult. I moved through a haze of need.

One night, while we were waiting for the evening service and dinner, she heaved a great sigh and pulled a crumpled piece of yellow paper from the depths of her skirt pocket.

"I might as well show you this about me," she said. "Let you know the worst."

I uncrinkled the paper and looked at it. It was a ticket issued by the Santa Barbara Police to her, Shelley Cameron. "Soliciting Alms," was the charge. I was outraged.

"You got ticketed for alms? My God, are we living in a police state? Tell me what happened."

"I'd been drinking wine with a group. Now you know, I don't really care for wine. Beer is more my drink, and vodka tonics if I can get what I want."

"So?"

"I was drinking with them. Well, it was for the company, babe. They starting saying as how they needed cigarettes, and I was out, babe. Flat out. So I went to ask for some."

"Where did you go?"

"In front of the liquor store. Do you know, babe, I asked a policeman. I thought that's what he was there for, you know, to give directions and to help out."

"Instead, he gave you a ticket."

"He did, babe. He said I'd have to appear on it too, and go to jail if it happened again. What do you think? Would I make it in jail? I don't want to go, babe."

I was determined to help Shelley with this ticket. I felt like a crusader against injustice. We'd go to the top.

"Here's what we do: write the President."

"What do we say?"

"Give me some paper."

She pulled a note pad from her voluminous pocket, and I began to compose a letter.

"Dear Mr. President,

My friend Shelley Cameron has been charged with soliciting alms. Sir, it is outrageous that a gentle lady in distress cannot ask a policeman for the help of—

Here I paused. "How much did you ask for?"

"Two dollars."

…for the help of $2 without being ticketed. Mr. President, we need help out here. It isn't easy to live on the streets. When we try to survive and, each time we turn around, get a ticket, it just isn't practical.

I ask you to cancel this ticket and get the issuing officer to apologize to Miss Cameron.

Sincerely,

Dr. Dee Williams

I signed the letter with a flourish. My title would lend weight to the petition, I was sure. I felt very important. This would get results; I would be a hero.

"There. Now ask Dina to help you mail this, Shelley. She'll have stamps. When it's time for you to go to court, tell them you're not guilty, and that you have appealed to the President. That oughtta shut them up." I was very pleased with myself for taking direct action.

"Thanks for going to the trouble, babe. Do you think it'll work?"

"Why not?"

***

Finally, the day came. My check arrived. Exultant, I tucked in into a pocket. Now, where to cash it? Ask at the Army? No—that would commit me to the place. How about the liquor store around the corner?

In my forays out from the Salvation Army, I had seen two places of interest to me. One was my immediate destination: the liquor store on the corner. The other was a bar right up the street which was named "The Office." From there, I had decided, I would set myself up in business. I could take on editing jobs, like I used to do. I would only drink enough to get rid of my nervousness, to satisfy the craving. And soon I'd be a successful businesswoman.

The liquor store was in a small stucco building. It was crammed full of merchandise. When I entered, I saw that the aisles were full of display cases holding cans of food, chips, toilet paper and the like. Refrigerated cases circled the inner walls; these were filled with beer and wine. It was reassuring just to be near the alcohol.

The counter was also filled, with large displays of magazines. Nude woman bent, pointed, leered and winked at me from the covers. Next to them were displays of newspapers from all over—The *New York Times*, the *Los Angeles Times*, a Chicago paper, as well as the local paper.

Behind the counter were the bottles of hard liquor. Guarding them was a lone man chewing on an unlit cigar. He had a surly expression which deepened when I reached into my poncho and pulled out my check. Uh oh. A hurdle.

"I don't deal with that. You'll have to see the boss." He leaned backward from his seat and stretched his neck behind the cash register.

"James! Someone's here about a check."

In a few moments, the owner appeared. He was a younger man, and dapper, with dark hair brushed back from his forehead. His bearing was elegant and courteous. I took a deep breath: he would be necessary to my survival.

I put on my brightest smile and pulled the stiff, formally stamped check from its envelope. Heavenly day! $500. I could get a motel room and stock it with booze. With a flourish, I could treat the whole bar. I could buy a new dress. I could live like a queen—and I would, I promised myself. Forgotten was my promise to my daughter.

"May I help you?" he asked.

"I hope so. I have a Social Security check I need cashed. I'm—the person the check is made out to."

James held up the check, inspected it.

"Looks all right. I'm like the bank, though—I also need some kind of I.D., some way of proving who you are. See, if I offered this service to anyone who walked in off the street, I'd be forever cashing checks. Just isn't practical."

"What kind of proof do you need?" I asked, desperation starting to grow in my gut and sound in my voice. Dismally, I pictured a whole day spent tramping around, trying and failing to cash my check.

"Well, a license or someone who lives here—someone who can vouch for you."

"A letter from the Salvation Army guy?"

"That might do it."

Frustrated, I took the check back. Then a low, gravelly voice sounded behind me.

"I'll vouch for her," he said. I turned, surprised. The speaker was the old gentleman I'd seen in the Army. His black and silver hair glistened with rain water. Small and wiry, he balanced on his two metal canes.

"I say she can be trusted. I've watched her. She's got good manners—not like some."

"I guess, Clifford, that your word is good enough."

The old man winked at me. His eyes were bright blue and snapped decisively. I was flooded with relief. I'd been rescued. And it had been so unexpected, so easy!

"That's it, then," he said firmly. "Help me first, then take care of her. That all right, miss?"

"Certainly." I stepped aside. What had prompted his kindness? All I'd done had been to give him a place in line. I was to learn that the smallest kindness was long remembered on the street.

Clifford winked again and held a finger to his lips.

"Give me a quart of vodka, James, two packs of rolling tobacco, and one 'a them buns for my breakfast."

James assembled the requested items, sacked them, and made a note on a pad.

My rescuer turned to me then.

"I run a tab here," he confided. "That way, I don't have to carry the cash. You might as well do the same. Why run the risk of getting rolled? Good luck to you, dear. Come by to visit when you're squared away. You'll find me at the Fig Tree in good weather; the train station in bad. That's where I'm headed now."

James looked around as if expecting someone else.

"You got anyone to help you carry this?"

"Nope. Couldn't find anyone I trust. Last guy I sent drank half the vodka on the way back. Need something done, do it yourself."

"That's the way."

"So just put it in one 'a them plastic sacks with handles, would you? I'll loop it around my cane. Oh. I'll take a coffee too."

"Sure you can manage?"

Clifford banged his cane impatiently.

"I'll make it. Made it here, didn't I? I'll just go slow. I'm in no big hurry, James. Got all day, don't I."

James laughed and did as he requested. Then he turned to me.

"So you know Clifford."

I didn't deny it.

"Best reference you could have on the street. He's been banking with me for years now. If he vouches for you, you're all right. Now the way I work it is this. I'll cash half your check and keep the other half here as credit."

"Credit?"

"Yes. You get $250, half the check, in cash now. The other half stays here and I'll start you a credit sheet. Whatever you buy gets deducted from your balance until the other $250 is spent."

"Fine," I said, willing to agree to any terms at all as long as I could have some cash in hand. I later learned that James' deal was standard check-cashing practice for street people. It was a way to guarantee that at least half an alcoholic's check would be spent at the liquor store.

"If you want, you can have the whole check sent here. That way, once I know it's coming, you can run a monthly tab like Clifford does.

One thing though: don't spread it around that you bank here, all right? I really can't do it for everyone."

I drew myself up, dignified. "No need for anyone to know my business."

He nodded and counted out $250 in twenties and a ten. I nearly gasped when he handed them to me, and I pushed them deep into my jeans pocket. Feeling deeply satisfied and very lucky, I walked out a wealthy woman. The day beckoned. I'd have an adventure, celebrate my good fortune.

There would be no railroad station for me, not today. I had business to take care of in the Office Bar. First, though, I hiked to the Social Security office and completed the paperwork to have my check come directly to the liquor store. With that action, I felt I had become a true Santa Barbaran.

Rain came down in sheets of water, and it was with relief that I entered the Office Bar a few blocks up the street.

The Office was venerable if shabby. It had wooden booths with cracked plastic seats, a long wooden bar with stools along one wall, and a speckled mirror behind.

Slumped rather than perched at the far end of the bar, her blonde curls drooping, sat Shelley. She brightened considerably when she saw me, and she waved me over. Above her head, the television flickered game shows.

"Babe! Come on over." She lowered her voice to a whisper. "I'm on my last beer—last of my change. I told you I got robbed, babe. Is it possible you came in here to buy me a drink?"

A generous mood seized me. I bought myself a bourbon, her a vodka tonic and, unable to resist showing off, unfolded the twenties from my pocket.

"My first check, Shelley. Would you like a loan until your next one comes in?"

"Would I ever, babe."

I gave her fifty, feeling very swank, and very much the lady of the hour. Such a good and generous person I was. Such a fine friend. Edging into my mind came the thought that I could now go and visit my daughter. Maybe look into renting a place. I banished it. Today was too rainy. She was busy with school. Besides, I'd just sat down and ordered.

Calmly, certain of my welcome here, I surveyed my surroundings. It was close to eleven and the bar was starting to fill. In the back of the room was a pool table; several young men were playing a game.

"Let's play next," I suggested, feeling bold.

She was willing, but the young men would not move. Shelley suggested that we go to another bar.

"It's a little place with a big pool table filling up the front, babe. The games really circulate there."

I was at that early, rosy part of a drunk where anything seems possible, including that I would win at pool. We bundled ourselves up and went out into the dark afternoon, which seethed with rain and thunder.

The bar Shelley had in mind was down even closer to the liquor store, which pleased me. I was already finding the few blocks of town which would become my turf. The bar was in a small, boxy building, narrow, with one large picture window.

As we walked in, I saw a figure crouched by the door, covered in plastic bags, the kind newspapers come in. He had covered himself entirely with them and sat like a guard dog at the door, his tongue lolling out of his mouth.

"Service you for a drink," he offered.

Shelley shuddered fastidiously.

"I wouldn't let you touch my hem," she said haughtily. I was annoyed with him for his obscenity, but I did think he was tame. He leered up at us as we walked in, his leathery face split with a grin, his wet tousled hair sticking out from plastic wrap. He's a gargoyle, I thought, guarding the cathedral-bar. What was it about leering gargoyles? Their ugliness kept the devil away.

Inside, it was dark, narrow, crowded. The long bar was to our left, with only a passageway in front of us. One large pool table had been set into the place's one window. It stood in the front, and from the window we could see the top of the gargoyle's head. He turned, sensing us watching him, and pressed his tongue to the glass.

"He's disgusting," said Shelley. "I've drunk with him and he always says the same thing. He's like a broken record."

She ordered drinks, squeezing us into the crowd at the bar. "This is the place where I got robbed," she whispered to me, "so hold onto your purse."

"I don't have a purse," I whispered back, feeling very wise and street smart. "Why did you want to come here?"

"I like the place," she continued. "Besides, my purse might not have been grabbed here. It might have been on my way back to the Army."

Her vagueness disturbed me. Didn't she know when or if she'd been robbed? Had she made it up? Was she conning me? Gloomily, I contemplated the draft beer she'd bought me, then downed half of it. Maybe I'd just been played for a sucker.

"Shelley," called the bartender. "You're up." She'd chalked our names on a board for the pool table. We headed for the table and played a few games. My confidence had proven to be greater than my prowess; we resorted to lifting the balls and dropping them into the pockets, laughing.

We got three games; then, it was the turn of the next people who'd chalked their names on the board. They turned out to be playing a tournament. We got ourselves fresh drinks and watched.

Shelley was cheering for one of the players, a rangy, coffee-colored man with a goatee. He was lithe, graceful, and a joy to watch.

"Go, George," she called, flirting with him. He smiled at her and kept moving—he was an angling of stick and body, always in motion. His opponent was a squat, older man whose face had been rearranged so many times it was an off-center splattering of parts. We decided to hate him, the villain, and root for George. Our villain, however, was mean and quick with the cue, and George lost.

"Cheater!" cried Shelley, slamming her vodka tonic down on the bar. I, too, felt a surge of resentment and a desire to weep that our favorite had lost.

"Settle down," said the bartender. "I'll ask you to leave if you make trouble."

My head was beginning to spin from the drinks, but I needed to take action. Shelley was snuffling into a handkerchief, desolate that George had lost. What could I do?

"He cheated," I asserted, to cheer her up. "Squish-face cheated, or George would have won."

"Cheater," she moaned, setting her face on her arms.

I couldn't bear the tears. Unsteadily, I rose from my stool and left. I went back to the liquor store and got a large coffee to go, needing to sober up for my next move. Perhaps I would challenge Squish.

When I re-entered the bar, Shelley was being comforted by George, who was laughing at her. Two people were racking up for the next match. On a sudden impulse, I drew back my arm and hurled the remains of hot coffee onto the pool table.

"If there's cheating," I declared, feeling like an avenger, "No one plays!"

Within moments, I felt myself lifted by the underarms. I'd not realized the bartender could move so fast.

"Out," he said to me, making it happen as he spoke. I was lifted up and bodily hurled outside.

I flew through the air, landing with a thud in the street.

"Mama!" called the gargoyle. "Mama! You got wings!"

I heard the impact of my landing, the thud of body on cement, but all the drinks had numbed me and I didn't feel anything but shaken. I was limp. "I'll just lie here awhile," I thought cloudily, "and pretend to be a bundle of old clothes."

But I was not allowed to rest. Strong arms were lifting me up, pinning my arms back, fastening handcuffs onto my wrists.

"Let's go," said a blur to my left.

"I didn't do anything," I protested weakly.

"You got thrown out of that bar," came the voice. "We were coming around the corner and saw the whole thing. You're drunk and disorderly. Let's go." My heart sank.

"I love you, mama!" called the gargoyle in farewell. "Do it again!"

I slithered wetly into the backseat of the police car. A mass of pink peered mournfully in at me and waved—Shelley. I slumped down and passed out to the comforting sound of rain on the car roof.

"I was in prison, and you came to me…Truly I say to you, to the extent that you did it to one of these brothers of Mine, even the least of them, you did it to me."
(Matthew 25: 36, 40)

CHAPTER 13

I had a sense of travelling far, far away. The Santa Barbara County Jail is located at the farthest edge of town, as jails often are. I thought this location was to make it more difficult for people to get back into town once they were released.

I remained limp and pliant. A dim memory arose: how outraged and panicked I'd been the first time I'd been taken to jail. This day, I just accepted my fate. I was a drunk: drunks went to jail. Simple as that. During booking, a jailer showed me my photograph. I stared in disbelief. It was a picture of a woman with wild hair, unfocused eyes, a gaping mouth. Hideous image. Why did I let myself get that way?

After being booked, I was escorted to a large cell, a holding tank for drunks. There was a stack of pale green mattresses on the floor. I took one, dragged it onto the concrete, melted into it, and passed out.

I was awakened by the annoying sound of someone talking and crying. Blearily, I rose on one elbow and looked around me. The cell was eight by eight feet, big enough to hold about ten people. There were four bodies in it now. One, a Hispanic woman whose long black hair flowed down to her waist, was talking on the telephone. She irritated me; she was disturbing my sleep. From what I could understand, she was trying unsuccessfully to talk someone into bailing her out. I wished she'd give up and be quiet. Who cared that she was in jail? It was no big deal.

The pay telephone was on the wall next to the locked, barred door. There was a low bench against the back wall, and the rest of the cell was blank, just stucco walls and concrete floor. On the wall by the telephone, posters advertising bail bond places were the only spot of brightness. They were a garish yellow. On the wall opposite me was a toilet, stark white. I hoped no one had to go.

The talker hung up, disconsolate, and came to sit fastidiously on a mat which she'd pulled to the wall opposite me, in the corner away from the toilet. She ignored me, hunching up with her arms around her knees and weeping quietly. I felt no compassion. She'd get over it. I've become hardened, I realized. When did it happen?

Next to me lay a woman on her stomach, snoring. Her shoes were half off, her clothing rumpled. On the bench, a skinny older woman in a long, tattered sweater coat sat muttering to herself. When I made out the words, I could tell she was chanting "Forty four bottles of beer on the Wall" and counting down. I resigned myself to it. Sleep was over. Welcome to the zoo.

"Four bottles of beer on the wall," she intoned finally. "Four bottles left, and one of 'em had to land on my head."

The Hispanic lady suddenly turned on her mat. "Shut up about it!" she pleaded. "Shut la boca!"

The older woman snorted. "I ain't done counting them bottles, chickie. Respect your elders."

The sleeper snorted. I sighed and sank back on my mattress. Here I was, in jail again. Some celebration on my first day with money. I'd looked forward to it so much. Was it bad for me to have money? Should I have stayed poor? Was it because I got drunk? Would it happen all the time? Why hadn't I tried to see my daughter instead? These thoughts bothered me, made me feel guilty. I pushed them away.

I dozed fitfully through the rest of the night. Our barred door showed only a wall and the edge of a corridor through which no one passed until early morning, when a surly contingent of trustees came rattling through with a cart of breakfast trays. They passed the trays through a small opening.

"Court bus comes in an hour," announced the guard who accompanied them. "We'll be by to chain you; you can go in street clothes."

True to her word, she returned with a huge length of chain. We sat poised on the edge of the bench, all in a row, while she cuffed our hands together and linked us together. I'd never been chained up before. It shook me up. I felt branded, and I was nervous. What if I stumbled and brought everyone down with me?

"Four little monkeys all in a row," cackled the old lady. "All dressed up and no place to go."

"You're going someplace, Geraldine," commented the guard.

"You're going to court, probably be out tonight. How's Harry?"

"Fool took my check again," the lady complained. "Hit me with a beer bottle when I told him off. Then your pal Officer Sam picked me up, and by the time I get outta here, the check'll be all spent. Harry drinks fast, and he invited the whole crowd."

"Officer Sam was trying to protect you, Geraldine. We don't want to find you dead out there."

Geraldine softened at that, and smiled. Most of her teeth were missing; the ones that remained were stained with tobacco.

"I know, sweetie. You mean well, that's the truth."

I knew there was nothing in my own pockets, but I had a vague memory of emptying them when I got booked. Oh! Half my check was still safe at the liquor store. I'd have that credit when I got out. Immensely cheered and pleased with the way I'd done business, I led the chain into the hall and then out to a waiting bus.

It was a large black and white jail bus, already filled with male and female prisoners in jail uniform. It surprised me that the men and women were being transported together. I asked Geraldine about it.

"The guys are housed next door to us," she explained. "We only see 'em when we all ride together to court."

The inmates were uninterested in us, the drunk tankees. They were trying to catch one another's attention, to pass notes back and forth, to get news of lovers and friends on the other side. They were making the most of this brief contact.

Awake for the ride into town, I tried to memorize the route I'd need to walk home once I was released from jail. The liquor store and the Office Bar were now going to be home. I wondered if Shelley had already spent her $50 and thought it very likely she had.

The jail bus barreled along, wipers going fast. We were two to a bus seat, with our chain looped behind us. The old lady was my partner.

"New to town?" she asked me.

"Been here over a week."

"I'd like to get through one payday without landing in jail. I used to do it just fine, but these days I'm not as quick. My old man is quicker— he gets that check off me every month." She laughed in appreciation of his skill.

She looked to be in her seventies, with a shock of straggly yellow-white hair which spilled out over her face and down to her shoulders. On her head I could see dried blood, the scabbed gash where the beer bottle had landed. Her sangfroid impressed me. Would I get to be as cynical as she?

The court building, which we circled before entering from the back, was beautiful, built in California mission style. Bright flowers graced the entrance, gleaming in the mist. When we parked, the Hispanic woman began to moan again. Her complaint was that people might see us when we marched out in chains. I was glad this wasn't my hometown. People who saw me wouldn't know me. There was no one to care, no one to be shocked. I had no need to be embarrassed.

Inside, the court was segregated. One section of the room was filled with citizens who were showing up for tickets received. The other was filled with people from jail. The two sections didn't have much to do with each other. Guards uncuffed us, and a man and woman gave us a lecture in Spanish and English. It was about pleas, lawyers, fines. We waited to be called.

The judge was a small man with spectacles; he blinked at us neutrally. When he called my name and charged me with drunk and disorderly, I pleaded "no contest," feeling very savvy. From what I'd understood of the preliminary spiel, this plea meant that I could not be sued later for damages. I didn't want to get charged for a pool table.

The bar, however, had not pressed any charges. The bartender must have thought he'd solved the problem by tossing me out the door. I was given a week for drunk and disorderly and placed on probation; any further disturbance would give me thirty days in jail. I felt let down; I'd hoped to get right out and back to the liquor store. Now I'd have to endure another week without any alcohol in me. Geraldine had a warrant—she'd signed a probation paper last time, she explained, and now she got ninety days in jail. She was philosophical about it. "Harry ain't here to see me, but then I didn't expect him. Just as well. My check's gone, and this way I'll be out of the rain for the duration.

It'll be hell to de-tox, but I done it before. Maybe they'll give me some librium."

She and I rode back out to jail in a small paddy wagon. The Hispanic woman who'd tried to bail out had also broken probation and was chained immediately to the uniformed jail women. The fourth member of the drunk tank stayed behind in court; I never knew what happened to her.

Back in jail, the admitting officer looked me over. "I don't think you're ready for General Population," she remarked. "I'll house you in the row of solitary cells." Why? Was I being punished? Was there something strange about me? Maybe it was because I had the shakes again.

She escorted me there. General Population was housed in the basement. Solitary was upstairs and was for people with medical problems and for those who'd been pulled for behavior problems. Which was I? I guessed the "drunk and disorderly" charge was understood by the jailers to be a warning—I might make trouble. I wondered if they viewed me as dangerous. Perversely, this idea pleased me. It meant I was not someone to be taken lightly.

I now had my own room: good. It was a single cell, with a bunk bed against one wall and a small metal writing desk next to it. Against one wall was a small toilet and sink; these faced the floor-to-ceiling bars of the cell and the corridor. There were five such cells in a row. I could not see the other inmates. Well, there'd be time to make their acquaintance.

I had a little stack of clean clothes: two pair of drawstring pants, a short sleeve sweatshirt and a longer one, two pair of socks, and a pair of tennis shoes. Clean clothes! What luxury. Especially the socks. I had a stack of bedding and two small towels. Outside, the storms of the rainy season raged, but I was housed. It was jail, true, but I felt strangely comforted. I'd be safe and warm in here.

I climbed onto the top bunk, clumsily made the bed, and crawled in. Hours later I awoke, drenched in sweat. Why was I so wet? I learned later to call these the night sweats; they were one result of de-toxing from alcohol.

I didn't know where I was when I first woke up. Then a single guard came through with a flashlight to check on the inmates. Where would she be thinking we'd escaped to?

I sat up in bed. "I'm up!" I told her cheerfully, hoping she might be game for a chat, but she just nodded at me and continued on her rounds. Unfriendly, I muttered to myself. I'd wanted some company. I tried to sleep again.

When I next awoke, it was to a clattering of the meal trays. Trustees and a guard rolled through the solitary cells, depositing trays of food. I took mine to my desk, luxuriating in having one. Breakfast was surprisingly good. As I ate my scrambled eggs and toast, sipped my coffee, spooned up my baked apples, I contemplated my new surroundings.

Perhaps I'd write a letter from my new desk. Hadn't famous works been written from jail? There was *De Profundis*, and there were St. Paul's letters. There was Martin Luther King. Well, I wasn't a philosopher like those guys. And I wasn't being persecuted. And I wasn't famous. But if I could write, write anything, I could stay sane here and avoid deathly boredom.

When the guard came through again, this time with cleaning supplies for our cells, I asked hopefully for paper, pen, and something to read.

"Tablets are sold in Commissary," she said. My heart sank. That posed a problem. I'd run out of cash. True, half my check was safe at the liquor store, but I'd come in this time with nothing on me. How had the money gone so fast? Had I bet on the pool games? Bought other people drinks? I couldn't remember; that first payday was mostly a blur that had landed me here.

***

Notes from Jail

I've got four pieces of paper here, so I have to write very small. One of the neighbors, third cell from the television, said she'd give me some paper if I'd roll up some tobacco she has.

Good deal: I can roll; she can't. She threw in a pencil if I'd give her my sugar from the coffee for my next three meals. So, I can survive in here. I know how to barter. Didn't used to, but now I do. This paper is gold to me.

Geraldine was right—detox is hell. I'm shaky. I woke up all wet from night sweats again. I hear things that aren't there. The best thing to do is keep quiet so nobody knows I'm going crazy. No! I'm not crazy. I refuse to be. I'll pretend I didn't hear the voices. If I write this, it'll keep my mind off the detox. That'll work. It has to work.

Sunday—I've met the neighbors. We get out for a shower once a day, one at a time. I had time for a quick shower and a tour of the row. Next to me is a very large woman—at first I thought she was Shelley, but she's somebody else. She's very different from Shelley—not sociable at all. She just lies on her bunk and spins fantasies. She'll lie there on her back for hours, kicking her legs and muttering that she wants a stun gun. She says she saw one advertised in a gun manual and it is the only thing that will make her safe with her boyfriend. They get into violent arguments when drunk, which is why she's here.

Question: Why, in that case, is *she* here? Why is *he* not here? There is no justice. People say "we were fighting" when they mean, "I got beat up." I hear violent stories in here. They really bother me, keep me awake obsessing over them. I'm starting to hallucinate bruises. When I look at someone, a guard or anyone, I see her face as if it were all bruised up. I hate seeing things. I can't tell anyone I do it.

Next to Stun Gun is a tall woman with a wild mass of hair, dark brown. She's okay sometimes—at others she just makes no pretense of being all right. She walks on her tiptoes and paces the cell, going three steps in one direction and then going three steps back. She complains that she's not making any progress. I think she hopes the guard will transfer her to a mental hospital where, she says, there's more room. Imagine that, actually wanting to go there to get shot full of drugs. Ugh, awful. No thanks.

The reason she's here also has to do with a boyfriend, as far as I can make out. They were staying in a residential hotel downtown. She got mad at him and locked him out. He broke in—she got a picture off the wall and bashed him over the head with it. Management called the police.

I asked her what the picture was. She said it was a landscape with poppies. She's on some kind of medication, and when they take her off to see the doctor, she returns much calmer and sleeps for the rest of the day. I hope they don't try to medicate me. They'd better not. I'll fight them off. I hope they're not slipping something into the food. Maybe they are—drugs to keep me quiet. What can I do? Not eat?

How about microphones? Are there hidden microphones? I won't say anything about myself in here, in case this paper gets confiscated. I'll just write it all down, my observations.

The third cell down is occupied by Lila, who traded me for the paper. I'd say she's the savviest of the bunch. She's in here for dealing drugs, and she started out in general population. She got placed in solitary because she brought down a tray of food on a rival's head.

I asked her what they'd had for dinner that night. Stew, she said, and the enemy got carrots and celery all down her sweatshirt, and a big glob of gravy on her nose.

***

Monday

Today a chaplain got locked in with us by mistake. It was pretty funny, although it's not nice to laugh. The chaplain is a woman named Bonnie. She looks like an athletic grandmother. She has gray-brown hair and dresses casually in pants and a sweater. She came in to talk with the Pacer. They discussed the state of the Pacer's soul for a while, and her needs. Then the big door which leads to the outer corridor slammed shut. It seems a guard, seeing it open, just closed it without checking who might be inside.

Bonnie turned pale. She tried the door, but when it locks that sucker is locked. She began to pace herself—she was praying like mad. She had a nice moment though; I have to give her credit. She turned to us and said, "Now I know how you feel. When I heard that door slam locked, I panicked. It sounded so final."

Well, in a way she might know how we feel. In a way, I'd say. All day long, we hear doors and gates slamming shut. We know each one is locking itself as it closes. We live inside a series of locks. She must have known she'd get out, and she did. She found the red emergency phone and called the guard.

She seems like an okay person. I might request to see her myself. She has a group that meets on Thursdays. Why not? It would be a way to get out of the cell for a while.

I asked her if she could get me something to read. The days are really long in here. She said she'd see what she could do. She gave me a Bible.

***

Tuesday

Chaplain Bonnie came back, just to see me! She told me an amazing thing. "You street people are very close to Jesus, because you live like he did. He didn't have a home; he lived outdoors wherever he could camp. Listen—" she read from the Bible—"'The foxes have holes, and the birds of the air have nests, but the Son of Man has nowhere to lay His head.'" She marked it in my Bible—Matthew 8:20.

Living close to Jesus! That makes me feel so special. No wonder I've so often thought of Him. Is it possible? Is it true? I think it must be. Now I know that Jesus understands me. That's what I felt at New Life. I was right. It's good to be right.

Wednesday

Got a sad letter from my daughter today. Don't know how she found out I'm in jail. Maybe through a school counsellor. "Dear Mom—when I was little, you were my hero. Now, I cry to think of all the times we have missed. I love you. I hope you get out soon."

I cried, too, when I read it. It broke my heart. She's suffering because of me. How could I allow that? What happened to my dream of making a home for us? Will I really ever do it, or will I just gravitate back to street life once I get out? Can I really change?

I really don't see the point of going to the Alcoholics Anonymous meetings they have here—told the guard no thanks, it doesn't apply to me. Alcohol is all I have to keep me going out there. Why would I quit? Anyway, I use it to maintain. That's all.

Then the guard pointed out that it would get me out of here for an hour. I guess they meet in the downstairs dining hall. I'll think about it. I guess I could go and fool them—pretend to be an alcoholic.

***

I'm running out of paper. Need to bargain for more.

Thursday

Still waking up wet with sweat. Makes me cold. Shakes are getting better. When I get morning coffee, I pretend there's bourbon in it. That's what I'll get when I'm released—bourbon, and lots of beer to chase it. Ah. Bliss.

Went to the A.A. meeting. Why not? Nothing else to do. The guard came up and got me. She took me downstairs to a room with metal tables—that's where General Population eats. There were some chairs set in the back, in a circle, and these two women in street clothes were sitting with a huddle of inmates around them.

The two in street clothes did all the talking. None of us wanted to reveal anything because who knows who might be listening? The two talked a lot about a higher power. Do they mean God? Do they mean Jesus? Hard to tell. It's confusing.

I don't really know why the two in street clothes are willing to give up a perfectly good night to come out here. They must like to talk about themselves because that's what they did.

At the end they do this weird thing: stand in a circle, hold hands, say a prayer, and then shake hands really hard, saying "Keep coming back." I started laughing to think they meant, "Keep coming back to jail."

I'm leaving tomorrow.

I'm ready to go. I don't know what to do with my Notes from Jail. Do I mail them? Nobody to mail them to. I'll take them with me.

I'll see how it goes.

"When He ascended on high,
He led captive a host of captives"
(Ephesians 4:8)

CHAPTER 14

SPRING, 1986

The morning of my release, a guard came for me right after breakfast. I was very pleased to see her, excited to be getting out. It had only been a week; it had felt much longer. I was weary of jail. She led me to the shower room and handed me my clothes.

"The trustees have washed them for you," she said with a smile. "We give good service here, don't you think? Try to stay sober, now. Try to stay out of here a while." I was happy about the clothes and touched by her pep talk. I would try—not to get caught.

"She'll be back," snorted a second guard who brought in another woman to be released. "She won't be able to stay away from us. Her kind always returns. You watch."

How galling. I ignored her, wouldn't look at her. She'd angered me and hurt my feelings, but I wouldn't let that show. She's trying to trick me into a display of anger so she can keep me here longer, I thought, warning myself. Let it go. What does she know, anyway? Stupid woman. Stupid mean woman. What did she mean, "her kind?" I felt hot tears well up; I turned my back to hide them and not show weakness.

When the first guard pushed my old shoes across the counter, I furtively slipped them into the trash. If I could, I'd walk out of here with the jail-issue tennis shoes, which were cleaner and much more comfortable. My pulse raced. Could I get away with it?

My companion was a short, bright-eyed woman who regarded me with interest. "Better to dump 'em," she agreed, once we were momentarily alone. "They're not your style." I changed swiftly, lacing up the tennis shoes.

We were led down a corridor and out to an enormous door, which clanked open and then shut behind us. We were out. I quivered with joy and anticipation. The early morning sun glinted down on us. We stood stunned for a moment on the pavement, not quite believing in our new freedom.

Below us, a large gate buzzed and swung open.

"Free at last!" cried my companion then, and I grinned at her with complicity. Yes! Freedom. Quickening our pace, we headed out, down the hill. The road was lined with eucalyptus trees; birds chattered noisily as we went. I was enthralled by the scenery, the fresh air. Every detail was in sharp focus; each leaf stood out. The sharp tang of eucalyptus was exhilarating. I inhaled deeply, marveling at how new the world seemed after release. Everything seemed possible at that moment.

My companion began to hum, breaking off to introduce herself.

"Name's Susan," she said.

"Dee."

"Charmed, I'm sure. Anyone picking you up?"

"No one."

"Let's walk into town, then. It's only a few miles. I've done it before—doesn't take long with company."

I was pleased and relieved to be with someone who knew the way. The hill wound down to a dirt road which we traipsed along, passing a grove, a trailer park, a small store.

"Too bad we haven't got any change," Susan said wistfully. "A drink would make the walk go easy. You aren't holding?"

I shook my head regretfully. I, too, longed for a drink. I could make the walk only with the knowledge that, at the end of it, was the liquor store on lower State Street. I focused intently on that thought. It was my beacon.

"Too bad. Maybe we can hustle some change on the way down."

We continued on, past a reform school for boys that was set back in rolling green hills.

"They're starting young," she commented. "How 'bout you? Been in long?"

"I was just in for a week."

"Me, I was just here for the weekend. Got picked up Friday night. The cop who took me in was real nice, didn't put the cuffs on too tight. It must've been a wild night; I don't remember it too well. Here—" she handed me a small photograph, "They let me keep my intake photo. What do you think?"

It was a small black and white photograph, the sort we used to take as teenagers at the beach. We'd go into the photo machines, after smearing on lots of pale lipstick so as to look sophisticated and accentuate our tans.

Susan's photo showed a woman in disarray. Her hair was tangled and matted, her eyes bleary, her mouth drooling. I was repulsed; it reminded me of my own intake photo. Ugly. Almost subhuman. How could we let ourselves get that way? Too repulsive. Today I'd just have one drink or two. Just enough to steady me, to maintain. I'd remain a lady. Building up these promises to myself, I handed the photo back without comment.

She laughed. "I could enter it in the beauty contest," she said. "Think I'll win?"

I remained tactfully silent on the subject.

"Where you headed?" she asked me.

"Downtown. I have some business to take care of," I said with self-importance.

"Me, I'm going back to camp. We've got a place out by the beach—well hidden. My old man called the jail and left a message for me to come on home, all is forgiven."

"What's forgiven?" I asked curiously.

"I don't know. We must have been fighting."

I wondered at her story. How likely was it that her old man, presumably a street person, had telephoned in with a message for her? Not very. I decided not to question her, though. Perhaps the fantasy that he was so thoughtful was necessary to her.

"Our camp is down by Ledbetter Beach," she offered. "We've got room. You need a place?"

I shrugged, unwilling to take the chance. She was being generous and I was grateful for that. But the last thing I needed was to camp out with a wrangling, fighting couple. I'd get caught up in the violence in no time. "I stay here and there," I said evasively, playing mystery woman.

"Come on and check it out with us if you want."

"Maybe sometime." I was noncommittal, not wanting to alienate her.

We continued on down the hill. Dawn was turning to day, a clear day. I rejoiced at the absence of rain. We were getting closer to town. Realtors' offices and motels dotted the sides of the highway. I noted the motels with longing. Maybe next check…

"We're dreaming of food stamp day again," Susan confided. "That's why he wants me back. I get the full issue. We'll probably do a barbecue at Ledbetter Beach. We always do; it's a tradition."

"I'll check it out." A party? Might be fun. I giggled to imagine us as two ladies planning our social calendar.

We passed a residential section. Large homes fronted the highway, their lawns and gates protecting them from the street. An orange tree grew along the side of the road, offering fruit. Susan reached up and picked two. We peeled and ate them as we continued on.

"At least it's wet," she said, slurping up the juice. "I get dehydrated after a night in jail. You?"

"Me, I get the sweats."

"Oh yeah, that's the worst. They don't know what they're doin', pulling us away from our people and our wine. We get all discombobulated in there. They think, you know, that they're doing us a favor, pulling us off the streets."

She laughed at the thought. "Well, I ended up with two nights at the Gray Bar Motel this time. The cops who took me in said they were protecting me. One guy said when me and my old man get into it, it looks like I'm going to be killed. How are they so sure he's not the one who'll end up dead?"

I was intrigued. Would she really murder in a drunken rage, or was this just bravado? Was I walking with a potential killer? "Ever considered it?"

"Plenty of times. But he's a sweetheart, really. I just gotta look real hard for his good points."

As we got closer to town, the houses becoming larger motels and storefronts, her demeanor changed. She had been relaxed on our long walk, her arms swinging at her sides, her step springy. Now she tensed as if coiled from within. Her eyes darted back and forth. She was readying herself for purposeful activity.

"Stop," she said as we neared a small grocery which advertised coffee and doughnuts. "Here's a good place." Cars were pulling in and out as people on their way to work went in for refreshment. She darted up to a man who was emerging from the store, balancing a coffee cup and a paper as he reached for his car keys.

"Sir!" she called out boldly. "Spare a dollar? Me and my friend are hungry."

He sighed, set his coffee and paper on the roof of his car, reached into his pocket. "You people are everywhere," he said, pulling out a dollar. "Here you are. See you spend it on food, now." I was impressed by his concern and bemused by his naivete. Surely he knew she was after a bottle.

"Bless you," she smirked at him, wheeling then to me. "Not bad for the first score."

Half my mind was still in jail; the other half was racing ahead to the liquor store where I had some money banked. Thus distracted, I held back as she went into a flurry of activity, asking everyone we passed for change. She paused to chide me.

"What's wrong with your voice? You ain't asking a soul—you're leaving me to do all the work here."

"I've got something stashed at the liquor store downtown," I said defensively.

"Smart."

I felt it would be only right to invite her since she'd been gracious with me.

"If you'd like to come with me…"

She hesitated, clearly tempted. Then, "Another time," she said grandly. "I'd love to have a drink with you, but I have to get back to the old man. I like to impress him, see. I'm trying to get enough for a pint here. We've got a few weeks yet to go before the stamps come in."

As we got closer to downtown, we parted ways.

I found it odd that she, in her morning's search for alcohol, had turned down my offer of a free drink. Then it occurred to me that she had not believed me in my talk of a bank at the liquor store, any more than I had believed her in her talk of her old man's telephone call to jail. It was comical. I laughed aloud to imagine that we had accompanied each other on the long walk from jail to town, neither believing the other but humoring each other to make for a pleasant time. Anything for peaceful companionship.

But when it came to survival, she did not trust me and I did not trust her. Why should she risk wasting time over a possible lie, my liquor store story, when she could ask for very real change and return the sooner to her enemy-lover? Why should I risk an uncertain welcome at her camp, when I knew there was a sure thing awaiting me at the liquor store?

It was the first time in my sojourn on the street that I had not gone along with another's proposal. Or so it seemed. I had been primarily a follower up till now, stumbling into adventures of someone else's making. Today, I had a plan of my own. The discovery thrilled me. It was highly gratifying. I was learning how to make it on the street, all by myself. I was a survivor.

My plan had been forming as we made our walk. First I needed a place to stay, needed to find an unoccupied car or doorway or encampment of my own. Going back to the Salvation Army was out of the question; there was a no drinking law. With deep certainty, I knew I'd break it today. Maybe I could use the Army later to get back with my daughter, but I'd postpone that a while. "Sometimes I cry to think of the times we've missed…" yes. Stab of guilt. She needed me. Needed a mother. I'd do something about that, soon. Very soon, I vowed. Today I was in no shape…

What I needed today was not someone official, like the Army, to interfere with my life, but a connection with people on the street. I needed a group of people who knew how to make it out here. Who could give me pointers. I'd attract them with a bag of groceries.

I found the liquor store without difficulty. It was on the corner of the main street in town, way down by the beach. Approaching it, I had watched as trendy jewelry and clothing stores were replaced by pawn and thrift shops. Night clubs gave way to sleazy bars whose signs had been maimed. " eer on Tap," announced one.

"Countrymen, give me your 'eers!" I shouted, glad to be free. "An eye for an eye, an eer for an eer! If you have eers to hear, listen up!" I was jubilant, feeling very clever and lighthearted.

"That's right, sister," encouraged a man who was lounging in front of the thrift store. "You tell 'em. 'ere, 'ere."

In good spirits, I entered the liquor store. The owner was working the counter this morning, a good omen.

"Good morning," I crowed. "I'm back. Do I still have my credit?"

"Yes, it's safe here for you. Welcome back. Been to jail, have you?"

I was taken aback. "How did you know?"

"When people disappear, it's jail or the hospital. Except, of course, for those who don't come back at all."

He was being too grim for me this morning. I didn't need to get depressed, to dwell on death. I nodded curtly and began to roam the aisles, choosing the items carefully. I wanted the shopping bag to be magnetic, drawing people to me.

I selected a case of beer, two cartons of cigarettes, two gallon jugs of wine, some bean dip, several packets of chips, some rolling tobacco, and a quart of vodka. At the last I added a pad of paper, so as not to be without. Today, I'd need to make no trades. It felt wonderful to be so purposeful and self-assured.

James matter-of-factly rang it all up, deducting the total from a slip of paper which represented my account.

The bag was heavy. I staggered with it out of the store and made my way farther south. My destination was a grassy knoll by the water where, I'd learned, it was legal to drink.

I shifted the bag to my hip, carrying it as I would a small child. It was precious cargo. When I'd gone half a block, I was hailed by someone across the street.

I recognized him as one of the people who'd spent the night on the Salvation Army porch. He loped across the street, grinning at me, holding out his arms to take my bag.

"That looks heavy. Let me help you," he offered eagerly.

He was very brown from the sun. I suspected he'd been outdoors so long that his color was permanent. He had long brown hair, which flowed to his shoulders, and a beard and mustache, which flowed over his face. His eyes were brown and lively. He looked like the picture postcards of Jesus. Instantly, I trusted him.

What I noticed most about him was his nose, which had been broken several times so that now it lay off to one side of his face. That part of him was not Christ-like. It was pure street.

"I'd love some help," I replied calmly, feeling a tremor of pleasure at the quick success of my plan. "I'm headed for the knoll. I'm just out of jail, and I'm celebrating. Care to join me?"

"You bet." We settled on the knoll. I spread out the goods: the beer to one side, the wine to another, the vodka in the place of honor. I set the chips and dip in the center and offered him the tobacco. Once I'd assembled the feast, others began to appear. I was delighted and gratified. It was just as I'd pictured it. No one could resist me. I was the center of attention, commanding respect.

Soon there was a group of us perched on the grass, enjoying the morning's picnic. From our position we surveyed the ocean behind us, the boardwalk in front. Tourists strolled or rode in bright bicycle carts which they pedaled industriously.

I felt very much the grande dame of the streets that day. I was in the position of honor in the circle. Yesterday they didn't know me, I thought with inner glee. Today, they all kow-tow. Superb. Nothing could get me down. It was a blue and cloudless day. The Pacific ocean sparkled nearby; the grassy knoll was soft and comfortable.

I noticed that Peter, the man who'd helped me carry the bag, had fallen silent. He'd drawn himself off to one side and sat, knees hunched up, gazing at me.

"What it is?" I asked, made uncomfortable by his steady gaze.

He was silent a few moments more. Then, "I'd like to cuddle with you tonight," he said shyly. "I'd like you to come back to camp with me."

Coolly, I considered my options. Here was an offer; could I afford to turn it down? My stash of cash at the liquor store would not translate into a place to sleep. At this rate, it would last only a few more days. Then I'd need to survive the rest of the month. I needed a place for tonight. And his offer was flattering. I looked at the brightness of his eyes and the bent nose, considering.

"All right," I said. I felt the words resound deep within me, as if I were sealing my fate.

A woman had joined our group. She had long brown hair that matched Peter's, although it was darker than his. She was long and lean and wore bubble-shaped dark glasses. I saw that she, too, was peering at me.

"Did you want something?" I asked her, annoyed.

She crinkled up her face. "What's going on with you and Peter?" she asked suspiciously.

"I'm joining his camp," I announced, making it a challenge. Did she have a claim on him? We'd see about that.

She removed her dark glasses and pointed to her right eye. Blood vessels in it had burst and leaked. It was completely red where it should have been white. I was shocked and repulsed.

"Peter did this to me," she said calmly. "He got drunk and began jabbing his fingers in the air. Then, he turned to me and got me right in the eye."

Was this true? I shot a questioning glance at Peter, who gazed at me soulfully.

"She's my ex-old lady," he explained. "She's going with Manuel now. She's—you might say she's prejudiced against me."

Manuel, a giant with a red bandanna wrapped around his head, nodded thoughtfully at Peter's assessment of the situation.

"She'll get over it," he commented, munching on a chip.

I decided to leave the woman, whose name was Caroline, alone for the time being. I wished she hadn't spoken. The evidence of her eye disturbed me deeply. Was she being spiteful? Did she want Peter back for herself? Or was she warning me? Peter'd offered me a place in a camp. That's what I'd wanted. He was being very peaceful now, very respectful. Just because it happened to her—*if* it had happened the way she said—didn't mean it would happen to me. I decided to risk it, need and desire overriding caution.

We went several times back to the store to replenish the supplies. By midafternoon, I was passed out on the wet grass. When I came to with a jerk, it was early evening. I was lying in a fetal position on the grass. Where was everyone? Had I been abandoned? No, Peter lay trustingly a foot away from me. The others had left.

We were surrounded by the debris of the picnic—empty bottles and cans, cartons of cigarettes ripped open and emptied. I felt desolate to view the mess and, irrationally, robbed.

He stretched. "Good party," he said. "Come on. I'll show you our camp." I remembered. I'd committed myself. Feeling very daring, I went with him.

We walked along side streets until we came to a ravine that was, I could see in the dusk, overgrown with vines of morning glories. Pretty. We walked through the gully to the end. He pulled aside a vine; within it was a sleeping bag and a cardboard box that had been upended to serve as a table.

"This is it," he said. "This is camp."

I felt a surge of relief and pleasure, mixed with self-satisfaction. I'd been successful. My plan had worked. I'd found a street home.

"The poor is hated even by his neighbor,
but those who love the rich are many."
(Proverbs 14:20)

Chapter 15

I woke up with the dawn, and so did the others. Others? There must be. I could hear them moving about and groaning. Disoriented, I blinked sticky eyes and looked around for a place to relieve myself.

"Over there, in the bushes past camp," instructed Peter.

I felt very awkward and withdrawn. We'd been intimate. Yet I didn't know Peter at all. What kind of person was he, really? What had I done on a drunken impulse? I had been so sure of myself last night. Now I felt exposed, intensely embarrassed and ill at ease. I didn't know what to say to him. And what about these others? Would they welcome me or shun me?

When I returned from the bushes, Peter was rolling a cigarette. Behind him was another couple. "Felipe and Maria, meet Dee."

They were a young Hispanic couple. In the morning light, I could see they had a crucifix and a picture of the Virgin on their cardboard table. These signs of faith were reassuring. I began to relax a little.

There was a shout, and two more people joined us, Caroline and her giant with the kerchief. I was startled to see them. Had I joined a whole group? So swiftly? This is what you wanted, I reminded myself. We sat talking, hunched under the morning glories. Peter showed me that, uphill and behind an apartment complex, was a faucet to splash off.

Caroline was cordial this morning. It was as if she'd forgotten the tension of the day before, had accepted me. I was relieved and decided to go along with her lead. She suggested we all go to the Wings of Death for breakfast.

"Wings of Death?" I asked incredulously.

"Wings of Love is its name; we call it Wings of Death. They serve vegetarian."

"Still, it's hot food."

"Yeah, but they don't open till 10. How 'bout the Rescue Mission?"

"Too far, and it's got that sermon."

"How 'bout the Starvation Army?"

Peter shot that one down too. "All they got's cereal in the morning, and really weak coffee."

The group didn't seem likely to move any time soon, and I felt stalled out. Impatient. We couldn't sit here all day. Boldly, I took the initiative. I spoke up to get us going.

"Let's go see if I have any more credit at the liquor store."

Peter laughed aloud. "I got a smart lady," he beamed. The praise warmed my heart. He was proud of me, he approved. But doubts arose too: how it would be between us when my money ran out? Would I still be a desirable prize? I wondered.

We all trooped through the early morning streets to the liquor store, which opened at 6. We got a bottle of cheap whiskey, several cases of beer, some white bread and lunch meat, more cigarettes, two gallons of wine. As I organized the shopping, I beamed at the others, feeling generous and charitable. I was being such a good provider. I was so pleased with myself.

"You're down to ten dollars," James noted. "Have you arranged to have your check sent here?"

"Yes," I assured him, feeling like an astute businesswoman and happy for a chance to show off in front of the others.

Caroline's giant wanted to go uptown to a park where it was legal to drink.

"No sense in risking a ticket with all this good stuff," he pointed out.

We wended our way uptown. I was glad for the men to help with the packages, which were very heavy.

Alameda Park, our destination, was in the northern part of town. Our walk uptown gave me a good look at Santa Barbara. It was charming, with broad sidewalks and gracious architecture. We passed shops and restaurants, many with flowers hung brightly in front. The streetlamps were designed to evoke a bygone era; the lush foliage and purple flowers made for light, bright color. It was a calm and peaceful place, resembling a Spanish outpost in the West. I walked along happily, enjoying the view, glad to be out of jail and in a new group. It's a new day, I told myself, feeling a rising euphoria.

The townspeople shunned us—crossed the street, even, to avoid coming into contact with us; pretended we weren't there. It was as if there were two worlds occupying the same space: theirs of normal citizens and ours of street people. The difference intrigued me. It was as if I were invisible. I'd had that feeling before on the street. In a way, it conferred freedom.

Our walk north was slowed down by Peter, who frequently set his bag down to dash up to passersby and ask for spare change. "God bless you!" he'd beam at them, whether they gave or not.

"He's a real pro at panhandling," Caroline remarked. "You won't have to worry about what to drink when you're with him. In that way, at least, he's reliable." She looked at him fondly, almost as a mother to a son. Hm. So her proprietary hold on him remained. I felt sharply, immediately jealous and insecure. She still loved him. Did he love her? Would they get back together, leaving me alone? It was troubling; my earlier euphoria turned to gloom and worry. We passed the courthouse, where I'd last been in chains.

"That's a familiar spot," said the giant. "Let's see whose names are up on the board."

Setting the packages down again, we walked through an elegant courtyard and around a corner to an indoor wall which had pages of small print posted on a board. Each page contained names of people who would be called in court that day.

"There's Felipe, and there I am," the giant announced. "That'd be for drunk in public. We were all together that day. Peter, did you find your name?"

"Not today. That last ticket hasn't gone to warrant yet."

I surveyed them sadly. I'd hoped for another day of celebration, not a day in court. Still, it seemed polite to wait for them to take care of their business.

"Will it take long?" I asked wistfully.

"Oh, we're not showing up. It'll take another week to issue warrants for arrests, and then they'll only pick us up if they find us. Adds a little excitement to life, running from them. I don't think I've ever shown up for a ticket."

Felipe, who'd found his name listed, snorted in disgust. "Forget it," he said. "I'm not showing up either. I'll run from them."

"My bandito," said Maria, hugging him.

It was a new idea to me, just not showing up for a scheduled court date. Reckless and wild. But if that was the street custom, I'd bow to their superior wisdom, I decided.

"I showed once," Peter reminisced. "Caroline had me up on an assault charge. Remember? It was when we had that apartment."

"*My* apartment," she countered. "I was only letting you stay there."

"What's yours is mine," he sang. "Forever after." I felt another sharp stab of jealousy. He was serenading her! What about what *we* had? What about these bags of goods? Did they count for nothing? I was growing angry now.

She tossed her hair and regarded him with half-closed eyes.

"I'd forgotten that time," she said.

"It was when you'd been flirting with Manuel here."

The giant grinned, then made a placating gesture with his arms as if blessing the group.

"That's all over and done with now," he soothed. "Let's get going."

I was glad for his presence. He acted as buffer between Peter and Caroline. Their past intimacy, their shared history, their easy banter and heckling disturbed me and made me feel very left out and lonely. With his intervention, though, maybe I could still fit in.

The group resumed its progress uptown. The courtyard, as we passed through it, was lovely. Early spring flowers festooned the space. The turrets were very grand. When I'd been taken to court from jail, my view had been blurred by rain, and we'd only entered through a service door. I hadn't realized I'd been in such a fancy place.

As we left, a tourist bus was disgorging its passengers to admire the spot. People strolled out with cameras slung around their necks, exclaiming at the bell tower and oohing over the flowers. They hastily looked away from us when we passed.

"Whatsa matter?" called Peter in a jeering tone. "Don't like the view? We're part of the tour."

"Don't play the fool," the giant admonished. "C'mon, let's get out of here."

We continued our uphill climb, led by the giant, who gave a shout as we approached a vast green expanse. "We're here!" he proclaimed. "Welcome to my estate."

A soccer game was going on in one corner of the huge park. The giant led us past it, to a cupola which was perched on a rise fragrant with newly cut grass. He placed his bag on its inner bench.

"Spring has sprung!" he hollered. "Let's get drunk."

I felt miffed and slighted, as if control of the party was no longer mine. I'd have to remedy that. I was the hostess, after all. This was *my* event. I'd make sure they knew it. Quickly, I pulled the bottle of whiskey from the nearest bag.

"Let's start with this," I said grandly. "Peter, will you bless the bottle?"

"Bless it?" Caroline said scornfully. I held firm, very sure of myself. With this party, I was buying my way into the group. I wanted it to be perfect. I wanted no fights, no outbreaks of violence today. Who was more powerful than human nature? God, of course. We drank the way others ate, as a daily necessity. Hence, a blessing was crucial.

Peter stepped forth with alacrity, winked at me, and held the bottle solemnly in front of him.

"Dear Lord," he intoned, "Thank you for this plenty. Please bless us as we drink it."

Triumphantly, I broke the seal, and we started in.

The cupola had been painted white and gold; I felt regal as I handed out drinks and food. Perched as it was on a hill in the park, the cupola gave a view of the city below. I relaxed, pretending to be mistress of all I surveyed. Queen of the hill, with her loyal subjects gathered…so the fantasy spun.

As we drank, Caroline began acting like a little girl. She scrunched her face up and tugged at Peter's jacket.

"I have to go to the bathroom," she whined. "Will you walk with me?"

"Always, for my little Caro," he said gently, slurring his words.

I was both enraged and desolate. Had I found a lover only to lose him the next day? To be humiliated? They were probably renewing their romance right now, behind my back. Almost, to my face. They were just using me, using my credit at the liquor store. They were making a fool of me. I was a fool.

Felipe and Maria were oblivious to my distress. They cuddled up to each other on the grass in front of the pergola. She was half asleep, with her head resting on his stomach. He sipped a beer pensively and stroked her hair.

Peter and Caroline staggered off down the hill to the public toilet. I glared at the giant. Why hadn't he intervened? Why hadn't he insisted on escorting her? He was supposed to be Caroline's now. I needed him to back me up.

He returned my look calmly, shrugged, and maintained a dignified silence. We sat there together, not speaking, willing the others to return—willing them not to linger by the bathroom. In their drunken state, they seemed to have forgotten they'd broken up. It wouldn't take long for them to become intimate again. I waited anxiously, suspiciously.

When they did return, their faces were solemn. "Couple cops coming up the hill," they announced.

"I'm gone," said Felipe. He rolled himself away from Maria and raced into the nearby shrubbery. "You haven't seen me."

Indeed, two uniformed officers were making their way uphill to where we sat. I saw their heads first, then their uniformed shoulders and badges, then their holsters swinging heavily, with sticks dangling at their sides. Last came their pressed pants and their shiny black shoes. One cop had a red face from the effort.

Caroline slithered to the floor of the cupola. "Someone else do the talking," she said.

I rose confidently. After all, I knew it was legal to drink here. "Afternoon, officers. What's the problem?"

The red-faced one grunted at the sight of our debris. "We've had several complaints from neighbors," he said. "You'll have to all move along now."

"But, officers—" I pleaded.

"No argument. Move it or come along with us," said the other cop firmly. "Which do you want? All the same to me."

I felt a flash of outrage that we should be herded away like animals. Our party was to end in jail, or threat of jail? We could just be chased off? No. I was determined to prevent it. We might be homeless, but we were citizens. We had rights, surely.

There came to me then a deep calm. It descended upon me; it must be the blessing, I thought. Inspired, I stepped up to the two cops, and the professional woman I had been years before emerged and spoke.

"I am Dr. Williams," I said formally, extending my hand. "You are?" They looked at each other in sudden confusion.

"And you are?" I repeated courteously.

"I'm Officer Hadley," said Red, "and this is Officer Burnett."

"Officers, I appreciate your coming by, but you have no cause for alarm here. I'm head of a research team. My colleagues and I are investigating the effects of alcohol on the homeless community. I assure you we aren't bothering anyone. Indeed, I'd be happy to reassure the neighbors. We're just enjoying a day in the park here and conducting our research."

They drew back and consulted with one another. Red got out a walkie talkie. He spoke briefly into it, listened, then nodded at me.

"Have a pleasant afternoon," I called victoriously after their retreating backs. Triumph! Since I'd just served jail time, I had no warrants. Since I was new in town, they didn't know me yet as a street person. I knew there was a university nearby. Apparently they hadn't wanted to risk offending me if I were legitimate. So my ploy had worked. Shakily, I sank back down on the cupola bench, my street self again, grateful to God for the gift of a professional demeanor when I'd needed it.

"How did you do that?" asked Caroline petulantly.

"I don't know," I said honestly, unscrewing a jug of wine. "It just came to me."

***

We stayed at the park the rest of the afternoon. We took off our socks and washed them in the goldfish pond, leaving them on rocks to dry. We lay in the sun on newspapers. We ate the sandwiches and drank the rest of the wine. We told stories that went on and on into the evening light.

The giant started the topic of being locked up. He'd been in a men's prison up north and talked about the music he learned to make there with spoons.

"I was locked up as a kid," said Peter, "for shooting my old man."

"Oh, not that story again," moaned Caroline.

"What happened?" I asked at the same time, shamelessly, knowing he wanted to tell the story and determined to be a good listener and show Caroline up.

"My dad was a big old guy, and he beat on my mother. One night he just kept hitting and hitting her, and he wouldn't stop. I grabbed the BB gun he'd given me for my birthday, and I shot him in the leg."

I was proud of his bravery. "Did that stop him?"

"He grabbed me and the gun, didn't even stop to put a coat on. Put me in the truck and drove me down to the sheriff station. 'You take him, Joe' he said. 'He's incorrigible.'"

"The sheriff listened to him?" I asked, appalled.

"They were old drinking buddies. I got sent away to a place for boys. Stayed two years."

I was touched by the story, and deeply reassured about my future with him. If he'd protected his mother that way at such an early age, I figured he'd protect me too. I'd be safe with him.

"I've never been locked up," said Caroline smoothly.

"Yet," said the giant. "You got a couple tickets now, for open container."

"They'll lose those tickets."

"Ha."

She tossed her head and, picking up a pencil she'd taken from the liquor store, began drawing on a paper bag. I looked over her shoulder. She was sketching the church tower that rose gracefully from the town below us. I was impressed.

"That's good, Caroline."

"Oh, yeah. I used to do this—worked as a lithographer. That's when Peter and I met; we were both working then."

"How'd you end up out here?" I risked asking The Question.

She shrugged, tapped the wine bottle. "I lost my job, then he lost his...then we figured we could make it, bumming around. We got, you know, heavy into sweet wine."

She added a bell to the church tower. "How about you? You weren't always a street person."

"No, I used to teach…then I had a home business for a while." The green lawns of the university…the excitement of preparing for a new class…the thrill of being called Dr. Williams for the first time…where had that life gone? Had I really lived it? I felt a sharp pang of loss. It hurt to remember. I longed to change the subject, to forget.

"You get tired of it?" she pursued.

"I got tired of the tension and the pressure to excel. Got tired of impressing people, I guess. I'd always wondered what it would be like to live out…you know, no worries." Ha. I was lying, or only telling part of the truth. It had been a matter of needing beer in the morning just to get going…of hitting the bar every night…of all the men I'd take home from the bar…of the panic each month over making rent… yes, the long, slow descent.

"So here we are."

"That's right."

Our conversation was unusual in that street people didn't normally talk of why they had become homeless. They recognized each other as kindred spirits and regaled one another with countless stories of past triumphs and tragedies, but no one probed into the events or motives that had led them to a life outdoors. Our talk of the past, I realized, was triggered by the emergence of my former persona when talking to the police.

Caroline and I sat a moment in companionable silence, our earlier enmity forgotten. Felipe returned from his hideout.

"We're going back," he announced. "Going to set up camp. See you there."

Soon we all began straggling back down the hill. I was hungry and said so.

"Hold on," said Peter. "I'll get you something." He zigzagged down a side street, ending up behind the kitchen of the Salvation Army.

"They're done serving," Caroline protested.

"That don't matter. Hey, Bert!" He leaped up to tap on the window, and a face appeared.

"What's up, man?"

"Give me a plate, brother."

"You know we're closed, man."

"Come on, bro. It's for my old lady. She's hungry."

I looked at Caroline in amazement. So he was claiming me after all. "He called me his old lady. We just met yesterday."

She nodded. "He's like that. It doesn't take him long."

The Army worker handed a covered paper plate down to Peter, who passed it to me triumphantly.

"You don't have to worry when I'm around," he said proudly.

"Thank you."

Caroline and the giant headed back then for their own camp. Peter led me through a maze of back streets and alleys. Dark shapes loomed; I realized I was seeing the backs of buildings and stores. The alleyways were narrow, gutted, filled with trash and empty bottles.

We ended back at the empty lot with the morning glories. Felipe and Maria were already in bed, taking up the space we'd occupied the night before.

Peter grabbed a few blankets off the top of them.

"We'll move upstairs," he said.

Farther uphill, in the roots of a tree, was a narrow space. Behind it was the dumpster for a set of apartment buildings. We built a nest there and went to sleep.

"…the younger man…squandered his estate with loose living…but when he came to his senses, he said…'I will get up and go to my father…'while he was still a long way off, his father saw him and felt compassion for him, and ran and embraced him…the father said to his slaves…'bring the fattened calf, kill it, and let us eat and be merry; for this son…was dead and has come to life again…" (Luke 15:20-24)

CHAPTER 16

FALL, 1986

When I awoke, my head was on the canvas of my jacket. I was groggy. A rock was sticking into my side. It hurt; I felt underneath myself to dislodge it. There. I was sleeping on a strip of cardboard with the blankets over me. We must have put the cardboard right on the rock. A typical drunken move, I thought with weary disgust.

Near my head, the gray metal of a large dumpster loomed.

It was early morning. The air was cold, and a loud twittering of birds met streaks of gold and pink in the sky. Pretty. My normal love for early morning returned.

The body next to mine stirred and then flung itself upward with a snarl. I flinched.

"Shut up, birds!" Peter yelled. He glanced at me, shook his head slightly as if to clear it and resumed his monologue, speaking in a loud surly voice.

"Damn birds. They woke me up. Didn't we save any of that wine? This is no way to start the morning. Why didn't you save any? You kept pushing me out of bed. I was rolling downhill all night. Damn mornings anyway."

At first, his early morning temper had shocked me and frightened me. I'd run away, only rejoining him when he'd gotten enough alcohol in him to calm down again. By now, I was inured to his daily blast of rage. I wouldn't respond, wouldn't get drawn into a fight, I resolved. Too dangerous.

Now he was muttering curses. It was this way every morning. Resentfully, feeling very put upon, I raised myself out of bed and reached for my shoes, ignoring him, not wanting to draw attention to myself and get him yelling at me again. I wanted to shrink into myself so as to escape his notice and his wrath.

"Use the stupid faucet. Here—" Peter stepped up behind the dumpster, where a faucet protruded. He turned it on and stuck his head under it; then, he shook himself like a dog, spraying me with shivery wetness. I recoiled.

Cautiously, I splashed off in the cold water and caught a comb he tossed me. It was black plastic and familiar—a jail issue comb. I pulled it through my tangled hair with difficulty.

"Let's go see if Felipe saved anything to drink—a wake-up. Felipe!" Good. His mood was changing.

A sound of weeping came from the camp below. Maria poked her head out of the shrubbery. I was alarmed. What was wrong?

"They came for Felipe last night. Didn't you hear it? Two cops came here and took him to jail. My baby's gone."

As quickly as it had risen, Peter's rage dissipated. He became solicitous.

"I musta slept right through it. They didn't come up here. He'll be back, Maria."

I was bewildered. How had the cops found Felipe? He'd hidden from them for months. Should I ask? Betray my ignorance?

"How did they find him here?"

Peter made a dismissive gesture. "They know where to look for our camps. They make raids at night and then run warrant checks on people."

Maria turned a tearful face upward. "He has six warrants and probation. That's why he was hiding from them. They'll keep him for months now. Will he be in court this morning? I want to go see him. Will they let me talk to him?"

Peter leaped down the slope with agility and, reaching her, patted her shoulder. "The chain for court won't get there until 8:30. You've got hours to wait. We'll go up with you to say hi to him."

We would? Here he was planning my day. My resentment returned. I'd thought of trying to get a little store credit today and maybe trying to find out more about the Dalton gang. A group that was so feared would be good to have as extra protection if I could get friendly with them. They might even act as buffer for Peter's rages, I thought cagily.

Maria's tears subsided. In response to Peter's questions, she found a half bottle of brandy that Felipe had stored.

"Oh, you beautiful woman."

"We were saving it for his birthday."

Peter took a long swig and passed the bottle to me. I drank deeply, gratefully. This would smooth out the day. My resentment vanished; good will rose up in me. Maria needed us? Of course we'd help. Be magnanimous. After all, we were all street people together here, part of the same camp. When trouble befell one, it befell all.

Maria pulled a mirror and brush from the cardboard box that served as her bed table. She began brushing out her long black hair and then expertly braiding it. Peter pulled long on the brandy bottle and watched her appreciatively. I felt a stirring of the old, familiar jealousy I experienced whenever he admired other women.

"Do we have time to get breakfast at the Mission?" Maria asked.

"Sure. Let's go to breakfast, and then we'll walk you up to court."

We headed out into the cool morning, Peter with one arm around each of us. He had turned ebullient, and I marveled at how quickly his moods changed. I was wary of him now, didn't quite trust him, but relaxed under the warmth of his arm and pretended all was well.

The Rescue Mission was located in a small stucco building that fronted the railroad tracks. An inscription on the door announced that God loved us. These words comforted me. Please do, I prayed. You're all we've got. (Since this writing, a larger Rescue Mission has been built in Santa Barbara, on the outskirts of town.)

"Let's go," said Peter, ushering us in. "The morning's not so bad here. The sermon's only half an hour."

The Rescue Mission was the only one of the soup kitchens open at 6 am. An assortment of people, mostly male, were straggling into its main arena—a whitewashed room with folding chairs facing a small wooden altar. Pulling my scattered wits together, I tried to prepare myself to worship.

We found seats in the middle. To my right was a screen; behind it came the clatter and hiss of breakfast preparations. I could smell the savory coffee and a sweet warm baking smell, and despite my earlier intentions to listen carefully to the sermon, I longed to burst through the screen to the food beyond.

"I know a guy who stayed here a while," Peter commented. "He said it was hell—they work you half to death. He had to get up early to make the breakfast, stay in to clean the rooms, then begin working on lunch…then he had to help with showers, wash the towels, and bam, it was time to start getting dinner ready." I was skeptical. The story, like most of Peter's stories, sounded exaggerated to me. "You've never stayed here yourself?" I challenged.

"Ha!" he answered scornfully. "Not me. I don't usually come for meals, either. The dinner sermon's an hour."

"Nearly six thirty now," said a grizzled man behind him.

"They make good pancakes, though," said Maria. "I hope they have those this morning, not hash. The hash is terrible."

"What I'd like," confided the man in back, "is chorizo and eggs."

"Yuck!" exclaimed Peter. "Don't you know what goes into chorizo?"

The fellow drew himself up with dignity. "It is not what goes into the mouth, but what comes out of the mouth that defiles."

I was deeply impressed and soothed by what the old man said. He was quoting Christ. Why did words of scripture have this power, this ability to comfort? I didn't know; they just did. I'd love to know the Bible that well. How did he do it? Doubtless, years of coming to the Mission—and maybe long hours in jail, reading the book.

I was still curious about the Rescue Mission. I might need it someday. "Have you ever stayed here?" I asked Maria.

"Oh, they don't let women in. Just for meals. They only have beds for guys. They try, you know, to rehabilitate the guys. Maybe I should send Felipe here." She laughed again. Her spirits had lifted. Was that due to Peter's ministrations? Again, I felt a spark of jealousy flare. He was so charming to others. I was the one who got the brunt of his rages. It was bitterly unfair. Still, I was curious.

251

"Where do the women go? If they need shelter?"

"They don't. They stay with their Felipes. Oh, the Sally Army has a long-term care, and then there's a battered women's shelter."

"You don't want to go there," inserted Peter quickly. "They lock those women up tighter than a drum. They don't even let 'em go to the market. I know a woman went in there; no one saw her ever again."

He made it sound as if the place had devoured her. I thought of the San Rafael shelter, its stringent rules. Would I have lasted there had it not been for the pneumonia? I doubted it. I sure hadn't lasted at New Life.

I reflected upon the irony of needy people and the places that tried to meet that need. It came down to rules. Street people distrusted rules; that's why they were on the street—to escape society's rules. Yet the missions believed that we needed rules and structure, needed to be brought back into society. So there had opened a chasm of misunderstanding.

The grizzled man tapped Peter on the shoulder. "Got anything?"

Peter glowed. "We had some fine brandy, man, but we drank it all up. Had to get ready for court—Maria's old man."

The man scowled. "You're a selfish pig. You ain't got no manners, son. You know you shoulda brought that brandy up here. Now I got me a few fingers of vodka left, but damned if I'm gonna share it with you."

Peter was contrite. "I'm sorry, Grandpa. I did wrong, I know it." I felt a warm surge of affection. I liked this about him, this willingness to admit fault.

"Yeah, you mumble a lot about sorry. You're lucky I don't hit you with my cane."

At the mention of a cane, I turned around in my seat to look more closely. Was this the fellow who'd talked James into cashing my check? I thought it was. He had the same silvery-black hair, but he looked more weather-beaten.

"You're the man who helped me get a check cashed at the liquor store."

"Is that you, girlie? What are you doing with this crowd? Come on by the train station and I'll see you're treated right."

Our conversation was interrupted by a young man, gawky and intense, who stepped up to the podium. He surveyed the crowd solemnly and then began to speak.

"I know most of you, and I know that when you get out of here, you'll go right out to drink, and you'll end up in the weeds. You'll pass out in the same weeds you piss in.

"I know you will because I used to be out there with you, up till two weeks ago. Brothers and sisters, I'm here to tell you that you can get out of those stinking weeds."

He went on for about ten minutes, the refrain "get out of the stinking weeds" repeating. I was offended. I knew the difference between the bathroom bush and the sleeping bush, for heaven's sake. So did everyone else. Why was he patronizing us? I felt a flash of anger.

"I know the guy," hissed Peter in my ear. "He won't last long here."

The next speaker was more seasoned. He told the story of the prodigal son and encouraged us to follow his example. I was lulled by the story. It ended so happily. Slowly, I considered it. Could it happen for me? Could I, should I, return to my family? Oh, no. There was no way back home for me. I was too deeply immersed in street life now. Still, it was a good dream...returning home to find a celebration and rejoicing. I let my thoughts drift.

The sparse crowd listened impassively, waiting for the guy to cease and for the screen to open. When the time came, we ate in shifts, half the room going in while the other half waited hungrily in their seats.

"Where's Mike?" Peter asked Grandpa.

"The fool never showed up. I was going to send him on a run to get my vodka. He's the only one who brings it back. Since he ain't around, I figured I'd get some food here and make the run myself." He turned his attention to me.

"How 'bout you, girlie? You got that check going to the liquor store now?"

"Yes, but it took some doing."

He shook his head in disgust. "They'll try all sorts of tricks. Tried 'em with me. I told them, 'Look. I'm old. I'm crippled. I need my vodka every day, and I need to be outdoors for my health and my friends. Send it to the liquor store direct.'

"That's the way, girlie. Gotta be firm with 'em, show 'em who's boss." I was impressed. Would I ever be so direct and outspoken? He really knew his way around.

Maria was devouring hot cereal and doughnuts. "Is it time for court? I don't want to miss him."

"We can head up there," said Peter. "The court bus might be early."

We pushed back our chairs and headed out. Three people stepped forward to take our place. We began the trek up to the courthouse. The route was growing familiar now—here was the Mission, there was the liquor store, there was the side street to the Salvation Army. There was the bar where I'd been pulled in for drunk and disorderly, there was the Mexican restaurant and the art store, there were the thrift shops with people eagerly entering for bargains.

Here, several long blocks up, was the courthouse. We sat perched on a ledge outside, companionably watching the traffic, until a big white and black bus pulled up, full of prisoners. A guard opened the bus door and led out the first chains of people.

"There he is!"

Felipe, clothed in an orange jumpsuit, lifted his chained wrists in greeting and blew a kiss to Maria. "They got me," he mouthed ruefully.

"See that?" said Peter. "They've put him in orange. That's for troublemakers. He must have resisted arrest."

Maria nodded. "He tried to kick the baton away," she said proudly. A guard stepped forward to prevent any further displays; Felipe marched in his line indoors.

After the men, the women filed out. So that's what I had looked like, coming off the bus in chains. I shuddered, glad to be free. Most of the women kept their heads down, as if afraid to see anyone they knew.

I recognized the older woman who'd been booked in with me, and I waved. She looked up with a smile.

"Time to get back inside," she called to me. "Rain's coming again."

So that's how she worked it? She tried to get taken in to jail to avoid the bad weather? Amazing. Indeed, the air was growing chill, and mist from the ocean was swirling around us.

"I'm going in to hear his sentence," Maria announced. "You don't have to wait."

"No," agreed Peter with some urgency. "We'd better get the bedding over to some cover. Maybe the train station is the best place. C'mon, Dee."

I bridled at being bossed around. Who said he was in charge of me? It was very annoying. Still, there was no point in lingering at the court, so I followed him. We made our way back to the ravine, gathered what bedding and cardboard we could carry, and headed back downhill past the Mission down to the tracks.

The train station had a roofed porch all the way around it, and today it was filled with street people. They'd rolled their bedrolls up against the wall and were sitting or standing in small groups, peering out at the unseasonable rain. There was lots of khaki, so the watching figures blended in with one another. I was a little intimidated by the size of the crowd.

"Let's find Grandpa and see if he's got any vodka," Peter suggested. "He's got to be here; he wouldn't go far in this weather."

We found him crouched on his haunches up against a wall, leaning back on a stack of bedrolls. Two pit bulls flanked him, one speckled and one jet black. The black one raised a sleepy head and sniffed at me. Was this the dog who'd come up to me on the Salvation Army porch? It liked me! Acceptance. I patted its bullet-shaped head.

"Down, Max," snarled Grandpa. "They left me here to babysit," he explained. "Left the old man to guard the stuff and mind the dogs. Sit down, get comfortable. How 'bout a game of hearts?"

We sat on our own bedding and played a few hands with him. He was sharp at cards and won. That's his due, I thought.

Peter's hope for vodka was thwarted. Grandpa kept a tight grip on his bottle, taking tiny sips from it throughout the morning.

Peter was increasingly restless. Finally he threw his cards down. "I need a drink," he announced. "I'm going out to see what I can do." Turning to me, "You got any credit left?"

"I don't think so." My stomach clenched at the question. I'd come to believe he was just using me, didn't really love me at all. Why had I ever thought he would? Despite the death of my romantic dreams, I had resigned myself to staying with him. I'd had enough of being alone. If he ever turned dangerous, I'd run. Anyway, here at the depot were too many people for him to get mean again.

Grandpa frowned. "You supporting him, girl? I thought you had better sense. Tell you what—just call James at the store and ask him."

"You mean the store will okay it?" I asked in wonder. Peter perked up.

"You gotta chance if James is working. Phone's right around the corner. Here, I'll show you how." Struggling to his feet, he gripped his cane and led me to a pay phone at the other corner of the station. He inserted coins and dialed, asking to speak to James.

"James, it's Clifford. I'm going to send somebody up your way, and Dee here is too. You know her, the one I vouched for." He passed the phone to me, and I negotiated with James for a small advance on my check. Feeling daring, I ordered a quart of beer and a pint of vodka.

Peter, on hearing we'd ordered, pulled up his collar and ran out into the stormy day. The old man called him back.

"NO you don't. We ain't sending you out on your own. You might not come back with it. Hey, Joe," he called to a figure huddled up in a sleeping bag. "Go with Peter here, pick up our order. I'll give you a drink for it." The man obliged.

"C'mere Dee, sit down here next to Grandpa. Now what you doing with that fella?"

"We've teamed up," I said defensively. I had my doubts about Peter but didn't want anyone else criticizing my choice.

"Well, you're young. I teamed up too, when I was your age. My lady's still in town, but she's smart. Says she's tired of living outdoors like an animal. When we got older, she saved up her check and rented her a room at the Californian Hotel up the road. Oh, I see her when she comes down for a visit, but they won't let me in the room. Maggie, that's her name. My lady love."

He sighed and patted his heart. "When we lived out here, we had us a little shack. It's still there, but it's boarded up now. We had us some good times. Now, mind you, I never treated her bad. Not like the boys do today, hitting their ladies and yelling. No ma'am, I kept my manners."

"He filling your ear with lies?" asked Peter, returning. He dripped onto the bedroll as he lowered two bags to the ground. I presented Clifford with the vodka, a gift which touched him.

"Now, that's really something. Everyone else forgets old Clifford. Only getting beer when they know I don't drink beer. But you remembered. See, I knew I wasn't wrong about you, girl. You were brought up right."

I glowed with the praise. But my motive had been less than pure. It had seemed to me that a gift would get this old man of the streets on my side. He had the air of a patriarch with his shock of white mingling in with gray and black hair, his bristly beard, his snapping eyes. The others, I had noticed, were deferential to him—an attitude he fostered by waving his cane at any threat.

The afternoon passed in card playing, desultory talk, and naps. The rain continued to pour down. The one train that afternoon held few passengers; these disembarked swiftly and headed straight for the inner station, keeping their heads up and their eyes straight forward. As a group, we were hard to ignore, but the passengers managed.

"Won't we get kicked out of here?" I asked, worried.

"Not in the rain. The city tolerates us here during a storm. When the rain stops, they'll clear us out. But we got us a good camp to go to. Come stay with us, Dee. You and lover boy here. We gotta family, like. It's safer, you know. We look out for each other." Sounded good. My hopes rose.

The black dog got up to stretch a few times but returned always to Grandpa's side. The speckled one stayed put, as if in a long afternoon's dog dream.

"She's pregnant," confided Grandpa. "We got her pups sold already, and they ain't even come out yet."

"What's her name?"

"Sharonna. The black one's Max. He's the papa of the babies. Right, Max? You sly old dog."

Max grunted and nosed in again on the other side of Grandpa, into the bedding. Periodically he'd rise and pace a few steps away, carrying a sleeping bag over his head. That gave the illusion that the sleeping bag was walking.

"He's a blanket thief," said Grandpa. "Max! Come on back with that bag. That's the only thing we gotta watch him for. Come night, it's good to have one of them by your side. They heat up the bed like a furnace."

Near nightfall, three men materialized out of the wet gloom. Grandpa introduced us. There was John, the leader, whose shaved and bullet-shaped head resembled a pit bull's. There was Mike, the tall blonde man I'd met at the Salvation Army. He was dressed in a long green jacket and looked as if he'd returned from a reconnaissance mission. I learned later that he'd fought in Vietnam. There was Eddie, small and quick, with a tattered baseball cap on his head.

I had met the Dalton gang.

"Who has wounds without cause?…
Those who linger long over wine…
'They struck me but I did not become ill;
They beat me, but I did not know it.
When shall I awake?
I shall seek another drink.'"
(Proverbs 23:29, 30, 35)

Chapter 17

The storm lasted three days. We huddled under the roof of the station. I used up all the credit the liquor store would give me and girded myself to survive until the first of the month. I was tense, on edge. It would be difficult, I knew, and it made me anxious. My panhandling skills had not improved. I had to hope that my largesse on the first of the month would be remembered, would carry me through.

One night when the rain had cleared, Peter and I were panhandling along Chapala Street. We were near a small market when he erupted. "You're not doing jack! You're letting me do all the work here."

"I share my whole check with you," I said angrily, feeling unappreciated. He was being unjust, I felt. He was good at this; why shouldn't he support us part of the time?

"I'm sick of hearing about that check. Where's the check now? How're we going to get more wine if you don't help me out here? Speak up and ask people."

I froze. I had a deep-seated unwillingness to beg. I watched people come and go from the store, but I could not ask them. In a daze, I smiled at them and let them pass me by unnoticed.

Peter grabbed my arm and pulled me around to the side of the store, where he began to bash my head up against a stucco wall. In horror, I felt the sharp points pierce the skin. I felt his fists thudding onto my skull. The wine I'd drunk all day numbed me. I could feel his attack only dimly, as if in a nightmare.

Finally, I ducked under his arm and ran up the block to a 7-11. I stood and crouched in its light, fighting off nausea and trembling and the awareness that I had been attacked.

No. I hadn't been bashed in the head. No. I was drunk; that's why my head was ringing. No. I was drunk and had imagined it, hallucinated it. That was that. I retched, fighting off the memory, feeling vulnerable and terribly alone.

"Mi amor por la vida," Peter would whisper to me at night, intensely. "Por la *vida*." "Por la vida," I'd echo back happily, lost in a dream of love. My lover for life. A rare and special love…that's what I wanted, desperately, for us to be a couple in love. So. Getting hit had been a hallucination, brought on by all the Thunderbird wine I'd had that day. Hadn't it? That was all it was. Wasn't it? All night I fought with myself, hurt and shock on the one side, a craving for love on the other.

The next morning I met up with Peter again. I was tentative. He was worried, with no memory of the night before.

"Where'd you go, Dee? I missed snuggling with you. Did you go off with someone else?"

I hesitated, unsure of my words and unsure of the truth, but pleased by his concern. "No. I stayed up all night thinking. It seemed like… someone was hitting me in the head. I ran off."

"Someone was hitting you? I'll kill him. Who was it?"

"I…don't know." My courage failed me. So it was that we conspired, at first, to hide the fact of violence that was to dominate our lives. I felt an urgent need to keep silent about it. If I said nothing, then the violence was as if it had never happened.

***

Spring, 1987

Right up from the train station was the fig tree, a huge old overbranching tree with a plaque to inform of its history. The tree had been a major tourist attraction until the street people took it over and began sleeping in its roots. (On my last trip to Santa Barbara, I noticed that the Fig Tree had been cleared of street people, its value as a tourist attraction restored.) The tree people showed us the value of the gas station which was at that time across the street from the tree. (It has since been torn down.)

The gas station was open all night, and so were its bathrooms. The owners kept a pot of coffee going in the lobby, and it became a refuge. During the rainy season, we trekked up there and back many times.

One day, I went up to use the gas station's bathroom. It was in disarray—paper towels pulled out and overflowing, floor streaked with mud, doors filthy with smeared graffiti. I would turn this mess to my advantage, I thought hopefully. I went to find the owner, mindful of my mother's stories of the Depression—how tramps had come to her mother, hat in hand, asking for work in exchange for food. I'd show some gumption here. I would do the same thing as those tramps. I couldn't panhandle, but I could work.

The station was owned by a middle-aged couple who'd retired from their previous jobs to run it. I approached the man, who referred me to his wife. She sat in the tiny office.

"I wonder if you'd like to hire me to clean the bathrooms," I suggested boldly, feeling very daring. "I'd do a good job."

She eyed me carefully. She was a solid woman with tight gray curls, a kindly face, and bright pink lips that matched her nails. I could tell she was impressed that I was asking for work; I knew she was approached daily for handouts and free coffee.

"It's true the bathrooms need help," she said. "Let's try it for a week." She showed me where the mop and cleansers were kept. I set to work, humming all the while, immensely pleased with myself for finding this solution.

It was satisfying work because the bathrooms were so grimy I could make an improvement at once. I started on the men's room and scrubbed the stalls clean of graffiti. Crude sayings came off with squirts of cleanser. Squirt! Scrub! I wouldn't put up with such language. The stench was overpowering at first, but I poured bleach and scoured. I felt very important. My job was necessary; I was making a difference. As I worked I went into a kind of trance state in which I imagined that my grandmother was looking down at me and blessing me, approving of me. That was a happy feeling and I looked forward to it.

After that, I went to the station in the early morning twice a week to clean. She paid me $5 on those mornings, and that increased my popularity on the street.

In the predawn a few weeks later, I got the cleaning supplies and headed for the women's bathroom. I did the mirrors last. I wiped the spray and there, looking back at me, was a woman with a split lip and a black eye.

Shock. How ugly. Shame. Everyone would know now; I couldn't hide it. When had that happened? I detached and examined myself scientifically. Looks terrible…try to clean off the dried blood…will it leave a scar?

My memory blinked on and off, allowing me only glimpses of the night before. I'd been running from Peter's fists. I'd tripped on a tree root and landed on my face. The damage was part from him and part from the tree.

Peter's favorite trick was to smash my head, one side and then the other. Those blows left no mark. They just left me with ringing ears, sadness, and a deep anger which I hid from myself. This was different. It showed. I was deeply embarrassed.

Fig tree tripped me…Peter hit me…Angry words…hard panting, hard running…here I am, now…wounded…it'll go on like this…go on and on. Bleak future, no escape. He's my old man. My security. It happens. Endure. Run faster next time.

***

Summer, 1987

Peter and I moved up the tracks to the Dalton camp. It was located in a eucalyptus grove just east of the train station, right next to the railroad tracks. Throughout the day, the train would come whistling through, and sometimes a conductor would toss out packages for us: drinking water, sandwiches.

The Daltons called their camp "The Jungle." It was the site of a traditional hobo encampment, being near the train. Incoming strangers would be announced by the Daltons' pit bulls and would be quickly chased away unless they were known and welcome guests.

The train tracks were on one side of camp; the highway was on another. We were near the ocean. Camp itself was a man-made shelter under the eucalyptus trees. The Daltons had dragged an old carpet out, and at night they unrolled their bedrolls onto it. Near the tracks was a cement block in front of which, each night, one of the gang built a fire to warm us and to cook the food that the others had scavenged.

It was Clifford, "Grandpa," who provided me entry to the Jungle. His word was just as good here as it was at the liquor store. If he vouched for me, I was all right. I became the only permanent female resident. Sometimes the men would bring women back, but they rarely stayed past the night. I felt pleased and privileged to be accepted as the lady of camp. It gave me a status I craved. The Jungle was legendary; I belonged. I also felt much safer. Peter didn't attack me around the others.

One night, Clifford drew me aside. "Dee, you and I and the rest of the men here, we're different. We're alcoholics, Dee. It's a terrible disease, 'cuz we gotta have the alcohol to live. I don't know the answer, Dee. But I pray every night, for you and Peter, to get free of it, Dee. I pray each night that you'll be okay."

I was deeply touched to think of this old man's sending prayers up every night. Prayers for me. Tears sprang to my eyes. I watched him now turn in; he curled up inside his sleeping bag with a bottle of vodka clutched to his chest as if he were cradling a baby.

***

Fall, 1987

As the first of the month approached, all the talk was of the barbeque on Ledbetter Beach. This must be the same party that Susan had told me about on our walk into town from jail. The idea was that people's food stamps would be pooled and used to produce a mammoth party. I was excited. A celebration! I loved them. Susan would welcome me; it would be fun.

Peter and several of the Daltons were receiving food stamps now. We went up to General Delivery to collect them, and then out to sell them. A buyer would pay in cash half the value of the stamps, which was as good a deal as we could get.

Then, laden again with drink and tobacco, we walked along the shore to Ledbetter beach. As we approached, we could see fire from the barbeque pits. We were hailed as we drew near.

"It's the Daltons! Bring the dogs?"

"They're following behind us."

"Come on in, grab some beach."

I sat at one of the picnic tables, complacent, feeling at peace with the world, watching pale-skinned chicken char. Then, to my left, I heard an uproar. I looked over to the lawn. A woman was pinned to the ground. I recognized her as Susan, the woman I'd left jail with.

"No!" she was screaming. "No, no!" Oblivious to her screams, a large man who was straddling her drew back his fist and proceeded to punch her carefully, methodically, in each eye.

Outraged, I rose in my seat to defend her and was pulled back down by Peter.

"Don't interfere," he commanded.

One of the Ledbetter group leaned over the table to get a beer.

"Why are you letting him hit her?" I asked intently, hoping to spur him to action.

He shrugged. "It's their business," he said calmly. "Want to help me turn the chicken?"

Peter relaxed his grip on my shoulder. I went over to her, but she was now in the company of an older woman who had her arm around her shoulder. Susan was looking out angrily at the world, her eyes red and swollen, her body shaking. Her attacker had rolled off her and joined the group by the barbecue pits, laughing, anger spent.

What had been her offense? She'd probably been slow to hand over her first-of-the-month money to the attacker. I was enraged and disgusted, and I longed for big muscles and a weapon so as to get revenge, street justice. How I'd longed to protect her.

Here I stood, half a warm beer in my hand, helpless to prevent such injustice. It rankled, and the beer tasted sour. "What about yourself?" whispered an inner voice. "You're a victim too…there's no difference." With an effort of will, I pushed the voice away. I was not a victim. It was only sometimes…and those were times to forget.

"Here," said Peter, joining me. "Come on, leave her alone. Have a plate of chicken."

I took a bite. The skin broke and oozed pink juice. I left it to congeal on the plate, reaching for another beer. For me, all the joy had gone out of the gathering. I felt helpless, and it rankled bitterly.

The Ledbetter gathering lasted well into the night. The violence I'd witnessed was only the first of many fracases. By midafternoon, men leapt on one another, kicking and punching and drawing knives. Peter vanished, to emerge hours later with blood dripping down his face from a cut on his head.

"Got into it with someone in the parking lot," he panted. I knew a good woman would be concerned, would apply first aid to her man, would take his side. What I felt, though, was pleasure and a deep satisfaction that he'd been hurt. He hurt me often enough. He deserved it, I thought darkly. It's his turn. I kept my feelings to myself.

In the late night, we wended our way back to camp and collapsed on the rug.

"That's the last time I'm going to Ledbetter," Peter moaned.

***

I came to dread the first of the month. It had too much pressure on it to be a good day. We would have all scraped by for a month, scavenging food from dumpsters and begging for spare change, drinking scant sips from a bottle that had taken hours to procure. All our hopes were fastened to the first of the month, an imagined time of plenty, when there would be abundant food and drink and creature comforts.

Those who received no benefits preyed on those who did: dazed recipients of "crazy money" skulked along, fearful of attack. Tempers raged: "Give up the beer! It's my turn." Fights broke out everywhere: once I came upon Jungle Mike with a victim on the ground. With one hand, Mike was punching him hard. With the other, he was groping for the guy's wallet.

It was, ultimately, the bloodiest day of the month. So while I, like the others, longed for it to arrive, I felt a terrible tension when it came. What fresh horrors would it bring? How long would I be allowed to keep my check? If I clutched the cash, would Peter break my wrist to get it? I knew I'd wake up a few days later, having survived all the fights, dismal and broke again.

***

Spring, 1988

That spring, one of the Daltons' pit bulls had her puppies. She had six of them, little squirmy rat-size creatures with big square heads. They nosed around blindly. All were spoken for; the presence of a pit bull was valued on the street. They made excellent guards of territory.

I enjoyed the puppies and volunteered to stay at camp while the others made forays out for alcohol and food. Someone always had to stay at camp with the dogs. Usually I wanted to go out, but for a few weeks I stayed within the parameters of the eucalyptus grove to be with the puppies. They aroused my maternal instinct.

Drunk one day, I stripped off my shirt and dribbled condensed milk on my breast to nurse my favorite pup. I pretended she was my daughter as a baby. I didn't tell the others; odd behavior was likely to get me beaten up.

* * *

We took the dogs to a big park on Cabrillo near the water. It was a regular park with a bandshell and baseball diamonds. Often we drank there; I'd get morose watching baseball and imagine the games my daughter might be playing in, games I was missing. I'd get drunker and drunker, unable to stop, nursing the pain.

One Sunday a month, a church group sponsored a charity event at the park. A preacher would speak from a microphone first; then, he and his crew would line up with food, hot soup and sandwiches. At the end of the line, while they lasted, were clean socks. It was a popular event and I looked forward to it.

The preacher looked with pleasure at the people sprawled on the grass, filling the park. I was reminded of a Sunday school picture of Christ speaking to the multitudes—there we all were, hungry and waiting for the preacher to multiply the chicken soup and bologna sandwiches. I giggled at the thought.

The preacher was a short man in a white buttondown shirt and a black clip-on tie. He had horn rimmed spectacles which he took off and polished before stepping up to the microphone.

"Brothers and sisters," he boomed. "I am here to tell you the good news of redemption. Yes! That means redemption for you. Brothers and sisters, the Lord sees you sitting out there in your misery. He sees your dirty clothes. He sees your wine-soaked thoughts. He knows your sins! He knows how you lie and beg and steal! He knows your hard hearts.

"Do you wonder, why am I so dirty, why am I so hungry, why am I brought so low? It's because you have turned from the Lord. Yes! You have turned your back on his saving grace, all for the sake of a bottle.

"My friends, I am here with good news for you: God can take your misery away. Yes. People, if you only turn to him, right where you are, and accept him as your savior, the Lord will take all your pain away."

"Turn, people. People, I implore you to turn to the Lord, and he will help you. The beginning of wisdom, people, is fear of the Lord. If you fear the Lord, you will not be able to go on living the way you do. You would be afraid, people, to steal and cheat and drink that wine. Fear the Lord, people, and he—"

A wildfire started in my heart. It crackled into being and roared through me as it consumed all inhibitions in its path. I jumped to my feet, rose up from the ground and began to holler back at him.

"Stop this talk!" I yelled, feeling that flames were shooting out of my mouth. "Stop insulting us! Why do you say we don't know God?"

Peter tugged at my shirt to pull me down. "Shut up!" he hissed. Oblivious, I shook him off and kept going.

"Of course we know God. How else do you think we get through the day? How else do we find blankets, escape danger, find food each day? How else do we survive, when people look and run away from us? We rely on God."

"Christ is our friend, Mister Preacher. Get down from that stage and ask us about Him, instead of talking down as if we were fools. Get down off that stage and let the people speak."

Grandpa began to laugh and to wave his cane in the air. "Bring on the soup and sandwiches!" he chortled. "Bless that chicken noodle and let's get on with it."

I began to spin in widening circles from where I stood, as if the fire inside me had turned to a hot white motion that would not be stilled. I felt ecstatic, having released thoughts long held. My heart was light now.

Peter, holding a beer bottle in one hand, grabbed for me again. "Sit down, Dee. Wait till he's done serving everybody. If you scare him off, he won't come back and feed us."

The preacher blinked uncertainly and brought his talk to a swift close.

"Let us pray. God, in your infinite mercy, bless this food to nourish and strengthen us all."

His helpers, women who were also dressed in black and white, took their places and began ladling out hot soup in styrofoam cups. People rose from their places to form a huge line.

"Stay put," said Peter fiercely. He had succeeded in bringing me down, and had one leg over mine so that I was pinned to the ground. "It's his microphone; let him use it. You always want to be in the spotlight."

"She don't need a microphone," Grandpa observed. "We could hear her just fine. Go get her some soup, lover boy. Dee will stay here with me, won't you Dee?"

I nodded at him, spent from my outburst. He patted my hand as Peter rose to get in line. I relaxed on the grass, feeling cleansed and free. Then doubt arose: what had I said? What had I done?

"Here," said Grandpa, passing me a pint of vodka he'd concealed in his pack. "God provides, sister. That was good entertainment."

Peter returned with soup and sandwiches, a frown creasing his face. He set down the food, sloshing the soup on me.

"Of all the stupid stunts," he complained.

Grandpa swerved his cane in Peter's direction.

"Watch it, lover boy," he said in a warning tone. "Drink your soup and settle down."

I leaned back against a tree trunk and let the soup quench the fire that had flamed within. I was thirsty, hungry. It tasted good. Mike, in passing, tweaked my cap off my head and tossed it up into the tree.

"Hey, Dee. What were you going on about?"

"She got the spirit," Grandpa announced. "It happens sometimes. Nothing she can do about it either, so shut your traps."

I bit into a bologna sandwich and felt the twirling words and the shaking subside. I was very grateful for Grandpa's protection, for now I was weak. After lunch, the Jungle men got involved with a game of soccer, leaving me alone with Grandpa. When he dozed off, I stood and paced around the tree.

What had happened? I had to figure it out. It was baffling. I'd gotten mad at the preacher, yes, for talking down to us. But he'd said something that intrigued me, too. What had I heard? "Fear of the Lord." What did that mean? I would ask. "Dear Lord, the Bible says to fear you. But songs say to be your friend. Do you want me to fear you? If so, please show me how. I really want to know." I paced out the words, letting each step be one word: Fear of the Lord. Big step, little, little, big. Soon, I was choreographing the phrase.

I paused for a rest and went on to the next question. "Lord, it says 'praise the Lord.' People say it and preachers say it. But they don't *do* it. To say "praise" is to give a command and follow it with real praise. So, I'll try, Lord: You are good and gentle and…and…you care about us, and…" I circled the tree and then joined Grandpa for a rest. I was all the way worn out. Religion had exhausted me.

"Blessed are the poor in spirit, for theirs is the kingdom of heaven." (Matthew 5:3)

CHAPTER 18

SUMMER 1988—SUMMER 1989

Spring became summer. The puppies grew and were sold. I was sad to see them go but knew we couldn't manage so many dogs. In the Jungle, our numbers varied as different members were picked up on warrants and taken to jail. The cops knew where we camped; if someone had a warrant they came to collect him. It was very predictable, and I'd long since lost all fear of the police. I simply accepted them. They did their job; we did ours. Our job was being alcoholics. "Being an alcoholic is a tough job, but somebody's got to do it," joked one.

After a few weeks in jail, the prisoner would be back out with us. Then we'd have fun with him: he'd come back clean and sober from a stay in jail. We'd get him drunk and see how soon we could get him scruffy again. At times I felt guilty for doing this. But why else would the freed prisoner return to us, if not to embrace our way of life?

One day, I looked up and saw the police coming in disguise. They had picked up branches and were holding them in front of their bodies as they proceeded on tip-toe. I was astonished. They were whispering and chuckling among themselves.

"The woods of Dunsinane advance," shouted one in triumph.

Mixed feelings. I wanted to resent their intrusion into camp. Technically, they were still the enemy. Yet I had to admire the literary reference and the clowning. Cops who performed Macbeth? Pretty classy. I was impressed in spite of myself.

"Let's see who's here," said the leader jovially. "Mike, you have a warrant. Time to come along with us."

Mike stood to be handcuffed. The cops surveyed the rest of us, who were trying to hide our morning beers.

"Open containers of alcohol—tickets all around."

It was convenient for them to have us all be in one known area, and it was easier for us not to have to run from them.

Peter, who'd been gloomy since the incident in the park, asked me one night if I'd like to go out to dinner with him. I was inordinately pleased. It was a gesture of peace, and I welcomed it.

What he had in mind was a tour of the dumpsters of the best restaurants in town. We visited Enterprise Fish and Little Joe's and Fiesta, sneaking around the back of each place to its dumpster. Since he'd invited me, he did the climbing in and scavenging. Then he handed out scoops of food to me, which I'd pile on used paper plates. I'd see the top of his head and his quick arms as he sorted through the layers to find the choice bits. I felt pampered and grateful—Peter didn't usually pay attention to eating, preferring to keep the alcohol level high. Clearly, he was trying to get on my good side, and he succeeded. I appreciated his work.

When we returned to camp, I was full with meatballs, fish curry, enchilladas and lots of rice. We were never ill after such forays. Living out, we had developed strong immune systems.

We rarely went to soup kitchens. The cost was a long wait in line, a long sermon attacking our way of life, and a steady, relentless pressure to change our ways. We preferred to be self-sufficient, operating from our home base of camp. I was proud to be part of the group, to be accepted. It felt good to know we were living by our wits.

Evenings, we'd drink whatever the panhandling team brought back. Our group split up the work by pairs. One detail would be sent out to bring back jugs of water for the morning, when the alcoholic thirst burned our throats. Another group went out to rummage through dumpsters, another to panhandle in front of the liquor stores. Another would be assigned the job of guarding camp with the dogs. I admired how streamlined it was to have a functioning camp. Whenever I returned from a foray out, it was reassuring to know that I had a home base. It comforted me.

When it grew late, we'd unroll our bedding onto the large carpet that lay under the eucalyptus and pass out.

James's liquor store opened at 6 am, and we had to be there when the place opened. It was our unwritten rule. We'd rise with the dawn, straggle over to the water jugs to splash off and to drink. Grandpa was firm about the necessity of keeping water at camp.

"We're alcoholics," he'd intone, "which means we get dehydrated. If we're gonna drink, we gotta have food and plenty of water to keep going." I respected his wisdom and experience.

When dawn streaked the sky and the birds started twittering, we'd rise. Mornings, I'd see the bodies strewn about the carpet, sleeping bags going in and out with the rhythm of the breathing within.

When all were awake, one group would clean up camp—start the fire, roll up the bedding, sweep off the carpet. Another detail would head out to James's liquor store.

Unless it was a bathroom cleaning day, I'd walk with two others, usually Peter and Mike, up to James' store. I loved the morning walk. On the way, Peter would pluck a flower from a garden we passed and present it to me with formal courtesy. I'd twine it in my hair. I came to crave the romantic gesture. "He can be so sweet," I'd murmur to myself, and try to forget the bad times.

When we reached the store, James would carefully mark down an amount that was our limit. We'd get Grandpa's vodka, cigarettes, and a case of beer. I'd get a coffee and an airplane bottle of bourbon for the walk back. Outside the store, we'd get newspapers.

Walking back, I'd sip the bourbon and coffee and feel with relief the liquor going into my system. Ah, bliss. My body would tingle; my nerves would unjangle; my mood would lift.

On our return, the dogs would run toward us, barking a welcome. Then we'd spread out on the carpet to drink, read the paper, and play cards until we'd drunk our morning's ration. I'd put my morning flower in water and join in on a card game.

Usually, about midpoint through the game, I'd feel myself slipping from high to drunk. The cards would blur and my moves would become increasingly haphazard. My mind would dim, my speech would slur, and I'd be gone: numb and out of it, ready to pass out.

On one such mid-morning, Grandpa nudged me. "Your daughter just went by," he informed me.

"Wha—what? Where?"

"A van from her school just drove by on the highway."

Dimly, I realized that the school must be making a field trip into Santa Barbara. She was so near and yet so far. We were geographically close, yet living in totally separate worlds. To numb my aching heart, I took a swig of Grandpa's proffered vodka and passed out.

Our routine was that later in the day, once we'd all come to, we'd disperse to go panhandle throughout the city. I usually went with Peter and Mike. Peter was an aggressive panhandler. He'd go rushing up to people. Once, as he lunged drunkenly toward a woman, she ran across the street to escape him. Undeterred, he kept going. I was in awe of his raw nerve.

I continued to hate panhandling and would often hide behind Mike, letting him do the talking. We'd all return in early evening to compare notes and prepare for the nightly ritual of fire and food. The predictable nature of our days soothed me.

There was a cement block in camp. At night, we'd build a fire up against one side of it. The block also served, on its top, as a catch-all. When people came and went from jail, they brought back combs and toothbrushes which ended up on the block. When John raided a newspaper stand, he brought back papers for everyone, and the unread portions remained on the block. When I found a treasure in the dumpster—a bookend, an earring, a box of bent paper clips—on the block it would go. These small treasures were dear to me, since they provided the illusion that I'd been able to create a home.

The block also held a mirror and a roll of toilet paper. Our morning ritual consisted, first, of our sliding down the bank to the creek below the bridge over which the train passed. We'd clamber down one by one, taking the roll of toilet paper with us. Then we'd climb back up, splash off, comb our hair, check our appearance in the cracked mirror that, when it was not on the block, would be fastened to a tree.

The Jungle was our home. We loved it. No matter where we went during the day, we'd always return to it, walking home along the railroad tracks. Following the tracks was the best way to find the place when it was late and we were unsteadily drunk.

Peter and I were linked now in an increasingly hostile relationship. Despite our romantic gestures—his morning flower to me, my daily walk by his side—I'd come to think of him as an enemy to outwit. I'd originally hoped that because he'd opposed his father's violence to his mother, he'd be a peaceful man himself, but Peter had turned out to be a volatile soul. He'd awaken enraged and stay that way until the first drink of the day was in him.

Late afternoons, when he awoke from passing out, he'd be in a foul temper and was likely to strike out. I had to stay alert to dodge his fists, which all too often connected. I'd try to arrange things so that, when afternoon came, we were surrounded by others who could stop Peter, pull him off me, get some drink in him. It was a daily challenge that kept me on edge, wary and suspicious, continually on guard.

I had wearied of being hit and, determined to change the situation, was learning how to wrestle from a man named Andy who was camping with us.

Andy was different from the rest. He worked part-time as a waiter at a bar, and he hung his pressed black pants and white shirt from a tree in the Jungle. He had, at one time, been an amateur wrestler. I'd talked him into giving me some training, and I decided I would become as good a wrestler as Jacob when he fought the angel. This dream sustained me.

I'd had several wrestling lessons and was feeling fine, well-prepared. One morning, on our run for beer and vodka, we'd picked up a newspaper, and I was reading about the upcoming presidential elections. The democrat's wife was showing up to functions drunk and embarrassing the candidate. I wondered if she'd rather be out here with us.

I wanted to finish the story before I got too drunk to read. Peter was impatient. He wanted my attention. He hated it when I was absorbed in anything besides him, and the paper was annoying him. He kept batting it out of my hands.

Irritated and fed up, I threw it down and leaped on him, trying to wrestle him down. He'd had a good many beers and was off balance. To my delight, I got him down to the ground easily. He pushed up on his elbows; I grabbed them and shoved him back down. I was prone on top of him, using all my strength. There! I had him. Overjoyed, I raised my head to announce victory. At that point, he too lifted up his head and clamped his teeth into my ear.

The pain was intense. When the others came over to separate us, I was missing part of my ear lobe. Shocking, bitter defeat. Our battles had reached a gruesome new low. I was devastated. I'd been so sure I'd win for a change. Now I was maimed.

I went up to the hospital that day, got the ear bandaged up, and was met outside by two police who wondered if I didn't want to file a complaint.

"You can get him on a mayhem charge," one offered.

I felt a brief flare of hope that arresting him might solve the problem. But then, "No thanks," I said wearily. Any small satisfaction I'd get from turning him in would turn to terror once he was out again, and out again he'd soon be, seeking revenge. Nor could I turn to the others for support once they knew I'd broken the rule of the street and had him put in jail. We were supposed to take care of our troubles on our own. I knew that much.

So I went back to the Jungle with antibiotics and pain pills which I took with beer. The others made room for me and we all played a game of hearts, Peter rather sheepishly losing.

"Did you tell them a dog did it?" he asked hopefully, trying to pretend. I ignored him coldly.

"A dog did do it," Grandpa cackled. "A dog named Peter."

My wrestling coach was unsympathetic. "You had him in a good hold," he analyzed, "but you forgot to block his head, girl. That's very sloppy. Now we have to call you Van Gogh."

I ignored him too, nursing my chagrin. I hated to lose in battle.

279

Despite the violence, I clung to my relationship with Peter with all the tenacity of one of the pit bulls. We were known as a pair, and that gave me an identity. I desperately wanted to believe that we were fated to belong together as a couple. The romantic illusion was necessary to me; it brightened my otherwise bleak life.

Because of my tendency to fight back and make sneak attacks on him, it also gave me a reputation of being a fierce woman, which I enjoyed. I was a Dalton now, and a person to be feared and respected.

One day in the big park off Cabrillo, we'd gone again to hear the Sunday sermon and eat soup. We'd managed to get a lot of beer and vodka that day, and everyone passed out after the soup. I came to with an unpleasant wetness on my back from the dew-filled grass. I was thirsty and my body ached; I needed more to drink. Blearily I wondered, had anyone saved a bottle? That's when I saw them.

Peter was still passed out, but he had another woman asleep across his legs, her head nestling snugly in his lap. I felt disbelief at first, then the sharp pain of betrayal. I lunged toward them in a wild rage and began kicking them about the head and shoulders.

"Wake up, fools!" I shouted. "Wake up, Romeo and Juliet!" I kicked them until they'd rolled shamefacedly apart.

"Remind me never to get on your bad side, Dee," commented Mike, handing me a beer. "When you go off, you really go off."

***

It was morning. As I was climbing unsteadily up from the creek, I heard the uneasy rustling of my fellow campers above. The dogs, who were barking loudly, were quickly silenced by John. I crouched behind a bush, cautious, uncertain of the wisdom of appearing. From my hiding place, I could see two policemen talking with the group.

"By tonight," one said. "It all has to be gone by tonight. The bulldozers are coming first thing in the morning."

John was trying to reason with them. "It's our place," he argued. "It's our home. You know we're out of the way here, and we don't bother anybody."

"Not up to me, buddy," said the cop impassively. I knew without seeing him that John would bridle at the "buddy." "It's Fiesta in a few weeks, and the City wants to clear out all the homeless camps. Then, there are plans to develop this property."

Camp was to be razed? Impossible. I began to shiver. I could see the tip of a cop shoe from my bush. It tapped impatiently.

"Just the way it is: If you're around here during Fiesta, we'll pick you up—it's that simple."

"Yeah," said John, in a defeated voice. "Thanks for the warning."

The cops left; I sidled out from my bush.

"I heard," I told John, fighting off panic. "What will happen now?"

"They've done this before. They're going to send a bulldozer tomorrow morning to clear out this camp. It'll all be an empty field by tomorrow. The cop said we'd better move anything we care about because when they come, they'll cart everything to the dump."

"What was he saying about tonight?"

"Cops'll be by tonight and take anyone who's still here to jail. Illegal camping."

I sank down next to him on the carpet, defeated. Our home was going to be bulldozed? I couldn't bear it, couldn't take it in. Briefly, outrage and protest flared.

"How can they do it, John?"

"Easy. Listen: I'm not moving. We can do a sit-down strike."

"Will we go to jail?"

"Sure, but I'll feel better about it."

I looked around. The dogs were surrounding John, trying to comfort him. Where was Peter?

"Did Peter go on a run?"

"No, Dee, they took him in. He had warrants up the yin yang. They took him right off, when you were down at the creek. He said to tell you he loves you."

"Cheer up, Dee," said Grandpa. "He'll be out in a few weeks. It'll give you a nice break from him, and he'll miss you, and he'll be all lovey-dovey when he gets out."

Peter's going to jail did not upset me. It would give me a vacation; I could relax my guard. What did upset me was the prospect of the bulldozers. How could I bear to lose camp? I watched a card game develop among several men on the rug.

"Hearts, Dee. Want to come in?"

"Next round, cut me in. Listen. Where will we go?"

"I'm staying where I am," Grandpa asserted. "John's right. No sense making it easy on them. So they take us to jail—I could use some regular food again. I'm an old man, Dee. I ain't going to run."

"What about the dogs?"

"John'll find someone to take 'em. By tonight we'll be in with Peter, Dee, and you can visit your friends on the women's side."

I looked at my flower, a yellow rose which was perking up in its can of water. The thought of leaving the Jungle deeply distressed me. It was our base of operations. It was good to return to, good to hear the barking of the dogs and the welcome of those who'd stayed in camp. It was good to decorate with a vase of flowers in water, with treasures found in the dumpster. I would miss it dreadfully—miss it more than

I had my last apartment. The apartment had been just a place to rent. This Jungle was ours; we had made it home.

That night we all gathered around a particularly good fire and roasted the ends of beef that John had scavenged. Grandpa boiled water and tossed a handful of coffee in.

"Don't take it so hard, Dee," he said in an effort to cheer me up. "Have a cup of coffee with some vodka. You know, I been living out for most of twenty years, girl. Places come and go. We'll find a new one. Home is where your people are, Dee. That's who we are: your people."

I nodded, huddling closer to the fire. I sipped the drink and let its warmth flood through me. What Grandpa said was true.

"You oughtta get away from that Peter, though, Dee. I've talked to you about this before. He don't treat you any better than a dog, Dee. He's just staying for your check, you know. Living off you. Get yourself a nice guy who gets a check himself. Not me, now. I'm too old for you. I love you Dee, but not in that way, if you get my meaning."

"I know what you mean, Grandpa." This advice was true too, but I lacked the power to make a break. I was suddenly filled with lassitude at the thought.

I got my blankets then and curled up on the carpet next to the others. The cops did not come until nearly morning. I awoke to a light shining in my eyes, and I stumbled into their van with the rest. No one struggled; our defiance consisted of simply remaining in the Jungle until the last possible moment.

The cops who came were used to the night shift; they laughed and joked among themselves as they herded us into the van.

I said goodbye to the men, my street brothers, outside the jail. They were taken to the men's side, I to the women's. I had no warrants, so I wouldn't be held long.

"It's Dr. Williams," said the guard who checked me in. "Say, did you know we've booked you in almost fifty times?"

"That many, huh." Despite my depression, the number impressed me. It was some kind of a distinction, after all.

"So what's up, Doc? Got any warrants?"

"None that I know about."

"You're clean—we'll keep you in the holding tank a few hours. If you're lucky, you'll get breakfast."

I was released later that morning, with a pink ticket for illegal camping. It was afternoon when I made my way back into town, and I headed for the Jungle. Viewing it was a shock. It had been transformed into an empty field. Our carpet was gone; our bedrolls were gone. All the odds and ends of our housekeeping had been dumped in the creek. It was a scene of desolation. Our home was a wasteland.

I walked along the track to the train station, and on around the corner to the giant fig tree. A scattering of homeless were there, leaning against its roots, but I did not see any familiar faces. Were all the Daltons in jail? I was very lonely and uprooted.

I spent that night in the Salvation Army. Later that morning, I made my way to James' liquor store and there, to my surprise and delight, met up with Mike. It was an intense relief to see him. He had both dogs on leashes.

"Dee, you're out. Good. I rescued some blankets—got out before the cops came the other night. Did they take everyone else in?"

"Everyone."

"I've found us a new place, over by the freeway offramp. There's a major growth of ivy there, and bushes, so we're hidden."

I was impressed and began to feel a stirring of hope that things would be all right again. "How did you accomplish all that?"

"Army training. Didn't you know I was in Vietnam? We were always having to move camp in the middle of the night. Who'd have guessed it would come in handy?"

Mike led me into the new place stealthily. We crept along side streets and made a curve, following the freeway, until we came to a mass of overgrown bushes and ivy. After carefully looking around to make sure we had not been followed, he ducked into the ivy, motioning me to follow.

The area was screened from the freeway by large bushes which grew in a tangle. Behind them was the ivy, which Mark had stamped out into separate rooms, each with a bush for a concealing front door.

"Here's the spot for you and Peter, Dee. Don't worry. While he's in jail, we'll take care of you. We're family."

Pleased, I realized that my status as Peter's old lady worked in my favor now. With him gone, I could even enjoy it. It lent me protection and respect, and I didn't have to put up with him.

Mike had salvaged some blankets from the bulldozing; each room had a couple of them. Gratefully, I settled into my new home.

"This poor man cried and the Lord heard him and saved him out of all his troubles." (Psalms 34:6)

Chapter 19

Summer, 1989

For the next month, I was sister to many brothers. It was a peaceful, companionable time. I reveled in the absence of violence and the sense of belonging. I could relax, free from worry and tension.

We lived in the ivy. Two mornings a week, purposefully, I'd rise and go to my bathroom cleaning job. Whether I was working or not, we'd head for the gas station's bathroom first thing, to tend to our needs and clean up.

"Cheeks, don't fail me now," Mike would yelp as we strode briskly toward the morning's goal.

I enjoyed the company of the men, yet I longed for female company. While I did not wish street life on anyone, I yearned for other women with whom I could talk, compare notes, confide. Lack of female friendship created a gap in my life, and I felt it keenly.

One day, I'd finished cleaning the bathroom and was on my way with Mike to the liquor store. We passed through the grass by the fig tree and there, screaming and leaping like a wild woman, was Lucy.

"Uh oh," said Mike. "Let's get out of here before that Indian wench spots us. She's got a big mouth."

Intrigued, I looked more closely. She was a tall, dark woman, and she did have a big mouth, full and beautiful. Today she was using it to defend a man who sat dejectedly on the grass behind her.

"How dare you kick him out of the circle?" she was yelling to a group of men. "You used his last change to get that bottle. Now you better give him his share. He and I panhandled that change, you greedy pigs."

I was impressed and delighted by her. Here was a woman ready to dispense street justice and protect the underdog, just like I'd wanted to do. Arms gesturing, mouth moving, she was fearless. I wanted to know her and learn from her warrior spirit. Maybe I could get to be more like her.

"Let's help her," I insisted to Mark, who sighed and accompanied me to the fracas. Lucy was up against four men who huddled tighter on the grass, trying to hide a small vodka bottle.

"What's up?" asked Mike. He loomed over the man holding the bottle, who looked up with a fatalistic expression. He knew he was about to lose.

"Ah, we asked them to leave. They were taking more than their share."

"Liar," exploded Lucy. "We gave most of the change that bought that thing."

Mike was firm. "If they helped you buy it, man, you gotta give them their share of it." Standing tall and straight, he looked like a preacher, enforcing one of the unwritten rules of the street: Those who contribute to the bottle share the bottle.

"Yeah, yeah." Glumly, the loser passed the bottle up to Lucy, who grabbed it and took a long swig, then passed it to the man who was hiding behind her.

"There," I said, deeply satisfied. "Happy ending." I turned to go, pleased by the resolution.

She beamed at me. "Thanks, baby girl. You off so soon? Later, then. Later days."

After our intervention I spoke often with Lucy, and was gratified when, within a few days, she moved into our freeway camp with another Native American she loved, Dano. He had long black hair and played the guitar for money. Because of his showmanship, he was fastidious, keeping his long hair and his fingernails clean. Clearly, he considered himself a step above the others.

He tolerated Lucy, who stood head and shoulders above him physically and, I came to believe, in worth.

Lucy and Dano had lived in the same reservation in the Three Corners area. She told me stories of what she called "the rez."

"Once we went out herding sheep, me and Dano. We ran like the wind, heading them out of culverts. We were faster than the sheep dogs."

I wondered, briefly, how much of her story was based in fact. When, for instance, had they gone to tend sheep? Our life on the streets had a timeless, eternal quality, one day blending into the next. We all had former lives. Yet these were part of a dim background from which, when the day grew long, we'd pull stories. On the factual basis of the tales, however, we never challenged one another. So I relaxed into the story, imagining myself there too, running like the wind.

Briefly, that summer, we had another woman staying with us in the freeway camp. She was beautiful, with long blonde hair and blue eyes. Incredibly, she brought luggage with her. She was just passing through, and she knew Mike from early days together in Long Beach—"the Wrong Beach," as they called it.

We liked her because she classed up our act, although I felt twinges of jealousy because of her beauty. Mike was elated by her presence; clearly, he was still in love with her. She did not have to tell stories; he told them for her.

"One time in Long Beach, we were winding up a week-long drunk. We'd been out by the pier, and she decided we needed more bourbon. Well, she walks into what she thought was the liquor store and smacks her money down on the counter. 'Give me a pint of your best bourbon,' she says. Only thing is, she'd walked into the police station. Guy says, 'Uh huh, right you are ma'am.' And he takes us all in."

Mike slapped his knee and guffawed; she smiled kindly at him and patted her hair, pleased to be the subject of a story.

One morning early, as dawn was just streaking the sky, Peter returned. I tried to be happy and welcome him, like I knew a good old lady should, but I experienced the sinking feeling that his homecoming meant an end to a peaceful interlude. The pleasant routine of days—liquor store, cards, sleep, Mission meals—was over, and it saddened me. I'd enjoyed a privileged status as a sister in the Dalton Gang. With typical street morality, the guys had respected me as "Peter's old lady" and protected me from any outside advances or attacks. Now that he was back, I'd need to be on guard again against his temper and his fists. My anxiety began to build. My heart hardened. Even as I embraced him, I tensed my feet, knowing I'd need them for running.

***

Nights, the Dalton gang revved up for high powered panhandling, recovering from the slump of the afternoon. We were all walking along a main street several blocks away from the beach. The plan was to make enough, not just for a bottle, but to get us all into a bar with a

289

beer apiece—once inside the bar, we'd hustle for more drinks. I was excited by the plan. It would be fun to sit inside a bar, like a lady.

"My alcohol level has dropped too low!" Peter was in a foul mood. Alarmed, I sped up to put distance between us. Looking back over my shoulder, I saw him coming at me with arms outstretched; I figured he meant to vent his rage by smacking me. Not this time, I vowed grimly. My courage rose, as did an inner resolve to thwart him. Just as he approached, I ducked down low and butted my head into his abdomen. With his arms raised, he was now off-balance, and as I connected he toppled off the curb and into the street, in the way of passing traffic.

Mike grabbed him by the elbow and dragged him back, shaking, onto the sidewalk. "Get out of here, Dee!" Mike yelled. Numbly, I watched the gang close ranks. They were expelling me for having endangered Peter. Without pausing to defend myself, to protest injustice, I fled. I'd be on my own that night, but I felt no remorse. I felt powerful to have repelled attack with a surge of adrenaline. The knowledge that I might have gotten Peter killed impressed me deeply. I hadn't realized the intensity of my rage at his attacks.

I was not out of the gang permanently. Our policy was that outrageous drunken behavior be dealt with at the time, then be forgiven and forgotten the next morning. Besides, I was the one with credit at the liquor store.

***

"Stupid birds! Stinkin' birds!" Predictably, Peter awoke in a temper. I knew that he'd holler and rant all the way to the liquor store. Once he got some alcohol in him, he'd quiet down. Once I got some alcohol in me, I could ignore him, tune him out. I tried to do that on our morning walk—tried pretending that his raging voice was just part of the background, like the sound of traffic heading to the freeway. I never responded to his outbursts; the wrong word might spur him to start swinging. I remained silent, insulating myself with a cold indifference.

"Every morning it's the same story, no alcohol in camp, nobody saved any, you are really stupid—"

"Hey, bro!" Mike came up beside us, swinging his arms to and fro. "Hey! Check out that couple up ahead of us—they look like they'd be good for some change. Let's hit 'em up together."

Gratefully, I followed behind as Mike and Peter raced up to panhandle. Reprieved.

***

Autumn, 1989

Lucy was all excited about the idea of going to San Francisco. She'd gotten word that there was a big homeless camp set up in front of the city hall there. The churches had organized a nightly soup kitchen right outdoors; AIDS activists had a booth for giving away free clean needles and condoms; the living was good.

We were sitting in a circle by the fire when she burst into the gathering.

"I've found a guy who'll give us a ride to San Francisco tomorrow morning! He's got a truck. Peter and Dee, come on with us. Dee, the Social Security is easy there. You can get your check sent directly to a p.o. box, and there's check cashing places all over town."

Peter's ears pricked up at that. Check to a p.o. box? Easy cash? He'd only have to fight me to get all of it, and that he knew he could do.

Resistance surged within me. I was very reluctant to go. Here I knew the group; I belonged. There were usually people around, especially Mike, who would pull Peter off me or distract him from a rage. Lucy kept after me, though, with assurances that life was good in San Francisco. A whole little city of street people, unity, privileges, solidarity. Eventually, worn down, I agreed to go.

When the truck and driver pulled up to the side of the boulevard by camp, we piled in. I rode in the back, feeling the wind whisk through me and grow colder the farther north we went.

I had been so often hit in the head by now that my infrequent speech was very slow and halting. There were large gaps in my thinking, terrains balanced on a bedrock of fear and held together only with the certain knowledge that soon I'd be hit again. Still, I tried to enjoy the scenery of the ride.

There was a snap in the air as we pulled into the city, and an underlying excitement which I caught. San Francisco was gray that day, but it held the tension and crackle of many souls hustling, hustling, and hoping that a big break in their luck was just about to happen. My pulse quickened. Maybe this change would be good.

We drove past the high towers of the Financial District; I shivered in its shadows. We pulled in, then, by the side of the vast park that fronted City Hall. It was true: A small city was there—row after row of sleeping bags and tents, with walkways in between the different camps. The homeless were making themselves unavoidable. I was in awe. No more hiding from the cops?

Lucy leapt from the truck and raced off to find her drug connection. Peter and I wandered aimlessly among the different camps, settling finally in an open space.

I had found a child's sleeping bag in the middle of bedding in the truck, and I zipped myself into it, curling into a fetal position. "I'm off limits," I said firmly. "And if you hit me again, I'm leaving. Understand?" He nodded. Good, I thought, drawing strength from my ultimatum. Good. New place, new rules.

The next morning, Lucy came to escort us to the Department of Social Security. She was counting on getting a cut of my check as well, since she'd done the research. I accepted that fatalistically.

From the City Hall, we trudged along a wide, open courtyard area. All the city buildings were close together, and soon we came to the multi-layered building we needed. I saw there many others who were in my position—being carefully watched and supervised by those who had designs on the coming check.

One woman obviously received the disability check; she was in a wheelchair. Her mate was pushing her roughly into the elevator when we arrived.

"Stupid," he hissed at her, giving the wheelchair a jerk. "You are so stupid. You could have asked them for a larger advance." She held herself still, masking her face in a stoic resignation which I instantly recognized from my own. It was the way my features felt. To talk back, to laugh, to argue would invite more blows, and she, unlike myself, could not even run away. So we stayed passive and remained in the hope, against all evidence, that our oppressors would change and become kind. For her sake, I wanted to upbraid the man who was jerking her around. I wanted to report him, to hit him, to get rid of him. I was filled with anger. But I did nothing, joining the ranks of those who would not interfere, and I despised myself for my inaction.

At the Social Security office, I found that Lucy had been right. The worker was happy to transfer the check and have it sent to a postal delivery box. He was pleased with himself, certain he was doing me a favor. I longed to tell him my real situation, to beg for help and protection, but torpor and resignation kept me silent. I thanked him and left.

***

In San Francisco, I became totally worn out from all the battles with Peter and from the daily struggle to survive without getting hit or kicked. Gone was the power of my ultimatum. I no longer cared; I was inured to abuse.

My silence was constant now, and people took to calling me "The Zombie." The name humiliated me, but I had lost all my fighting spirit and defiance. I had become completely numb and existed in a void. When I dared to feel, despair was the only feeling.

"Hey, Zombie! Get up." Peter's voice rasped in my ear. I was loathe to get up. It was early afternoon, but I'd crawled into the sleeping bag nevertheless. More and more, lately, I'd craved unconsciousness. Why stay awake? What was there to live for? Nothing.

He prodded my bag. I rolled slowly out of it and rose to a half crouch.

"The reporters are here. Newspaper and tv—see the camera?"

I looked where he was pointing. Reporters from a local station were standing over at the edge of the park, with their large cameras set up and whirring.

"Let's go get famous," said Lucy excitedly. I went over to the drinking fountain to splash off. Someone had left a toothbrush in the basin.

Lucy came up behind me. She was quickly running a comb through her hair.

"Come on, Dee. Let's get on the evening news."

I thought about my family, whose members were scattered throughout California. I didn't want any of them to flick on the tv and see me onscreen as a battered homeless woman. It seemed a cruel thing to do to them. I headed in the opposite direction, but a reporter waylaid me.

"Hi!" she said brightly. "Do you live here?"

"For now I do."

She thrust a microphone to my mouth. I jumped back at the gesture. The mike was dark, rounded at the tip.

"Don't be scared," said the reporter warmly. She was dressed in a yellow blazer and navy pants which were smooth and uncreased. She had a blue and gold scarf around her neck. Her face was young and intense, with reddish gold hair falling softly to her shoulders. I caught a whiff of light perfume as she stepped closer to me.

"Would you say women have a harder time of it out on the streets than men do?"

What a question. A hard question. How would I know? I only knew this life as a woman. If I said it was harder, would people sympathize and come up and give me money? Or would it just anger the guys? I'd try to answer.

"Yes and no. It's easier for women to get benefits. It's harder for women because there is so much violence everywhere."

Peter materialized at my elbow. Reflexively, I jerked. Now I couldn't say anything because I might say the wrong words and pay for them later.

She nodded encouragingly. "What's been your worst experience?"

Desperately, I searched my mind for an answer. The worst moment had been to think I was winning the wrestling match with Peter, only to find that his teeth had clenched onto my ear. Here he was, grinning widely for the camera. In front of him, I couldn't talk about the violence. It would only get worse if I talked.

"There was a time…"

She pushed the mike closer.

"There was a time when a group of us were camped out. A man sneaked into camp and went up to one guy with a knife drawn. Luckily, we had the dogs with us then, and they chased him away.

"Would you say there's a lot of danger, then?"

I stared at her. Words began to push their way up my throat. "Get me out of here!" I wanted to scream at her. "Take me home with you! Protect me! Feed me!"

Peter shoved me to one side. "She's not too great at talking," he said. "Danger? We always have to be ready to defend our lives. But it's like a family out here—I want to make that clear. We stick together like a family."

I ducked my head as the camera whirred, and then it was over.

"You'll all be on the six o'clock news," called our interviewer as she moved away with the others.

That night a church group set up a table in the park with big vats of hot soup. I sat on a bench by a pathway, half comatose, sipping it from a styrofoam cup. I could feel it begin to revive me. As I slurped down the last noodle, a woman came frantically up to me. She looked like she'd just gotten up. Her long, matted hair was sticking out in all directions. She had an army blanket over her shoulders like a shawl, and it dragged behind her as she walked.

"Got a comb?" she asked me. "I want to look nice in case the cameras come back."

"No," I said coldly. She repulsed me. Even so I had to recognize the irony of my emotion: I was in the same state as she.

With a sigh, she plopped herself down on the bench beside me, wrapping the blanket tighter. "I need a comb," she sighed. "My own radio show comes on in about fifteen minutes."

"Radio show?" I was alarmed. She was nuts. I looked around for Peter. He'd gone back into the line for seconds on soup. She began to swing her legs to and fro.

"Don't you want to know about my show?"

"Not really." I clutched my torso with my arms to isolate myself from her.

"Sure you do. It's a radio show, see. I got my own channel. The transmitter is planted in my brain."

Just as I'd feared. "I already gave an interview today," I told her firmly.

"Oh, a celebrity. I thought so. I've seen you around with that cute guy. Are you married?"

"Might as well be."

"He doesn't hit you, does he? I'm always getting hit. I'd like to find me a guy who isn't a hitter."

"They all do it," I said wearily. "They give each other lessons, I think."

She looked morose. "If you see one who isn't that way," she sighed, "send him my way. I get lonely in my sleeping bag. Uh oh, Time to go on the air."

She began humming, stopping every so often to announce "Ding, dong" in a high falsetto. I edged farther down the bench.

"Welcome to K-God Radio," she called out brightly. "All your dreams come true on this show. Remember to put in your requests early, folks, because this is K-God and anything can happen."

She thrust a fist at me; I supposed it was wrapped around an invisible microphone. "Got any requests, little lady?"

Might as well play along. "I request that I escape the danger."

"Good prayer on K-GOD! Now, hold on, folks. Here comes a public service announcment—" she tapped her fist experimentally.

"Combs needed! Yes folks, there is an urgent need for combs out here! Just bring them by the station."

Peter came back, balancing a cup of soup and several slabs of bread.

"Get away from my old lady," he said gruffly.

"Threat!" she sang out. "Threat! To freedom of the airwaves."

"I said get lost!" Peter shouted.

She scuttled behind the bench and then waltzed away, humming.

"Take some bread, Dee," Peter said. "You don't even have the sense to get in line, do you? Good thing you have me."

I lifted a slice of bread from his plate. In the distance I could hear the K-God lady going for the high notes of "The Star Spangled Banner."

"Shut up!" Peter yelled into the gathering dusk. Turning to me, "You're a zombie and useless, but at least you don't sing."

***

Publicizing the homeless camp had a short-term and a long-term effect. Immediately, people from the town's social services roamed the park in front of City Hall, offering blankets and trying to sign people up for foodstamps. The town's churches redoubled their efforts to send out teams to stand at night ladling hot soup. During that time, the homeless camp felt indeed like a privileged small town within San Francisco.

However, the long-term effect was that, in a few weeks, the City Council voted to clear the area.

The police came by in teams, giving us a deadline of noon to clear ourselves out. After noon, they said, any people would be taken to jail for loitering and all bedrolls and tents would be confiscated for a police auction. I felt no resistance, no outrage. We were back to normalcy: "Move on, move on, or go to jail."

We cooperated and moved with many others to Golden Gate Park, which, being much larger, provided more hiding places. During the day, we sat in small groups on a large grassy area bordering Haight Street. At night, we disappeared into the depths of the park.

Lucy had found her own group, but she came by one day to visit. "Let's take a walk, Dee." We went out of the park, into the residential section, around the block. She stopped in front of a white house with a green door.

"If you ever need it, this house does counseling for street people. They make referrals. I think, too, they give shelter for battered women. You've got to be careful, though, with them—they're into rehab. I know a woman who went in there, and it was months before we saw her again."

I shuddered. Just what I needed, to get stuck inside a place for rehab. Sounded like jail to me. No drinking. Anyway, battered women...I wasn't...but I was. The certainty of it coursed through me. "Thank you, Lucy. I'll remember."

Our home base became a children's playground located on the northeast side of the park. We'd stash our bedrolls behind the public restroom during the day. At night, we'd pull them out and arrange ourselves in the playground. I usually ended up underneath the slide. I'd curl up on the sand and fantasize that I was a clean-cut, happy young mother taking her child to the park. "Swing me higher!" my daughter would chortle. Thus, I lulled myself to sleep.

One of our members was a man named Tim who'd followed us up from Santa Barbara. Most people, I included, feared him. He was a stocky guy and deceptively jovial most of the time. We'd hear him laughing one moment; the next, he'd be slamming his fist into somebody.

To avoid the constant fear, I became completely numb. I paced through the day in silence. My eyes darted right and left in an attempt to avoid blows. I began to pray. I formed very simple requests: Keep me in wine and out of danger. May Peter pass out so that he is no longer a threat to me. May I pass out and forget where I am.

Tim, who resembled a wrestler in a carnival, acquired a grocery cart to hold all our bedding during the day.

"This way, when we get asked to move on, it'll be simple to move," he pointed out.

I had no objection as long as he pushed the cart. Even though I was a homeless woman, I resisted making myself really obvious as one. To push a cart was an identifying tag: "I am down and out." I would not push it, I decided. I would keep my pride intact.

One night, we were walking in a group through San Francisco. The cart creaked along on the sidewalks, full of our bedding and squeaking from one wheel.

My thoughts were racing out of control. My mind was filled with scenes of disaster coming, with an oppressive sense of doom. I was sure I was dying or about to be killed. The certainty of it was like being filled with cold ice. That night, Tim pushed the cart through Chinatown. We passed Chinese grocery stores with ducks strung up in the windows. I looked at their bodies—they seemed shellacked, they were such a deep brown. They were headless. Their feet had been stretched up to a hook which hung them suspended from the ceiling. They horrified me. I imagined that I would share their fate—be butchered, tanned, beheaded, and strung up to hang in a shop window. The fantasy was intense and very real to me. It lingered for hours, holding me in the thrall of pure terror.

We were out panhandling along Haight Street when Peter rebroke my right wrist to show me never to hold out on him. He pulled me around a corner into an alley, grabbed my wrist. I heard it crack as he slammed it into the pavement. I whimpered, too weak to protest or fight back. What has happened to your spirit? I asked myself dimly. Wake up! Slowly, a sense of outrage and injustice began to build.

In pain, I cradled it as we returned to the park to seek out a nearby place to sleep. We were both too drunk to find the children's playground that night. We ended up in a low-lying gulley near a bridge that led to the Chinese gardens. Near us were a multitude of broken bottles. Peter cleared a spot and soon began to snore.

My pain was constant and I was soon filled with a cold, focused, murderous rage. I stayed up all night, fantasizing killing him. I could take a bottle with my good hand and smash it with all my strength into his skull. I would take the broken end and push it into his heart. Joyfully, I would watch him die. Then I would run. I replayed the scene over and over, savoring it.

Or should I go find a hospital? Beg them to take me and hide me? Make me safe? My wrist throbbed with a sharp ache. I lay on the twigs and considered what to do and moaned softly. In the end, I did nothing. My nemesis, passivity, won.

The next morning, there he was, not dead but awake and snarling for a drink.

"I need to go get this wrist set...it really hurts."

"Quit complaining. It's no big deal...it's only sprained." Maybe if I got a drink, it would quit hurting. We made our way through the park and found the others. It was to be another day of wheeling the cart through the city to panhandle.

"Hey, Zombie," hollered Tim that evening. "It's your turn to push the cart. This thing gets heavy. Peter, make her take a turn."

I sat stubbornly where I was on the grass. I would not push it. No one could make me. Someone hit me hard from behind, and then a fist connected with my eye. Defeated, I staggered up to the cart and pushed it toward that night's destination, the children's playground. "You've lost again," slurred a voice in my head. "You will always lose. Accept it."

Bitterly, I rolled under the slide, hunching up, trying to make myself into as small a ball as possible and therefore less of a target. I slept then, with troubled dreams about little children who wanted to play in the park but could not because we had taken it over.

"I want to slide down," said a small girl in the dream, "but that woman's in the way."

"I'll move," I told her. "I'll play with you."

She ran away.

I awoke with sand in my face. I could not open my left eye. In resignation, I knew from its stickiness that it had swollen shut. Peter looked at me with revulsion and pity.

"What happened to you?" he demanded. "Who hit you?" I didn't answer because I didn't know. I thought it likely that it was he. It had been Peter or Tim: What did it matter? Nothing would change. I failed to care who'd done it. It was a fact now.

This morning I was silent. I shook my head and went to the drinking fountain to splash off. There will be a little peace now, I thought with relief. There always is right after an attack.

The others woke then, and we all sat dejectedly on a bench facing the swings. No change.

"Tomorrow's the first of the month," said Tim cheerfully. "Let's just take it easy today. Dee needs rest; she looks awful."

My relief deepened. Just before the money came in on the first, people tended to be solicitous toward me. They wanted to treat me well so I'd go get the check cashed and bring it all back to them. The others agreed with Tim's plan, and by late morning we'd drawn out all the bedding and set it up in a grassy area a little away from the playground, facing the basketball court. By noon, everyone had passed out.

I came to in the late afternoon, refreshed. A sharp breeze blew my hair into my eyes and rattled some fallen leaves toward me. Slowly, cautiously, I sat up in my sleeping bag and looked around me. All was peaceful. In the basketball court, some young people were shooting baskets. To my right was a row of sleeping bags. I could see bits and parts of the people in them: there was the top of Peter's head; there were Tim's dirty tennis shoes sticking out of his bedroll. Several others, who had joined the group last night, were only lumps inside their bedding. I surveyed them calmly, dispassionately. They were nothing to me.

The wind blew a leaf onto my leg. I picked it up in wonder. How very lovely and subtle: deep green at the center, shading into yellow, then red at the outer edge. And there were the veins, branching delicately out. Was this God's creation? I marveled at such beauty.

I sat still; it felt as if the wind was blowing right through me. Whole sections of me were shifting, leaving wide open spaces within. I sat quietly, feeling the spaces. What was happening? I was changing. It felt marvelous.

I moved my hand over the grass. It was soft, green, not yet damp with dew. How splendid.

I got up out of my sleeping bag and took a few tentative steps away from the others, out into the new world. Why stay here? I asked myself.

I took a few more steps. "Nothing's keeping me here," I whispered in awe. I looked at the others. They remained asleep, as if they'd been held in position. I had the strong sense that God was keeping them asleep. I walked more quickly to the street. Looked back. No one was following me. No one was stopping me. "I'll leave," I said calmly, confidently. I walked farther, and as I walked, I felt a strong presence surround me.

It was loving, peaceful, protective. It felt like a shield. "What's this?" I asked, startled. The answer came. "This is prayer. Many people are praying for you."

I had now walked out of the park, feeling victorious. Behind me, the bodies that would ordinarily have rushed up to stop me, to hold me with them till payday, lay prone and oblivious to my escape.

I walked up a street where narrow houses were squeezed in next to each other. There was the white house with the green door that Lucy had shown me. Counseling...referrals...I went up the stairs and knocked. There was no response. Undeterred, I pressed my finger on the bell to the side of the door. I heard its sharp ringing from deep inside the house.

The door was opened by a slight man wearing reading glasses.

"May I help you?" he asked pleasantly.

"I'm escaping," I said simply, trusting that I'd be understood.

He lifted his glasses up to the top of his head and motioned me inside.

"Come with me. I'll see if I can get you into a shelter."

Shakily, impressed with my daring, I followed him through the lobby and up worn carpeted stairs. He led me into a dining room where an assortment of people were sitting. He pulled out a chair for me.

"What happened to you?" asked a black woman who had a pile of knitting in her lap.

I shrugged and sat in silence, hands folded in my lap.

"It doesn't matter," said the man, returning. "She's had enough of it. Here," he said, handing me a piece of paper. "This will get you into a woman's shelter. I've called you a cab. Just go where it takes you, all right? They'll find you a bed there."

I sat very still, waiting. When the cab came I got in and rode to a section of town I recognized. The cab pulled up to the curb across from the Pussycat Theater. To the right, a large, shabby building loomed. It was a place that served lunch during the day, but now there was no line in front.

"It looks closed," I said, achingly disappointed.

"Ring the bell. They'll open for you when they see your referral slip."

I did as he instructed. The door did open, and a woman led me down a long walkway and into a large dining room from which all tables had been cleared.

"At night, we're a women's shelter," she told me. "Get a mat from the pile over against the wall."

My vision came into focus then, and I saw a group of women sitting on mats. Some were coming in and out of a door; those going in carried soap and shampoo; those going out had wet hair and looked scrubbed.

"Showers are inside that door," said my guide. "Get yourself cleaned up. We'll have a snack and then bedtime in a little while." These were simple instructions. I could comply. Feeling protected, I did.

I stayed under the hot water as long as I could. I let it wash away all shakiness and doubt. When I emerged, damp and shiny, I took a nightgown from a hamper full of them and slid into it.

When I came out of the shower room, someone handed me an apple and a sandwich. I sat on my mat and munched the food, looking neither to the right nor the left. I'll just follow the rules, I thought firmly, and I'll be all right. No one asked me who I was or what had happened, and I was grateful for that.

My hearing began to buzz and ring. Why? Withdrawal? Aftereffects of violence? Through the static I heard a woman announce that it was time for a bed-time story.

I looked around then and noticed that along with the women were a group of children, who all looked up eagerly at the mention of a story.

I lay down on my mat, soothed, and listened to the woman read "The Story of Pippi Longstockings." When she read about Pippi and her pancake batter, I closed my eyes and was soon asleep.

I woke up to the clattering of dishes. I raised myself on my elbows and looked around, confused. Where was I? Over in a corner, several women were setting out cereal bowls, milk, and oranges. The floor near me was strewn with mats, each one holding a woman or child. Some people were already stacking their mats in the corner. Feeling small and obedient, I copied them.

The woman who had let me in the night before clapped her hands to get our attention.

"Time to get up, ladies. Please take all your belongings with you; we have no storage here. Come back by 5 tonight if you want a place in the shelter." My heart sank. What would I do all day?

In the shower room was an assortment of clean clothing; I helped myself and dropped the nightie in a laundry bin. The clothes I found were a large sweatshirt lettered with "I Love San Francisco" and a pair of baggy jeans. Pleased, I surveyed myself in the mirror. "There," I told myself. "It's a new you."

When I went to get an orange, the women and children were already filing out the door. I grabbed my fruit and followed them.

Outside, I saw a small group of people lounging in front of the Pussycat and sharing a bottle of wine; I walked by them swiftly. Not today. "This is a new day," I repeated firmly to myself.

"Hey, Mama!" called out a black man, tilting his worn cap at me. "Come hang out with us." I shook my head and kept walking. I skulked along city streets until I came to the place where I'd rented a post office box. With joy and a huge release of tension, I saw that it held my check. Farther down was a place advertising "Checks Cashed Here!" I used it, stuffing my pockets with cash. Now what, in my new life, would I do?

Suddenly, I was stricken with sharp guilt. Today, I believed, was Peter's birthday. How could I leave him? We'd been partners so long. What was I thinking of? I'd better take the cash right now and go find him.

I got on a bus to the park. Once I entered, I grasped onto a pole and looked around. Across from me was a black woman, neatly dressed. She gazed at me and I saw a look of startled horror cross her face as she registered my bruised face. I was ashamed. Then, to my amazement, she closed her eyes. I realized that she was praying for me.

I was deeply moved. Here I was, heading as for a magnet to the street people. Here she was, a stranger, beseeching God. A memory flooded me: yesterday, I'd escaped through prayer. I clutched the pole more tightly and joined my prayer to hers. "Oh God, please—don't let them be there," I asked fervently, feeling that my request resounded to the bottom of my soul.

I exited at the front of the park and made a quick search. No one I knew was to be seen. They should have been there. They were not there. Very well. My prayer was answered. Thanking God and trembling with the realization, I caught another bus to the Greyhound depot.

Buses were already pulling out of the station. I stood in a short line and purchased a ticket for Los Angeles. My bus left in an hour.

Feeling breathless, I ducked into the ladies' room. My right eye was vividly colored; parts of it matched the purple lettering on my sweatshirt. I hid in the restroom, very afraid that someone who knew me might spot me and drag me back to the park.

Then it was time to board. I climbed on boldly, found a seat near the front, and held on tight.

The bus lumbered out of the station, with much clashing of gears and belching of smoke. I was out of the city soon. With relief and joy I watched the driver take us onto the freeway south. My old life was behind me. Ahead was the unknown.

It was nighttime when we pulled into Los Angeles. I found a small hotel near the station and sat hunched over on the bed. I was afraid to take off my clothes. What if someone crashed in during the night? So I pulled a blanket over myself and rocked to and fro until I fell asleep.

"Peace I leave with you; My peace I give to you; not as the world gives, do I give to you. Let not your heart be troubled, nor let it be afraid." (John 14:27)

CHAPTER 20

The next day, I found a city bus that went out to the suburbs. My thoughts were scrambled, but one idea broke through and led me powerfully: I would go to my mother's house. Doubts churned but I set them aside, remembering the return of the prodigal as preached at the Rescue Mission. I had to try. I felt compelled.

The bus driver was shocked when he saw my bruised face. "Who did that to you?"

I was touched by his concern. Here was a stranger who cared. "A man I've left behind. I'm going to family now to heal and get help."

"Best thing you can do. That's what families are for."

Comforted and encouraged, I settled in for the long drive up to South Pasadena. I recognized the stop, got out, and began walking to my mother's condo, uncertainty and anxiety growing with every step. I knew she had long resigned herself to my being lost on the streets. What would she say now? Would she be glad to see me, or would I be an unwelcome bother?

When I arrived, she and my stepfather were just sitting down to afternoon tea. She held me by the shoulders and surveyed me calmly. "What a beautiful black eye. Come sit down. Would you like a cup of tea?" I was amazed by and grateful for her gracious welcome. No questions, no fuss, just serene acceptance of my presence. Gradually, I began to relax.

As I sipped the hot beverage, I screwed up my courage. "I ran into some trouble out there. It's too much for me. I wonder if I could stay here a while?"

She did not hesitate. "Yes," she said firmly. "Stay. You're safe now." My stepfather just grinned and nodded his assent. I later learned that he'd been praying every night for my return.

***

For the first month, I was too self-conscious to leave the condo because of my bruises. I just luxuriated in hot showers, good food, a warm bed. "I'm going to snuggle in," I'd murmur to myself at night as I climbed under the covers. "I'm going to snuggle my buggle in." The nonsense rhyme delighted me and lulled me to sleep. I began, tentatively, to accept the fact that I was safe and secure.

During that month I experienced a buzzing in my brain, along with thoughts racing out of control. This phenomenon troubled me deeply. I had so prided myself on my mind. Was it gone? Would my thoughts never clear? Had I damaged my brain irreparably? On an impulse, I took a Bible from the bookcase and clutched it, then leafed through it. I was too unfocused to read it chapter by chapter, but turning to the Psalms I found this phrase: "Thank you for your unfailing love." I latched onto the sentence with fervor. I repeated it over and over, letting it lodge in my mind: "Thank you for your unfailing love; thank you for your love unfailing." Over and over I'd murmur it and let it lodge in my mind, where it began to quiet the buzzing. One morning, I awoke to blessed mental silence. I felt exultant to have discovered such powerful words. Victory!

When my bruises had faded, my stepfather began a campaign. He was a recovered alcoholic, a member of a group whose sole purpose was to help people get sober.

"Why don't you come to a meeting with me tonight?"

I balked. "I don't think so, thanks. Don't much want to be around people."

He persisted. "I spoke to a woman about you, a friend of mine. Told her you'd come home. She said to tell you she would save you a seat at Friday's meeting. Don't you think it would be rude not to show up if she's holding you a seat?"

He had me there. Despite my reluctance, I had to agree. It would be rude. That Friday night we went out to a local church where the group was gathering. There were so many people! I found it overwhelming and regretted being there, but there was no way out now.

My stepfather spotted his friend and, taking my elbow, guided me toward her and made introductions. She was an elegant blonde, very poised, beautifully dressed in purple. Her eyes sparkled as she welcomed me to the group. Next to her, I felt shabby and awkward.

What to say? How to act? What would she think of me? To my dismay, I felt all my social skills had deserted me. Without a drink to smooth things over, I was lost. From deep inside came the instruction: "Take a chance. Tell the truth."

"I'm…I'm pleased to meet you." Long, excruciating pause. Suddenly, I stammered, "I've spent a lot of years drunk." There. My confession was out.

Her response was, incredibly, laughter. "So have we all, dear. That's why we're here. You're in the right place. Get yourself a cup of coffee and come sit down by me."

Hands shaking, heart pounding, I complied. Tried to focus on what was going on during the meeting. Missed a lot of it. But one thing I heard. A tall, lovely black woman was speaking from the podium. Near the end of her talk she paused and spread her hands. "I have this to say to the newcomers. Don't leave before the miracle happens for you."

That struck home, straight to the heart of me. There was a miracle waiting to happen for me? For me personally? Oh no! What if I'd given up and left? Then it would happen, my miracle, and I would not be here to receive it. Just my luck, I thought ruefully. What a sad waste that would be. I couldn't risk it. I'd better stay, I decided firmly. Strange though this all is, I'd better stay.

***

With my stepfather as my guide, I began to attend many sobriety meetings, one and sometimes two a day. At peace, I simply submitted to a barrage of new ideas. I let them wash over me and felt my spirits lift. I'd find myself smiling for no reason. Gradually, I began to understand the process recommended by the group: Admit defeat with alcohol. Surrender to God and let Him heal your mind. Survey your life and admit your failings to God and another person. Make restitution for harms done. Strengthen yourself with prayer and meditation; reach out to others.

At first, it was daunting. So rigorous! How could I even begin? It soon became obvious to me that I'd need help if I were to go through such a program, so I asked a woman to sponsor me. I chose her by attending a woman's meeting and listening to all the women speak in turn. The woman I chose was heavyset, with a pillowy bosom and a good-natured grin. She impressed me for two reasons: she loved to laugh and she was comfortable speaking of God. When I got up my nerve to ask her, her response startled me.

"Let's do it on a trial basis. Call me every day at 10 in the morning. If you can do that, that'll show me you have the discipline to carry on."

Miffed by her assumption that I might lack discipline, I vowed to call her every day and made good on it.

"What was your favorite drink?" she asked one day.

"Beer and bourbon."

"Did you have any control over what you drank or when?"

"None. My whole life was given over to getting the next drink. That mattered more than anything else—daughter, family, work."

"What was the worst part of your drinking?"

"The awful depression, the shutting down of all my faculties, the deadening of my soul. And the violence. I was always dreading it, never knowing when the next blow would fall."

"Are you ready to be free from all that?" she asked gently.

"Yes."

"Then you're on your way."

Did I dare believe it? Yes. I was on my way. But people still scared me. The size of the meetings scared me. Conversing scared me. What on earth to say to people? They all seemed so relaxed and comfortable; I still felt ill at ease around them.

It was approaching the holiday season. So I stood in front of the mirror at home and practiced two simple words: "Happy Holidays." Then, whenever I'd go to a meeting, I had my greeting: "Happy Holidays," I'd pronounce carefully, and head for the coffee before things got any more complicated than that.

One Saturday night I was at a mixed meeting, men and women. On my way out, I tripped on the pavement and started to fall. A man walking out at the same time caught me and steadied me. I was so used to violence from men that his gentle protectiveness moved me to tears. Here, truly, was a new way of life.

My sponsor challenged me to have no sexual relationships with men, no dating, for the first year of my sobriety. I was stunned. How could I do that? I'd always been linked to a man. Calmly, she explained: "Give yourself a year to get right with God first. Being with a man would only distract you. Of course, if you can't do it..." she teased.

I bridled. Not be able to do it? Of course I could. Thus began what for me has become a marvelous adventure: a life of chastity. I came to realize that once I stopped looking at men as substitute saviors, once I stopped looking at them as sexual objects, I could view them as potential friends. My life became enriched.

Early on in sobriety, I felt an urgent need to contact my daughter and somehow make amends for the years I'd abandoned her. The task seemed immense. How could I ever make it up to her? Nevertheless, I called her. I had to try.

By now she was attending a college back east. I told her, "There's no excuse for my leaving you. You never deserved it. You deserved a much better mother, one who was present. But I want you to know that during all those years, I never stopped thinking about you and I never stopped loving you. And all I can do is be the best mother I can, starting now."

To my amazement, she was willing to listen to that tentative beginning. I wrote often, and during vacations we visited. The first summer of my sobriety, I took a bus to where she was staying, at her paternal grandparents. We all went out to the lake. I was swimming with her. She dove into the water and as she came back up, head glistening with drops, she beamed, "It's good to have my mother back!" My heart leaped with joy.

***

One day in early sobriety I was out walking about town with no specific goal in mind. I felt happy and carefree. I stopped by a garden to look at the flowers. Peering deeply into the center of one, I saw an image of Christ. Stunned, I blinked. It was just a flower again. But I knew what I had seen. Very determined now, full of need to know more, I continued walking until I came to a church. I entered. To my immense relief, the pastor was in, a gentle man with kind eyes. Could I speak with him? Yes, certainly. He'd be delighted.

I drew a deep breath. I had to find answers. "I saw an image of Christ in a flower. Am I crazy?"

He smiled. "Not at all. Many people find God in nature. God leaves His fingerprints in the natural world. After all, He created it all."

Soothed, I decided to push further. "Is it possible—to speak with Christ?"

"Certainly. We call that praying."

Such a simple answer. So that's what happened in prayer. That's how I got freed from my street life. That's why I had this chance to start over. I was elated.

"Shall we pray together?" he suggested.

"Yes."

"Dear Lord, thank you for revealing yourself to this your child. May her faith grow and be strengthened with each day that passes."

And so it was that I found my church home. I soon discovered that the combination of church and sobriety groups was a good one. The two activities mutually supported one another. Sobriety groups pointed me toward God; the church took me deeper, into the Bible and into discussions about Christ that I was hungry for. Together, they gave structure to my life, and I realized to my surprise that I now craved structure.

Months passed; I was keeping my life very simple and basic and I was happy. I found myself laughing a lot, singing a lot. But one day I woke up to the fact that I was bored. I was going to meetings. I was going to church and prayer group and Bible study. These were good things. But the day was long, with many hours. I needed something else.

I took the problem to prayer group: "Could we pray that I find a job?"

"Paying or volunteer?" asked the pastor thoughtfully.

"To start with, volunteer. I understand that if we put spiritual things first, the material things will follow. And I'm still living on the SSI check." Also in my mind was that a volunteer job would not be as arduous as a paying job.

He nodded. "We support a ministry here in town. It's a publishing company for the blind, producing Christian books and magazines in Braille and on tape. If you're interested, I'll go with you tomorrow and introduce you."

"Yes. I'd like to try it." I was excited and apprehensive at the same time. Would I be able to do it? It had been a long time since I'd worked. Would I fit in?

The company was small. The boss was a large man with mocha skin who was blind and yet navigated gracefully around the premises. He was genial and kind. Then there was a small, thin, pretty Albino woman, who specialized in Braille and was initially very shy. Still, "I wish we had more people like you," she murmured. "We need the help." Last was a wiry Hispanic man who ran the printing press, very much in charge of his domain. They needed someone to manage the database, run the library, and pick up the slack in other areas.

I was intrigued. I started with two days a week and before too long was going in every day. The work captivated me, and I enjoyed the people.

One day, I was helping put Braille magazines together and the young Albino woman, Debbie, opened her heart to me.

"You know, I've always believed and gone to church. But one day I realized that after his death, Christ actually came back to life and that He is alive today, as alive as you and me. And that I can talk with him just like I'm talking to you, friend to friend. That's when my real faith started."

I felt a jolt of energy from her words. Christ, alive and present! My faith leaped forward.

One day a week, I left the publishing house and walked to a friend's home. She and I would go to a noon meeting together. After the meeting, she'd drop me back off at work. It bothered her that I was volunteering.

"Dee, these people are taking advantage of you," she insisted. "I know, because I used to belong to a church, and I was always getting stuck with kitchen duty and child care. I'm warning you: if they know you're ready to volunteer, they'll just pile more and more work onto you."

I considered her warning. I didn't feel used at all. How could I explain what it was like for me?

"Mary, you're worrying over nothing. These people are giving me so much. I get to read the magazines onto tape, and the articles teach me a lot about faith. It's exciting. I end up with the feeling that Jesus came to earth just for me."

She sighed. "I guess—I envy you that."

How to convey the love of Christ? How to spark, in another soul, a craving for that love? I tried with Mary and failed. She chose a different path, that of the Dalai Lama, and it became comical the way the two of us tried, each in her own way, to convince the other that she had found the truth. Yet our friendship survived and thrived.

***

As I approached my first sober year, my stepfather became very excited. It was customary, in our sobriety meetings, to celebrate years sober with the giving of cakes. The birthday person would choose someone to hand her the cake with candles.

"Who will you choose to give you your cake?" he'd ask hopefully.

"I'll choose you," I said, smiling. And so it was. Exuberantly, I blew out that one candle and honored him.

***

I had expressed to my sponsor my desire to make amends to the city of Santa Barbara. From my years there, I still had outstanding warrants for drunk in public, illegal camping, open container of alcohol. These nagged at me, and I wanted to clear the record. She'd advised that I wait until I had a year of sobriety under my belt, and after I turned one she agreed it was time.

So, feeling very grown up and determined, I called Santa Barbara, scheduled a court hearing for all my warrants, and made the trip up there. My sponsor accompanied me, as did another sober friend, a lawyer, who came along "just in case." I felt fortified and comforted by their presence; the closer we got the more my butterflies increased.

It was a beautiful day for the trip. The skies were blue, the ocean sparkled, and, as we neared the courthouse, the bougainvillea flared purple and red. I remembered all the previous occasions when I'd

318

entered the court handcuffed, with a chain attaching me to the other prisoners. It felt strange but good to walk in unencumbered.

We entered a crowded courtroom and sat down. With a start, I realized that I recognized the judge. He was a small man with a mustache and a vibrant bowtie, and I'd stood before him many times in the past to be sentenced for drinking in public.

When my turn came, he perused the list of my offences and then looked at me. He smiled, recognizing me too.

"Well, Dee. It's been a long time. Where have you been?"

Confidence rose up in me; I spoke up loud and clear. "I've been working and getting sober. I'm here to clean things up."

"Very well." He paused, then added, "I see many cases come through this court, and it's very rare to see someone come back to clean up past mistakes. We're all the better for it."

I thrilled to his words and hoped fervently that some people in court that day might understand that it was possible to break free of the cycle of offenses and begin a new life.

He offered me a choice between community service and a fine. I chose the fine. My sponsor insisted that she would pay it in full and that I could pay her back in installments. "That way, you'll be free and clear," she said. I accepted gratefully.

We left the courthouse and went to a restaurant near the ocean where I took my friends to lunch. It was a symbolic place for me in that many times, in the drunken homeless years, I had passed it and longed to go in and be an elegant lady dining with friends. That had been an impossible dream; all I'd been able to do was gaze through the window, yearning. Here was the dream fulfilled—a simple dream, a simple lunch, but very meaningful to me.

***

I made another trip to Santa Barbara right after that first year. The more I reveled in my new sober life, the more pleasure I took from church activities and work, the more joy I derived from calm and pleasant times with my daughter and family, the more I thought of Lucy. I loved her, and I longed for her too to enjoy a life like the one that had been given to me. This desire haunted me, and finally I decided to track her down.

There was a chance, I thought, that she'd migrate back down to Santa Barbara for the winter. It was a saying on the streets when we wanted to find somebody: "First check the hospitals and jails." I tried the Santa Barbara County Jail and sure enough, she was in there. So I made the drive up, alone this time.

I arrived just as visiting hours were starting. With the other visitors, I rode downstairs in a big elevator and waited to be called, marveling at the difference between being a visitor and being an inmate. Soon, I was seated on a wooden chair facing a window, and I saw Lucy being escorted down the hall to sit on the other side. She was stunned to see me, disbelieving at first.

"I didn't know who had come to see me. Dee, is that really you? What have you done to yourself? You look really good."

"Lucy, with God's help I've gotten sober and begun to build a new life. I've been hoping and praying that you would do the same."

"That's so weird you would say that. I've been meeting with the jail chaplain. He's been urging me to accept Christ. He's really nice to me, but I'm not sure what it means, to accept Christ."

How to explain it? Oh words, please come, I prayed urgently.

"Well, Lucy, that's what I've done, accepted Him. Christ came to rescue sinners, and you know me from my old life—I was one.

Remember when I tried to kill Peter by pushing him into the street? I just didn't give a damn. And I just forgot about my daughter."

"Sure, I remember."

"When Christ died, he took our sins with him, and when he came back to life, he offered us the same—to be reborn in hope and love. That's what it means to me, to accept Christ. It means to accept his gift to us. The difference you see in me is the difference it makes to be reborn. To accept him? It's a decision only you can make, Lucy."

"Well, like I said, the chaplain is really nice. And I may take Jesus up on that offer. Meanwhile, Dee, since you're here…I could really use some cigarettes. Would you put some money on my books?"

"I already did," I said, laughing. "I already did."

To this day, I wonder about Lucy and pray for her. Did she take Christ up on his offer? Did she find a new life? Or did she slip back into the old life once she was released, just as I'd done time after time. I may never know. We pray for people and sometimes that's the best we can do. We don't get to see the results.

***

In my years on the streets, I was completely alienated from my family, as most street people are. In those sad years I would sometimes spend whole afternoons thinking about my family, missing them, gazing off into the horizon as I longed for them, ignoring the shouts and catcalls of Peter and the others who tried to distract me and pull me back into street life and the need to go out on a panhandling trip.

As my sober year became two, then three, I was able to reunite with family and build back up a solid relationship with them. It took time, and it took being present where once I had been absent.

My sister and her husband had adopted one child, a boy, and were looking forward to adopting a second. On the day they picked up their new daughter, they came by. I was ready with a bouquet of balloons and a dish of chocolates shaped and wrapped as pink baby shoes. What a thrill it was to hold the new one and be part of the celebration, knowing I'd now be involved with her and her brother's lives.

My brother, after years of bachelorhood, decided to marry a lovely woman with two young boys. Together with my mother and stepfather, I flew up north to attend the wedding festivities. There were parties, there was dancing, there was the wedding itself. It was a joyous time, and I was there, fully conscious and clear headed.

One evening, a few years after the wedding, my brother called. His wife's father had died, and she and he had to travel to Oklahoma for the services. Would it be possible for me to come and stay with her two young sons, my brother's stepsons, while they were away? I'd be needed for three to four days.

"If you can do it, Dee, it would really help us out."

"I can do it. I'd love to."

To be needed and to be trusted—how wonderful. What a privilege to be asked. I took a flight up to San Francisco the next day, where my brother picked me up. He filled me in on the drive to his house. The boys needed haircuts, and the oldest one needed help with a school project. I could use my brother's car, and here was cash for any supplies. My brother had to fly out early the next morning.

Those days passed quickly. The boys were friendly and eager to talk about the events in their young lives. One evening the oldest answered the phone, listened, and replied, "My parents are out of town. My aunt is taking care of us." How good that sounded. Me, a reliable woman in charge.

Back home one day, wanting to solidify our relationship, I asked my daughter if it would help her to tell me what it had been like for her during my street years. She took a deep breath.

"I think it might help, yeah. But I have one condition. When I'm through, you can't say, 'I did the best I could.' Because you didn't."

"No, I didn't. I promise not to say those words."

She talked for an hour, describing her loneliness and fear and confusion. One story she told me affected me dramatically.

"In high school, we took a day trip into Santa Barbara. I was walking with a friend up State Street and I saw you from a distance. You were sitting on a wall, panhandling. I grabbed my friend's arm and said, 'We've got to get out of here. I just saw my mother.'

'Your mother? Let's go say hi,' said my friend.

'No, no,' I insisted. 'You don't understand. I don't want her to see me.' So we turned and ran."

I am very grateful to my daughter for this story. I can imagine it from her perspective: there was her mother, a frightening presence with leathery skin and wild hair, begging for alcohol. A being to flee from, instead of what she needed: a comforting person to turn to. I use that story as a touchstone as I try, today, to be a good mother and lead a sober life.

***

One summer, at work, my boss called me aside. He steepled his fingers and rested his chin on them as if pondering how to begin.

"You know, I used to be a guidance counselor. How about if I give you some counseling?"

"Sounds good."

"I know you used to be a college teacher."

Uh oh. Memories of failure, of potential not lived up to. "Yes, many years ago. A lifetime ago."

"Still, I believe you'd be suited for it. Here's what I have in mind. My wife works in the administrative side of the Los Angeles County Community College district. She could get you an application for a teaching position with them. Then, if a job came up, you could take it. They pay a lot better than we could ever pay you here," he added practically.

I dared to hope. "Well—I'm willing to try."

Sure enough, the application came. Carefully, I began to fill it out. There was a huge gap in my employment history, of course. I wondered how I'd explain that. Then came the major snag. Had I ever been arrested for a misdemeanor?

With a sinking heart, I thought of all my jail experience. Hardly the sort of experience they were looking for. Should I lie? Gloss over it in some way? I prayed for the right response. Then, deliberately, I filled it in: "Many arrests for drunk in public, 1979-1989." The application invited me to explain any yes answer, so I wrote: "I went through a period of acute alcoholism, which led to my arrests. I am now recovered and have been sober for five years. I hope this bleak period in my life will not prejudice you from hiring me." And I mailed it off.

A month later, while I was working on a grant application for the publishing house, I got a telephone call.

"Hello, Dr. Williams?"

Who on earth knew me by my professional name? "Speaking."

"This is Al Wilson over at LA Mission College. I have your application in front of me. Would you be able to come in for an interview sometime this week? We have a need for part-time faculty in the English department."

Joy, anticipation, disbelief. "Yes—yes, I'd love to come in." In a daze, I managed to set a time and get instructions. With trembling fingers I set down the phone, then turned to my boss and told him. He boomed out a belly laugh.

"It feels good to be right," he pronounced.

Later that week, I went in for the interview and to my amazement was hired on the spot. Incredulous, I learned that I would begin teaching that fall, two courses.

***

One day, in my first semester teaching, I was standing in front of the class explaining about apostrophes (my favorite punctuation mark) when suddenly I experienced a disassociation. It was as if my consciousness had left my body. Even while I went on calmly about possession (dog's house) and contraction (let's go), I was separate from myself and able to observe myself teaching. "This is really you, Dee," I thought. "This is really you up in front of the class. Isn't it incredible?"

After I'd been teaching a year, I began to apply to other colleges close by. Sometimes I'd get rejected, but sometimes I'd be hired for a semester or more. So, by piecing together courses at different schools, I became what is known as a "freeway flier" and was able to work the equivalent of full time.

Teaching kept me busy; I enjoyed the responsibility and cared about the students. It was fun to chat with other faculty and compare notes.

Then came a blow. One night, alone in my own apartment by now, I was jerked awake by the sound of loud voices outside my window, speaking about me and jeering about my past. I knew they weren't real. Yet, while I could hear them, I was trapped in fear of them, just as if enemies had gathered to torment me. The next morning, I was able to dismiss it as a nightmare. But then it happened again, and again.

What started as an interruption to sleep spread into the day. When I was walking along the street, I'd see people coming toward me, quite ordinary people. As they approached, I'd see bruises and welts forming on their faces. That wasn't real either, but it shook me to the core.

I'd go into a restaurant full of people to meet a friend for dinner. On my way to the booth, I'd hear people talking about me, strangers weaving my name into their conversations.

Clearly, something was wrong. I went to my doctor and told her everything. She was very gentle with me and laid her hand on my shoulder.

"It's a really good thing that you told me. We're going to get you help. I will refer you to a very good doctor, a psychiatrist. I'd like you to see him this week."

I went to the new doctor, very frightened. What if he could not help me? What if I were doomed to hear these unwanted voices and see these unwanted visions? Would I have to live in a nightmarish world? Would I have to give up teaching? Would I have to hide out in the house, huddled in a corner?

He listened to me describe my symptoms and was blessedly unsurprised. I suppose I'd feared he might regard me as a freak. He wanted to hear all about my years on the street. Had I hallucinated then? Yes of course, but I'd thought it was the alcohol.

"You have a form of mental illness that is very treatable. I'm going to start you off on a new medication that is very effective in treating hallucinations."

"A medication? I don't want one! I've seen people on medications and they shuffle and drool."

"We've come a long way since the early psych meds. If you have negative side effects with this one, we'll try another until we get a good match for you."

Still I balked. At that, his kind sympathy vanished, to be replaced with steely resolve.

"You know you're an alcoholic. To recover from it, you had to accept the fact of your alcoholism. In just the same way, you need to accept your mental illness, and you need to be prepared to take medication for the rest of your life. I suggest that you go home and talk with your sponsor about it. Ask her to help you with acceptance."

I left his office stunned and shaken, a prescription stuffed into my purse. One thing he'd said had penetrated: call your sponsor. I did. Thankfully, she was home.

"You'd be amazed, dear, at how many alcoholics also experience some form of mental illness. You are very fortunate to be living in an age where these medications exist. God gave us good doctors, and He gave us the meds too. There's no shame involved in taking them."

I filled the prescription and began the regimen. A month later, my symptoms had gone. The side effects I'd dreaded never materialized. I just felt like myself again. I was profoundly relieved.

Still, recovery has been sometimes rocky. Once I went off my medication and had to be hospitalized. Another time, a doctor prescribed too high a dosage and I had to be hospitalized again. Finally, I was diagnosed as a manic depressive with schizo-affective tendencies and got the medications that were right for me. Today, I am on an even keel. I am able to work and enjoy it and to function normally. I understand now that it was a combination of mental illness and alcoholism that contributed to my street years.

People have asked me if, during my years of recovery, I have missed the street life. Yes and no. No, I don't miss the hunger and the dazed, crazed mental state. Nor do I miss the daily fear of violence and the relentless preying of the strong upon the weak.

Yes, I do miss the adventure of setting up camp, sleeping outdoors, and the strong sense of community—being one member of a group intent on its own survival. But mainly, I miss the people. They were wild, often destructive, rude and crude. Yet, I loved them. Despite the rough and tumble, they were capable of much kindness to me and to one another—small things like making sure there was water in camp, like sharing food, like holding aside branches so that I could enter camp. Every day, I think of those people whom I knew and with whom I lived. Every day, I pray for them.

Today, I've spent more years in my new life than I did on the street. I recall a phrase that came to me and comforted me during those years: "As low as you go, that's how high you can fly." I think that's true. I went about as low as one can get. Now it's time for flying. Flying to me is experiencing the flood of joy that sometimes overcomes me in worship. Flying to me is having my normal state be a calm, content, and peaceful life.

***

One spring day in my early recovery, I went to board a city bus. Seated on the bench was a homeless woman. She had wrapped herself in an old blanket. She smelled of neglect. Her hair, matted and greasy, fell over her face.

I sat next to her and heard that she was murmuring to herself, carrying on a dialogue. Then she turned to me, fixed me with a piercingly blue gaze, and chanted, "Remember. Remember. Remember."

This book is the product of that remembering.